AT THE READY

AT THE READY

GLOBAL SECURITY UNLIMITED 3

SHARON MICHALOVE

Published in the United States of America

Editing by Karen Hrdlicka, Barren Acres Editing

Cover by 100 Covers

ISBN: 978-1-7369187-7-7 (paper)

ISBN: 978-1-7369187-6-0 (ebook)

ISBN: 978-1-7369187-8-4 (hardbound)

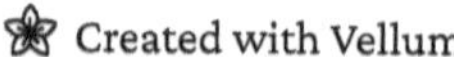 Created with Vellum

PRAISE FOR SHARON MICHALOVE'S GLOBAL SECURITY UNLIMITED SERIES

At First Sight

If you are a fan of romantic suspense with a hunky Global Security hero, a successful determined author, supportive friends, creepy stalkers, danger, secrets, bravery, a loving family, and a HEA that will leave a satisfying smile on your face, then you will love Cress and Max's story.—Goodreads Review

Sharon Michalove takes the hindsight fantasy of what may have been and polishes it up with a thrilling dose of it's clear to see, we were meant to be.==InD'Tale Magazine

The story does a masterful job of slowly building trust while the danger lurks, getting closer and closer. —Goodreads Review

At the Crossroads

[T]he story building is fantastic with immense suspense and action, with the perk of hearing the perspectives of both Max and Cress. Gripping and delightful!—InD'Tale Magazine

The author did a great job of writing flawed characters who come together to form a strong relationship.—Goodreads Review

EPIGRAPHS

If it be now, 'tis not to come: if it be not to come, it will be now: if it be not now, yet it will come: the readiness is all. The rest is silence.

    William Shakespeare, Hamlet

Each player must accept the cards life deals him or her: but once they are in hand, he or she alone must decide how to play the cards in order to win the game.

    Voltaire

Thanks to my Dark & Stormy critique partners.
So glad we found each other.

READER'S NOTE

Some of the timeline overlaps with *At the Crossroads*. I've tried not to repeat scenes, or at least give them from a different point of view. If you want to know more about the terrorist plot that threatens Max, or what happens to Cress in Paris, please check out *At the Crossroads*. You can find out how Max and Cress got together twenty years after they first met in *At First Sight*.

If you want to know what Stanley's was like, check out this video of Joel Quenneville singing "Sweet Caroline" in 2012.

FRENCH-CANADIAN SWEARS

The most common long-form swear among French Canadians.

Osti de tabarnak de sacrament, de câlice de ciboire de crisse de marde!

Quebec swear words, or in French sacres, are pretty much just words that go against the establishment; adjectives, verbs, and nouns deemed inappropriate by the general population. Or those who govern the general populace. Swear words are meant to stick it to the man, whether that be your parents, the government, or in the case of early Quebec, the Catholic church.

In Quebec's past, the church was running the show. The clergy controlled nearly every aspect of society in 19th century Quebec, which understandably pissed off the Quebec people. Taking words deemed sacred or holy by the Church, Quebecers recreated these untouchable sayings into harsh profanities. If you've ever wondered why Quebec swear words have a religious tinge, now you know it's basically because they wanted to give a linguistic fuck you to the Church.

Michael D'Alimonte, mtlblog.com

Frequently Used Words

    Câlice = Damn

    Crisse = Christ

    Tabarnak = Fuck

    Osti (also ostie or esti) = another equivalent to the F-word

    Ciboire = another equivalent to the F-word

Any others you find in the text will be equivalent.

For more about Quebeçois, check out this article from Atlas Obscura.

CHAPTER
ONE

One secret of success in life is for a man to be ready for his opportunity when it comes.—Benjamin Disraeli

Chicago, February 2014
Micki

TODAY'S THE DAY. Best suit. Flawless hair and makeup. Every inch the polished senior associate. No four-inch heels. Frederick Lanscombe, managing partner, is a little sensitive about his height. At five seven, stilettos bring me close to six feet. I tower over him. Not a good look since this meeting is the crucial first step in the campaign to be the next partner at Miller, Lanscombe, Baker, Francis, Masters, and Hargrove.

The door to the small conference room is wide open, an open box from Do-Rite gracing the polished mahogany in the middle of the room. Three partners sitting in judgment.

Fred at the head of the table, eats a maple-bacon donut. My mentor, Rebecca Masters, smiles and gives me a small thumbs-up. Tyler Miller, associate managing partner, nods to acknowledge I'm here.

I'm more than here. After a hundred years, this firm is still a boys' club, but I'm determined to crack into the top echelon and become the second woman to make partner.

Hayden Forbes-Cartwright barrels into me. I fly through the door and end up on hands and knees. When I look up, Fred's mouth and donut haven't met. Rebecca's hand is over her eyes.

"What an entrance, Micki." Tyler's mocking laugh pricks my balloon of confidence.

A snigger erupts from Hayden as his big hand reaches down to pull me up. "So sorry, Micki. Couldn't put the brakes on in time."

Upright, my ankles wobbly as I balance on my low-heeled shoes, my glare has the heat of the Milky Way. Not that Hayden pays any attention. His bogus concern is yet one more layer of deceit.

Points to him. I'm the klutz and he's the chivalric hero. "Have a seat, Micki, Hayden." Fred gives us each a once-over. Dressing well is one of the unspoken rules. Hayden's navy-blue pinstripe is comparable to my silver-gray jacket and matching pencil skirt—points even on wardrobe. My phone in my lap, I pull up my spreadsheet. I've kept score since the first time we met. The advantage has seesawed back and forth, but we're competing for the pinnacle in the stakes race, so I'll have to up my game.

Hayden and I were adversaries from the get-go. We started here, on the same day eight years ago. Me half an hour early. Hayden fifteen minutes late, strolling in with his uncle. All my muscles clenched when he looked me over with his trademark devil-may-care smile.

"I know you both received the memo. With Sonny Philips' retirement, the firm will promote one associate to partner this year. As the two seniors, you will be the leading candidates."

Hayden stops fiddling with his Chicago Yacht Club tie. "Does that mean you'll consider other associates?"

"Technically, yes, but in reality, you are the only ones qualified right now. The partners will evaluate you on several criteria besides the competencies you've shown in your time here."

He pauses.

Hayden rushes into the momentary silence. "Does every partner vote?"

"You know they do," Tyler chides his nephew impatiently.

"Are some votes weighted more heavily than others? Like seniority?"

"No. Please go on, Fred." Rebecca's eye roll should send a message.

When I glance toward Hayden, he shows no embarrassment, not even a slight flush. Most lawyers learn early to put on a neutral face. I permit myself a tiny smile. Minus five to Hayden.

Fred looks at the sheet in front of him, then from Tyler to Rebecca. He positions reading glasses firmly at the end of his long, narrow nose. "The criteria includes enthusiasm, treatment of others, the opinion of your mentor."

He places a finger on page, then clears his throat, glances around. "Also, maintaining personal control, commitment, successful building and protection of your reputation and that of the firm." Another pause.

Tyler breaks in. "We're looking for consistent hard work, always available, constant improvement, and most important— being perceived as trustworthy." He gives an oily smile, staring at me as if he doesn't trust me at all.

Hayden's eyes dart like tiny silverfish, his tell when he's calculating his chances for winning. I put in the long hours and never turn down a request. Hayden skates by, taking credit for the work of junior associates. He boasts about staying late when he disappears in the middle of the day.

When your uncle's name is on the door, you have an extra pass. Tyler Miller will definitely push for Hayden to be the next partner.

Fred is still talking, and I wrench my attention back to his droning monotone. "Besides the formal evaluation, the other piece is assisting Rebecca with a high-profile insider trading case. It's more than usually sensitive because our client is a candidate for a Senate seat. He says it's a setup. Not necessarily a strong or provable defense. You'll be combing emails, social media, accounts, and documents to find evidence."

I suppress a shiver. The sensation of a bucket of night crawlers being dumped down my spine short circuits my thoughts. Then I remember what Mom used to say when I lost confidence. "Be your own cheerleader." *Rah, rah.*

But I'm beaten to the punch. "What a great opportunity for us to show what we're made of." Hayden's wide smile and crackling delivery are as phony as a carny barker's come-on.

Our managing partner nods his head approvingly. Hayden is his favored candidate too. Fred and Tyler have some kind of mutual admiration society and Hayden benefits.

Yeah, he's a suck-up.

My turn. *Say something but avoid the gush.* I clear my throat as quietly as I can. "This is an amazing challenge. I really appreciate the chance to work on a case so important to the future and reputation of the firm and, potentially beyond, Fred."

Kind of stiff. Fingers crossed I've hit the right note. The knot in my chest loosens when Rebecca winks.

As we walk out, she stops me. "Micki, I have a lunch appointment, but let's have a drink after work." She looks around. Tyler's just going into his office, not paying any attention to us. "We haven't had a good chat for a while."

"Great, Rebecca. Just come by my office when you're ready to leave."

Then I cancel my date for the evening. Work comes first, always.

After-work drinks have replaced the three-martini lunch, unless you're Hayden Forbes-Cartwright. He indulges in both. An unwind is just what I need along with a heads-up on what I can expect in the next few months as we grind through the promotion process.

The Gage is lively at five thirty. A millinery shop in the early twentieth century, the transformation into a happening bar and restaurant on Michigan Avenue in the twenty-first includes historic framed ads for hats.

Rebecca pushes through the crowded room after the hostess, who seats us at a quiet table in a corner near the tile fireplace. We won't have to shout and have less likelihood of being overheard.

Our waiter arrives in classic server attire, pristine white

shirt and black slacks. His curly red hair is a Raggedy-Andy mop.

"One Paris Rose, one Jabberwock, fried pickles, and a cheese board." Rebecca hands back the menus and lets out a breath.

Then she pulls out a legal pad. "Thought we could go over some strategies for the work. You can work on the emails, social media, anything online, and whatever documents we can upload. That way, while you're traveling, you'll have plenty of material to access."

"Great. I've been anxious about being away at such a crucial point in my career."

The pencil between Rebecca's fingers moves up and down like a seesaw. "Thanks to technology. Years ago, we were tied to the office, the library. I'm glad you can go to the awards ceremony. Kind of like the Oscars for authors."

"Yeah. Still, five working days away…"

"I'll make sure you're front of mind for all the partners. As far as the work, our new legal research assistant is already busy organizing everything as documentation comes in."

The barman puts the flute containing the Paris Rose cocktail in front of Rebecca. She hurriedly pushes her legal pad to the side, but not before a few drops splash onto the paper, leaving a light pink trail. She takes a sip just as the server deposits the cheese board in the middle of the table, along with a basket of fried pickles. Meanwhile, the barman has brought my Jabberwock in its coupe.

No time for lunch and my stomach growls. Cheese is a magnet for me. Hence my passion for pizza. With grabby fingers, I snatch some almost before the server gets the platter on the table. "Sorry," I mumble my apology through a mouthful of cheese. "Starving."

Rebecca nibbles on a pickle. "Simon Greenberg is an attorney with Talcott, Maier, a state legislator, and the front-running Republican candidate for Senate from Illinois. We went to law school together and have faced each other in court many times."

She places cheese on a couple of pickles and pops them, one after the other, into her mouth, then sighs with satisfaction. "The SEC received a tip claiming he made use of private information to trade stocks from several companies he represents. After an investigation, the Commission decided on civil charges. Unfortunately, because his candidacy has made him a public figure, criminal charges are pending as well. There may well be some questions about election finance, too."

"Wait. Shouldn't Hayden be here?" Not that I want him, but if we're a team, he deserves the same explanations.

"Hayden has already been briefed."

Be professional. In control. Pretend it doesn't matter.

"Oh. I see." But I don't. Not at all.

Rebecca takes a huge swallow of the pink liquid. "Not by me. After our meeting, Tyler and Fred took Hayden to lunch and briefed him there."

How does she know? Or is this an assumption? My heated protest escapes before I can rein it in. "But it's your case."

She waves the comment away. "He was so full of himself when he got back. Swanned into my office. 'Simon Greenberg, huh? I wondered after the rumors flying around. Good for us.' Then he laughed and walked out."

Her scowl could freeze the Chicago River. "I was sure Tyler at least would make sure he's up to speed, and I wanted to put you in the loop right away. Fred and Tyler are bound to give Hayden some instruction on how to handle things, and he will take advantage of the time you are away in April."

My cocktail beckons and I chug it down, sputtering slightly as the potent alcohol burns the back of my throat. "Should I cancel the trip?"

She ignores that. "You'll meet the client tomorrow, so make a powerful first impression. Wear good jewelry and heels are fine. Simon is tall, so he won't mind. Red lipstick if you have it. He respects women who can stand up for themselves—usually."

Mindlessly curling my hair around a finger, I muse about wardrobe when I should be concentrating on the facts of the case. Rebecca has moved on and I hurriedly refocus.

"You'll have plenty of work to do while you're out of the office. Have a tech set up your laptop with VPN. It will be your lifeline to the firm. Video meetings will help too. Make sure you can report on progress every day. You need to maintain a firm, visible presence while you're in Paris."

We see the waiter in the distance and Rebecca catches his attention. Once we have refills, she takes a sip, then leans forward. "Show you're dedicated to the firm and the case and you can work without supervision. I'll try to schedule the meetings first thing in the morning to mitigate the seven-hour time difference."

"And the other complications?"

"Hayden is one, as I'm sure you've guessed. More in terms of your selection as partner. The bad news is the partners decide long before the case ends. But he'll try for every plum he can pluck. The other is, because of the election cycle, Greenberg is pushing to clear it up or bury it quickly. News of the pending charges will hit the papers tomorrow."

Why haven't they leaked already?

Rebecca must be a mind reader. "The papers are planning front-page splashes with stories, commentary, and reactions on at least two inside pages."

I can picture the *Tribune*. Huge headline and photos on their broadsheet front page. Stories about the investigation, the campaign, lots of background on the candidate, a piece where the rest of the field comments. Then an editorial on the op-ed pages. Maybe a political cartoon. The *Sun-Times* tabloid format will be just as comprehensive in a more compact form. "Collusion?"

"Cooperation." Her forehead wrinkles, brows touching. The corners of her mouth turn down.

"Keeping him from making incendiary comments is going to be a job in itself. We want as little coverage as possible while we work on clearing him—if we can. The damage to his reputation is a gift to the other contenders. He's been the front runner, the poster boy for the party."

In two swallows, the Jabberwock has disappeared. I order another, then, still hungry, I pop more bread and cheese into my mouth.

"Hey, guys. Didn't get the memo." Hayden pushes into the tufted leather booth and reaches for a pickle, almost knocking me to the floor. "Uncle Tyler thought you might be here, Rebecca. Said it's your usual watering hole." His stress on "uncle" makes my blood feel like ice water.

"A casual afterwork drink." Rebecca's voice is flat.

Hayden reaches over and taps her legal pad. "Sure you aren't strategizing?" The twinkle in his eye shows malice, not amusement. "By the way, I met Laney this afternoon. She's a cutie."

"Laney?" The name is unfamiliar.

With a leer, he says, "Our legal researcher. Fresh out of her paralegal program."

The server comes by with my third drink.

"Are you running a tab?"

Rebecca nods.

"Two Satan's Whiskers. Need to play catch up with these two." His smirk makes my skin crawl.

"How appropriate."

He snickers. My snarky comment bounces off his crocodile hide.

Before the drinks guy can take off, I hold up a hand. "I'd like to order something to go, please."

Pad out, he looks a bit like a bird, head to the side.

"Shrimp cocktail with no sauce, and the apple salad. Just put the shrimp on top of the salad with the dressing on the side."

"You got it."

Hayden puffs out his chest like a pouter pigeon. "Me, I have a date as soon as I finish these truly spectacular drinks."

"Drinks named just for you."

He grins. "You know it. Scary but seductive. And I have some seducing on tap."

Probably with our new researcher. I push the sour feelings back. "Have fun."

"Oh, I intend to."

Rebecca's warning look doesn't make any impression either. She grabs her coat off the empty seat. "Off to have dinner with my hubby. He's cooking tonight."

I trudge to the office, take-out container in hand, ready for a little research of my own.

CHAPTER
TWO

Smell is something that attracts me instantly. So if the guy smells nice, there is an instant attraction.—Alia Bhatt

March 2014
Micki

JL Martin, a new friend I'd like to know better, asked me out several times in the last month. Good thing he's persistent because getting up to speed on the insider trading case is kicking my butt big time. Today is Sunday and I'm giving myself the evening off. I worked for five hours earlier, but tonight's the night.

Except for a few dinners at my parents' house, I spend every waking hour at my office. Just hours of research, meetings with the client, too much time with Hayden, and at least one meeting a day with our team of seven. We've added a legal secretary, a file clerk, and a first-year associate.

No friends, no hockey either at the arena or on TV. All my meals are delivery, or just bowls of cereal. Three boxes of Chocolate Chex stashed in my credenza help with sudden hunger attacks.

JL is just my type. Not breathtakingly handsome like my friend Cress' boyfriend, Max. I don't need movie star good looks. He's got that craggy jawed, French-Canadian hockey-player aura. He's well-muscled but not muscle bound. No visible tattoos. Cropped brown hair, sprinkled with gray. Deep brown, almost black eyes, like pools of dark chocolate, complete the package. My heart stutters every time I see him. *Take a deep breath.* Then snort as water goes up my nose.

I met JL last December. He's a security specialist. His company, WatchDog, Inc., supplied bodyguards to protect my best friend. A narcissistic lunatic, someone we went to school with, tried to destroy Cress' life and career. Still entangled with my now-former boyfriend, the immediate attraction unsettled me, and I buried it deep. Now that Sam is an ex, I dig it up. JL can be the safety valve to relieve the pressure of work.

Water drips down my long hair into my face. My eyes are squeezed shut to keep errant drops from seeping in. The slick, soapy granite surface means one hand stays flat against the marble cladding, so I don't slip and fall. I fumble to find the knobs that shut off the multiple sprays. When the hot water stops, the immediate sensation is ice coating my skin. Shivers run through me while I grope for a towel. Any old piece of cloth in a storm would help at this point.

Where the fuck is it? I know I put it in easy reach. But

this master bath is so much bigger than the normal-sized room in my former condo that I feel spatially challenged. The walk-in power shower is at least three times the size of anything I've ever used before. Too many months alone, my mind wanders in sexy directions. If things move along well, JL and I might have fun in here.

That's all I want. Some fun. After the shit show that is Sam Beamer, I deserve a bit of no-strings happy.

My feet start to slide, and I grab on to the edge of the glass with my left hand, grope with the right, and dislodge a soft French terry textile that I catch just before it hits the floor. I wipe my eyes, then rub the cloth against my dripping hair. So what if it's the bath sheet. At this point a washcloth would do. I wrap the cotton fabric around me and notice, my eyes now open and dry, the hand towel is right where I put it for a quick pick up.

Bending over, I use the newly rediscovered hand towel to wrap my hair in a makeshift turban, tighten the bath towel around my quivering body, and step out into my slippers. At least they're where I expect them to be.

The frustration that made my heart pound leaks away now I've reestablished control. The weakness in my limbs subsides and I don't need the wall to prop me up. The generous bath sheet starts to slip, and I readjust it once more before walking into the bedroom. That's when I hear shouts. Not screams of distress or pain. More like the insistent howl of an angry predator spewing pure vitriol.

"I know you're in there, you fat slut. Show yourself, bitch. I have things to say to you." A drawl. How does he do that? Howl with a Southern accent?

Sam. Can't believe he found me. Goosebumps march up my arms and across my chest, the good-old-boy accent sending me into high alert. I force myself to keep my hands down so I can't put my fingers in my ears, then slip behind the edge of a long curtain, craning my neck to peek out the window.

Dancing in rage on the narrow sidewalk, Sam's hand curls around something, but from this distance, no glasses or contacts, I can't make out what it is until the former baseball wannabe does a wind up and lets the object fly.

The condo I'm subletting is on the top floor, and he throws like a girl. That's why he's a wannabe. No way that missile is going to reach me. When the projectile hits the wall two stories below, I see it's a small rock. Not only is he incompetent in throwing, but he didn't even use something that would cause much damage.

"Where are you, shyster? Stop cowering and show yourself, you filthy cow." His invective might make a passerby think he was harassing his lawyer instead of his former girlfriend.

I edge away from the window, flop onto the king-size bed, let the towel drop to the floor, and wrap myself in the royal blue velour bedcover. The velvety feel is comforting as I try to ignore the epithets and relax into the luxurious warmth. The memory of our next-to-last encounter sweeps over me.

A cold, sunny December day and we've had an early adjournment, so I decide to surprise Sam with a lunch date. Opening the door, I hear loud noises. "Sam," I call out, wondering if he's sick. When I walk inside... Surprise.

Sam's not alone. His companion's red hair splays out against the deep plum of my new couch.

Startled, I scream, and he lifts his head, a bald spot outlined by the straggly, shoulder-length hair. Hazy eyes stare into mine. His thick, gravel tone is accusatory.

"What the hell you doin' here, Micki? Shouldn't you be at work?"

"Yeah. Who are you?" The redhead's voice is high and nasal.

I straighten to my full five foot seven and, with a glare so hot it could set the furniture on fire, I tell her, "I am the owner of this condo. Until just now, I was also the partner of this douche."

"I live here, baby." He stares as if daring me to contradict him.

With a swallow and a deep breath, I summon all the flair I use in the courtroom, snapping, "You don't live here anymore, you bastard. Out." My forefinger points to the still ajar front door.

"But, Micki, darlin', I need to..." He grabs for the bib of his overalls, voice a combination of whine and wheedle.

"Scram. All you need to do is leave and never come back."

He scrambles up and faces me. He's trying to pull up his boxers with no success. "Back off and let me explain." He gives a menacing growl.

I step forward, my stilettos pushing down into the denim of the overalls that pool on the floor, and shove farther into his personal space. The bright red nail of that same forefinger pokes at his chest. "You need to leave. Right now."

He backs up, and a ripping sound makes his face redden. "You tore my pants, bimbo,. These are fucking expensive," he snivels. "Prada."

My disbelieving gasp turns into a laugh. "How the hell do you afford Prada? Save up from all the meals I've paid for? The rent you've saved living here? A wealthy patron you never mentioned? Certainly not from the mediocre art you produce." My eyes narrow. "Oh, I know, they're knockoffs. Should be more careful with your money, Sammy."

His enraged growl makes me expect he'll shake his raised fist at me, but he hauls off and punches me in the face. Shocked, I put a hand on the arm of the couch to keep my balance, taste blood as my bottom lip catches between my teeth, and don't make a sound.

"You'll be sorry," he yells as I slam the door on his fingers. He yelps and steps back, so I close the door, set the deadbolt, and sink onto the floor, trying to block out his banging fist against the wood.

I shudder with frustration as they clatter down the stairs of the six-flat building. That's when I realize he still has a key, but I'm too discombobulated to deal with it now. Instead, I call my best friend, Cress. She promises to come right over.

I drop my head into my hands. Can't hold back the tears and I start to bawl.

THE VISIONS DISSOLVE as I hear Sam, still screaming like a banshee. A hail of pebbles smash into the building. Then another rock hits, this one bigger. I pray he hasn't caused any major damage. I crack open the window and yell. "What did you expect? You cheated on me and ruined my couch, you fucker." Pulling the window back down, I reach for my cellphone and dial 911.

～

JL

When the woman you lust after agrees to a first date, you feel you've won the World Cup. Micki and I met last

December when Max's girlfriend, Cress, faced accusations of plagiarism, a threat that could have destroyed her writing career, and eventually escalated to physical violence. Cress' best friend came as part of the package. She was a magnetic field that drew me in, although she had a longtime boyfriend, Sam.

Our uneasy relationship, built on mutual friends and embarrassing circumstances, has been tentative, even after Sam turned out to be a total douche. The day she found him having sex on her couch, she threw him out, but not before he hit her. Despite her reluctance, Max and I convinced her that a trip to the emergency room had to happen. Her belligerent attitude made the staff happy to see the back of her. Since then, I've given her space but, three months later, I'm ready to try for a goal.

Last month, standing in front of Max's Gold Coast mansion, she was a vision in a chic emerald-green wool coat, unbuttoned so I could admire the stunning blue silk wrap dress with the deep neckline that matched her Pacific-blue eyes. Her long, straight, honey-colored hair curved below her shoulders, swinging slightly when she moved. Short enough to fit under my chin, I itched to hold her gentle curves.

Heat rose from my feet to my face. Instead of repeating the greeting, what popped out was, "Micki, ma chère, I want to take you out sometime." At least it wasn't what I'd been thinking. *I want to take you to bed, right now.*

She blinked. Then blinked again. "Uh, yeah, sure." Sparkly nails in some kind of graduated blues pushed back flying silken strands. Her words were so tentative, I followed up with the inane, "Really? You're sure?"

"Sorry. You surprised me. But yes, I'm sure."

That's when I screamed victory, waving my arms in the

air like a madman, only slightly constricted by the stiff leather of the new jacket Maman sent me for my birthday. No butter-soft hide for her. It's rich, dark-brown, textured like tree bark. The look sharp. It would wear into suppleness eventually, but not for a few years at least. I would never tell her I would have preferred something more pliant. Pre-ruined, a term a friend coined.

Micki's reaction was adorable. Shock, delight, and amusement flitted across her face in rapid succession. Her eyes sparkled as she tossed her head, silky tresses flying in all directions. In the end, we both doubled over laughing.

Moaning, she held her side. "Damn it. I have a stitch. Laughter shouldn't hurt."

I tried to nod and straighten up at the same time, gasping from the pain. "Calisse," I grunted. My face was wet. Never believed cry laughing was real until then.

"Just so you know, I'm planning on karaoke." I crossed my fingers, hoping one of my favorite things appealed to her, too.

A mischievous grin touched her lips. Then, fists raised, she screamed, "Score!" And we dissolved into new paroxysms of laughter.

A door slammed, and Max ran down the steps. No coat. He started shivering as soon as he stopped. "Bloody hell." He rubbed his arms. "What the fuck do you maniacs think you're doing? I'm sure people can hear you all the way to South Shore."

Micki giggled. "Bit of an exaggeration, Max."

His chest made a rumbling sound. "Come in out of the cold. Cress has rum hot toddies ready."

"Not whisky?" Max's impressive collection of rare whiskies impressed the select few allowed to share the treasured elixirs.

"None of my single malt is going to be wasted like that." He turned and ran up the stairs as if Jack Frost was nipping at his nose.

ALL THIS FLASHES through my mind as my new Italian beauty, an Aprilia RSV4 motorcycle, idles at a red light. I can see the drivers around me staring at its sexy shape. It is a heavy bike, and not as fast as some of its competitors, but the four-cylinder engine produces a sound that makes your neck hair stand on end. It's compact, so it works well on city streets. My chest thrums with pleasure, seeing the desire and envy of the surrounding drivers.

The vibrations keep me in a constant state of physical awareness at this very long red light. So long I count with the longest swear I know under my breath, "Osti de tabarnak de sacrament, de câlice de ciboire de crisse de marde!" Finally, after what seems like infinity but is only five times through the litany, the light changes. I rev the engine, producing an operatic peal, bob and weave past the slow-moving buses clogging Inner Lakeshore Drive, crawl through several intersections, and head toward the Gold Coast.

The Drive has more traffic than I expect and I'm running late. When I turn onto her street, I can see the impressive Parisian-inspired condo building just down at the corner. Micki rents a condo with an option to buy.

As I reach the intersection of Goethe and Stone, a fracas erupts just outside the building entrance. The concierge tries to tackle someone throwing stones at the façade. I roar up, tires squealing, tear off my helmet, and run toward the combatants. Behind me, the bike is on the ground, writhing from the throbbing engine. In the distance, sirens wail as I pull the two men apart.

The concierge steps back, uniform looking the worse for wear. The other man is Micki's cheater ex-boyfriend, Sam Beaton, in his usual country hayseed outfit of sloppy, tattered overalls and a red-checked shirt with frayed collar and cuffs. Both are paint splattered. He's a "naïve" painter, although I think he's just bad. The fake good 'ole boy persona is part and parcel of the presentation.

Sam looks me over and drawls, "Weel, if it ain't the Frenchy."

"French Canadian, tonton." It means boob, which amuses me.

He glares and takes a swing. Unprepared, I end up on the pavement at the wrong end of a punch on the nose. Sam cackles. "Serves ya right, ya filthy Canuck."

I ignore the pain, push myself up, and slug him in the jaw. He tumbles to his knees like garbage down a chute. I push him onto his back with my foot. Only then, with my foot resting on his chest, do I pull out some tissues to sop up the blood I can feel dribbling out of my nose and trickling down from my lip to my chin.

The police surround us. One latches on to my arm and moves me away. The other pulls Sam to his feet. One officer, hands on his hips, says, "We got a 911 call from this location. What's going on?"

Sam opens his mouth. I know he is going to blame me. But before he gets a word out, the concierge takes charge. "Officer, this man." He points a shaky finger toward the slob, who adjusts the bib straps on the overalls. The concierge quivers with rage, his voice rising to falsetto. "This man came into the building asking about one of our residents. When I refused to give him any information, he ran out and threw rocks at the windows. Screaming obscenities. I was trying to stop him when this gentleman arrived and subdued him."

"You made the call?"

"No. I don't know who called. Probably a resident."

Just then, Micki, feet bare, runs out the door. Her hair is half up, face bare of makeup, allowing a stunning flush to show through.

"Thank God you're here," she shouts at the officers. She points at Sam. "This jerk has been stalking and harassing me. I even have an order of protection out against him, but he just ignores it. Mostly he yells at me from a distance, but attacking the building, well…" We all look where Sam had been throwing rocks. A pile, like a miniature cairn, sits on the edge of the lawn. The concierge winces at the sight of the pockmarks in the lintel over the door and fine cracks in the ornate fanlight.

Micki turns toward me, recoiling at the sight of my damaged nose. "Sam, you dirtbag. I hope you go to jail for assault and vandalism. Maybe you'll learn a lesson." She moves closer and dabs my nose with her right forefinger.

"I'm so sorry," she whispers to me, standing on tiptoe to kiss the side of my cheek.

"All better." I grin.

"Yh, ri-" Sam jeers, his words blurry from his broken jaw. "I knkd oo dn, sshoe."

Micki looks down at her bare feet and frowns. "If I had my stilettos on, I'd make you sorry, Sam."

He tries to snicker, but a groan of pain is all that comes out. Mighty struggles don't make any difference since he can't squirm out of the grip of the cop holding his left arm. Now cuffed, the cop hangs on to him.

"That was a tap. No harm done." I see worry clouding her eyes. "Don't worry. His jaw is worse off than my nose."

"Jus' way. Oo'l paaa." Can't tell whether Sam's unintelligible mumble is a threat or a complaint.

I hold my body still and bite my inner cheek. Micki takes no prisoners. She walks up to the balding man with the beer belly hanging over his belt and pokes him in the gut. "Shut up, jerk."

"Ore," Sam spits out. Then groans.

"Pot, kettle." Micki sends back a sizzler.

Wailing sirens distract all of us as two ambulances skid to a stop, tires squealing in counterpoint.

"We're transporting him to emergency to have his jaw checked out before we charge him." The senior cop loosens his grip as the EMT comes over. He focuses on my nose and the contusions on my cheek. "You need to be checked out, too?"

When I remove the tissue, the bleeding has stopped. "Can't tell till the swelling goes down, but I think it will be fine. I'll have a doctor check if something crops up."

They wrestle Sam into the ambulance. The cop turns back to me. "We'll need a statement from you. Meet us at the Eighteenth Precinct on Larrabee. Check in with the desk sergeant and tell him you're there. See me, Sergeant Lam. He'll know to expect you."

I call after him, "Fine. I'll be right behind you." Crisse, this messes up my plans.

"Have Max and Cress pick you up," I yell to Micki as I race for my bike. "I'll meet you at the bar when I'm done."

"I'll take an Uber." Her arms are tight across her chest.

"Please." My sad hound expression must work because her arms drop, and her stony face softens.

"Okay. Just because you asked nicely."

I give her a thumbs-up, then follow the blue and white down the street toward the police station. In my rearview mirror, Micki dwindles into the distance.

The building that houses the Eighteenth Precinct is fairly new and I stop by the long, raised counter inside the door, helmet under my arm. A woman in uniform leans over a partition and I let her know I'm here to see Sergeant Lam. She points me to the waiting room, chilly in the cold March evening. A cup of coffee would be welcome, but the pot has been sitting too long, smells burnt, and when I try to pour out the inky black liquid, it's almost congealed. With a small twitch of my shoulders, I put the foam cup down on the table.

I alternate between sitting in one of the vinyl chairs and pacing back and forth, the heels of my boots clacking against the beige linoleum tile flooring. Two groups huddle in different corners of the room, ignoring me but occasionally looking over to stare at each other. Several of the women have swollen eyes and tear-streaked cheeks, mascara melted into blotches. The men keep their distance from the women, forming several smaller groupings close by. All I hear are occasional swear words and some sobs. I wonder if there was some incident they were all involved in. Yelling comes from the hallway, in some language I don't know. It gets louder, then gradually fades.

When Lam calls me in, my body floods with relief. This is a crap way to have a first date. I stand, find I'm stiff, and stretch out my back before following him back to an interview room. The other guy is already there, a notebook out. "I thought you recorded these things now," I say.

"We do. But sometimes I want to make a note." He taps the ballpoint against the stiff green cardboard cover.

I didn't see Sam when I came in and when I ask, they

tell me he's still at the hospital. "You wouldn't have seen him, anyway. We take suspects through a different entrance."

Knowing I won't find out any more from them, I finger my nose, trying to decide if it's broken or bruised. It feels swollen but not too disfigured. Breathing is laborious. I tell them my story, then wait for them to produce a statement. I sign and rush out the door. Before I go to Stanley's Kitchen & Tap, I have to go home. I can easily wipe the blood off my jacket, but I need to change. I like tie-dye, but a blood-spattered shirtfront is not the look I'm going for.

CHAPTER
THREE

*I don't run away from a challenge because I am afraid.
Instead, I run toward it because the only way to escape fear is
to trample it beneath your feet.—Nadia Comaneci*

Micki

REGRET MAKES my chest ache as JL recedes into the distance on his snazzy red-and-black motorcycle. A sense of yearning fills me with the desire to ride on the back of it, arms tight around his waist, one cheek pressed against his back. My imagination gets the better of me, and I fantasize about the thrum of the engine through my core. I start to tremble with desire. Once he is truly out of sight, I trudge back into the building, only partly successful in skirting rocks and broken glass. Tommy brushes down his uniform and mutters curses under his breath and little drops of blood deface the lobby floor.

My mouth droops as I apologize. "Sorry about that, Tommy. I never expected Sam to find me here."

"What's wrong with the jerk?" Around sixty with short silvery hair, Tommy is originally from New York and thirty years in Chicago hasn't affected his Jimmy Cagney accent. He sticks out his chin pugnaciously, and with his boxer's stance, looks ready to go fifteen rounds with Mohammed Ali.

"It's a long story. He's aggrieved that I kicked him out."

"Aggrieved, huh? This looks more like a convention of ticked off cabbies. Wad he do to ya?" Tommy gives free rein to his curiosity as he digs deep into his Lower East Side roots.

"He had sex on my new couch—and not with me. Let's just leave it at that."

Tommy surveys me, lips curved up in appreciation. "Dirty, yellow-bellied rat." His Cagney imitation is a little shaky. Then he switches back to his normal voice. "Okay. He was always a jerk, not just a jilted lover."

"Right. And now I need to finish getting ready to go out with friends." I move toward the elevator, but Tommy stops me.

"Your feet. Can you manage okay?"

"I don't expect you to carry me. I got into the building by myself. Just sorry for messing up the floor."

He looks down, then shakes his head. "Custodial staff will take care of it, no problem."

I move closer to the elevators.

Just as the doors open, he lobs another question. "Who's the guy who helped me out?"

Not sure how to categorize JL, I pause. "He's a karaoke buddy. Not the best start to the evening." I move into the car before the doors slide shut and push the button for the third floor. No more questions, at least not until I call Cress.

Besides the tacky feeling as I walk across the marble floor, my feet are icy. I run down the hall, fling open the door, and slide into the fuzzy slippers waiting next to the opening. *Bliss.*

Once inside the palatial condo I call home for the moment, I wrestle out the phone trapped between the couch cushions. It landed there when I threw it down and ran out the door after calling 911. Then I walk into the bedroom and throw myself onto the bed.

"Hey, Siri. Call Cress."

"Calling Cress," the obedient bot responds.

She answers almost immediately. "Micki?" Her voice is breathless with concern. How could she have heard anything yet? Unless JL called Max on his way to the police station.

"Why are you upset?" I ask.

"We're supposed to meet you at Stanley's, and you're calling. Something must be wrong."

Cress always imagines the worst, although in this case she's not wrong. Her intuitive leaps are too much. I rub the small of my back, trying to dispel the creepy crawly feelings up and down my spine.

I take a deep breath, then plunge in. "Sam found me, somehow, and laid siege to the building."

"He what?"

"Laid siege to the building," I repeat, trying to keep the impatience out of my voice.

"What the hell does that mean?"

Rolling over to my stomach, I groan. "You're pretty obtuse for a historian. I assumed you knew what a siege was."

"I do, but he's only one guy. Sieges are conducted by armies. Over long periods of time."

"He's an army of one. Throwing rocks at the building, bellowing threats. Like 'Monty Python and the Holy Grail.'"

She sniggers. "'Your mother was a hamster and your father smelt of elderberries!'"

I hoot. "'Go away before I taunt you a second time.'"

"Rocks and epithets. Anything else?"

"He attacked the doorman when he came out to quell the disturbance. I saw it all from my window and called the police. By the time they arrived, JL was on the scene. Sam broke his nose, but JL broke Sam's jaw. EMTs took him to the hospital."

"Sam or JL, or both?"

"Sam. JL had to go to the police station."

"Why?"

"He had to make a statement about what happened. Pretty standard procedure."

"Oh my God." She's hyperventilating. "Are you okay?"

"I'm fine, unlike the combatants."

"JL's with you, then? Are you canceling?" She sounds disappointed. I'm surprised since karaoke isn't her thing.

"I told you, he's at the cop shop, telling his story."

"Sam's in jail??"

"Not sure if they arrested him already or if they're waiting until after the doctors wire his jaw. Anyway, JL suggested you and Max should pick me up. He'll meet us there."

"Okay."

"Thanks."

"Max is eager to see your new digs. And maybe you need GSU to provide extra security."

I bite my lower lip. "Can't see why. Sam will be in jail."

"You know better than I do that he'll probably be out in a day or so."

In a grudging tone, I agree, "Guess so. But he violated the order of protection. Maybe a judge sympathetic to persecuted women will give him 90 or 120 days. Or something for the vandalism."

Background noise on the other end makes me ask, "What's happening, Cress?"

"Max was just talking to JL and says to tell you we'll be over in twenty minutes. Finish putting on your going-out face."

"Byeeee." I click off the phone, ready to paint my face. Once the mascara, a light dusting of foundation, highlighter, and blood-red lipstick are on, I grab my hairbrush.

Ninety-eight, ninety-nine, one hundred. My arm throbs, but my hair looks fab. Beauty is hard work. I add sparkly clips to each side, slip into my totally impractical stiletto-heel nude sandals, and finish with gold hoop earrings and a necklace of lapis lazuli chunks and gold beads.

Buzz. Buzz. Buzz. Must be Max and Cress. I fumble the clasp in my haste to push the entry button. I've just gotten it fastened when rapping starts against the door. I yank it open just as Max raises his fist to pummel the inoffensive wood again.

"Come on, Max. It's a door, not a percussion instrument." The grumpiness in my voice doesn't go unnoticed.

His breath slowing, Max whips out his latest quip. "I was out with some friends, and one pulled out of singing at karaoke at the last minute."

Cress and I look at each other. "Huh?" we say at the same time.

"Snap," Cress crows.

Max snickers. "I had to duet myself."

Cress grimaces. I give Max a small smile. One thing I've

learned, since meeting Max's family, is telling jokes is deeply embedded in the Grant clan's DNA.

"Don't encourage him," Cress warns.

Ignoring her, Max continues, "A karaoke singer stayed with me once, but I had to ask him to move out. He never knew when to come in and could never find the key."

"Boo. That was terrible," Cress says.

I'm giggling. Max smirks in triumph, and I know he will do at least one more.

"Chap I know went to the doctor and said, 'I keep singing "The Green, Green Grass of Home" at karaoke.' The doctor said, 'You've got Tom Jones syndrome.' Got that from Dad."

Cress has been moving around the living room, straightening ornaments, and plumping throw pillows. "Brian is a terrible influence. Anyway, bad things always come in threes. You've had yours, so stop now."

"Fine. Micki's amused, so my work is done. Show off your digs, then we'll go."

A ding heralds a text message. Max pulls out his phone. "JL says he's waiting to sign his statement. Give us the thruppenny tour. Then we'll make tracks for the bar. I hear they have the best karaoke in the city."

I usher them toward the dining room, outfitted with a table for twelve, and holding a matching breakfront and buffet. The kitchen is just behind. No galley kitchen. This is a large space with top-of-the-line stainless steel appliances, granite countertops, cherry cabinets, and laminate flooring that looks like stone. There is an island in the middle with stools set on one side.

Moving toward the double doors on one side, I say, "Drumroll, please. The pièce de résistance." I pull them open with a flourish. Shallow shelves display a startling array of food, mostly jars, jewel-tone colors of jams, preserved fruit, containers of grains and cereal, bags of coffee. You name it, it's probably there. The owners are obviously foodies. Too bad I don't cook. At all. Ever.

"Nice," Cress comments, picking up a jar and examining the contents. "Preserved lemons. Guess they like Moroccan food."

"Can we liberate a few things?" Max asks. "Or do they know their food stocks will remain unviolated while they're away?"

I snicker. "They didn't padlock it."

"We'll come back and do our shopping here."

"Would that be all right?" Cress sounds unsure.

"The owners are hoping to sell the place, so I don't think moving the food is on their agenda. Besides, they'll be out of the country for a year. By then I hope I'll be able to afford a down payment."

"Isn't this extravagant?"

"Says the man with the many-roomed Gold Coast mansion."

"And the extensive family." He folds his arms with a mock glare.

"I want the aspiration home. The place that shows I'm confident enough to be the next partner in the firm."

Cress breaks in, "We'll buy the couscous and preserved lemon tomorrow so Max can fix a Moroccan feast. I haven't had Moroccan food for an age."

"Hmm. I could certainly do a tagine and a b'stilla." Max's voice follows me as I turn out of the kitchen, motioning them to follow. The food talk is not all that interesting, although if they invite me to eat it, I won't say no. Probably beats cereal or toast, my two standbys.

"Not sure tomorrow will work. I'll probably go in early and come home late."

A hand grabs my arm and Cress pulls me around to face her. "Don't drive yourself into a cesspit. If you're dead, you lose." Her fingers continue to press into my bicep while we walk toward the other side of the condo. When she finally lets go, indentations remain on my skin.

French doors close off the sleeping corridor. There are three bedrooms, each with its own private bath, plus a half bath in the hall. The primary bedroom is humongous, with oversized furniture to match. The bathroom has a Jacuzzi tub and a shower.

We move on to the next bedroom, which is the one I'm using. Set up as a guest room, it's big but not outrageous. The bathroom has a modest tub-shower combination.

The owners converted the last bedroom into a study. Book-lined walls make the space feel cozy. There is a wooden desk and a computer table with an iMac. Two filing cabinets sit under one set of hanging bookcases. In a corner, a wingback chair rests at an angle with a floor lamp behind and a small table next to it.

"Very impressive," Max says.

"Not as impressive as your house." He shrugs off my comment.

We return to the living room with its stone fireplace, grand piano, and large sectional sofa. A sixty-five-inch television hangs on one wall, an oversized sound system underneath.

"Fully furnished is nice." Cress gestures around the space. "But where's your stuff?"

"In storage. I don't have much anyway. I sold almost everything when I moved. Once I have a place of my own, I'll buy whatever I need."

"And you're hoping to buy this?" Max moves over to one couch where he'd thrown their coats, then picks up a long deep red woolen balmacaan and shakes it invitingly.

Instead of answering the question, I squeal in delight at the garment. "You replaced the coat."

I walk past Cress to grab my jacket from the hall closet. The stars in her eyes transfix me and I have to remind myself to move my feet.

Max's soft expression matches the one on her face. "She adored the original. But no one could fix it and the dry cleaner advised us the blood wouldn't come out. I went back to replace it, but they were all sold out. Sold out everywhere."

"He contacted the designer and had this made for me." Fairy dust sifts down everywhere.

All this mushy emotion makes me eager to reunite with JL. Not sure why I feel this way since I see this as a fun interlude in my life. My priority is to make partner at the firm. With a fifty-fifty chance, I need to be on my game.

I'm not sure whether the evaluation or the insider trading case is the more important piece, but I need to work two-hundred-percent, even though I know Hayden won't play fair and has two partners in his pocket.

Cress suddenly looks down at my sandaled feet. Her own are in practical ankle boots and I bet she has socks on too. Fortunately, she can't see the bandages across the cuts and abrasions on my soles. I try not to wince as I walk toward the door. At least the antibacterial cream has helped with the pain.

"Aren't your feet going to be cold?"

I shrug, pushing my right arm into one of my coat sleeves. "We're going to be in the car, then inside. No big deal. My feet won't have time to freeze."

"Onward, ladies." Max opens the door with a courtly sweep of his arm. I make sure I have the door key. We hear the click as it locks behind us. The entire building can probably hear Max as he sings "I'm Gonna Be" by the Proclaimers—the song he used when he apologized to Cress at Christmas last year. Warming up for karaoke, I join him in the chorus as we troop out of the building. Cress stomps ahead, pretending she's not with us.

I've been to karaoke nights a few times, but Cress has always refused to go with me. "Hey, Max." I want to find out why they're going along.

"May I help you?" His formal response cracks me up again.

"Cress treats the idea of karaoke like a dreaded disease. So why are you two going?"

"JL's my best friend, so of course I said yes. Cress just wants to horn in on your date." His raucous laugh streams down the street into the cool night air.

A door slams. Cress has already climbed into the back seat of the SUV.

CHAPTER
FOUR

Always remember: if you're going through hell, keep going.—
Winston Churchill

JL

THE TEXT from Max arrives as I rush past the desk sergeant on my way out. I wave, but she doesn't notice.

> MAX: We're here. Getting the ladies settled.

I try to breathe a sigh of relief, which hurts. My nose is sore and before they carted Sam off, the EMTs confirmed the break. Not the first time, but it's never fun. Just hope the new shape isn't too terrible and I don't need any cleanup surgery. I'll ask the bar for some ice and a glass of water for the painkillers. Hope it doesn't impact my singing. Winning tonight's competition would be some recompense for a more than average shitty day.

ME: Need to change. I'll be there soon.

I slip the mobile into my pocket, rev up the bike, and take off for the short ride to my condo in River East. In less than ten minutes, I've stripped off my shirt, examined my nose, put on a turtleneck, and got back on my bike, heading toward the flatiron-style building on the corner of Lincoln Avenue. After I park, I salute the mashed potato mural on the side and set the white rocking chairs in motion as I walk through the doors.

The hostess points me to the back. Micki jumps up from her seat in a red vinyl booth, waving her hands wildly above her head. Plates of shared food sit on the table. Stanley's specialty is down-home Southern cooking, and the platters include andouille corn dogs, fried dill pickles, and God's Own Mac and Cheese. Even though Max ordered Stanley's Tots Poutine just for me, Micki spears a tot from the platter and waves it at me.

"Not authentic." She frowns at my assessment.

Max taps my shoulder. "Let's move to the bar and order the first round. And pick up some ice for that elephant trunk."

At the end of the bar, we each pick up a shot glass and pour in some bourbon, a lagniappe Stanley's provides for customers who know to look. We down them while we wait for our beers, wine, glasses of water, and a small plastic baggie of crushed ice. The place is hopping, waiting for Sunday night live-band karaoke as we thread our way into the back room. My skin damp from the rising heat from so many bodies. The smell of savory fried chicken and melted cheese mingles with spilled beer, too much after-shave and perfume, and the slightly sour smell of too many people in too little space. I'd pick up the pace if I could, but many human roadblocks clutter our path.

"I want to assign some guys to Micki," I tell Max, then raise my voice. "Excuse me. Could you let us by?"

A guy turns with a glare, then sees the load we're trying not to spill, pulls at his pal's arm, and moves out of the way.

"You think she'll accept that?" Max sounds dubious.

Not at all sure how she'll react, I straighten my shoulders and pull on my cloak of confidence. "She was all for it when that nutcase, Tina, threatened Cress."

"That was Cress. Doesn't mean she'll be receptive when it's a question of her own safety. Look how she fought when we made her go to the ER after Sam slugged her last December."

"This crazy attack is a definite escalation."

By now, we're back at the table.

"Think we'll see any celebs?" Micki twirls her glass of wine, a bold Zinfandel, and takes a sniff. Max carefully puts Cress' glass down where she can't inadvertently knock it over.

I give a noncommittal shrug as I pull off my jacket and drape it over the back of the chair.

"Chris Chelios sometimes comes in." Cress' face flushes with excitement at the possibility.

"If he's in town. Doesn't live in Chicago now." Micki's little smile and the way she buffs her nails against her collarbone, as if she's won some contest, are charming.

"Wish they hadn't traded him to Detroit." Cress gives a mournful sigh.

"That was fifteen years ago. Let it go." Micki pats her on the shoulder.

Replete and warm, we sit around waiting for the entertainment. Once the band sets up, we'll move to the front room and grab some stools at one of the cocktail tables.

"Do you want to sing with me?"

Micki turns, eyes sparkling, and my body fizzes like I've just downed an entire bottle of vintage champagne.

"What do you have in mind?"

Several French titles run through my mind, but in the end I say, "How about 'You're the One That I Want'?" I waggle my eyebrows suggestively.

She crosses her hands over her heart, and wiggles like she's restraining herself from jumping up to dance. "Oooh, John Travolta and Olivia Newton-John."

Max smirks while Cress' jaw drops, eyes wide and staring.

Finally, she gives a little mouse squeak. "Are you singing, Max?"

Lines crinkle around his eyes. "'Annie Laurie,' I thought."

We gaze, astonished.

"What? Cress wants me to vary my repertoire."

"Not so appropriate for karaoke," I tell him.

"Why not? I've seen people win with opera arias." His jaw hardens.

"'Annie Laurie" isn't 'Nessun Dorma.' It's too lachry-mose. People want something upbeat." Cress' dryly, acerbic observation makes Max wince.

He glares at her and rubs the back of his neck. Then, in a kind of metamorphosis, his eyes twinkle with a new idea. He starts to make another suggestion, but Cress puts a palm against his lips.

"Not the Proclaimers. Or 'Scotland the Brave.'"

Max scowls and she slaps his arm.

Eyes squinched to show she's thinking hard, she

pauses, then mimes a lightbulb going on. With a mischievous look in her eye, she makes another suggestion. "How about 'Chelsea Dagger'? The Fratellis are Scottish."

"And it's the Blackhawks goal song," Micki adds. "Double points. You can sing it together, Cress."

Once he gets over the outrageousness of the suggestion, Max gazes at her like a dog begging for a piece of bacon. "Please sing with me," he murmurs.

"Yeah, okay, if they have the words for us."

Micki's long nails click on the screen of her phone. "Got it," she says, waving the instrument in Cress' face. "Just take this up with you. I bet everyone here will sing along."

Cress puts her hand out, palm up and Micki gives her the instrument.

With her hands free, I lean forward and slip Micki's hands between mine to capture her attention. My voice sounds like gravel when I tell her, "We need to talk."

Her eyes glaze into icy pools. "What about?" She removes her hand from mine with a grimace, scoots back on the banquette, and crosses her arms.

"You need protection for when Sam's released on bond."

"He's not that dangerous," she scoffs.

I huff, "He seemed plenty dangerous tonight."

"Small rocks, name-calling, and a not-very-successful fight." She waves her hands as if shooing something away. "He didn't bring a gun."

I point to my nose, glaring. "He might next time. Let me arrange some coverage for you."

Her lips thin and she spits out, "I don't need your help. I can take care of myself."

Cress grabs Micki's arm and makes her look into her eyes. "That's what I thought last year and look what happened. JL can arrange this. If nothing happens, great. But if something goes down, you'll be glad to have someone around."

She hisses. "I need to make the right impression at work. Not just to make partner. How will it look if I come in every day with my bodyguard? Like a liability, that's what. So, no."

"We can have guys outside the building." I fold my arms and shoot some visual arrows.

"You think he couldn't elude them around the Aon Building?" Her mocking expression is like a red cape to a bull.

I open my mouth to argue when a guitar riff warns the band has come in. They warm up. We hustle to grab our stuff and find seats in the main room. We snag some stools right under the noses of a group of wannabe tough guys. They try to move in, but one bouncer makes an appearance, and they back off.

People shoulder to shoulder press in. Max and I fight through, waving to the emcee to add our names on the list while Cress and Micki guard our seats. He nods at our choices and notes that we will do duets. Numbers six and seven. Not too bad. The earlier songs should warm up the crowd, but not to where the audience is jaded by a long evening of singing.

"Anyone famous coming in?" I ask. "My girlfriend is hoping for a celeb or two."

"Maybe. It's not like they call and tell us. But I heard Bill Murray might be in town. He's known to drop in."

The owner's been threading his way around through the crowd and is now standing near us. I point him out. "Too bad the Blackhawks are playing away. I heard Coach Q sang here a couple of years ago," Cress says.

"Quenneville? Yeah, he was a hit singing 'Sweet Caroline.' But the Hawks don't hang out here much anymore. All high-end steak houses these days."

"That's too bad. These ladies are big hockey fans." I clap a hand on his shoulder. "If someone should come in, could you give us a high sign?"

He looks over at Micki's and Cress' eager faces.

"I'll see what I can do. No one calls to tell us they're dropping by. Unless it's the President. We don't clear the room, but we limit the numbers."

With a riff on the snare and crashing cymbals, the band plays Guns 'n Roses "Welcome to the Jungle," and even shouting would be useless. By now, the crowd presses together with no space to fit in anyone else. At least that's what we think until two enormous guys push in. Somehow, they squeeze into the crowd and belly up to the bar.

Once everyone has settled down, the emcee introduces the band members. Then the first performer is called up. The crowd is quiet as he sings The Proclaimers hit and I punch Max in the shoulder. He laughs as I hear Cress tell him he does it better.

Finally, Max and Cress sing "Chelsea Dagger," the crowd sings along, and it's our turn. The band plays the intro, and we start. The crowd claps as we make a few dance moves. As we near the end, a commotion starts near the door.

A monster in green stomps in. Can't help but notice his lack of shoes. His feet leave wet blobs on the floor. Big body, in a coverall, potbelly hanging down. The hood covers the head. Features obscured by a full-face gas mask, goggles, and thick gloves. One gigantic hand pushes people out of the way as if they're foam blocks.

"Hey, guy. It's not Halloween," someone in the crowd yells.

Seconds later, the guy is on the floor; the monster stepping on him as it moves forward.

Micki's strained whisper sends icy trickles down my spine.

"It's Sam." Her eyes are wide, and she trembles against me.

"How can you tell? With that getup, it could be anyone."

She crosses her eyes in disgust. "It was his Halloween costume last year."

I'm convinced. But how did he find us? He should be in the hospital or in jail.

All the hubbub stops as the band tails off. In the sudden silence, we hear a high-pitched scream. "Tole you to move, din't I?" sounds like "twww uh tah muv." The swollen jaw makes him almost impossible to understand, and I'm not sure how he can even keep his tongue in the space.

A guy collapses to the floor, whimpering. Sam stomps up toward the stage and I try to head him off. He stops, his eyes moving toward Micki. Before I can react, he pulls something out of his pocket and throws it over his shoulder into the crowd. A blinding flash and unbearable noise, then smoke fills the space.

Calisse. Should have guessed from the 'costume.' My eyes sting and water from the chemical compound. I can't see or hear anything, but I feel a big body rush past, dragging something...or someone.

Blindly, I reach out and feel cloth that reminds me of Micki's outfit, but it slips through my fingers. Cursing, I stumble after, but I've no idea where I am in the room.

All hell breaks loose as cops swarm in. I'm wiping my streaming eyes and looking desperately for Micki. Max grabs me and pulls me toward the back room, where Cress hugs her. We're all coughing from the smoke, but in here the air is clearer. Sound filters in.

"What happened?" They don't respond and I'm not sure they can hear me as they sniffle and hug. I want Micki to hug me, damn it, not Cress.

Eventually, they collapse onto a banquette while I bring back glasses of water and damp bar towels so they can wipe their faces. Most of the patrons are gone and the cops continue to take brief statements from people who know nothing and saw even less.

Max, who has been hanging out with a senior officer, comes in with two large whiskies, puts them on the table, and punches my shoulder. He presses a finger against his ear. "Sorry, still feeling some pressure. Anyway, I just finished getting briefed." He motions for us to take a couple of chairs not too close to the girls. "What a piece of work. He managed to slip away in the emergency room. The cop told me that while he was waiting to be seen, he snagged some of his clothes and ran out. Didn't even wait to have his jaw wired."

"Wasn't he guarded?"

"They didn't want to go into how he eluded the cop who was supposed to be watching. At any rate, he never found his boots or shirt."

"Bare feet?"

"He's just wearing socks. You'd think he'd be smart enough to go home, but all he did was call an Uber. His truck was still sitting at the Press house. Had an extra set of keys hidden in it. He'd stashed the mask and stuff there too."

"Dumbass."

"After he let off the smoke bomb, Sam grabbed Micki

and started dragging her through the crowd. Fallen bodies formed a barrier across the room that kept him stalled. Trying to move people aside and hold on to her was too difficult. His grip slipped and Micki got away, but not before she showed him he'd picked the wrong girl."

He can't stop grinning. "Sam definitely miscalculated. She stomped on his foot with one of her high heels. Just socks on his feet. The spike went right through. My hearing had just come back and that scream. She inflicted some serious damage. Anyway, he was in so much pain he fell over. Micki ran, right into Cress."

Sam screams incomprehensible curses as he's cuffed and hustled out. Adrenaline must be blocking the pain. Cops come over to take our statements. By the time we're finally able to leave, everyone is exhausted. Micki gives me a world-weary headshake when I offer her the chance to ride on my bike.

"Go home, JL. Max and Cress can drop me off. I have a busy day tomorrow and I just want to go to bed."

"That's not happening. I will see you back to your place and make sure you are safe."

She snorts. "He'll be in jail. And I did fine. I can take care of myself."

Putting my hand on her back, I steer her toward the door. "See you later, Max."

Micki grinds her teeth but says nothing. I take out the helmets and put one on her, tweaking the chin strap to make sure it's snug. Then I adjust mine and throw my leg over. "Arms around my waist, s'il te plaît." She hesitates, then complies, and we roll down the street.

∼

Micki

The bike sits under a streetlamp, gleaming with a promise I'm too tired to appreciate. Once JL starts the engine, the thrum of the bike engine causes vibrations that trigger sensations I don't even want to acknowledge. My arms have his waist in a death grip. With my cheek pressed against his back, the intoxicating scents of leather, beer, and whatever aftershave he uses make my senses reel. Even though the ride from Stanley's to my rented condo is only about seven minutes, staying mad at JL is impossible. By the time he helps me off the bike, I am trembling as he gently guides me into the lobby of the building.

I squeeze my eyes shut against the glare of the overhead chandeliers, still feeling effects from the flashing lights, noise, and smoke. There's been a changing of the guard and as if from a distance, I hear the sound of the night concierge.

"Evening, or maybe I should say good morning, Ms. Press." I squint and make out Nate, sitting on a high stool behind reception.

My throat is scratchy, voice hoarse. "Morning, Nate." Unlike the older concierge, Nate is a clean-cut college student from the Chicago suburbs. He's a second year at John Marshall Law School and occasionally asks me questions about points he's studying. With an engineering background, I'm not surprised his focus is on patent law. When I asked why he was working here, his answer was unexpected.

"My grandparents own one of the condos and arranged this with the management company when I told them I wanted a job. Nights mean work doesn't interfere with classes and I usually have plenty of time to read."

"Where could we go for a really early breakfast?" JL asks.

"I'd say Tempo Café over on Chestnut. They're a twenty-four-hour place. Pretty good food, too. World-class waffles and three-egg specialties."

I move slightly away from JL and turn to face him. "You're hungry?"

"I could fix something for you if you prefer. I'm a dab hand in the kitchen."

"You sound like Max. Anyway, there's nothing here to fix. I don't cook, so I just have cereal." I don't tell him about the fully stocked pantry. Or that I don't want to risk having him come upstairs, where we might just fall into bed. This is a first date. Even though I've known him for a few months now, it's too soon. Especially after the two run-ins with Sam.

"Bien. Let's go eat eggs and drink coffee at Tempo Café." He grasps my hand in his, ready to turn toward the door.

Tempo is busier than I expect. Fortunately, a booth opens up. "Breakfast all the time." The server places small dishes with an orange slice, a prune, and two roasted chestnuts next to the fresh water glasses.

"Coffee," I croak. "With cream."

"You want coffee too?" she asks JL, examining him with interest. With his cropped dark hair, high cheekbones, long narrow face sporting the swollen nose and scruff he'll shave off soon, liquid chocolate-brown eyes, and a crooked grin that would make any woman melt, he's quite a dish.

"Certainement. Café au lait, s'il vous plaît."

"You're French? Wow." She is gushing now.

"French Canadian," he tells her with a comic leer. "We're much more romantic than the French." Then he winks. Winks!

With a giggle, she turns away to fetch our coffee.

I focus on the menu, so I don't have to look at him.

"You're still angry with me, ma chouette?" JL taps his fingers against the laminated card.

"Schwet? Sounds German. What does it mean?"

JL's smooth pronunciation caresses my ear. "C-h-o-u-e-t-t-e. It's a small owl. A term of endearment."

"A little soon for that."

"Not at all. I see this as a beginning. The timing is perfect." He pats my hand just as our coffees arrive.

"Cream?"

She points to a small dish with creamers. I don't see any half and half. "Do you have real cream? Or just some milk?"

"Sure, just a sec, and I'll bring you some."

When I see JL's puzzled expression, I explain, "Don't like artificial creamers."

He nods as the woman comes back with a small pitcher that turns out to be heavy cream.

I pour a dollop into my cup. "Do you want one too?"

"One what?"

"A nickname?"

JL wipes foam from his lips. Even that move seems sexy, but it could be the exhaustion giving me hallucinations. "No rush. Whenever you feel comfortable."

"Sure, Beau," pops out of my mouth. Where did that come from?

"Guess you feel comfortable enough." He empties the cup. "Now, let's talk about protection."

I take a deep breath, then blow it out in a teakettle whistle. "You're right. They will probably release Sam on bail this morning, and there's nothing to stop him from showing up again. The order of protection, while a legal nicety, will not keep him away. If he gets a gun, he could kill me before the police could act."

"I don't think his aim is to kill you, at least not now." JL's face is serious. "If he gets too frustrated, that could change."

"Well, that's a relief," I say sarcastically. "Why do you think he isn't interested in killing me now?"

With his next words, I remember JL has a doctorate in psychology. "Speaking with my psychologist's hat on, I think he wants you back, not dead. But over time, if he accepts that's not an option, then he might be angry enough to kill you. He won't want you to be with anyone else. I'm already a goad for him." Our server comes back.

"Ready to order?" she says, taking her pad and pen out of an apron pocket.

JL glances at the menu. "Steak and eggs look good. I'd like the steak rare, and I think we both want hash browns and toast."

"We have white, raisin, wheat, rye, and English muffins."

"A muffin for me, and a small bag of ice." He points to his nose. "How about you, ma chouette?"

"Scrambled eggs with chicken livers. The mushrooms, onion, and green peppers make it really yummy."

"Toast?"

After a short internal debate—raisin or rye?—I plump for neither. "Wheat toast, please, with the butter on the side. And do you have any jam besides grape or strawberry?"

"Blueberry?"

I give her a thumbs-up.

"You got it." With one more long gaze at JL's arresting, if

somewhat disfigured, visage, she hurries off to the kitchen to put in our selections.

He stares at me, brow furrowed. "Probably shouldn't ask, but what did you see in that asshole?"

"You probably shouldn't." I sip my coffee. Then I look over the rim of the mug into his burnt-sugar eyes. "I was ready to settle. He was convenient and convinced me he wanted me. In the beginning, he wasn't so bad. By the time I noticed the changes, inertia had set in. He was the easy option."

JL's mouth droops, but then he recovers. "You should never have to settle. Never. You deserve everything."

"Hah. The guys I dated in college and even in law school always told me I was too dedicated, too ambitious, too competitive. When I made my choice, career came first. Sam was the only guy who didn't seem to care I earned more money. He liked the idea of being a kept man. Settling for him felt like my only option if I didn't want to be alone."

After a sip of his cappuccino, JL wipes the foam off his lips. But he says nothing.

"And you?" I challenge. "How will you feel when work is my focus?"

"I believe you can have both," he says, sounding so sincere, so honest. His words warm me for a second before an icy trickle replaces it.

He's a man in a man's world and doesn't know what women face, especially professional women. The condescension, the backlash. And how long will it be until he wants the attention, complains about the long hours, tires of pitching in?

I shake my head and drink my coffee. His vision is a pipe dream, and he'll back away soon enough, find someone who can put him first.

He glances at his phone, turns the conversation to practical matters. "Still too early to call the office. After we eat, I'll take you home so you can prepare for the day. In the meantime, I'll go to my place, shower, and change, then pick you up and take you to the office. Once I arrive at GSU, I'll organize the arrangements. It will be three guys in rotation. Once I have everything in place, someone will brief you on the setup."

His take-charge, businesslike manner is another turn-on for me. Everything about him produces electric shocks and I have to concentrate on not salivating when I picture him in a well-cut suit. *Just lust and a yearning for some fun. Nothing serious.* If I say it enough, maybe I'll believe it.

He's not looking for permanent either. Cress told me his fiancée dumped him when he was serving in Germany. Serial dating is his speed now. Keeping things light and casual will make this so much easier when we're done. Satisfied I've quelled my inner siren, I dig into the Continental. What a treat. I'd never be able to make this, nor do I want to. Having others cook for you is the height of decadence for me.

"Micki, are you listening?" JL sounds both worried and irritated. Guess my lascivious thoughts are translating in a worrisome way.

I give him a sheepish grin. "Sorry, lost in thought."

"About Sam?" He sits rigid, back taut, shoulders sky-high, his tone sharp, acid.

Startled by his vehemence and obvious jealousy, I snap, "What makes you think that? Sam was the farthest thing from my mind."

"Sorry, but he is the only guy under discussion." Shoulders dropping from his ears, JL's eyes soften as he picks up a piece of steak, perfectly encased in charcoaled crustiness that contrasts beautifully with the deep red interior. He pops it into his mouth. "Parfait."

I excavate a piece of chicken liver from the enveloping eggs and relish the texture, smooth on the outside, soft and melty within. Sautéed and seasoned with a little balsamic vinegar, it's heaven on my tongue.

JL looks around the cheerful, brightly lit space, then gazes into the darkness beyond the window. "Nice place. Good food." He switches from the steak to pick up an English muffin, half slathered with butter and marmalade. He gestures with it, careful not to let anything drip. "Knowing you'll be protected after I leave for London eases my mind. After all, I'll be gone two weeks before you land in Paris." He pins me with a heated gaze. "I wish you could do the entire trip with us."

"Me too. But I can't take that much time off work. We have a big case on, and the client is pushing for a swift resolution. I can't even do my usual things—watch hockey or join a geocaching group."

"Geocaching?"

"It's a kind of treasure hunt. You use GPS to find hidden containers. I downloaded a free app. Locate the coordinates and use those to find the caches. Sometimes you add your ID to a log. Sometimes there's an item. If you want to take it, then you need to leave something comparable."

"What's in your kit? Do you need a shovel?"

"No shovels necessary. People hide the caches but can't bury them." I smile, thinking of treasures I've found. "If we have time in Paris, we could hunt."

"In Paris?"

"Caches are everywhere." But I can't do it. "I'll probably be working most of the time, but maybe one of these days..."

"Working most of the time?" He sounds miffed.

"Oh yes, I'll be doing that. There's this guy..."

"What guy?" His hyperalert expression gives me goosebumps.

"He's my competition for the partner position. I'm worried about him undermining me while I'm away."

"But if you're the best candidate, they would promote you, right?"

I do my party trick, crossing my eyes and puckering my lips. "He has a couple of partners pushing for his promotion and he'll schmooze the others and bad mouth me."

JL's face reddens. "Will you be totally invisible?"

I can see the supportive façade crumble and almost cry out with the pain.

"Video meetings at least once or twice a day. And Rebecca, the partner who's my mentor, will advocate for me."

"Then come with us to London. Max would make the arrangements for you so you could attend his father's birthday. I'm sure Brian and Viktoria would love to see you at the celebration, then stay with everyone in the Highlands."

He doesn't seem to understand the inflexibility in my position, and I try to control my irritation when I answer. "The time I've planned is all I'm willing to take. The managing partner sets the tone, and he is like a goddamn concrete post. I don't have the wherewithal to chip away at him from afar. He hardly tolerates women as anything more than secretaries and legal assistants. Hayden, my rival, is his favorite. If I want any chance to move up, I need to make the best impression possible, which means being in the office where I can be seen."

"You need most of the partners on your side to scotch his plan."

"Exactly. That's why I can't be out of the office for too long."

"Or find a firm that will appreciate you."

I startle myself with the growl that rumbles out of my chest. "Law jobs aren't a dime a dozen. I'm at one of the most prestigious firms in the Chicago area. Can't just take my marbles and go home." I wince at the number of clichés pouring out.

JL puts down his fork and takes my hand, squeezing gently. "We'll have to make the best of the next few days. Once I leave, I'll call you every night from wherever we are. And hold my breath until I join you in Paris."

A cough spurts out. "Hold.. .your...breath. You'll... be... DOA." The words are choppy as I try to hold in the bubbling laughter that overtakes me. "DOA," I wheeze.

"Okay, okay." He holds up a hand, palm toward me, in a stop gesture. "I won't be holding it literally, but figuratively, yes. I'll be counting the hours, maybe even the minutes, the hundredths of each second. You've bewitched me, but I don't want to escape your spells."

A little warning bell rings. His feelings are stronger than I thought. "Wait a minute, Beau. We've only been on one date. Too soon for those kinds of protestations. Can't we just have fun and see if it leads anywhere?"

"Since I've known you for a few months, I suppose I feel we're already getting close. I'm a sprinter, not a marathoner, but I'll emulate the tortoise rather than the hare if that makes you more comfortable."

"After tonight, and all the turmoil over the last few months, I need a breather. And my energy has to go toward promotion. The handwriting is on the wall. If I don't make it this time around, I won't make it at all, at least at this firm."

Back at the building, he walks me into the lobby. It's 4:00 a.m.

"I'll be back at seven," he says. Then kisses me on the cheek. I watch him until he's swallowed up by the darkness.

CHAPTER
FIVE

*God grant me the courage not to give up what I think is right
even though I think it is hopeless.—Chester W. Nimitz*

Micki

WAKING up at 6:00 a.m. when I didn't arrive home until four is not the best way to prepare for an important client meeting. Even though I took a shower to rinse off all traces of Sam when JL delivered me to the condo, I take another boiling shower to wake up, wrap myself in one of the huge bath sheets I favor, and make a mental note to buy a few more when I have my own place again.

My hair wrapped in a towel, I make my way into the kitchen for coffee. I have a dozen different choices of Keurig cups. Every day I choose a different dark blend. Today it's Emeril Lagasse's Big Easy Bold. Once I bolt a cup down, doctored with some cream and hazelnut syrup, I fix my hair, then put on my best professional suit—chalk stripe on a dark blue double-breasted, slim jacket and a matching

55

pencil skirt from Brooks Brothers. The perfectly pressed bright white shirt with a narrow-pleated front, navy heels, and nude pantyhose complete the ensemble. I fasten my small diamond studs into my earlobes and put on my lucky diamond starburst gold necklace, rubbing the charm. Almost seven. JL should be here any minute.

Not hungry after our meal at Tempo, I know I should make myself eat something before the presentation, but I don't bother. Shrugging on my wool overcoat, I pick up my brief bag, then put it down when the ringtone for my parents, the Beatles "Come Together," sounds from deep in my purse. I scrabble in the bag's bottom, noting I need to recharge it soon. I send it to voice mail, then send a text.

> ME: On my way out the door. Call you back in a few.

> MOM: Just wanted to wish you luck in the client meeting.

I send thumbs-up and crossed finger emojis with a heart.

Another ding.

> JL: Downstairs.

> ME: Okay.

> JL: I couldn't sleep last night, thinking about you.

I read this over several times. Not sure if this is concern over what happened yesterday or another declaration of feelings. I decide to treat it as if it's the former.

The intercom rings.

"Ms. Press, Mr. Martin is here." Antonio, the morning guy, has a voice like gravy.

"Thanks, I'll be right down." JL, smart in a gray tweed overcoat, leans on the counter, chatting with Antonio. The latter gives me a wave and JL turns with a big smile. "Ciao, amico," he calls out to Antonio as he moves in my direction.

We meet in the middle of the space.

"How're you doing, Beau?"

"I've had a lot of coffee. Two hours of sleep. Probably should have just sat up with you. More refreshing, ma chouette. You?"

"Same."

No motorcycle this time. We walk out to a black SUV complete with driver. JL holds the door and settles in next to me. When we pull up in front of the office building with a flourish, he walks me to the elevator, rides up, and trails me into my office.

"Are you planning to hang out here?"

"No, I have to go to work. Now that you are safely delivered, I'll set up your bodyguard rota. What time is your meeting?"

"Ten." I feel my stomach plummet.

"Someone will be at your office at nine to bring you up to speed on the arrangements."

I walk him back out into the empty reception area. We aren't open until nine, so everything is dark.

"Lock the door behind me." He gives me a peck on the lips.

I push him out and ostentatiously turn the locks while he watches. Then I make myself walk back toward the corridor before I can run out and ask him to stay.

With a sigh, I slip my laptop out of my bag, log in, and start reading preliminary documents about the case. We've had several meetings with Congressman Greenberg and he's a piece of work, hiding under the demeanor of the ever-helpful Boy Scout. To everyone's dismay, the media coverage has been relentless and brutal as the other contenders for the nomination lambast him. Insinuations are rife. With a sigh, I prepare to read today's stories.

Just as I pull up the websites for the daily papers, "I'm Too Sexy" announces another text message. Dealing with all this right now is just too much. I click the message app. Cress. Now what.

CRESS: LET ME IN

ME: Where are you?

CRESS: In the hallway. Can't you hear me pounding on the door?

ME: Hallway?

CRESS: Outside the firm's office, dingbat.

Crapola. Just what I need.

ME: Be right out.

When I let her in, Cress makes a beeline for my office. She trips on a wrinkle in the carpet. "A little dark, don't you think?"

"We're not open." Irritation makes me snappish.

She follows the rectangle of light shining from my open door and safely makes it to my guest chair, after throwing her coat onto the tree in the corner.

"Do you want coffee?"

"That would be great, thanks."

I turn and practically run down the hall to the kitchenette. We have two machines, so I place the cups, load the capsules, and press the start buttons. Since she didn't follow me, I have a little breathing space before whatever inquisition she has planned.

Finally, the coffees appropriately doctored with cream and sugar, I carefully transport them back. As I hand one to her, I ask, "What are you doing here?"

"Breakfast." She takes a box marked Toni's Patisserie out of her oversized bag. Inside nestle a croissant and an eclair. Just to wind her up, I reach for the eclair while she excavates for napkins.

When she sees my hand hovering, she snaps, irritated, "Hey, that's mine. Take the croissant."

"Fine." My grumble is pretend. She always gets the eclairs. All that chocolate glaze and custard. Not for breakfast.

I put the pastry down next to my cup and tap the laptop case. "Just getting started on today's reading. Greenberg will be here at ten for the next briefing."

"Do clients usually come in so often?"

"No, but our congressman is in a hurry. The flames are fanned every day and his numbers are tanking. He insists it's a frame-up, but I'm finding some suspicious emails from an anonymous account that just happens to be on his laptop."

Cress takes a bite of her eclair, face suffusing with color, not from embarrassment but from pleasure. The moan that follows the track of the pastry is probably what Max hears from her in bed.

Carefully, I bite into my buttery croissant, quickly

brushing pastry flakes off my skirt into the garbage container I pulled in front of me for this purpose.

"What are you doing this morning?"

"I plan to pack and write at home. This was my constitutional. Come by for a drink later. Maybe stay for dinner."

"I might need that. Between Hayden's antics and Greenberg's demands, the day will be pretty taxing."

"Think positively," says my friend, the ultimate pessimist.

I look at my watch. "I'll walk you out. JL has someone coming to see me in about ten minutes."

As we walk out of the Aon Center, the building we call our home away from home, my right heel gets caught in the space between paving slabs in the building courtyard facing Randolph Street. When I yank it out, it snaps off. Fuck me.

Cress, who has already gotten ahead of me, looks back. "Micki?" Her eyes widen as she sees the disaster.

"Don't worry." I wave her off. "I have another pair in the office."

She bites her lip. I make pushing motions with my hands and eventually she runs to catch the bus she needs as it appears in the distance.

JL

Light traffic this early in the morning makes the drive to the office quick. I park in one of the public lots near the Rookery Building, in the heart of Chicago's financial district. The GSU offices occupy the entire fifth floor of the historic late nineteenth-century structure.

The lights in the coffee room are dim when I fetch my

first coffee of the day. "Call building maintenance and have the lights fixed," I tell myself. When I'm back at my desk, I contact Liam and give him instructions, then tell him to meet Micki at her office at nine.

The coffee is lukewarm. A sip proves it undrinkable. I walk back, make another, sip the perfect liquid in situ. Paradise.

The distinctive voice of Edith Piaf singing "La Vie en Rose" trickles out of the pocket of my black gabardine slacks. Maman. Her favorite song from her favorite singer. Their similar backgrounds attracted my mother to Piaf's music. After Maman's parents died, she lived in precarious circumstances in Quebec City, until she met my papa. I slip a capsule into the coffee maker and press the start button for the cup I'll take back to my desk. Then I grab the phone from the counter.

"Bonjour, Maman. Ça va?"

"Ça va." But instead of saying, "Et toi?" I hear a grumble, then a scolding squawk. "Tu es très méchant, mon bout de chou."

I wince at a name I haven't heard since I was about seven.

"Maman! I am no longer a child." She doesn't answer.

I try again. "Pourquoi?"

"A week. You haven't called in a week."

"Désolé, Maman. Mea culpa, mea maxima culpa." My very Catholic Maman will appreciate the apologetic words, even if I can't tell her why I have been too busy to call. To confess about the threat Micki faces and how it affects me is out of the question. She doesn't even know of her existence, and this is not the time to enlighten her. The terrorist threatening Max is another issue I can't say anything about. I'll have to come up with a few white lies.

"I'll be leaving for London in a few days for work. Getting ready for the trip means cleaning up a few jobs and making sure everything is in order with my guys. And you know how Clay is about loose ends."

"D'accord. I forgive you." She uses her magnanimous voice and I squirm like a small child being punished. "How is your friend, Max?"

"Merci, Maman." Forgiveness accepted, I go on with the small talk my maman lives for. "Looking forward to his dad's birthday party. We're going up to Scotland for a few days after all the business is done. Cress is excited about the awards dinner in Paris."

"That is the girlfriend?"

"Fiancée," I correct.

"And he is younger than you!" The implication is clear, but I ignore it.

"How old is his papa?"

"Seventy-eight. All five of the children will be there, along with the grandchildren." I put a hand over my eyes. I should have censored myself. Bringing up grandchildren in a conversation with Maman is like crashing into a beehive, so I'm shocked when she doesn't follow up with any more than a sigh.

"And you are flying here from Paris?"

"Oui. I'm booked on a flight two days after the dinner. Max and Cress are going on to Venice." I click over to the calendar on my screen. "I'll be in Vancouver in less than a month." I toy with the idea of telling her I might bring a friend, but there's no guarantee I can convince Micki to take the extra time.

"Perfect. I have a surprise for you." She sounds gleeful and my heart sinks.

"What kind of surprise?"

"If I tell you, it won't be a surprise, mon chou. But I'm sure you will like it."

I suppress a sigh. Pursuing this would be profitless so I move on to another sticky subject. "Is my uncle still with you?"

"Where else would he be?"

Calisse. Of course, he's still there. When he was released from prison in Quebec, Uncle François arrived on her doorstep like a homing pigeon, and she'll never kick him out. "Is he drinking?"

"Not too much," she tells me, her voice low.

"How much is not too much?"

"Just some beer. Not here. He goes to the bar with his friends."

And comes back drunk. But she's not telling me that. No point asking about drugs, either. I pray he's not selling them out of her house.

"Maman, has he hit you?"

"Non." Her voice rises an octave and gets louder by at least twenty decibels, a sure sign she's lying. "There is nothing to worry yourself about, JL. Everything is fine."

Prickles break out on my chest, and my breathing is heavy. I slap the phone down on the desk. Then I rub my chest with one hand, while sipping coffee from the mug I hold in the other. If I could, I'd be on a plane tonight. But I'm leaving for London on Sunday. Can't be in two places at once and if I go to Vancouver first, I'll be stuck there. Ostie de Tabarnak.

"JL?" Her voice is apologetic. Not the Maman I expect. "He needs to be somewhere safe. And he doesn't have anyone else."

"I know, Maman. But he doesn't make life safe for you."

Stronger and sharper, she snaps at me, "I can take care

of myself, Jean-Louis. Just make sure you keep in touch while you are away." I hear the receiver bang down.

Coffee mug in hand, I pace. Cancel the European trip and leave for Vancouver now? Or take her word and see her in late April. The worry over Maman's safety tangles with anger as I think about how easily she gives in to him. Why she feels any loyalty to my father's brother, I can't fathom. He's always been a cheat and a liar. It's his fault Papa died, an innocent bystander when a criminal rival tried to shoot Uncle François, who got away without a scratch. I had just joined the army and couldn't return for the funeral. I've never forgiven him for that.

Cup empty, I walk back to the small kitchen area, set the vessel in the sink, and start down the corridor to see Clay. Halfway there, I stop, turn around, and go to Max's office instead. He's leaning forward to study the big screen that takes up the side portion of his desk and tapping quickly on the keyboard in front of him.

A rap on the door gets his attention. "You need something, JL?"

"Just got off a call with my mother and I'm worried. Maybe I should cancel on Europe and go to Vancouver instead. I still might be able to make Cress' dinner in Paris."

"Is it an emergency?"

"No. My uncle is staying with my mother, and he's an alcoholic. Sometimes he just sleeps off a bender, and sometimes he is a nasty, threatening drunk. I worry about her safety." I decide not to mention the possible criminal activity.

"You have clients to meet with in London. A little late to cancel, don't you think?"

"Mince!" I hit my palm with the fist of my other hand. "Maybe we could send someone else?"

He laughs. "Who? Clay? No chance he's going anywhere with Kath pregnant again. None of your blokes can negotiate the contract and sending someone lower level will rankle the bankers."

Max takes off his glasses, then pulls out a microfiber cleaning cloth and a small spray bottle. He sprays the lenses and rubs them clean. After he finishes one side, he does the other. Finally, he slips them back and returns the cloth and bottle to their assigned places in his desk drawer. Then he tents his fingers, resting his elbows on the top of the blotter.

"And my parents would be very sad if you weren't at Dad's party." He searches my face as if looking for buried treasure.

"I know. Your family has been very kind to me, and I would hate to miss spending time with them. But she is my flesh and blood."

Max looks pensive. "If you really need to go, we'll figure something out. Did she ask you to come? Give you evidence your uncle was being abusive? Was this a call for help?"

I shake my head no. "She told me there's nothing wrong and she can take care of herself and she'd see me when I return."

He turns back to his screen, relief in his voice. "Nothing to cancel, then. If something happens, you can cut the trip short."

Failure should be our teacher, not our undertaker. Failure is delay, not defeat. It is a temporary detour, not a dead end. Failure is something we can avoid only by saying nothing, doing nothing, and being nothing.—Denis Waitley

Micki

I PICTURE my office and visualize the extra pair of shoes I keep there. Not my usual stilettos, but acceptable low-heeled black pumps. The idea of spending the day in my bare feet is so horrifying that relief floods through me, knowing a bit of leather stands between me and utter humiliation. I limp back into the building, swipe my ID, and hobble to the elevator that will return me to the sixty-first floor and the law offices of Miller, Lanscombe, Baker, Francis, Masters, and Hargrove.

When I reach the glass doors etched with the firm's name, the lights are on. I peer in, hoping the receptionist isn't there. No luck. She's perched on her high chair, above the long, polished marble counter. Twenty-five or so, but looking fifteen, she has magenta curls that cascade down below her shoulders and clash with the orange, yellow, and purple of her patchwork-print dress. She raises one pierced eyebrow. "Why you standin' out dere, Ms. Press?"

I straighten my shoulders and march in as if I don't have a care in the world, my shoes gripped in the fingers of my left hand. Cold feet from the granite floor is the least of my problems as I glare at her.

Her voice is identifiably Bridgeport Irish, and I wonder how many partners heard her. None, I hope. The senior ones won't be in yet.

Wrong. A tap on my shoulder. I turn and practically bump my nose into Tyler Miller's chest.

He looks at my hand, shoes dangling in my fingers, then at my bare feet.

"Stop at Oak Street Beach on the way here, Micki?" He shakes a finger at me. "Don't get sand all over the foyer."

I choke back a curse. "Morning, Tyler."

He sniffs and pushes me out of his way when I don't address the issue or apologize.

"Morning, Elspeth," I greet the broadly grinning receptionist, attempting a breezy air I don't feel.

She looks around. Tyler's already at his office door. "That Mr. Miller's a piece of work."

Shifting back and forth on my bare feet, embarrassment isn't strong enough. I held my feelings in so Tyler couldn't see, but mortification is the emotion of the moment. "I'm expecting someone from Global Security Unlimited any minute. Just send him back."

With a smirk, she asks, "Is he cute?"

"No idea. I don't know if I've ever met him."

"So naht the guy you're going out wit', den." The smirk

has morphed into a high-pitched giggle. She leans over the counter and her gardenia perfume wafts in my direction. I move back from the overwhelming scent.

How does she know about JL? Not like he hangs around the office.

"He's already in the lounge." Unlike my esteemed colleague, she doesn't point out the inappropriateness of my attire. A latter-day wild child, Elspeth has her shoes off all the time, cramming them on if she has to leave the security of her desk, backs broken from the practice. Fortunately, none of the lawyers come around to her side of the counter. I'm not sure what attracted her to work for an old-fashioned stuffed-shirt outfit like this.

"Fine. I'll collect him when I'm ready."

Once my sensible flats are securely in place, I walk back to the front desk.

"Hey, Elspeth. Could you do me a favor?"

She doesn't even hesitate. "Sure."

"Could you call a shoe repair place and find out if they fix Louboutin shoes?"

"Can you spell that for me?"

"L-o-u-b-o-u-t-i-n."

"Got it. I'll call around."

After locating and slipping on my spare shoes, I go to the lounge. A burly guy in a gray suit looks up just as I walk in. "Hey, Ms. Press. Good to see you."

I know him. Liam was one of Cress' bodyguards last year. Now I guess he will be one of mine.

"Coffee?" When he nods, I fire up both Nespresso machines once more. He takes his black. I add a lot of cream to mine.

Back in my office, Liam following on my heels, I slide behind my desk.

"JL says someone's stalking you."

I nod, rotating my chair back and forth. Liam, sitting in one of the leather chairs on the other side of the desk, follows my movements. Bodyguards are a complication I don't need. Sudden anger at Sam blows up in my chest and I gasp from the pain.

"You okay, Ms. Press? You're not looking so good."

"Fine," I squeeze out on a breath, rubbing my chest, trying to ease the pressure.

Damn Sam and his bullshit. Who the fuck does he think he is, threatening me? He didn't want me when he had me, so what's changed? I feel heat surge up to my neck and my ears start to burn. *Think cooling thoughts. Picture an icy stream, a snow-capped mountain, a Starbucks Frappuccino. Let the shit go.*

A text message dings.

> JL: Sam was bailed this morning. Liam there?

I'm not surprised but my anxiety is now sky-high. My fingers shake as I tap out a response.

> ME: Just arrived.

> JL:

Liam's ringtone, "Burnin' It Down," starts. "JL," he tells me with a grin. "Yeah, Boss?"

Silence for several long minutes. Then Liam puts the phone back in his pocket. "Okay. I'll be here until JL takes over. Can I hang out in your office? Or do you have somewhere I can be close by but not be in your way?"

"You can stay here for the moment. I have a meeting in

the conference room soon. We can figure something out later."

"Cool. JL is going to take you to lunch and will be with you overnight. Case will take over in the morning. Dirk will be the third man." He snickers, enjoying his own reference to the Orson Welles film. Clearing his throat, he continues, "With JL leaving at the end of the week, three will be the minimum and we can bring in someone extra if we need to. JL will give you the complete schedule."

"Is this going to extend to my trip to Paris?"

"To O'Hare and an escort onto the plane. GSU will have someone pick you up at De Gaulle and take you to the hotel. JL is the man when it comes to organizing everything."

"Thanks." I pick up my iPad. "If you want more coffee, the machine is in the staff lounge."

"Great. All right if I hang out there?"

"No problem. If anyone asks, just tell them you're waiting for me.."

As I walk out from my office, I hear Elspeth call me. "Hey, Ms. Press." She must be psychic or have CCTV in the corridor since she can't see me from her post in the foyer, and yet she knows I've left my office.

With a frown, I change direction. "What is it, Elspeth? I have a meeting in a few minutes."

She huffs, "Just doing your favor." Then she sits there, staring at me.

"Favor?"

"Yeah. Your shoes." She looks at my feet with a frown at my conservative, low-heeled, black pumps.

"Oh, right. Thanks for looking it into it for me."

"There's a place you can send them for repair." She dangles a Post-it note then pulls it back. "Just leave them here and I'll arrange for a pickup."

"You're a lifesaver," I gush, then run down the hall for the meeting.

The partners' conference room is overheated, and I feel moisture collecting by the time I take my seat, halfway down the left-hand side of the mahogany table. Rebecca sits at the head. This part of the meeting is pre-client strategizing.

The table seats twelve, but there will only be eight of us, plus the client. The three unused chairs sit against a wall, a minor blockade in the narrow rectangular space. I've been in this room three times—when I was interviewed, when I was formally introduced to the partners and staff on my first day, and when I was promoted three years ago from associate to senior associate. Now I'm placing my foot back on the ladder, hoping to move up to non-equity partner, where I don't have to buy into ownership until I can afford to move up another notch. This promotion would show the equity partners have confidence in my abilities and give me options for more lucrative cases. If Hayden gets the spot, he'll be an equity partner for sure.

While I've been woolgathering, the rest of the team have taken their places around the table—Laney, our researcher, Blaine, the file clerk, Mario and Francesca, the junior associates, legal secretary, Tulia, and puffing in at the last minute, Hayden. He's wearing a suit I've never seen before. It looks custom tailored. Dark gray with a subtle eggplant-colored stripe, matching vest and slacks, with an eggplant-colored shirt. Black, high-gloss patent leather shoes. The outfit's so sharp he could cut himself. Ten points to him for style. I sigh and add them to the spreadsheet.

"Where's the donuts and coffee?" He glares at Mario and Francesca. "That's one duty of junior associates."

They trade mystified glances. Rebecca raps on the table

with her knuckles. "If you want coffee and donuts, Hayden, call Do Rite or Stan's for delivery. The associates are not required to feed your face." The asperity in her voice sounds like the harbinger of doom.

I look out a window, barely able to see my reflection in the glass. Not for the first time, I wonder whether I belong at a firm where someone like Hayden can flourish.

"What kind of donut do you want, Micki?" Hayden's irritating rasp makes me snap to attention.

My response isn't fast enough. With a snap of his fingers that bumps my nose, he repeats, "Micki, donut, wake up.

"Chocolate old-fashioned."

"Can't hear you," he roars.

"This is not a pep rally, Hayden. Sit down and shut up. There will be no food. When the congressman arrives, please offer him coffee, Tulia."

"Sure, Rebecca." Her breezy attitude is diametrically opposed to the edginess Hayden and I exhibit.

Hayden glowers. My stomach rumbles while I worry my bottom lip.

"Micki, Hayden, do you have anything to request from Congressman Greenberg?"

"I'm finding some anomalies in his email correspondence."

"Like what?" Hayden crosses his arms.

"He told us he has two email addresses. One for his office and a personal one. But I've found four."

"So?"

"So, he lied. He must be hiding something."

"What am I hiding?" The voice is mid-range and irascible. Congressman Greenberg is in the room.

A cool voice cuts him off. "Good morning, Simon."

"Hello, Rebecca. Seems I arrived too early...or too late.

"Perfect timing as always, Simon," she drawls. "Hayden, would you start, please?"

He straightens up, even though he hadn't been slouching, his voice almost apologetic. "We've had preliminary discussions about interviews with family, friends, and colleagues. Now I need to start setting up the appointments, but you haven't provided the list yet, Congressman. I'd like to begin with your former firm and the members of your campaign staff."

"Liaise with my secretary." Greenberg's dismissive tone is meant to show that, as the client, he has the upper hand, at least over us menials.

Rebecca ignores the power grab. "Micki, do you have any issues?"

"Congressman."

He eyes me.

"Right now, I'm tasked with checking all of your email correspondence."

"I know, and I don't approve. My privacy is being invaded."

"True. But you're facing both civil and criminal investigations, which means, in essence, you have no privacy." Rebecca, palms flat on the table, snaps, "You should know that Simon."

He glares.

"Unless you want to plead guilty, suck it up."

He looks like a sulky teenager, mouth clamped shut.

I know he's hiding something. Financial shenanigans? An affair?

Rebecca throws me a look and I continue.

"There are at least four email accounts going through your desktop computer. You told us you only have two."

"The others belong to my wife and daughter. No big deal."

Then why lie about it?

"Do they know you have access to their accounts?"

"None of your business. My family is not to be involved." His low, angry tone reverberates in the stillness.

He pushes his chair back, fists resting on his thighs, moistening his lips, ready to keep going. A glare from Rebecca and his mouth snaps shut like a mousetrap.

"I've been accessing your laptop, but I also need to access your desktop. We can have our technician set it up remotely since I'll be away for a few days."

"The email accounts would be the same."

I lift a shoulder. "There may be other things we need to see."

"And you're going away. Unbelievable."

"Not a problem, as long as I have my laptop and full access."

"I hope it's a family emergency and not you on the beach somewhere."

"Paris, she's taking off for Paris." Hayden sends me a snarky look.

Greenberg scowls. "A vacation? At the beginning of the case. I told Rebecca time was of the essence..."

Rebecca raps her knuckles on the table. "Be quiet, Simon. Our associates aren't prisoners. And Micki has a very important event coming up in Paris. As she told you, working remotely is still working, and our team will meet every day by video call."

The congressman's look is sullen. Being schooled by your lawyer is not fun. I think there must be some history there.

"Explain again why you need access to my office machine?"

"There may be other material on that computer, different from your desktop. And I haven't even started accessing the files."

He glowers.

"If you have your laptop with you, I'd like to have our tech guy clone your hard drive. And send someone over to your campaign and congressional offices as well. We need to start evaluating files."

Before I can continue, Greenberg interrupts, "No, I'm playing golf after this. My laptop is at home." His impatient tone doesn't bode well. "Rebecca, I didn't want to bring this up here, but I'm pressed for time."

She raises one beautifully sculpted brow. "Go on, Simon."

"I'm not sure having Ms. Press on the team is a wise idea."

Hayden fails to suppress a grin while I clench my teeth to keep my jaw in place.

"Why is that?" The temperature in the room has dropped into the minus zone, and yet I'm overheated.

"I have it from a reliable source she is in her own legal difficulties."

What the h...?

"I'm not aware of anything." Rebecca's expression is neutral, but I can hear the tightness in her vocal cords.

"Ms. Press." He turns his inquisitor's face to me. "Isn't it true someone is stalking you?"

"That has nothing to do with your case. My 'stalker' isn't interested in my legal cases."

"How can you be sure, Micki?" Hayden barely disguises

his gloat. "Perhaps sabotaging the firm would be great for getting revenge on you."

The conference room door opens and Tyler Miller walks in. "Sorry to interrupt, but are you finished? Simon and I don't want to miss our tee time."

Rebecca takes a deep breath. "Run along, boys. I'd hate to interfere with your golf game."

Greenberg pushes his chair back. "Think about what I said, Rebecca."

"Oh, I will, Simon. Enjoy the fresh air while you can."

"Hayden," Tyler calls. "Is your bag in the office?"

"Yup."

Meeting adjourned.

JL

I call Micki for the third time, but she doesn't pick up. Then I make a call to the office number and ask to be connected, my eyes mist with red at the response.

"Sorry, sir, but she's already left for the day."

This is strange. I call Liam.

When he answers, I say, "Where are you?"

"With Ms. Press. Why?" He sounds puzzled.

I take a deep breath. At least I know nothing's happened to her. "Where is she?"

"At her condo. On Goethe." He says Go-ee-thee. I've heard it as Go-ith and Go-thee as well. And a few Chicagoans, and the CTA, use the correct German pronunciation, Ger-tuh.

"Why didn't you tell me plans had changed? I was just getting ready to take off for her office."

"Sorry, Boss. She got some bad news, but she said she'd let you know. Text or something."

"She's not answering her phone. Tell her I need to talk to her."

He clears his throat, clearly uncomfortable. "She told me she was going to take a nap and didn't want to be bothered."

"Tabarnak." I clench my teeth briefly. "I'm coming over." I pause. We were supposed to have lunch. She'll need to eat, and I know she doesn't have any food. "Did you pick up anything?"

"Nah, just wanted to take her home. We can order out later."

"I'll take care of it. What do you want?"

"Where are you going?"

"I'll stop at Portillo's."

"Italian beef, fries. And a large Coke."

Eager as I am to leave, Micki is in expert hands, so I make sure I have everything covered for the rest of the day. Then I put on my jacket, put Case in charge, and tell my secretary and the receptionist I'll be out for the rest of the day.

When I arrive at the condo, the concierge I helped yesterday is at the desk and tells me to go up without checking my ID or calling. Terrible security. I want to tell him that, but concern for Micki overrides everything. When I see the elevator doors are open, ready to whoosh me up to the third floor like Superman, I run over.

Liam knows to expect me, but he not only checks through the peephole, but opens the door with the safety chain fastened. I position myself where he can see me, but I can't see him. Once he's sure I'm alone, he takes off the chain and lets me in.

'Good thing you're here. That asshole at the desk waved me up with hardly a second glance."

Shoulders shaking with suppressed laughter, Liam says, "Well, he already knows you as a good guy."

"Sorry. I guess it's just trotte dans la tête."

"It's???"

"Stuck in my head, bee in my bonnet."

"The French sounds cooler."

I snort. "I'll teach you a few phrases so you can annoy Clay when you see him." Then I dump the takeout on the coffee table and survey the living room, empty of life. "Still sleeping?"

"She isn't making any noises, so I guess so." He's rooting through the bags. "This mine?"

"If it's Italian beef. What set all this off?"

"No idea. She stormed out of the conference, found me in the staff lounge. 'We're leaving,' she said. Then collected her coat and purse but left her briefcase. Locked the office and we skedaddled. She was moving so fast I could hardly keep up with her."

"Which is her room?" I'm going to storm the fortress. If she's had more threats, I'll tear Sam limb from limb.

He points to a corridor. "It's the middle room back there. Guess she didn't want to sleep in the primary room."

Interesting quirk but no time to examine her reasoning. Instead, I stride down the back hallway and try the knob. It's locked. My knock goes unanswered. "Micki," I call out. "Please let me in."

"Go away," sounds muffled by pillows, but I can hear the catch in her voice.

"No, not going anywhere. Just open the door. Or come into the living room. I need to know what's wrong."

A meaningless "nothing," is the only reply.

I examine the lock. It's a typical bedroom handle with a pinhole on the exterior. My small set of screwdrivers has one that fits into the hole. Once it catches, I hear the mechanism pop. When I open the door, Micki sits with her feet under her, the duvet draped over her shoulders. Disheveled hair and blotchy face.

With no tissue in sight, she wipes the back of her hand across her nose, grimaces, then pushes the duvet to the floor. As she drags herself toward the bathroom, I can't take my eyes off her defeated posture until she disappears through the doorway. When she finally reappears, looking a little more composed, I take her in my arms and hold her loosely.

"Is it Sam? Did he manage to contact you, threaten you?"

"No. I haven't heard from him. I blocked his number, so he'd need a new one."

"Then what is it? You look like your entire world has blown apart."

"It has." A new sob bubbles up and she rests her cheek against my chest while her whole body vibrates with distress.

I can't even imagine what could have happened and have no idea how to console her. "Are your parents okay? Did someone die? Tell me what's wrong."

"Don't want to talk." She backs away, arms out, palms facing toward me in a gesture of denial.

"Please, talk to me," I plead. "Just tell me what's going on."

She pushes me out of the room and slams the door, then pushes a chair against it.

I retreat to the living room and slump onto the couch in defeat.

CHAPTER

SEVEN

When you have expectations, you are setting yourself up for disappointment.—Ryan Reynolds

Micki

WHEN HAYDEN and the congressman walk out the door with Tyler Miller, I know I've lost the partnership battle.

"Don't be ridiculous, Micki." Rebecca sounds bracingly down-to-earth.

"Golf. They're playing golf. It's an old boys' club and I'll never break through."

"I did, and you can too."

Easy for you to say. Fingers turn black with mascara when I rub my eyes. Just one more indignity. "I have to go wash all this stuff off." I hustle away, but Rebecca is right behind me.

The ladies' room has a lounge-like atmosphere with two comfortable love seats. Rebecca plops down on one while I grab paper towels to clean my face. The mirror shows ruined makeup, so washing it off is the best course.

Meanwhile, Rebecca raises her voice over the rushing water. "You need to show how good you are, Micki. You're a much better lawyer than Hayden, and his uncle being a partner should not be the deciding factor. Neither should his golf game—or yours."

"Don't play golf." My sullen mutter is too soft for her to hear.

Her brisk voice makes me want to claw the walls. "Send Tom over to Simon's office and home for the computer files. Eventually, we can have Blaine camp out with the paper files."

"Why is Greenberg being such a jerk? If someone really framed him, wouldn't he want us to turn over everything to find out who, and how?"

"You'd think so, but perhaps he has something else to hide."

I snuffle back the tears when I see the pity in her eyes.

"Anyway, take the rest of the day off and start planning the next step. I'll meet you at Lou Mitchell's for breakfast. My train gets in at seven thirty."

If I ever come back.

When Liam comes to find out where we're meeting JL, I panic. Stomach in turmoil, lunch isn't an option. A white lie rises to my lips.

"We canceled. I'm leaving for the rest of the day and working from home."

After an incredulous look, he puts on the jacket hanging from one finger and escorts me to the SUV.

Back in my temporary home, the guest bedroom suite is big enough for me to pace. I need to decide, act. Should I settle for a permanent position as senior associate now that the handwriting is on the wall? Or figure out how to maneuver past any roadblocks Hayden might cook up? Can I convince Greenberg to come around?

I'm sick of hiding in my room, debating whether I can face food—and JL. Rebecca told me to ignore what happened with Simon Greenberg and Hayden. If only forgetting was that easy. Not a handwringer by nature, if I squeeze my fingers together much more, they'll turn into misshapen lumps.

When my phone rings, I startle, fumbling with the device. "Hi, Cress. What's up?" The words come out in a shaky treble rather than the upbeat tone I reach for.

She gets right to the point. "Okay, I take it the client did not greet you with 'well done' or 'brilliant ideas' or 'we'll get right on that.'"

How did she know? Probably JL told Max. Instead of grumbling about gossip mongers, I admit, "No one bandied those phrases about."

"Well, fuck them." Cress' bluntness makes my heart lift briefly. "One reason I like to work for myself."

"But you don't."

Her tinkling laughter drowns my protest. "If I don't like what a publisher is proposing, I can tell my agent to rene-gotiate or try another house." Her smug tone makes me wince. "And I can self-publish. That's gaining some traction these days."

My snort clones itself as feedback. "Being a bestselling author doesn't hurt. Anyway, you've convinced me working for yourself works for you. I don't have the funds for a startup and the clients I work with would be too high powered to come with me. Starting over at forty-six is an unattractive option."

My exasperation must show because instead of arguing,

she's silent for a beat. "I'm sorry. I wish things had gone your way." She pauses and I hear her deep breaths. "Face it. You work for a big, stuffy, conservative law firm that would rather have a man as a partner than a woman."

My stomach suddenly gurgles. It sounds like a noisy drain.

"What the hell was that?" Cress shouts from the other end.

"All I've had today is that croissant from this morning. Guess my body insists I find some food."

"Well, that's a relief. I thought your plumbing had suddenly gone kablooey."

Her word choice makes me smile for the first time in hours.

She goes on. "I called to see if you want some distraction this evening. You might enjoy helping with my tutoring session in the literacy program. Give you that sense of doing good in the world. Then I'm meeting Max for dinner."

When I say nothing, she wheedles, "You have nothing in your place to eat, so you might as well accept."

My voice sounds too mouselike for comfort. "Tutoring and dinner. Max is paying, right?"

Cress laughs. "He'll pick up the tab. We're going to Brindille."

I withhold a groan. What I don't need is a romantic restaurant where I will be a third wheel.

"Put on a nice outfit and meet me at the State Street entrance to Harold Washington library at four forty-five. Be there or be square."

"Max is rubbing off on you." I end the call.

After bathing my eyes in cold water, I emerge from my lair and walk into the living room. JL sits on the couch, laptop open on the coffee table. He frowns at the screen but looks up when he hears my footsteps on the terrazzo floor of the kitchen.

"Sleeping Beauty." He narrows his eyes as he looks me over. "Are you hungry? You look pale and interesting, but I'd rather see you happy and satisfied."

"You look grouchy."

"Just some work complications. We have a minor problem with a client in Hong Kong."

"Will you have to go there?"

His eyes widen in surprise. "No way. I have clients to meet in London next week. Someone from the Tokyo office will take care of it. Warn the client, if he continues to ignore our advice, two things will happen. One is we will end the contract, and the other is he will probably be dead."

"And your expected result?"

"He's heir apparent to the family company. I expect his father will bring him into line. We can't protect people who evade us and take dangerous steps."

His warning tone seems aimed at me as well. I wince.

His voice warms. "I brought some food from Portillo's. Would you like some?"

"What is it?"

"Ribs, onion rings, and chocolate cake. I can reheat the ribs and rings. You can eat the cake while everything warms up."

"When in doubt, eat dessert first. Perfect."

I curl up in an armchair and watch him come toward me with a gigantic piece of cake, a fork, and a couple of paper napkins. "Tuck into this and I'll reheat the rest." He moves toward the kitchen.

"Thanks. But don't bother with the rest. I'm going out to dinner with Cress and Max." He turns back, eyelashes at half-mast, hooding his eyes and signaling disappointment. Since the space is open, I can watch him move purposefully toward me, his thigh muscles bulging under snug slacks. When he sees me staring, he gives me a salute.

"What are your plans before dinner, ma chouette?"

"Why?"

"I'm your bodyguard until Case shows up tomorrow. Wherever you go, I go too."

"Meeting Cress at the library at four forty-five," I mutter. The way I feel right now, I both welcome JL's hovering presence and resent it. Why can't life be uncomplicated and fun?

He's standing so close I can feel his breath. "What?"

"Meeting Cress." I enunciate, slow and loud.

"Parfait. And we leave when?"

"Around four thirty."

He takes the now empty plate from me and hands me a glass of water. My spine tingles as our hands brush. I try to distract myself with a sip of water. The shock of icy liquid briefly blocks out the unwanted feelings that keep rising.

JL

Micki and I have just entered the building and we watch Cress check her watch as she waits just inside the grand replacement for the former library, now the city's cultural center.

"What time does the tutoring finish?"

She startles, then glares at me.

"They'll clean everything up by six fifteen. Max should be here by then." As we walk toward the room designated for the tutoring session, I scan the area. Several security guards form a little pod. I kiss Micki lightly on the cheek and go over to talk to one of them.

The guy writes on a clipboard and looks up as I close in. Holding out my ID, I say, "Hi. I'm JL Martin from Watch-Dog, Inc." When he looks blank, I add, "Our parent company is Global Security Unlimited."

"Heard of your outfit. Looking for a new job?"

"Not exactly," I say with a laugh, then point to the room Micki and Cress are in. "Just dropping off some friends who are in a tutoring session over there."

"You waiting for them?"

I chew on my lip. "I was going to check in with my office, but..."

"They should be fine here. Our security is first rate."

"I'm sure it is, but a stalker has been threatening them."

"Give me the deets and I'll watch out. You're coming back, right?"

"Six fifteen, they told me, but I'll be back a bit earlier."

He brandishes his pen. "Go."

"Mid-forties, about five foot ten or so, slouches, light hair, balding, paunch, and dresses in overalls."

"Got it. We'll keep an eye out. See you in an hour."

With a sketchy salute, I walk out into the chilly darkness, signal a passing cab, and take off for the office and the mass of paperwork I'm sure awaits me.

Forty-five minutes later, I'm on my way back to the library, this time with Max. We're dropped off at the entrance and Sean, one of my new guys, hovers at the curb. Business is booming and I've been on a hiring spree. The security guard greets me. "All quiet on the library front," he says. We give him a thumbs-up for the à propos twist on the literary reference.

The door to the tutoring room swings open and a group

of noisy kids spills out, followed by the tutors. Micki and Cress are talking with a well-dressed man carrying an attaché case. They stop a few steps away from the door. After a few minutes, he waves and walks off. Cress spots Max and gives a little squeal as she rushes in our direction. Micki seems more relieved than anything when I look into her eyes.

"We left the SUV waiting outside," Max says, herding us toward the door.

"Thanks for keeping an eye out," I tell the guard as we pass.

"Always vigilant, that's us," he says. "If you ever want a job, just let me know."

We smirk at each other, while Max's eyes narrow and he whispers, "What porkies have you been feeding him?"

I elbow him in the ribs. "La blague seulement."

"A joke, huh?" But he doesn't laugh.

The walk from the entrance to the Uber is short, but I can't help scanning the area constantly, especially the ragged-looking guy approaching. When he gets close enough, he's holding out *Streetwise*, the Chicago paper that raises cash for services to help the unhoused. Micki already has her wallet out, but I put a hand on hers and shake my head. Max hands over more than the requisite amount. Putting a hand on Cress' back, he steers her into the SUV and crowds in next to her. We hop in from the other side.

When we pull up to the curb, Max holds up a hand, then opens his door, checking carefully for oncoming traffic. Once on the sidewalk, he walks all the way to Maggiano's on the corner and back past the doorway to the other end of the block, with a casual glance around as if trying to find an entrance. When he gets back, he opens the passenger side door and helps Micki, handing her over to me before retrieving Cress.

"Thanks." He slams the door, then motions for the driver to park. By then, Micki and I are at the entrance and Max waves us to go in before putting his arm around Cress and guiding her forward. A little icy rain makes the sidewalk slick and Cress has taken a tumble or three in the past.

We're welcomed into the sophisticated soft gray interior and seated in the slightly secluded back alcove of the intimate space. I look out the long open view to the large windows facing Clark Street. A vision of a face pressed against the droplet-dappled glass proves to be a trick of the light. Not knowing when or where Sam might pop up gives me jitters. I want to pack Micki into my suitcase and take her with me to London. The two weeks before we meet again in Paris will be hell.

Cress leans forward and looks narrowly at my girl. "What happened today, Micki?"

"I learned that tutoring is amazing." Her smile is so bright I can't help wondering what she's covering up.

"The meeting?"

Micki gives a comme ci, comme ça gesture, then changes the subject. "Are you still planning to buy a new place in London, Max?"

"If we have time to look. Ian spends so much time out of the country, he's happy to put our Clerkenwell house on the market."

Micki taps one long, red fingernail on the table. "That's your older brother?"

"Yeah, the annoying one." Max's tone is light, with a slight hint of irritation. Mostly good-natured bantering and a bit of one-upmanship seems to be their MO. Ian's the temporary British consul in Chicago and is flying to London with us. I look forward to his stories of the trials of being the representative of every British person in the area.

"Ian has been dealing with the fallout of a British teenager accused of vandalism. He's a minor and his father took him home before the police could arrest him. Ian's the negotiator for having him sent back to stand trial. The whole thing's a tangle because his mum is a consulate employee and claims diplomatic immunity, but the kid's not eligible. Not sure he'll sort it out before we leave for London."

While Max, Cress, and I delight in Brindille's French delicacies, Micki moodily stirs her soup but only has a spoonful and pokes at the salad. Even her favorite entrée, lacquered duck, doesn't tempt her. When she refuses dessert, Cress presses her.

"At least share the clafoutis with me."

"Sorry. Not hungry. JL plied me with a huge piece of Portillo's chocolate cake not that long ago."

By now we're finished with the meal. Over coffee, I take Micki's hand. "Ma chouette, you didn't say how the client meeting went."

Her eyes flash with something I can't read. Anger? Frustration? "I told you it was okay. Nothing else to say."

Cress frowns. "Was this just another preliminary thing with the client?"

"Hayden and I told Greenberg what kinds of access we need to people and files. He wasn't happy. Kind of strange for someone who says he has nothing to hide." She shrugs. "Then he went off to play golf."

On that note, we leave the restaurant. Two GSU vehicles idle at the curb. Sean sees us and pops the door locks. Max and Cress take the second one.

Atmosphere like a heavy fog rolling in from the lake

constricts my chest and makes breathing difficult. I try to catch Micki's eye, but she's looking away. Her face is like marble, the sorrowing Madonna of Michelangelo's *Pietà*. When we're at her place, maybe I can coax her to talk about whatever is weighing on her soul.

We pull up to the building and she climbs out before I can move around to help her down.

"Go home, JL."

"Can't. I'm tonight's bodyguard, and I'll drop you at work in the morning."

Sean has opened the trunk and hands JL a gym bag.

"See you at the office tomorrow, Sean."

He gets back into the driver's seat, produces a small wave, and takes off at speed.

"Need to discuss that with him," I mutter.

Once upstairs, I make myself at home in the living room, ready to worm the truth out of her.

CHAPTER
EIGHT

The absence of old friends one can endure with equanimity. But even a momentary separation from anyone to whom one has just been introduced is almost unbearable.—Oscar Wilde

Micki

A GLARINGLY BRIGHT Sunday morning crashes my eyelids way before I'm ready to get up. Last night, Cress and Max had dinner for his coworkers—and me. I was there as Cress' friend and JL's something. We have no definition yet. Maybe Paris will clarify things. Unfortunately, a big blow-up at the end of the evening cast a pall over everything. Today the traveling band leaves for London. I should go to the airport, but my defender and I pick up a drive-through breakfast and go into the office to prepare for the Monday morning meeting.

Unexpectedly, I notice a few lights visible through the frosted rectangles of glass set into the paneled oak doors.

"Who would be here this early on the weekend?" Liam's murmur shatters the stillness.

"No idea," I mouth.

Thick carpeting helps us move soundlessly down the corridor to my office. My chest pounds, my hand shaking as I focus on opening the door. When I fumble, dropping the key as I try to fit it into the lock, I drop to my knees. The desperate scrabble in the dark leaves me breathless. Once inside, I collapse, unable to move another step.

When "Oh Canada" pours out of my purse, I can hardly lever the phone out and accept the call. A gurgle is the most I can manage.

"Micki? Ma chouette? You there?"

"Y-e-e-es," I manage through the lump that is clogging my throat. I slide off my knees and sit on the floor with my back against the wall, legs stretched out.

"We're taking off in a few minutes. I wanted to say goodbye. If I could, I would kiss you senseless and drag you onto the plane, so I suppose the fact you are not here is saving you."

His voice is soothing, and my heartbeat has finally slowed. "I wish I was there too," I say, a little hitch in my voice. "Two weeks and we'll be in Paris."

"If we had time, I would show you everything. Three days isn't enough, especially with the dinner."

Maybe we can find time to go back. Fingers crossed, I don't say it out loud. Who knows how long this will last? I'm starting to think my investment is greater than I imagined. A scary thought since I'm really not ready to jump into a new relationship this soon. Between my job issues and Sam, too much is already going on in my life. JL would be an additional complication.

"I will call you every day," he promises.

"Safe travel," I tell him and ring off.

Minutes pass, but I'm paralyzed.

Liam comes in with coffee to go with our rapidly cooling breakfast sandwiches. Once he's put the cups down and closes the door, he glances down. "Need some help up?"

I reach up a hand and he pulls me to my feet.

Then someone knocks on my door. Panic rises back up from my gut. Lights off. Who would even know I'm here? Sam? He would have had to follow me, but I doubt he could have gotten past the guard who checks visitors in and out. Especially on a Sunday.

Another knock. "Hey," a familiar voice calls. "I'm pretty sure you're in there, Micki."

A bolt of adrenaline surges through me and I pull open the door. Hayden. Fuck. Just what I don't need.

"You want me to scare him off?"

I can't tell if Liam is serious or joking. I'm tempted but shake my head no.

"Thought you'd be here," he says smugly.

Self-conscious that I'm dressed in sweatpants, New Balance walking shoes, and a long-sleeved tee emblazoned with "Looking for Cache in the Wrong Places," I gaze at my colleague, who's dressed for a weekday business meeting in a navy jacket that looks vaguely nautical, beige twill slacks, Oxford shirt, and deck shoes. Deck shoes?

"What's the shirt mean?'

"Geocaching. I've done it a couple of times and got a shirt at an event."

He gives me the "that's really boring" look and barely keeps from yawning.

"Going yachting?" I ask.

"I am, as a matter of fact. Fred has a boat out in

Montrose Harbor and invited me for a little boating party he's having. It's kind of work. A few of the partners will be there, and our favorite congressman."

"I didn't think the boats were out yet."

"He had it down in Florida and now it's back here. Didn't need to wait for bridge day."

Shit. Is this feeling FOMO or a premonition that no matter what I do, my future has already been deep-sixed?

"What made you think I was here?"

Instead of answering, he moves forward. "Can I come in?"

Hayden crowds me back, so I turn and sit behind my desk, creating a barrier. He takes a client chair, positioning it directly in front of me. Liam takes the second client chair, his arm almost brushing Hayden's, who ostentatiously moves slightly to the right. His mouth twists as he brushes at his sleeve.

"Did you come to ask me to join your boating party?" I brush my hand against my inappropriate outfit. I could wear it.

"No. I think if Fred had wanted you as a guest, he would have invited you himself."

"Then why were you looking for me, and how did you know I came into the office?"

"I have my ways."

What? Does he have bugs to overhear conversations? I give Liam a speculative glance. I can ask whether GSU can sweep the offices after hours.

"Invest in some gear if the rumors about your ex are true. Your pal here could install something for you."

I play dumb. "What are you talking about?"

"Come on, Micki." He smiles at Liam.

When I don't respond, he crosses one leg over the other

and tents his fingers under his chin, giving me a long look. "Fine. Let's move on, shall we?"

I cross my arms and rest them on my desk.

"Look. I have nothing against you, but you will never make partner."

I fight hard not to react. He looks disappointed at not getting a rise out of me. "Come on, Micki. Don't play coy. The whole firm knows."

A dull ache throbs in my temple. Coming in today was a bad idea. Except, now I have a better idea of how difficult staying on at the firm might prove.

Brick by brick, I build my fortifying wall. Then my eyes shoot flaming arrows. "And how do you know this?"

All this summoned scariness is worthless. He laughs. "Seriously? My uncle will make sure it's me. This has been my future ever since I started law school. If you think you will weasel your way into my birthright, think again."

I choke, but when I grab the coffee mug to relieve the coughing fit that just won't stop, it's empty. *Crappity, crap, crap.* Hardly able to see Hayden as the coughing makes tears run down my face, I grab the cup, round my desk, and run out to the water fountain. I take huge gulps, then fill the mug. Once I regain my composure, I walk carefully back to the office and resume the stare down of my unwelcome visitor.

His sangfroid is admirable. Frost edges his voice as he says, "I just want to caution you to watch your step if you want to stay on with the firm—as a senior associate."

Pushing my chair back, I stand, hands curled around the edge of my desk. The wood presses painfully against my palms, reminding me to stay strong. "Thanks so much for the heads-up, Hayden." I pause. "I've finished here for the day, so I think I'll just go home. Enjoy the boat and don't fall into the lake."

He bounces up, turns toward the door, opens it, and as he steps through, he looks back at me with what looks like pity. "Just be careful, Micki, or you'll be out of here. I can imagine Fred letting other firms know they might not want to hire you." With a swish of his perfectly gelled hair, he's gone.

I lean against my desk for a few seconds, then retrieve my jacket and bag from the floor before walking out. Liam follows, practically stepping on my heels. "Case has the SUV downstairs. Faster we leave here, the better."

It's nine thirty, and I've done nothing except listen to Hayden's threats, but who cares? "I'm starved. Let's find brunch."

CHAPTER

NINE

Love is a fire. But whether it is going to warm your hearth or burn down your house, you can never tell.—Joan Crawford

Micki

FOR THE NEXT FEW DAYS, time crawls. Even though JL calls every morning, being without him causes a constant ache of longing. This is the first time in a relationship I have felt cherished and protected. Even though I try to fight against the neediness, the battle already seems lost. With him away, my emotional state is one of loneliness and sensations of abandonment wash over me.

Work is a never-ending series of ice floes with treacherous semi-frozen water between them getting wider and wider. The biggest ones have polar bears, menacing in the distance. If I lose my footing, I'll drown or die of hypothermia.

By the weekend, almost paralyzed with indecision, and no Cress to turn to, I take off for my folks' house in Evan-

99

ston. Liam is my bodyguard again today, so we're in another black SUV. I wish, not for the first time, I could just hop in my little red vintage Karmann Ghia, but it will sit in the parking garage at the condo for the foreseeable future.

As a consolation prize, we drive through Dunkin' Donuts on Broadway, just south of Devon, then continue up Sheridan Road. Liam picks up black coffee, sandwiches, and a box of donut holes. I nibble on one of the golf-ball size treats as we negotiate the heavy traffic through Rogers Park.

"I'll stay in the SUV. That way, I can make sure no one approaches the house. Sam knows where your parents live, right?"

"We were together for eight years. He's been there lots of times."

"Would he threaten your parents?" When I glance over at him, his face is serious.

"Never thought about it." A tremor runs up my arms. Would he? The Sam I thought I knew wasn't that person, but maybe I never really knew him at all. "Maybe?" I say uncertainly.

"Do they know about his threats?"

"N-o-o. Didn't want to worry them."

"Hope you're planning to tell them now," he chides.

I throw down the donut hole I just picked up and clench my fists. *Who are you to judge me?* A lightbulb goes off. *Oh yeah, the person who has to protect me, even when I'm stupid.*

Mom and Dad never really liked Sam, although they tried hard to be pleasant when they saw him. We met in 2004 at a found-art exhibit and he'd already cut ties with his parents, telling me their middle-class Lake Forest life-style stifled his artistic temperament. I'd laughed; he didn't.

Mulling it over, I still don't understand what attracted

me. No one ever courted me with such persistence. I never had a love-at-first-sight, stars-in-your-eyes romance. Sam was abrasive and opinionated, always willing to dictate and criticize. Maybe it was his single-mindedness. Or the rough exterior he presented to the world. A safer walk on the wild side?

The guys who attracted me in high school and college seemed vapid in retrospect. All of them were smart, clean-cut, Ivy League, dressed-for-success types with perfect manners and probably a 1950s mindset about the perfect "little woman." When I mentioned law school, some backed off, some looked skeptical. By the time I met Sam, I was clerking for a judge and interviewing for a more permanent job in a city firm.

I never thought it strange, the way he popped up unexpectedly, always acting as if we'd made some kind of date. We circled around each other for a couple of years before finally hooking up.

Soon after I gave in, the warning signs were there—the subtle undermining of my self-confidence, the attempts to isolate me from my friends. Refusing to believe someone so buffoonish could be dangerous, I brushed them aside. Made excuses to my friends—and myself.

Besides, wasn't he what I deserved? Even though lots of women were going into law, I felt uppity with ambition. A partner who kept my inflated ego in check was perfect. Now that I was dodging Sam, Hayden reminded me every day.

I barely notice we've arrived until Liam parks at the curb. My parents have a bungalow on Forest Avenue. Over the years, they've remodeled the place and added a heated back porch, where I find them sitting on the couch. Dad watches Northwestern basketball and Mom, noise-canceling headphones blocking the sound, reads.

I step through from the kitchen and the door snicks behind me. Dad looks up at the sound. "Micki," he says, nudging Mom with his foot.

She frowns at him, then when she sees me, turns it into a smile as she pulls off the headset, and gets up to give me a long squeeze.

"What brings you here, darling?" I don't usually come without calling first, so I know they wonder if something is wrong.

"Are you ready for your trip to France?" Dad says.

"Yeah." I curl up in one of the bright red Adirondack chairs and chew my lip.

"It's less than a week away. You don't seem very excited." Mom combs her fingers through her long, gray hair. A sure sign she's upset.

"I am. But there's other stuff going on and I need some advice."

"You got it." Dad loves giving advice. A counselor for a nonprofit, he counsels indigent clients on everything from jobs to housing to food pantries and fast-food giveaways five days a week.

He reaches over for the remote and hits the off button. The Wildcats disappear from the screen.

Their expectant faces don't comfort me. After a long silence, I say, "First, and I don't need advice on this, Sam is stalking me."

Dad, face turning red, starts to speak, while Mom's jaw drops. My hand goes up like a school bus stop sign. "Don't need advice on this. Cress' friend Max works for a security company. He's arranged bodyguards for me, so I'm safe." They've met Max and now is not the time to mention JL.

"How safe was Cress when that madwoman shot her outside the Palmer House? Didn't she have bodyguards?" Dad's voice is a gravel rumble.

"No one can ever be one-hundred-percent protected," Mom counters.

I raise my voice to speak over them. "You need to know, because if he can't grab me, he might try to do something to you."

Dad sputters, then yells. "The hell he will."

Mom says, "Where's this bodyguard of yours?"

"He's in his vehicle, watching the house."

Mom gets up. "I have to see for myself." She takes off at a fast clip toward the front door.

I trail her out to the sunroom, facing the street. The black SUV sits right where Liam dropped me off, behind the fire hydrant, so there is plenty of space if he needs to exit quickly. He looks like he's writing emails, or maybe playing *Angry Birds*.

"The black SUV?" Dad comes up behind us, casually dropping an arm over Mom's shoulder.

"Why don't you invite him in?" Mom smiles, always the hostess.

"He can protect her better from out there," Dad tells her as we move back to the porch. "Let's sit down and Micki can tell us what she needs advice about."

"First, do you want protection, too?"

"No." Dad's face has turned a blotched cherry red.

"Well..." Mom's expression is doubtful.

"He hasn't made a move, Alice." Dad sounds assured and reassuring, but the shadows I see in his eyes tell a different story.

When Mom shuffles her feet against the floor, he snarls, "Stop fidgeting, Alice."

She looks shocked at his tone and hurriedly rises from the couch. "I'll make a pot of coffee. And we can try those macaron cookies I got at Trader Joe's. A little French treat for Micki's Parisian adventure."

When she comes back with the coffeepot, three mugs, cream, and a plate of macarons on a tray, we settle in. I take a deep breath.

"You know I'm in the running for partner?"

Mom nods while Dad says, "About time too."

"Yeah, anyway, there is another candidate besides me." I stop, overcome with the memory of Hayden's threats.

"You mean that cretin Hayden Forbes-Cartwright? He's been a pain in your butt since you started there."

"Hayden, pooh. You're the best candidate." Mom, always the cheerleader.

"Anyway, I have significant challenges—Hayden, a few partners who already want him, and our new client doesn't like me."

"Why not?"

"New client?"

Mom and Dad speak at the same time.

"Congressman Simon Greenberg." The sourness in my mouth squirts out like verbal lemon juice.

"You mean the insider trading thing?"

I jerk out of my pity party, but I can't force any words out.

"Jerk. I don't understand how he gets elected."

"Really, Des," Mom says. "Just let Micki tell us."

He glowers and takes a vicious bite of a lemon macaron. Light yellow pieces of pastry crack and shower onto his shirt. Mom glowers as he brushes them to the floor. I restart.

"Uh. Well. Hayden is working to undermine me. Being

away won't affect my work, but he can ingratiate himself with the partners. And he's already been golfing and sailing with Greenberg," I end on a wail.

"What about your mentor—Rochelle, Rachel?" Mom can never remember her name.

"Rebecca's handling Greenberg's case, and Hayden and I are assisting. She's great, Mom. Definitely on my side. But I'm not sure she can bring any of the other partners with her.

The light of battle shines out of Dad's greenish eyes. "A bunch of old white men."

I swallow an involuntary giggle as I look at him. The personification of older and white, although he has nothing else in common with the firm's partners.

"It's not the right place for you. Come work at Advancing the Common Good. Let your social conscience run free."

What the... I know my parents wish I didn't work for a big-deal Loop law firm. A perception I sold out their principles colors every conversation. Their disappointment I'm not being the social activist they brought me up to be pervades our whole relationship. Even lots of pro bono cases never seem enough. Years of weighty judgments press down on me.

All this subtext is one reason I don't come home that often. I miss the free and easy days of my childhood when everything I did was golden. Before the wrong turns and bad choices, as Dad never tires of telling me.

I hold up a hand to forestall the offer I can see is bubbling on Dad's lips. "Tempting, but I don't think I want to work for my dad. Right now, my best option is to do stellar work and make myself indispensable."

"So, what advice do you want, then?" Dad looks primed to give me his opinion, whether I still want it.

"I appreciate the advice you've already given me. I think talking it out has clarified what I need to do." I struggle to my feet, planning to put my cup in the sink and take off.

"Where are you going?" Mom asks.

"Home. I need to pack. Thanks for the treats."

"You're not leaving for a few days. Stay for dinner. You'll have plenty of time after that." We jump at an explosive noise outside. Too loud for a car backfiring.

"Damn kids. Parents probably drove them over the border to buy fireworks." Dad charges toward the front of the house.

Mom runs after him, mumbling, "A little early? It's months until the Fourth of July."

"They don't care. Just like making noise and scaring the hell out of everyone." Dad skids to a stop, if you can skid on carpeting. Growls. "What the fuck?"

Fireworks are not the problem. The haze in the air as we tumble into the living room clouds the picture window. The couch smolders yellow, the chemical reek of burning polyurethane foam signals the release of a toxic stew.

I peer through obscuring smoke. A movement catches my eye, and my mouth drops open. A flameproof suit lies discarded on the lawn and a bulky figure in overalls disappears into the neighbor's backyard.

Dad herds us back to the porch and out the back. "Go outside. I'll find the fire extinguisher."

"Too late for that," I pant, then grab his arm, pulling him out the door.

As we round the house and head for the street, he pulls away and dials 911, staying on with the operator. He mouths that police and fire departments have already been alerted and are about five minutes away. I run over to the SUV to check on Liam, and see the windshield in shards, Liam slumped over the steering wheel. Then I glance around in case Sam has doubled back and is lying in wait. My imagination in overdrive, I seem to hear laughter in the wind, but no sign of my persecutor. When I pull open the door, Liam has his hands over his ears, moaning.

"Liam." He doesn't respond. Shaking his arm, I yell, "Liam." He jerks away, but the reaction seems to be from my pressure on his arm, not because he's heard me. When I finally catch his eye, I point toward the house and, even though he's shaky and unbalanced, he pulls himself out of the door. He tries to totter toward my parents, surrounded by neighbors, but ends up slumped against the truck. I can see flames shooting through the roof. We've moved into conflagration territory.

Mom is being comforted by a few of her neighborhood friends. She moans, trembling, arms wrapped tight around herself.

"Thank God everyone is okay. But I wish the damn explosive had blown up in his face.."

Startled, I stare at her. The venom is so unlike my kind, forgiving mother.

Turning her tear-streaked face to me, she scolds, "I told you Sam was bad news years ago. You wouldn't listen."

"I never thought he'd try to blow up the house," I whine. *Shit, I sound like a sulky teenager.*

Liam, still shaky, leans against the car, putting his fingers against his ears, trying to clear them.

A cacophony of sirens heralds an ambulance, three fire engines, and two police cars. All the emergency strobe lights combine in blinding intensity. Once the police find out the criminal has left the area, the firefighters put out the blaze before the house burns down.

The fire marshal tells us it will be at least tomorrow before they can assess the damage.

"Probably a small incendiary device. Maybe a grenade or something homemade. Pure luck it landed on your couch."

"Luck?" Dad sputters.

"For the guy who threw it."

Cooling down as fast as he heated up, Dad asks, "Was it like a Molotov cocktail?"

"Could be, or a homemade grenade. Maybe something bought on the black market. We'll know once we've examined the remains."

Liam walks over from the ambulance, phone to his ear. The EMTs have just finished checking out his hearing and the cuts all over his face from the shattered glass. "He threw a flash-bang at the SUV. Cracked the windshield." He shakes his head. "The sound waves..." He stops. "My ears are still ringing."

Dad's face screws up like he's been eating lemons. "Guess that's why you didn't run after him."

"Des, you don't need to take your anger out on Liam. None of this is his fault."

"Sorry," he mumbles, holding out a hand. Liam shakes it.

"Stressful situation."

A police sergeant comes to join the confab. "We'll need to take statements from all of you. I understand you know the guy who did it?"

"Yes," I practically shout.

"Calm down, honey," Dad says, patting my shoulder.

I twist away. He wants to treat me like his little girl, and I am so beyond that.

I open my mouth to respond, but Dad continues, "It's her douchebag ex. He's been stalking her and now he's upping his game."

"We found the fireproof suit. Was he wearing it when you saw him? Did you see his face for identification?"

"The suit was on the grass when I saw him. I didn't see his face."

The cop frowns. "Then how did you...?"

"Look, I've known the guy for ten years and was with him for eight. Believe me, I can recognize him from the back or the front."

"Right." He makes a note. "Have you reported the stalking?"

Dad folds his arms and lets me respond. "Yes, Officer. To the Chicago police. I live in the city."

"We'll be in touch with them." Then he focuses on my parents. "You won't be able to stay here, Mr. Press. Do you know where you want to go?"

Before Dad can answer, I butt in, trying to assert control. "Stay at the condo. There's plenty of space. And you can hang out there, even when I leave for Paris."

"Yeah, I guess we can do that," Dad agrees, but I can see the unwillingness in the set of his jaw. Just like I don't want favors from them, he doesn't want them from me.

The sergeant takes down the address and says he'll arrange for an interview. The cops and firemen will be out here for a while. Dad goes to pull out his car from the garage around the back. Liam and I slip into the newly arrived SUV, Case at the wheel. While he points the black behemoth toward Sheridan Road and the Outer Drive, I dial my favorite pizza place.

"Just calling Pequod's for delivery." The thought of the caramelized deep-dish crust filled with pepperoni, mushrooms, onions, green pepper, sausage, black olives, and extra cheese distracts me from the chaos. "No food in the house, and we'll need sustenance to muddle through this."

Mom and Dad arrive an hour later. They stopped at Target to pick up clothes, toiletries, etc. Dad's rage, which had dampened during the hours with the authorities, reignites as he flings the plastic bags into a corner. Mom is barely holding herself together.

"Alice, it's just a building. We can have it fixed up. Thank God no one died."

"We moved into that house when Micki was two. Forty-four years." Her eyes leak a steady trickle down each side of her nose. "It will never feel the same." She gulps. "It's like someone died."

I hand her the box of tissues. Dad takes a defiant bite of pizza and talks around it. "If I catch that bastard…" He stops at Mom's shocked look.

"You will call the police if you find him." Her tone brooks no arguments. Then she dissolves into a sobbing mess. Dad puts his arms around her, head pressed against his chest, rocking her back and forth.

For me, this assault brings back memories of Cress' condo after Tina left it a shamble last year. All her belongings smashed, clothes in shreds, books burned. Now she's moved in with Max, I bet she'll sell it or make it into a rental unit.

I ponder the extent of the damage to our house—mostly superficial or a huge restoration project? Numb, I wonder if eventually I'll feel desolate like Mom? Does it matter to me now that I don't live there?

I grab my laptop and pull up the folder of pictures. We

had everything digitized a few years ago. It's all happy families—unbearable. My deadened heart revives, and pain with it. My skin is sensitive, my clothes chafe. When I click off, waves of muscle contractions ripple through my arms and legs. While I've fretted about work, Sam is the bigger threat. Hayden might blow up my career, but Sam is blowing up my life and family.

Leaving my parents to a grief that pierces me but I can't completely share, I lay out clothes for the voyage to come.

CHAPTER
TEN

When you play against an experienced opponent who exploits all the defensive resources at his command you sometimes have to walk time and again, along the narrow path of 'the only move.'—David Bronstein

Micki

IN THE DAYS before I leave, living with Mom and Dad in the condo isn't quite as bad as staying at the Evanston house would have been. Dad's pretty territorial, but we're on neutral turf, so he's tiptoeing around the perimeter. After our session with the police came the good/bad news from the fire chief. The house is salvageable, but there will be a lot of work before they can move back in. The fire spread as far as the kitchen and downstairs half bath, so Mom and Dad have decided on a remodel, resigned to a long haul.

No sign of Sam. Where he's gone to ground is a mystery. His studio is empty, and he doesn't seem to have a new apartment. Maybe he's hanging out with one of the women I never knew about. Could he have scared himself when he blew up my parents' house? Even with bodyguards, I'm on constant alert in any public place.

I dread going into the office before I leave for Paris, but Fred demands my presence. 10:00 a.m. At nine forty-five, Case lounges against the open door to my office, sipping coffee, waiting to take me to the airport for my afternoon flight. An itch develops between my shoulder blades, knowing he's watching me walk down the broad hallway toward the biggest corner office in our suite, where the spider that is Frederick Lanscombe weaves his web.

Fred has floor-to-ceiling windows that face east. Out of the corner of my eye, the lakefront shimmers in a weak April sun. Lemony air freshener scents the space, as if to greet me. I wonder if Atalanta, his administrative secretary, got a call from our receptionist, warning her I was on my way. Her eyes like burning coals, she glowers at me—Hera confronting Echo. Depriving me of speech, she's up from behind her desk. "He'll see you now," she lets me know he's been waiting and I'm late, even though I'm actually early.

I cross my fingers on each hand, arms straight down. Pull back my shoulders and hold my head high. Like I have to impress his minion. I manage not to slump as this thought crosses my mind.

Fred could be right off the screen as a television lawyer. Even sitting—and he doesn't stand when the Greek goddess ushers me into his office—he is noticeably tall, thin, and angular. A hawklike, patrician face with hooded, chilly blue eyes that have an avid, predatory expression. His pearl gray custom suit screams expensive and is complemented by a blindingly white shirt, and heavy gold cuff links adorning the French cuffs that peek out from his jacket sleeves. Intimidating is the best one-word description of the man who holds supreme power over my career at the firm.

Don't fire me today. And please, please, please let me make my plane.

"Thank you for coming in, Micki." His voice, as always, undermines the carefully cultivated look and the mansion on the lake. He has the same Bridgeport accent as the late Mayor Daley, underlining his Chicago roots and crafty political savvy.

Waving a long hand with thin, slightly knobby fingers, he says, "Siddown, siddown. I know we're short on time. When is your flight again?"

"Three. I need to be at O'Hare…"

"I know, three hours ahead. That's bullshit timing. But this won't take long."

My face hardens to stone while hairs bristle on the back of my neck. I press my lips together, catching the lower one between my teeth. His expectant look stiffens my determination not to respond. I'm not a brilliant chess player, but I have a few moves in my arsenal.

"Well." He clears his throat. Then taps his fingers against the pristine green blotter on his desk. I watch his eyes move to the pen, placed just so next to the yellow legal pad, covered with a neat, precise script. He almost reaches for it, then folds his hands and leans forward.

"Ms. Press. Dis is merely an informal chat."

I keep my interior chuckle to myself. He tries to use as few words as possible that highlight his pronunciation.

"Yes. Informal. Just a reminder. We expect you to work on the case while you're away."

I hold up my laptop case in acknowledgment, unsure why he thinks reminding me is necessary.

He pauses, eyes narrowed. "Fortunately, Hayden will keep an eye on things here."

"Isn't that Rebecca's job?" This is weird.

He moistens his lips. "Ah, of course. But Hayden will be her unofficial second-in-command since you'll be traveling." As if hinting it would be my position if I were staying here.

Fat chance. I should have taken Hayden's warning to heart. Have I already fallen from the ladder and down the chute? Is Fred's subtext that partnership is out of my reach?

While I've been panicking, he's still talking. "Rebecca can pass your progress on to the client. He's dealing with campaign fallout and congressional commitments, so the team won't meet with him in the near future."

Well, that's good news. I don't need Greenberg's scowling face on my screen. "I'll be meeting with the team on a videoconference every day."

He doesn't look at me. "Right. Of course. Enjoy your trip, Micki. Don't forget to bring chocolates back for the staff."

Dismissed. What a useless exercise. Except as inference and intimidation. I grit my teeth, keeping in the frustration I would spew, if I had the time and the guts.

Case stands in front of my office door, my coat over his arm, and goes for an elevator as soon as I walk out Fred's door. Once inside, he helps me into the coat, then we run when the doors open. The limo is at the curb in front of the building, Liam at the wheel.

He hands me into the back seat and climbs in front.

"You want lunch on the way? We have time?"

"I can pick up something at the airport."

Case gives Liam a look. "That okay with you, man?"

"Yeah. I'll drop you off, then stop for a bite. Just text when you want me back."

Damn it. Ms. Insensitive strikes again. "You're just dropping *me*..."

"Wrong." Case's response is loud, drowning out my words. "I stay with you until you're on the plane and the doors are closed."

"Seriously?"

"Yeah. Seriously." He slams the door shut and Liam edges out into mid-morning traffic toward the expressway. Speedy but careful, we're there in just over half an hour. Liam pulls in at departures. Case grabs my luggage and waves his colleague off.

"I'll text you and meet you right here."

Good thing I can drop off my bag at the door and go through TSA Precheck. The security line is much shorter, and I just have my purse and computer bag. Case takes out a pass and the agent allows him to accompany me to the gate. He'll leave once the plane's doors close. GSU will have someone waiting for me at Charles De Gaulle too.

Gurgling erupts from my stomach. The astonishment on Case's face makes me giggle. "Hungry, I guess."

We decide on Romano's Macaroni Grill.

"Do you really think I need protection in Paris?" I ask him. "I can't imagine Sam would follow me there. For one thing, he doesn't have the money."

He shrugs broad shoulders and takes a bite of his Penne Rustica. Case is built like a wrestler with the face of a poet, a long oval, a wide mouth with thin lips, long lashes that practically brush his cheeks. Instead of what I think of as a bodyguard uniform—black suit, white shirt, skinny tie—he's wearing tight Levi's, a gray heathered Henley, and a jean jacket. "He's an artist, right? Maybe he has friends in Paris to help him out."

A mouthful of spinach and shrimp salad barely gets down before I laugh, but it's really not that far-fetched. Sam spent a year studying art in Paris before we met, and he could easily keep in touch with his friends. Just because I don't know about them doesn't mean they don't exist. On the other hand, would his artist friends be willing to menace me?

At the gate, Case takes my ticket and goes up to the counter. He hands the paper to one of the agents and, with many hand gestures, explains something, occasionally pointing to me. I try to avoid looking at them, try to feel normal, try not to think Sam is lurking and ready to jump out. I tell myself Case and the ticket agent are flirting, and this is nothing to do with me. Then she picks up the mic.

"Ms. Michelle Press, please come to the ticket desk." People look around as I grab my bag and jacket and move next to Case, who hands me my ticket, takes my arm, and leads me through the door and down the jetway. First on the plane. This is all new to me. "First class?"

"Yeah, JL arranged it." He locates my seat, puts my things within easy reach, and makes sure I'm settled in.

"I'll be watching everyone board and once the doors are closed, I'll radio in and take off. Have an enjoyable trip." With a kind of salute, he ambles off the plane and disappears.

~

I'VE NEVER BEEN out of the U.S. Overnight and over water—yikes. Two preflight cocktails, courtesy of first class, settle the jitters while I glue my eyes to the safety video.

I've always envied the businessmen who settle into their seats, take a pill, and sack out, waking up rested and ready for their first meeting of the day. I never sleep on planes. Never. Until this trip. Don't even take a pill. One minute I'm trying to find the perfect reclining setting for the bed-like seat, and the next, someone or something, is shaking me.

I open my mouth to scream as Sam's face, painted like a clown, leers down at me, hands like claws moving toward my neck. I jerk upright, or at least as upright as I can manage from a fully reclined position.

"Are you all right?" A soft, female voice penetrates the fog. A face crinkled with concern peers at me.

I rub my eyes. "Uh..." My voice is thick, and I have to cough a few times before anything intelligible comes out. "Sorry. Bad dream, I guess. I rarely sleep on planes."

Soothingly she says, "We'll be landing soon. For breakfast we have omelet, fruit, a croissant, juice, and coffee or tea."

My stomach grumbles. I haven't eaten since lunch yesterday. "That sounds great." I'm still trying to push away the vision of Sam as killer clown.

Just before we're told to stay in our seats, I make it to the first-class toilet, wash my face, and put in my contacts. The world looks clearer, but I'm still exhausted. I close my eyes, but Sam's face comes back. The bastard's got me, even if he is over 4,000 miles away. I wonder if he feels it, as if he's hooked me with an invisible line and can reel me in any time he wants.

By the time we're parked at the gate, I'm paralyzed.

"Are you sure you're okay?" The concerned flight attendant is back at my seat. "I can call for assistance if you need it."

Unable to speak, I slowly struggle to my feet. Finally, I choke out, "Thanks, but I can manage."

Her frown tells me she's not reassured but she steps aside as I grab my bag. Stumbling slightly, I manage to deplane and walk down the jetway. An agent and a short burly guy in a long-sleeved T-shirt and jeans stand at the entrance. The agent checks a clipboard. "Mme. Michelle Press?"

Still finding speech difficult, I nod, then flinch as the short guy takes my arm. "GSU," he says shortly. When I finally move, he continues, "This way, Ms. Press. We have a vehicle outside waiting. Let's go down to baggage claim." He walks away at a brisk pace. I rush to keep up. Then he takes my arm to move me along. His warm breath and growly, slightly accented English are too close to my ear. "I'm Kurt, by the way."

I move my head and mumble. "Nice to meet you, Kurt." We're silent down to the carousels, where my serviceable bag slowly revolves.

"That it?" Kurt points toward a glittery gold roll-a-board.

Tells me he thinks I'm a ditzy blonde. I frown. "That one." I point at my medium-sized maroon Samsonite soft side, scrapes and rubbed spots showing its age.

He grabs it and we go off to find the GSU car. A black Renault SUV sits at the curb. Kurt opens the back passenger door and hands me in before putting my bag into the trunk. Then he hops into the front. "Henri, this is Mme. Michelle Press. Ms. Press, Henri Delaunay."

"Bonjour, Madame. Enchanté."

"Enchantée aussi, Henri," I say in my bad French accent. Instead of turning up his nose, as I expect, he smiles.

Once we've navigated out of the airport and onto the A1, Kurt says, "It's still too early for you to check in to Le Pavillon de la Reine. JL said you've never been to Paris, so would you like a private tour?"

Two hours later, we've driven up the Champs-Élysées, around the Arc de Triomphe, past the Opera House and Notre Dame, over the Pont Neuf, and through the Latin Quarter. Then Henri drives us up near the funicular at the Place Saint-Pierre, which takes us up to Sacre-Coeur. "I'll be waiting near the bottom. Just let me know when to pick you up."

The breathtaking, late nineteenth-century white church, Byzantine in style, is swoon-worthy. I spend too much time enjoying the mosaics in the late nineteenth-century house of worship. Then we walk up, and walk down, and walk up again, enjoying the outdoor artists, the shops, and the village atmosphere. After we finish climbing, I newly appreciate why it's called La Butte. My head whirls like the windmill of the Moulin Rouge.

When Henri finally catches up to us, I scramble into the car with relief. "You are staying at Le Pavillon de la Reine, Madame?"

"Oui, Henri." But then my French deserts me.

"You will enjoy it. Very chic and historic at the same time. Built by le Roi, Henry Quatre, in mille six cent douze."

"He's Parisian, and proud of it," Kurt says. "Personally, as a German, I don't really understand the concept of nationalism. That's not part of our ethos anymore." He flicks a finger at Henri. "En anglais, s'il vous plaît, Depp!"

Probably doesn't mean Johnny, but I'm not sure what the word translates to. Henri gives him a punch in the shoulder, then catches my eye and winks. "Désolée. The king, Henry IV, had it built in 1612 to be called the Place Royale, but it never became the royal residence as intended. Place des Vosges is the oldest square in Paris. There are many places in the city that are older, but no squares older than that."

Once we arrive near the Place des Vosges, he finds a place to park. Kurt retrieves the suitcase.

"You can take off, Henri. I have to stay to guard Mme. Press."

Henri gives a fake yawn. "Au revoir, Madame. Watch this one. His hands are quick."

Kurt's face screws into a scowl. "Miststück." Henri starts the car and drives off, laughing.

The sight of the hotel takes my breath away. This stately, white, ivy-covered building looks old, in a square filled with old buildings.

I tear my gaze away from the courtyard and turn back to look at the Place with its mown and rolled lawn and the ornamental fountain in the middle with small children wading while their parents watch.

The walks are filled with people promenading and window shopping. Kurt stands next to me and points to the right. "Down there is the house of Victor Hugo, the author of *Les Miserables*. You know it?"

"I saw the musical."

He rubs the back of his neck. "Of course. Everyone likes Andrew Lloyd Webber." After a pause, he says, "That is where the awards dinner will be. Very convenient for you."

At that moment, my continuing exhaustion takes over and my body slumps. Kurt grasps my suitcase in one hand and takes my arm with the other. Quickly moving through the courtyard, I make it through the heavy glass doors and collapse onto a couch in the foyer.

"I'll check you in and collect your key." Boot heels clack along the tiles as I lean back with my eyes half closed, trying for deep breaths. When his hand falls on my shoulder, I jump up, heart racing.

"Let's go." He dangles an actual key. "A porter will bring up the bags."

Once I'm in my room, suitcase and computer case delivered and on the luggage rack, I slip off my shoes, sip a glass of water, and try to focus. The junior suite has an original beamed ceiling and a collection of fine antique furniture. The carpeting is plush, the bed a combination of modern mattress and antique four-poster. No bed curtains, which suits me just fine.

I'm too tired to appreciate the finery, except for the amazing bathroom. Marble walls, floor with tiny tiles, shower, tub, toilet, and bidet, I can see myself enjoying the luxury, eventually. I'm sure the amenities are top notch, but now I'm dog-tired, even after sleeping on the plane. After a few minutes, I put my phone next to the bed, and set the alarm. A quick nap might perk me up.

The sound of "Viva La Vida" shakes me awake. Darkness all around makes me wonder if someone came in and blindfolded me. The only breathing I hear is my own, but I still can't be sure I'm alone. My heart races. When I put a finger up to my face, all I feel are my eyelashes. A rush of heat flows through me, making my cold extremities tingle.

Rolling to my side, I fumble around for the phone. When the screen lights up, the time is four-thirty. Missed call. Rebecca Masters. Butterflies start up in my stomach, but not the good kind. This has to be bad news. Maybe my latest case has some new twist. I can only hope that's all it is as my finger stabs call back.

"Micki." My mentor's smooth contralto offers no clue.

"Hi, Rebecca. Sorry I missed your call."

"No problem. It's early in the day here."

"You must have called at the crack of dawn."

"Umm," she says, noncommittal.

"Something urgent? A problem with the case? Or do you just want to know how I like Paris?" I can hear a quaver in my voice that undercuts my stab at light banter.

"Micki, you know I've always been your strongest supporter in the firm. After all, I hired you when I was managing partner, even though I had to push several members of the partner committee to support me."

"They were?" This was news to me. The firm never divulges committee votes, just the outcome.

"I heard about your meeting with Fred." An excruciating silence ensues and I'm not sure of the protocol. Should I say something or wait for her to continue? Rebecca is a stickler for following correct procedure, and this situation is out of the realm of my experience.

"Yeah."

"How much do you want this promotion?'

"I want it more than anything." And it's true.

"You're going to go through hell for this effort. Even if you get the promotion, the environment will stay hostile as long as Fred and Tyler are around. You know that, right?"

I squeeze my eyes shut. "The same, or worse?"

"Hayden will lay traps and bad-mouth you. Anyway, after Fred spoke with you, I was livid. Told him off. But it won't do any good. You really will need to watch your step because he and Tyler are determined to have Hayden as the next partner. He's been canvassing the partners, and I know he has a lot of votes."

"What do you suggest?" Numbness washes over me. "Should I sue for gender discrimination if the partners choose Hayden?"

"No point. If you sue, you might win, but you will never work here again, no matter the outcome. Beside the fact that you won't find a talented lawyer willing to take the suit. And a court case will deter other firms from hiring you." She heaves a sigh. "I shouldn't even be telling you this. But if you threaten to sue, they'll offer you a payout—generous but not enough to retire on."

I take a deep breath. "I don't want to give up. If I'm not promoted, I'll figure out the next step."

She clears her throat. "My advice is, show them how brilliant you are, but start looking around for other options. You want to leave on your own terms." We're both silent for a while. "You might find something even better." Her encouragement rings hollow.

The phone is on the bedside table because my hand trembles too much to hold it steady. I don't want them to win, but I realize I'm at the endgame and my throw of the dice was craps. But I'm not ready to give in yet. Maybe, with luck on my side, Hayden will make a major misstep. It's happened before.

"By the way, there's something fishy going on with the case."

"Oh?" Her comment piques my curiosity.

"Fred and Tyler have some financial ties with Greenberg. They deny its anything important, and he's not saying anything at all. Could you flag anything suspicious that comes through on the emails? Maybe from those anonymous accounts."

"I'll dig through and see what I can find. Do you think they are involved in the insider trading? We'd have to look at their financial records and investments, and somehow I don't think they'll be cooperative."

"Not sure. But something doesn't add up." She sighs. "See you tomorrow on the video call."

I choke out thanks and end the call, throwing myself against the pillows, engulfed in a stew of rage and despair, finally slipping into a restless nap.

When the phone alarm goes off, I groan, turn it off, and burrow back under the covers. Ten minutes later, it goes off again. My eyes are so puffy they open into slits, and I can barely read the numbers on the screen. After a little effort, they unscramble six thirty. What's so important about that? "Siri," I croak, "what's on my calendar?"

The robotic voice tells me I have an appointment in less than an hour. Fuzzy, I have to focus on this unremembered obligation. Finally, I give up and look at the calendar through my swollen orbs,

Shit, I have a ticket for a pricey bateau-mouche dinner cruise at seven thirty. I really just want to hibernate. Be your own cheerleader, my mom's voice says. Go. Take your mind off the firm for an hour or two.

I need to change out of my travel clothes and find the boarding quay. Groaning, I roll off the bed and totter into the bathroom to bathe my eyes. Maybe that will take out the redness. Then I remember Kurt, but I only booked one ticket.

I'm sure Sam isn't around. I'll try to ditch Kurt. Henri was right. He is handsy, something I really don't need.

I pull on my dress, slip into my shoes, and take a cursory look at my face and hair, putting on lipstick and pulling my hair into a messy bun. Then I grab my coat and purse and wrench open the door. Kurt lounges against the wall near the door to the room opposite.

He looks at my outfit. "Going somewhere?"

"Reservation for a dinner cruise and show." I dodge past him and rush downstairs.

Racing after me, he yells, loud enough for the whole hotel to hear. "You can't go alone."

Other room doors open, guests peering out at the disturbance. One man clumsily buttons a dress shirt. Stocky, with a fringe of gray hair that stands up around his head like an aureole, gives a contemptuous sniff. "Foreigners. Don't know how to behave."

I can't answer, at least not right away. My face red with exertion and embarrassment, I skid to a halt at the concierge station. Kurt catches me there and puts a hand on my arm. I jerk and move away. "I'm secure in Paris. You can stand down or whatever it's called."

He huffs, "JL would fire me."

My eyes dart around the room, looking for someone who works here. "Pardon," I yell into the empty space. My small store of French inaccessible to my brain, I continue bellowing. "Is anyone around?"

From some back room, the concierge and the desk clerk appear. Their faces look questioning, then morph into pleasant smiles rather than the 'damn American' look I'm sure they're suppressing. "Pardon, Madame. How may I help you?" The concierge's English is excellent, of course.

"I have a ticket for a dinner cruise and show."

I begin to ask for directions, but Kurt smoothly interrupts, "But Madame's reservation is for one person and there are two of us. Can you help?"

"Of course. Do you have your voucher?" He holds out a well-manicured hand to me.

Swallowing my chagrin at being outmaneuvered, I hand over the folded piece of grubby paper. He glances at it and picks up the black phone sitting on the desk. Once he has the connection, his rapid French leaves me completely in the dark. Finally, after listening to the person on the other end, he says, "What is the name of your guest?"

Kurt's triumphant expression tells it all. "Meisner, Kurt Meisner."

The concierge repeats the name. "Bon." Then he turns back to me. "Do you want this put on the card you used for the initial reservation?"

Another unexpected expense. Damn you, Sam. "That will be perfect," Kurt responds. Now everyone will think he's my toy boy. When he gets off the phone, I say, "We'll need an Uber to be at the quay on time."

"Fait accompli," my German companion murmurs. "Your carriage awaits." Kurt gives a bow toward the front entrance.

Why did I book this excursion? Oh yeah, it's a way to use up the evening and not have to deal with dinner separately. Seemed like a good idea. Now not so much. I'm ready to kick myself. Somehow, among all the couples taking this romantic evening adventure, going with my bodyguard is going to be a letdown.

Morning hangover. The meal was superb. Foie gras and oysters for the aperitif, lobster ravioli entree, fillet with a Périgord sauce and haricots verts as the plat principal. Then salad, a cheese course, followed by île flottante for dessert, in the French manner. The accompanying champagne, red and white wines including a Sauternes with dessert, and after dinner liqueurs, was a blowout.

When I got back last night, I drank a huge balloon glass of water and took two ibuprofen. My head keeps pounding. I guess it didn't do the job. Especially the ringing in my ears. I grope for my phone, trying to turn off the alarm, until I realize the room phone is ringing, and ringing, and ringing.

When my eyes unstick enough for me to see the evil instrument, I stumble over the ornate table it sits on. "Oui?" The croaking sound is barely comprehensible to my own ears.

"Madame, this is the wake-up call you asked for. The buffet breakfast is available for your pleasure."

"Merci." I want to slam down the receiver and go back to bed. I start to pick up my cell phone, looking for missed calls from JL. He's called every day since he left for London. Could I have slept through the ringing? Instead, I head toward the bathroom. I can check later. Right now, a full bladder is urgent.

That taken care of, I start the Nespresso machine and dress to the sound of JL's voice. He called four times last night, twice while I was cruising. The last time, he left a voice mail. "Kurt tells me you're safe in your room, so I am going to assume you're sleeping. I can't wait to see you tomorrow, ma chouette. I hope you have sweet dreams." I play it over and over, reassurance oozing through me at the sound of his voice.

After the last play through, I hear voices in the corridor, then a sharp rap. I pull the belt of my robe tighter. "Hello?"

Kurt's voice is loud and clear through the heavy wood door. "Ms. Press, did you order room service?"

"NO," I yell back.

I hear murmured conversation.

"Open the door, please." Kurt stands, grinning, next to one of the hotel servers.

Still fuzzy from the effects of last night's overindulgence, I ask, "What is this?"

"Breakfast, Madame."

"I see that, but why is it here?"

Kurt is still grinning. "JL ordered it for you. So romantic, yes?"

It is romantic. But I'm still not sure whether I'm ready for this much romance.

I move out of the doorway. The cart that rolls in has everything I might want and looks much more appetizing than the food on the plane yesterday. Definitely on a par with last night's gourmet meal. The server rolls it over between the two chairs. "Madame. Bon appetit."

I thank him and hand him a small tip, then sit with my now tepid coffee as he and Kurt leave. "Make sure you put the chain back on," Kurt calls out as he leaves.

Setting down my cup, I pick up the phone, planning to listen again to JL's message. I see two more calls from an unknown number and block them. Then I notice a stream of text notifications from someone unknown, or at least not in my contacts. As soon as I open the first one, I'm sure they're from Sam. Goosebumps break out on my arms, and the smell of bacon, warm pastries, fruit, and eggs turns from enticing to nauseating. Even the well-sugared and creamed coffee tastes bitter as I roll through the lines.

How did you like the fireworks? Good, huh?

Too bad you tried to block me, bitch.

My breath hitches.

Think you can escape.

You can run, but you can't hide.

I'm just an old hound dog but I'm good at
sniffing things out.

The Elvis reference is so Sam that, despite
myself, I want to laugh.

I will track you down.

Now I'm shaking, but I can't take my eyes off the screen.

Feel the hot breath on your neck?

Can't stay away forever.

Or I'll hop a flight to Paree.

A wave of dizziness washes over me as I picture Sam
striding through De Gaulle, clown mask in place, ready to
hunt me down. I throw down the phone, but almost immediately pick it back up.

How 'bout a dip in the Seine?

Watch for me in the shadows.

I'll find you when you least expect me.

I can play this game forever.

Why can't he let this go? His amour propre must be in
the stratosphere and totally tied up in getting me back at
any cost.

I look through the peephole in the door, but all I see is
Kurt in the otherwise empty hallway.

After a deep breath, I read the last few.

I'll be waiting for you.

I can wait forever.

No escape. Never.

Disgust makes my stomach heave. My phone hits the plushly carpeted floor as I run for the toilet.

CHAPTER

ELEVEN

Secrets travel fast in Paris.—Napoleon Bonaparte

JL

THE EUROSTAR IS BETTER than flying commercial. Instead of being crammed into a tiny seat in a narrow space, I pace, restless. The closer we come to Paris, the more I move up and down the aisle. I tell Max I need to stretch my legs, but he just snorts. Curious passengers watch me from behind newspapers and books or over their laptops as I plod back and forth.

When the food trolley comes through with Business Premier meals, Max growls, "Sit down, JL."

I clench my jaw. "Can't." Then move away from the glare burning into the back of my neck and retreat to the other end of the wagon. Coming back, I push past the server to return to my seat. The meal looks more appetizing than I expected. Hoping to quiet the buzzing in my chest, I gobble it down. No such luck as we pull into the station in Calais. The brief stop seems interminable, and I must remain in my seat. Half the passengers disembark to shop at the hypermarkets and bring home cases of cheap alcohol and luxury items like marrons glacé and goose liver pâté.

I tap my fingers on my thighs until Cress reaches over and captures my hands in hers. "We're all eager to see Micki," she says. "It won't be long now."

The aisle clears and the tightness in my chest loosens as I switch the grip and squeeze her hands. After a few seconds, she pulls them away and waves them at me, her engagement ring catching sunlight filtering in through the window. "Go walk, at least for a few more minutes. Just ignore Max. Not sure why he's so grumpy."

Max grabs her around the waist and starts kissing her. "Not grumpy," he says, coming up for air. "Just a little concerned about getting through the Gare du Nord without incident."

"I have guys positioned there in case Nasim Faez comes out to play," I tell him. Ever since Max started receiving threats from the escaped terrorist, GSU has been on high alert. Since his house in Clerkenwell was hit by a terrorist bomb while we were dining close by, everything has been stepped up. The racetrack fiasco in Scotland amped the level again. The fact Faez was able to follow us to Scotland and shoot at Max during a family celebration means heightened vigilance. Warnings of planned attacks in Paris in the next few days have us past red alert.

Police and Interpol have found no trace of Faez, but we're sure he's teamed up with some terrorist group. Ten years in a maximum-security prison with nothing to do but reflect on ways to avenge the death of his brother. He's had plenty of time to make connections and refine his plan.

"Allan Mason is coming over and will liaise with the French. We don't want to step on any toes and MI6 has already contacted their security service. If there's an incident, Clay doesn't want GSU directly involved."

"Bien. Of course, if you are the target..." Then I get up and pace again. Worry about Micki takes all my concentration and energy. Reports from Case tell me no one has seen Sam since the attack on the Press house. He's gone to ground. The police have an APB out, but they haven't found him either.

For all we know, he's lurking in Paris, ready to pounce. He seems to have sources of intel on her and may be staking out the hotel. Max says he hasn't shown up on any flight manifests, but I wouldn't put it past him to have a stolen passport and a flight booked under that name.

At least I'm not in charge of the security for Cress' dinner, where we think Faez will target Max. I am no fan of Allan Mason, but to have someone else in charge of Max's problems is a relief. A conductor announces Gare du Nord. I come back to the seat and grab my duffel and one belonging to Cress. Max takes her other bag plus his.

"Hey, guys, I can carry luggage." We both exhibit selective hearing, ignoring her protest. As we stand, waiting for our turn to disembark, I say to Max, "We should do another background check on Sam. I have a feeling we may have missed something, and Micki might not know as much about him as she imagines."

Overhearing me, Cress says, "They were together for eight years."

"That doesn't mean he doesn't have secrets. I think his good-old-boy façade hides a much darker interior."

Max drops one bag and slips a finger under his glasses so he can rub his eyes. "I'll see if Jarvis can assign someone from the team once we check in. With this flap on, it's all-hands-on-deck, and I'm not sure who'll be available."

I let out a hiss. "Not acceptable."

"Unfortunate, but I can't promise anything, and I can't contract it out. You can hire someone on your own dime if that helps."

"Non. The fewer people involved, the better. Can't Jarvis look into it?"

"He's too bloody busy to look for Sam. I know this is urgent, but he's doing the bulk of the recoding."

"All right. Let's see what looks workable. Just don't give him the details," I warn.

"Cool down, JL. This is bollocks. How the bloody hell do you expect him to find anything without the details?"

He's right but I'm a boiling kettle. Cool and down aren't helpful words. Max and Cress forge ahead, probably worried I might lose control completely. Under my breath, I curse. "Osti de tabarnak de sacrament, de câlice de ciboire de criss de marde." I chant it over and over until we reach the GSU limo that will take us to the hotel.

The hour-long slog into Paris feels like a lifetime. As soon as we reach the Place des Vosges, I'm out the door and into the square, where I do a lap around the arcaded walkway to retrieve my equilibrium, dodging the flâneurs. When I reach the entrance of Le Pavillon de la Reine, I rush through the gates and into the secluded courtyard. Micki is standing there waiting and as soon as I drop my bag, she jumps into my arms.

I press my lips against her neck in a soft kiss. "I've missed you so much. I was in agony the whole time."

"So glad you're here," she whispers between kisses all over my face. When I put her down, Kurt comes over.

"All quiet?" I ask.

"Yeah. Ms. Press and I went on a Bateau-Mouche dinner cruise, but otherwise she stayed in her room. We had someone outside the door all night."

"You did a dinner cruise with Kurt?" I look at her with mock outrage.

She shrugs. "I had a ticket, but I couldn't go without my bodyguard, so I bought him a ticket, too."

I focus my death-ray glare at Kurt. "You should have put it on expenses."

"Sorry, Boss. We were rushed, and I didn't think." His rough voice heightens his German accent.

Scowling, I turn back to Micki. "Give me the receipt. You shouldn't have to pay for him."

Max comes over with Mason. He was a burr up our butts in London, followed us to Scotland, and now here he is in Paris. Not even trying to keep the irritation tamped down, I grouch. "Tabarnak. Can't we have a few minutes alone?"

"I know it's cobblers," Max says with a drawn-out sigh. "Needs must. Cooperation with French security and MI6 is essential, so suck it up, mon vieux." He turns to face Allan, who introduces Inspector Poulliot.

"We'll meet you in the café in an hour. Nice to meet you, Inspector."

The cop slopes off to smoke while we make our way to the registration desk. I'm in Micki's room, so they just hand me a key and we leave Max, Cress, and Allan to their fate.

An hour isn't nearly enough time, but it will do as a stop gap. This is our first time in bed together and I wanted to take it slowly and savor every minute, but we don't have time. We just cuddle, touching and kissing with abandon, then share the magnificent shower, washing each other, getting to know each other's bodies. Tonight, we can abandon ourselves to pleasure.

When we reach the lobby, Max and Cress are waiting on one of the deep sofas. "About time you got down here," Max calls out when he sees us exit the elevator. René has replaced Kurt.

I clap him on the shoulder. "Salut, René. This is Michelle Press. She's a most precious jewel, so guard her with your life."

René St-Pierre is a tall, middle-aged man with a youthful, reddish complexion. A neatly shaved fringe of white surrounds his bald head. Face creased into a broad smile, René takes Micki's hand. "Enchanté, Madame." He bows and kisses her knuckles.

"Not part of the training," I tell him.

"We French are trained in how to greet a woman," he says. "You Canadian pretenders have no manners."

Cress interrupts. "Come on, René."

Her mouth quirks into a sly smile as he says, "Oui, Madame Taylor."

"We're going to the Carnavalet, then a patisserie, then to the Sainte-Chapelle."

Micki gives her a tap on the arm. "Don't forget I have a meeting at 3:00 p.m. and I'll be working at some point this evening."

Cress knits her brows together in irritation. Micki is so focused on work and the brass ring of promotion, I fear I'll hardly see her. This interlude should bring us closer together, but it may drive us apart.

"No arguments," Cress tells her, slipping an arm through Micki's, and practically drags her through the glass doors and out through the courtyard, my man trailing behind.

Max slaps me on the back. "I'm parched for a cuppa. Let's meet Allan and the Inspector."

∽

Micki

Once we're out of view, I pull Cress down onto a bench. René hovers nearby, pretending to watch the kids playing. "Okay, tell me about the ring, and the proposal."

She holds out her left hand, where the antique opal and emerald engagement ring flashes in the sunlight. "It's a Grant family heirloom."

"Did Max drop to one knee?"

Her laugh competes with the water streaming from the fountain. "He came looking for me in their family conservatory. Then he just blurted it out—marry me." Her eyes are unfocused. "And I said yes. It was so romantic. Even his father warned me that when I agreed to take on Max, I got the rest of them as a package deal."

Wow. I hope someday I'll find a guy who'll propose like that. But who am I kidding? The promotion probably means being an old maid. I think back to my conversation with JL at Tempo. I know the pattern. At forty-six, with my career uppermost, no man is going to take a chance on me.

I must say it out loud, because Cress punches my arm. "Nonsense. Rebecca's married, isn't she?"

"She got married in law school. Totally different." That reminds me of her interactions with Simon Greenberg. Maybe he proposed and she spurned him. The thought makes me giggle.

"What's so funny?" Cress gives me a cross-eyed glare.

"Just thinking about Rebecca and her law school classmates."

A text message interrupts.

REBECCA: Meeting canceled. See you tomorrow.

"Important?" Cress asks.

I honestly don't know, but the pattern sends up warning flags. "I don't have to meet with the team, so I'm at your disposal."

"That's good. We don't have to rush." She settles back on the bench, swinging her legs. "Getting back to engagements. Max and I have a bet going on how long it will take before JL lets you know he's serious." She titters, then glances away moistening her lips. "You'll be my maid of honor, right?'

"Of course. Who else?" I want to know the rest of the deets on the trip, but I need her take on Sam's threats. And I should probably mention how things stand with the firm.

René loiters just out of earshot but close enough to counter any danger. I don't expect Sam to pop up from one of the hedges. He never has much money and I let him mooch off me for all the years we were together. I'm sure that's one reason he wants me back. I'm not rich, but I have a very comfortable income and a place to live. He has neither and can't live with his parents since he rejected them a decade ago.

"Something wrong, Micki?"

I can't blurt it out, so I pull up the text messages and let her read them.

Her mouth drops open. Once she finishes and hands my phone back, she yelps, "WTF." The sound is shocking in the courtyard's seclusion of one of the grand maisons. "Has JL seen these?"

"No."

"Why not?" The accusation in her voice makes me wince.

To pull myself back together, I take deep breaths of the magnolia and rose-scented air. In response, Cress sneezes, saving me from having to answer. She grabs a bunch of tissues out of her tiny bag, blows her nose, then mops her face.

"We can't stay here. Let's go to the museum, and then we can discuss your plan of action over pastries and coffee."

The Carnavalet comprises two seventeenth-century houses, the Hôtels Carnavalet and Le Peletier de Saint Fargeau, on the rue de Sevigné, a four-minute walk from the square. René continues to trail behind us, far enough back that anyone watching would think he was just another stroller, out to enjoy the fresh April afternoon.

When we reach the entrance of the museum, he hangs back on the street while we go through the courtyard to the ticket office, following on a bit later, so he doesn't seem like a stalker. Discreet surveillance must be an art and he is well trained.

As we wander through the lower rooms of the old-fashioned, musty space, I can see why Cress likes to come here. True to form, she gives me mini lectures along the way.

"The original part of the museum was built as a private house in the sixteenth century but not finished until 1660. The famous diarist, Madame de Sévigné lived here from 1677 to 1694."

She roots around in her bag, muttering. "Where the eff is it?"

I roll my eyes. "You're not going to read me excerpts of her diary, are you?"

Brandishing more tissues, she sneezes again. "No," she manages between the attacks and the congestion. "But I can lend you a volume when we're back in Chicago. Max has the full set in his library. Of course, it's in French."

"Aren't all his books about car racing or spy novels?"

Her laugh resounds through the massive, high-ceilinged, fortunately empty room. "Well, he has those, but his degrees were in languages and literature, so he has an extensive collection of books in French, German, Italian, Turkish, Arabic, Russian, and a smattering of other things. He may not know much about pop culture outside of James Bond, but he's read *Crime and Punishment* several times—in Russian."

As we *flânon* through the museum, a verb I learned from JL, René, fades out of my consciousness and into the woodwork. I wonder if I stayed here for a few months if I'd feel Parisian. Morning coffee and croissants at my neighborhood café. Shopping at the boulangerie for baguettes and the fromagerie for cheese. Late afternoon wine, sitting outside a bar. The idea of being a lounger, a stroller, in Paris, is oddly appealing.

Cress must have a similar thought. "When I was younger," she says, "I read several books of Janet Flanner's *Letters from Paris* that had been originally published in *The New Yorker*. I thought being that kind of writer, an eyewitness to both history and everyday life, was the best career you could have."

"I think I'd rather just have the experiences and not have to publish them," I reply.

"And I'd rather not stand up in a courtroom grilling

people and trying to make the opposition into the personification of evil."

After we cover the history of Paris and the artifacts from various archaeological digs, we gawk at the campaign kit belonging to Napoleon I, mementos of the French royal family and the revolutionaries, Emile Zola's watch, and the bedroom and personal effects of Marcel Proust. I imagine him dipping a madeleine into his tea, setting off the memories of the past that became his magnum opus.

Cress, examining the recreation of his room, says, "I remember reading *Waiting for Gertrude* by Bill Richardson. It takes place at Père Lachaise cemetery. All the characters are cats."

Cress and her cats...

"Anyway, the souls of famous 'residents' of the cemetery are reborn into the cats and Marcel Proust has a leading role as the postmaster."

"Who's Gertrude? And why are they waiting? Is she Godot and never comes?"

"She's Gertrude Stein and the main character, Alice B. Toklas, is waiting for her."

"Why? Where is she?"

"She's going to be reborn as a kitten."

"How could I not have guessed that?" But that leads me to wonder if we have time to visit Père Lachaise. JL told me his mother's favorite singer, Edith Piaf, is buried there. I could take a picture for her. One step toward smoothing the way.

Cress looks at her watch. "Let's go to Mariage Frères for some tea."

"I thought you wanted coffee."

"That was before. Now I want tea. Mariage Frères is one of my favorite stops in Paris. The salon du thé has wonderful treats and there is a tea museum upstairs." She raises her voice so our lurker, who is studying prints of the siege of Paris in 1870, can hear her. "Onward to Mariage Frères. It's just a short walk from here."

We pick up our pace as we move back toward the courtyard and exit the building. Out of the corner of my eye, I see René following at a distance.

I'm not a huge fan of tea, but the shop is entrancing. Mariage Frères is a tea lovers' delight. Seductive scents waft through the shop space—black, oolong, green, and white leaves with their own herby, medicinal scents. Spices, flowers like lavender and bergamot, and dried fruits perfume the air. Scents of orange peel and candied ginger echo Cress' ginger-orange cologne.

We spend time in the shop, inhaling the aromas of some of the over six hundred teas in their signature black canisters. Every time someone asks for a blend, the employees scoop it into old-fashioned scales. We watch as the teas, marbled with dried fruit, spices, and herbs entice the eye, as the mixture spills out into the pan until the level reaches the correct weight.

René stays downstairs when we go up to the museum. Cress oohs and aahs over all the tea-making accoutrements, but I just want to stuff my face with pastry in the tea salon. With a little effort, I coax her down for some sustenance. The shop has dark wooden counters, long tables displaying products like jam, cookies, and special tin collections, as well as shelving that houses each tea canister in its own cubby.

Cress points out the different Marco Polo teas to me when she suddenly spins around. I see René moving toward us as a shortish guy with ink on his wrists, takes his hand off Cress' shoulder. He's dressed in jeans, an untucked

Oxford shirt with a frayed collar, and a worn cardigan that strains against overdeveloped biceps and quads. Deep grooves around his mouth and a gray cast to his skin give him the air of a man who has spent too much time indoors. Silver threads through his thick black hair. He's got a day or two worth of scruff.

"Yavuz," Cress exclaims. "I forgot you were coming to Paris."

"I thought I'd already be back in London, but Emre wants Tanik and me to stay for another week. Even though his studies keep him occupied, he's homesick." His English is excellent, but he has a strong accent I can't identify.

René bristles with suspicion. Cress gives him a bright smile. "René St-Pierre, this is Yavuz Arslan, a friend of Max and JL. We spent some time with him in London."

René nods but doesn't stick out his hand. "Heureux de faire votre connaissance."

"Ravi de te rencontrer également," Yavuz responds.

"We're going to have a girls' tea, Yavuz, but perhaps you'd join us tomorrow for the awards dinner at the Victor Hugo House. It begins at 7:00 p.m. If you come to our hotel, Le Pavillon de la Reine, we can have a drink at the bar and walk over together."

"Delighted. I will see you at six thirty."

"Dress is formal. I hope that's not a problem."

"No, of course not. Thank you so much for including me." He smiles. "Güle güle. Bonne journée. À bientôt." We watch as he walks out of the shop, his slightly rolling gait hinting at some old injury to his left leg.

"What was that first part?" I ask.

"He said goodbye in Turkish before he switched to French." René stands stolidly, arms crossed, projecting an air of disapproval.

"Turkish. Is he connected with Nasim Faez?"

Cress pulls a face. "Tangentially. Zehra, his sister, was in one of the Jeeps blown up in the terrorist attack in Istanbul that Faez engineered in 2003. She was Max's girlfriend."

"Max had a girlfriend? Complicated."

"Yeah, well..."

We watch him turn left off the Rue Bourg-Tibourg, "I can't imagine he has a tux."

"Rentals, Micki. Rentals."

Through an archway, we enter a room with mustard-colored walls, formal tables covered with potted palms, an atrium-style window, starched white tablecloths, and rattan chairs that recall the French colonial past.

Cress studies the menu. "Is it too early to have the Afternoon Tea with First Flush Darjeeling?"

"Pas de problème, Madame."

I ask for the same.

"How did Max meet this guy?"

"Max got to know Yavuz when he was working in Turkey in 2003." She presses her lips together. Guess there's more to the story she's not telling me, but I decide not to pursue it. I only know a little about Max's time in Istanbul, but I know some difficulties they had in their relationship were because he was so secretive about that part of his life.

"I'm surprised you invited him to dinner."

She shrugs. "We have an extra seat. Allan is probably going to be behind the scenes, and I hate to think of the opportunity going to waste. I don't like Yavuz much, but he and Max do have a connection."

Once our selections have arrived, she changes the topic, going immediately on the attack.

"Why didn't you show JL the texts when we got in? You had an hour before we met in the lobby"

I cross my arms over my chest. "We had sex instead."

She flushes to the roots of her hair. "TMI, Micki."

"Besides, if Sam's holed up somewhere in Chicago, it's not an immediate threat."

She continues to glare. I shift uncomfortably. "Look, I'll tell him when we're back at the hotel. I'm not planning to keep them secret. We had better things to do. I'll bet you and Max did too."

Her flush receding, Cress laughs. "We did. But we also didn't have any big secrets that needed to be divulged. We're past all that."

"Really?"

Cress scrunches her face. "I hope so. Max still has this idea he needs to protect me by keeping me in the dark. Anyway, no secrets at the present time. At least that I know of."

I snigger as she picks up a miniature eclair and pops it into her mouth. "Too bad they don't have bigger ones."

Like a cat toying with a mouse, she swallows the tiny treat. "When are you going to show him the texts?"

I shove a pastry in my mouth, then sip the tea, so I don't have to answer. The rest of the time, we gush over the sandwiches and the rest of the pastries, as well as the quality of the tea. She's finally gotten the message I don't know exactly when I will talk to JL about Sam's latest transgressions.

Before we leave, Cress buys two Marco Polo tea blends and some Thé de Noël. We walk out, collecting our shadow along the way as we cross the bridge to finish off at Sainte-Chapelle on the Île de la Cité, an island in the middle of the

Seine. René glances in windows as we walk to watch in case Yavuz follows us.

The Gothic chapel, with its trove of stained-glass, sky-blue ceiling adorned with gold stars, and a huge collection of relics might be the most beautiful church interior I've ever seen. No one else is around. Such luxury.

We don't know where to look first and spend more than an hour in the small space, soaking in the glories that surround us. Heavy footsteps come up the stone steps. René. He suggests we visit the conciergerie, where Marie-Antoinette was a prisoner, then have ice cream from Berthillon on the adjacent Île St. Louis.

Cress rubs her stomach. "I'm pretty full, but I do love the glaces from Berthillon. Maybe I'll work up an appetite touring the mementoes of the Revolution." She takes my arm, and we walk to the nearby Conciergerie. The first room is the guard room, a big space, filled with arches and columns, that is used for exhibitions. It's empty after a big modern art show that closed in January. We check out the artifacts in the museum of the Revolution, which seem to hold more fascination for René than for either of us.

"Madame Taylor, you are a writer of history, non?"

"Historical fiction, yes."

"Have you told the story of Marie Antoinette?"

"No, I have written enough about queens for a while, and somehow she has never interested me, cake notwithstanding."

"Dommage. Her story is so poignant, even if you are a revolutionary rather than a monarchist." He presses a hand to his chest near his heart.

Cress shrugs. "Perhaps in the future something will suggest a story about her court. But I doubt she would be the main character. Perhaps a young revolutionary in love with an aristocrat's daughter."

On that note, we troop over to the long line of eager customers waiting to order cups or cones of ice cream. Cress insists on treating us and a certain amount of palaver ensues while she places the order in halting French. Once she hands us our choices, we eat them quickly before they melt, as we meander back to the hotel with no Yavuz in sight.

TWELVE

Paris is a city where even the most outrageous story... is greeted with a verbal shrug: 'Mais c'est normal!—Edmund White

Micki

Is JL BACK? I wonder as I push the old-fashioned key into the lock. My heart hiccups when I see him lounging on the chaise, legs hanging over the end, feet flat on the floor.

"Micki? C'est toi?"

I throw my bag onto a small table just as he jumps up, grabs me around the waist, and swings me in a vast arc until we collapse onto the floor, heads spinning, laughing like loons.

When we finally come down from the heights, he says, "I've been dying to do that for ages."

"Glad you had the chance before you expired, Beau."

He looks intently at my mouth. "You had ice cream, I see."

"How do you know?"

With his thumb, he wipes the corner of my mouth. "Physical evidence." He licks his thumb. "Cassis. Excellent." Then he presses his lips to mine, gently pushing his tongue forward to coax them apart. "You taste like cassis, too. Perfect."

We embrace for a long moment, then I pull away. "You taste like cappuccino."

"Bien sûr. I had several during the tediousness of meeting with Allan and the Inspector."

"That bad?"

He shrugs. "It was important, but Allan is un criss de cave."

I cross my eyes.

"A jerk," he says. "Let's forget about Allan. I'm much more interested in you, ma chouette." He holds me at arm's length, the deep gaze mesmerizing me like an invitation into a magical forest glade.

"I thought you needed to be back for a meeting over an hour ago."

"Canceled."

Face crinkled in thought, he finally asks the million-dollar question. "Dangerous situation at the office?"

"No idea. Just a text from Rebecca. We'll meet tomorrow. She said not to worry."

"But you will." He takes my hand and tries to move me toward the bed.

I plant my feet firmly. "We met a friend of yours."

"A friend? In Paris?" He looks surprised.

"A friend of Max's anyway. A Turkish guy, Yavuz Arslan. He was at Mariage Frères."

He lets go of me and collapses into an armchair. "We knew he and his brother Tanik were coming to Paris. Their youngest brother is here studying. Still, I'm surprised you ran into him. Especially at a fancy tea shop."

"Don't Turks drink tea?"

"According to Max, they drink tea all the time. In glasses, using samovars, like the Russians. But a place like that isn't his style."

"Maybe he wanted a gift for a lady friend?"

Now he paces, and I wonder if there's something shady about Yavuz.

"Do you not trust him?"

JL's face scrunches. Then he rubs a fingertip over his lips. "He shows up at unexpected times. But then I can be a suspicious bastard. Goes with the job, I'm afraid."

With a gulp, I decide not to tell him about the dinner invitation but resolve to tell him about Sam's texts. "JL." I stop because I'm not sure what to say.

"Hmmm?" He grabs me and leans in for another taste, but I put my hand up to his mouth. He moves back in surprise. "Wha-at? Is something wrong? Don't give Yavuz another thought."

I walk over to my purse, pull out my phone, and open the text messages. Then I hand it to him and flop into a chair, my eyes squeezed shut.

The sound of him huffing with outrage as he reads what Sam sent me makes my chest tighten.

"Tabarnak. What the—" I look over. He's holding the case so tightly I wonder if he'll crush it. Which text is he reading?

"How does he know you're in Paris?"

"No idea. Maybe he overheard something."

"Where would he overhear something?"

"I don't know." Exasperated, my voice rises. "Asked around my office? Hacked my email? Bugged my phone?" My pissed-off level rises rapidly at his attitude.

He throws the device onto a soft chair. "No escape. Ever," he says slowly, enunciating every syllable. "I think he means if he can't have you, he'll kill you."

I double over, gasping, as if I had taken a blow to the solar plexus. "Are you serious?" I still think of Sam as the clowning guy I met all those years ago. Never really serious, even about his art. Certainly not a secret killer.

"Didn't he just set fire to your parents' house? This escalation is, is..."

"Concerning?"

"More than that." His laugh is short and unhumorous. "These are anonymous. Are you sure they're from Sam?"

I roll my eyes. Who else would send me texts like these? "I can't imagine them coming from someone else."

"Isn't he blocked? Tell me you at least did that."

"New number," I say tiredly. "I blocked the last one, and the one before that, and the one before that. It's a game he plays."

"Why haven't you changed your number?" He sounds censorious.

Bristling, I snap, "No fucking time."

"Crisse de câlice de tabarnak d'esti de sacrament de trou vierge," he mutters under his breath. "You need to make the time. Can't you just call?"

"No, I have to go to a store and have them do it. They need to swap the card."

"Did you block him again?"

I take back my phone and copy the texts, putting the document into my notes. Then I block him, deleting everything.

"Now I have." I slip the phone back into my bag. "As soon as I'm home, I'll go in for a new number." After I deal with whatever the fallout is at work.

Bossy boots has another idea. "Cancel your service. We can provide a burner phone for a while. As long as you keep to just a couple of contacts, he can't find you."

"No way. I have to be reachable by my office."

He rubs the back of his neck. "Tabarnak. Can't you keep in contact by email?"

"No. We have these video calls every day—well, except today. Would the burner number work with my computer? Would I be able to give them that number?"

"No, the whole point is to limit access. I'll talk to Max about options."

"Stop treating me like I'm some irresponsible teenage girl. You're not my dad and you can't tell me what to do."

"I am your protector, so I definitely can tell you what to do if it will keep you safe."

"Maybe I need to have my own room for the rest of the trip."

Now he looks like a sad raccoon. Dark circles stand out under his eyes. "Look, I'm under a lot of pressure right now, and all I want to do is wrap you in cotton wool and hide you away from the world."

My blood turns to fire and my lungs can't get enough air.

He takes my hand and starts thumbing circles around the back. "Please try to be patient with me. I don't believe Sam is here, but all these texts are a way of tracking you. I am trying to give you the access you need without endangering you at the same time."

Nodding, I settle back. "I'm sure my office won't give out the number." I try to sound more confident than I feel.

"Maybe, maybe not. After all, he could have called impersonating a potential client and someone may have told him you are in France."

"What do I do? I'll continue to have meetings. And send reports."

A ding interrupts us. JL checks his messages. "The local office is bringing over a computer. You can log onto your meetings with it. It's set up with VPN that will hide the IP address."

"What a relief. And you'll stop lecturing me?"

"I'll try. Worrying about you is taking years off my life."

He continues with more warmth. "I'll be with you until we leave Paris. I'm concerned about you going back to Chicago alone. Cress and Max are going to Venice. Come with me to Vancouver."

My heart stops for a second. Since I can continue working remotely, maybe I should take more time and not go back right away. I push aside the temptation. Then I think of Hayden and his underhanded tricks. Being in the office might ease that pressure.

JL points to the device sitting loosely in my hand. "Turn off your phone. No calls, no texts."

I want to remonstrate, but he silences me with a look that's a mixture of hurt I won't go with him and irritation he has to explain. "We need to make things as difficult for him as possible and keep you safe." Then he takes the phone, puts it in his pocket, and checks his watch. "Calisse, we're late."

"For what?"

"To meet Max and Cress for a drink."

"I need to change and freshen my makeup," I protest.

He gives me a long, assessing look. "No time. Besides, you are perfect." He steps close, pulls his fingers through my hair and gives me the sort of kiss that leaves my lips tingling and swollen. Greedy for more. If it wasn't a mess before, my face is now. After an appreciative look at his handiwork, he grabs my hand and drags me out of the room.

AFTER AN AMAZING PRIX fixe tasting menu at Verjus on the Rue Richelieu, Cress and Max go back to the hotel. We have all the wines with the nine-dish offering, and even though I never finished any of the selections, I drank enough that trying to work will be pointless. JL and I decide to stay on at the wine bar in the cellar and try several interesting wines by the glass.

Long wooden tables line the walls. Facing each other, we are so close I can feel JL's breath caressing my cheek.

"Before I left Chicago, there was a report of terrorist bombings in London. What happened?"

JL winces. "There were four different incidents around the city. A few injuries, and two deaths. One was at Lambeth Palace, but the Archbishop of Canterbury was fortunately not in residence and the damage was minimal."

My hand slides over his and I hook our pinky fingers together. "I hope you were far away from all of them."

"Practically down the street from the one in Clerkenwell." JL clenches his hands and I can see a muscle twitch in his cheek.

"But no one was hurt?"

"Only a couple of cars, and one was a Smart Car, so no loss there. But the bomb was just outside Max's house. We were at a restaurant, all of us, even the Grant children. And Allan had somehow invited himself along. Yavuz was there for dinner but had left to meet his brother at the train, King's Cross, I think." He squeezes his eyes shut briefly, then focuses an intense gaze at me.

"We were just eating dessert when there was a loud explosion. Allan got some intel almost immediately and advised we stay put for the time being. Hours and an ocean of coffee and tea later, we sloshed out to see the damage because the bombed street is where Max and Ian have a house. An immense crater made the street impassable. Difficult for the fire service. And of course, a cold rain started up. We were like icicles by the time we found somewhere warm and dry."

Pressing my nose into his chest, I have no words.

JL gulps down the rest of his glass of Sauternes and motions the server over. "Un autre, Monsieur?" the man asks.

They start a conversation about what else to taste and decide on an organic red from around Toulouse. I savor the last sweet drops from my glass while we watch the balloon glasses fill. JL sips the new offering and nods. "Très bien." I wait for him to continue.

"We left for Scotland the next morning. Allan had already arranged for the front of the house to be boarded until they can hire a contractor. After a few days, Ian went back to London to take care of everything. They were planning to sell the house since Max and Cress want something of their own. Not sure about Ian's plan. He's hardly in London and could share with his sister, Margaret."

A quartet of preppy-looking Americans, reminding me of Hayden, has been perched next to us on the backless stools flanking the narrow wooden counters that run along the rough-hewn stone cellar walls. This is not a Parisian hangout. Like us, everyone here is a tourist.

Now one of the twentysomething men leans over. "Did you say you were involved in that terrorist attack in London?"

JL's eyebrows go up as he crosses his arms. "I was in the vicinity, eating dinner. Why?"

"Just wondered what it was like, being near an explosion like that."

"Think of an earthquake—shaking, loud noise, things falling on you. The feeling the land under your feet might crack apart at any moment." He turns his back. The guy taps him on the shoulder, seemingly avid for more detail. JL glares.

Hands raised, palms out, the guy says, "Sorry, sorry," and goes back to his conversation with friends.

As a diversion, I gush over Cress' ring. "I saw the engagement ring Max gave her. Gorgeous. So Scotland was a relief."

"Some of it." The flatness in JL's delivery tells me there is more bad news to come but his next comment has me smiling. "Max taught Cress a bit of driving, so that was good. Although, where that man gets his patience, I'll never know."

"Cress drove?" My voice squeals with excitement.

JL's smile is tentative. "Automatic transmission would have been easier, but all of their vehicles are standard. Took her half a day, I think, to be able to shift."

"She can practice on my Karmann Ghia."

"You have a car?"

"Yes. I have nothing against driving."

"How do you have a Karmann Ghia? The company stopped making them decades ago."

"It's vintage. Dad and Mom got it for me when I graduated from law school."

"After the disaster when we had a track race for Max's birthday surprise, don't be too sure you'll ever see Cress behind the wheel."

"Oh no. Did they crash?"

"Not the way you might think. Cress was sitting in the grandstand with Max's parents, one of his sisters, and his sister-in-law when it happened."

Chills alternate with hot flashes as I try to imagine what the incident was. "Go on," I say, my voice tremolo.

"We were driving vintage Minis, like in that film, *The Italian Job*. Allan Mason rode shotgun with Max but the rest of us were solo. I don't remember which lap it was, maybe the third, when shots rang out and bullets hit Max's tire. The blowout caused Ian to crash into him, and Max's car flipped. The gas tank exploded, and Max and Allan barely got out."

Hopeful this was just an accident, I say, "Scottish Highlands, careless hunters, I guess."

"No, Max was targeted. The police identified where the two snipers were waiting. They left the rifles, but the guns weren't registered and there were no fingerprints. The assailants, who may have been staying at the hotel that has the track, vanished. A very sad end to our visit."

I can feel moisture trickling off the end of my nose and I taste salt on my lips. The linen napkin blots up everything, including some drops of blood from where I bit my lip. With a gulp, I say, "Makes my problems seem trivial."

With a frown and a gentle touch, JL holds a fingertip to my bottom lip until the bleeding stops. "Not trivial," he says. "Not trivial at all."

CHAPTER
THIRTEEN

Terrorism is the tactic of demanding the impossible, and demanding it at gunpoint.—Christopher Hitchens

JL

THE AWARDS DINNER at the Victor Hugo House is impressive, even though the other people at our table aren't. A pompous writer spends her time getting in digs at Cress about her book.

"Of course, you are the rare American who can actually write a decent sentence." She smirks. Cress makes no response.

Her husband drinks steadily and ignores her, while her son indulges in bad behavior. My maman would have smacked my bottom and taken me home. At the least, she should remind him of how to act in public.

Bored by the formality, I gaze around the space. The

house on the Place des Vosges was rented by Hugo in the 1830s and 40s. We are in the Chinese Lounge, which, along with the Red Lounge, makes up the space for the sit-down dinner for the eighty attendees. Hugo covered walls of the Red Lounge with red damask and portraits in the heavily carved gold frames common for the period. He originally designed the furniture in the Chinese Room for his house during his exile in Guernsey. Later it was moved to the Paris along with Chinese panels designed by Hugo.

Sounds of boots on the tiled floor of the entryway heralds the eruption of chaos, at odds with the genteel nature of the event, and makes the gunfire even more shocking. Several terrorists come into the room, brandishing automatic weapons and shooting over the crowd. The host of the event screams at the attackers in a language neither French nor English, who fire a hail of bullets into him.

Faez's vendetta convinces me Max is the target. He's looking for Cress but she's invisible as I concentrate on getting Micki under the table.

"She's probably already down there." I grunt and give Micki a final push before pulling the tablecloth down to cover her.

We need to find a path so they can crawl to safety. With Micki down on the floor, I turn my attention back to one of the tallest men in the room. Max has paid no attention to my comment on Cress' whereabouts and stands like a telephone pole, eyes darting, head on a swivel, daring them to shoot. He pushes back when I try to wrestle him to the floor. Cress and Micki are not there. When I try to swallow, my throat aches from the constant shouting.

I stand behind Max and shove him to the floor. "Move. We need to reach the corridor."

After some resistance, belly to the floor, he slithers from under one table to another, avoiding legs and feet. I follow, trying not to imagine the worst.

By the time we crawl out, Micki is in the corridor with Allan Mason and Inspector Poulliot, and they lead us out to the street. Cress has disappeared, along with Yavuz. Max, looking like Mel Gibson in *Braveheart*, keeps shouting, "Where the bloody hell is Cress? Where is she?"

Police swarm everywhere, trying to keep the crowds of onlookers at a distance. An American voice yells, "What's going on? What happened?"

Another, more feminine one, pipes up querulously, "We're already late for our dinner reservation."

"Merde," Poulliot swears under his breath. He motions over a uniformed officer. "Maurice. Quel bordel."

"Oui, inspecteur. Que devrions nous faire?"

Poulliot flaps his hands in the crowd's direction. "Try to move them on. Show them the best way to leave the Place. If they have a reservation at a restaurant in the arcade, explain they're closed, and to move along. Escort hotel guests so they can reach their rooms. But don't form a phalanx. This is a not a mob." As Maurice walks over to a knot of cops standing nearby, I hear Poulliot mumble, "At least not yet."

Allan has a restraining arm on Max's shoulder. "Keep it together, man," he grunts. "Poulliot is trying to see if any of his men know where they are. No point shouting."

Max gives him a pained look and snaps his mouth shut.

"We are locating them now," Poulliot says, phone pressed to his ear. "Où sont eux? Goussainville? Putain! Oui, c'est bien. Nous allons vite."

I'm still not clear on what happened while Max, Allan, and Poulliot take off to chase Yavuz and Cress. Did Yavuz kidnap her, or did he go to protect her against someone else? Are they both victims? Human shields or bargaining chips?

Micki

When the terrorists enter the dining room, JL immediately pushes me under the table, the long white covering hiding me from sight. Cress doesn't join me in the barely adequate hiding place. I panic and back out to see what's happening. The sight makes my stomach heave, and I squeeze my eyes shut as the tears trickle out.

"Micki, drop and try to crawl to the side door. Stay as low as you can."

Max stands stock-still, his eyes roving the room. "Where's Cress?" I scream. There's so much noise, it's the only way to be heard.

"Isn't she under there with you?" JL sounds surprised. Max grimaces and keeps looking.

"No." The two-letter word comes out as a long wail.

"Calisse. She must have gotten out already, but Max doesn't know where she is either." The desperate expression on Max's blanched face chills me.

Tears keep falling and my breath comes in shuddering gulps.

"Go, Micki. I'll be right behind you."

They say recovering old skills is as easy as falling off a bike. My infant crawling skills seem adequate and, with some shredding of my pantyhose and scraping of my knees, I wriggle out the side doorway and onto the cold tiles of the corridor. Allan Mason and Inspector Poulliot are there and pull me to my feet.

"Are you all right?" Allan's voice is chilly and he seems too distracted to care about my answer.

"Fine," I tell him through chattering teeth.

I look around the doorframe for Max and JL, but I only see other people screaming, trying to run out of the room. Gunshots sound. The French police pound in. They yell at the diners to get down, then I hear shots—four of them.

Max and JL appear, crawling toward us. Poulliot looks into the room, then turns with satisfaction.

"Our marksmen are parfait. All four terrorists are dead."

Then he pulls Max and Allan aside. They confer for a minute and run out toward the Place. I look at JL.

"They're going after Yavuz and Cress."

"Were they both taken? Or was Yavuz part of the plot?"

JL shrugs. "I'm wondering the same, but I have no idea. We need to go back to the hotel and wait for the dénouement."

The trudge down the short distance is like plodding through mud. My feet, in the fancy red high heels Cress gave me last fall, drag and wobble, but JL keeps a tight hold on my arm. Grateful for the support, I lean in. The scent of birch, cardamom, vanilla, and oud from Tom Ford's London calms the goosebumps that erupted all over. In the courtyard of Le Pavillon de la Reine, I collapse onto a chair, unable to take another step. I picture Cress tied to a chair, a gunman standing over her. My head drops to the wrought iron café table and I sob.

JL

As we move toward the hotel, Micki says she thinks Yavuz had a gun, but in all the confusion she isn't sure. My arm grasping her bicep, we slog down the arcaded walk past a line of police officers, our feet as heavy as our hearts. At the hotel, we sit in the courtyard and wait and wait and wait, wondering who is alive and who is not.

Micki has kicked off her shoes and alternates rocking and pacing, tears pouring down her cheeks. I want to hold her. Still her incessant movement. Assure her everything will be fine. But of course, I have no way of knowing if that's true or just a forlorn hope.

I sit in a moderately comfortable chair, the sensation of pins and needles attacking my arms, my legs, and the back of my neck. I try shaking them away, to no avail. Max hasn't called. I wonder where they are and if they'll be in time.

When Poulliot was talking earlier, all I heard when they ran off was Goussainville, which I assume is a place. I google it, and blink at the photo on the web. About thirteen miles from the capital and spitting distance from Charles De Gaulle, the old city is a ghost town with a modern village next to it.

I look over to where Micki is pacing again. "Come here, ma chouette. I'm looking at where Poulliot thinks they were taken."

She moves like a sleepwalker, glancing at my screen. Seeing the abandoned site, she draws in a breath and snaps into the present. "I'm sure Yavuz is behind this," Micki snarls, eyes still wet but burning like brands.

"Why do you think so? Because you thought you saw a gun?"

"Yavuz is out for Yavuz. If he's not involved, I'm sure he would have left Max to take care of Cress."

A reasonable assumption. "Maybe he wants something from Max and is using her as bait."

Eyes spangled from the courtyard lights, Micki's face is thoughtful. "What if he's working with Nasim Faez?"

My face muscles tighten. "That would be a twist." She might be on to something. All these fortuitous meetings. Perhaps not so coincidental after all. Max said there had been a traitor in their group in 2003. Yavuz? No, they killed his sister. He constantly shows how important his family is to him, so he wouldn't have wanted that.

Looking at the ruined grand maison, little more than a façade, next to a creepy overgrown graveyard. Behind is a church that at least looks intact. What happened to this place? I've seen a lot of scenarios, both in the army and since, but this is one of the most unsettling in my memory. I put down my phone and hug Micki, love and comfort enveloping me as I try not to reflect on possible endings.

As we try to blot out what we imagine happening in this macabre setting, I read her the story about the plane that crashed in the village during the Paris Air Show in 1973. The crash killed all eight on board. This catastrophe and construction of Charles de Gaulle Airport, with the noisy flight path over the village, ensured almost all the remaining inhabitants moved away. The authorities left the houses to rot, even though the airport had signed a contract agreeing to maintain one hundred of them.

"Do you want to see more photos of the village?"

Her face screws up. "I don't know. Maybe... Yes. Let's pull off the bandages and see what's there."

"Or what's not." I pull her into my lap to look at a website filled with pictures of the abandoned old village. Occasionally, a photo is so moving she runs a finger down the screen. Oddly enough, the modern city that has grown up around it has train service for the popular tourist attraction, for the ghouls who want to gawk at the site of a tragedy.

I check the time every few minutes on my phone. When it rings, the sudden sound of "Maxwell's Silver Hammer" makes my stomach jump into my throat. "Max, is that you?"

"We're on our way back. Hold tight."

"Are Cress and Yavuz with you?"

He's terse, but I hear an underlying hint of satisfaction. "Cress, yes. Yavuz is dead."

Urgently, I ask, "Faez?"

"Dead too. It's a long story. Talk when we're there." He cuts the call.

I caress Micki's tear-stained face, pull her close, kiss the tears away, and whisper, "They're on the way back. Everything is all right." We hold each other until footsteps sound on the flagstones. Then Micki pulls away. Unconcerned about the ruined makeup, she rubs at her face, wipes her fingers on her elegant silk cocktail dress, and tries to put on a cheerful expression.

Standing, I move toward the quartet that has just come through the archway. Micki pushes past me, seizing Cress for a long, tight hug.

"Oh my God, Cress. When you disappeared, I..." She can't finish the sentence. Instead, she takes a lingering inventory of her friend. Voice clouded with suppressed emotion, she gives an assessment. "I see you broke a nail. And your clothes, well you won't be wearing that dress again. Too bad because it was perfect for you."

Cress grimaces and wraps her arms around herself.

"Cold?" Max asks, peeling off his jacket.

She shakes her head. "I just need to go in. Change."

"Right. Thanks again, Poulliot. See you tomorrow."

"Wait—" Allan has his hand up.

"Come to our room," Micki says. "We can confab there."

"Anything else can hold until morning. Cress needs sleep." Max slips his jacket over Cress' shoulders and walks her toward the doorway, but she turns back.

"No, Max." Cress' voice is firm. "We'll go to Micki and JL's room and talk about everything. Is an hour from now okay?"

"Of course." Allan can be conciliatory now that he's getting what he wants.

None of us can take our eyes off them, Cress leaning heavily against Max, until they disappear into the depths of the lobby.

"Blast him. I want a statement now."

Poulliot lifts one shoulder nonchalantly. "We can wait. Only cleanup to do. I will return in the morning. You may tell me everything then."

"Fine." Allan turns on one heel and stumps away into the building. Poulliot lights a cigarette, gives a little wave. "Á bientôt."

"Á demain," I say and lead Micki back to the wicker couch.

Trying not to show the pain and urgency I feel, I pick up her hands and start kissing the knuckles. Then I gaze into eyes still shimmering with the remnants of tears. "Ma chouette, come with me to Vancouver."

"No, I—"

One of my hands cups her head, the other covers her mouth until I lean forward and stop the words with a kiss.

"Please come with me. Just text your office and tell them something has come up. They'll see the story of the attack on the news."

"I need to be there." Her wail is muffled by my chest as I hold her close.

"What's the worst that could happen?"

Face pale and drawn, she looks like that would be the end of the world.

"Isn't your managing partner making it easy for you to stay?"

"Yeah, if I'm there, it will be more difficult for him. Being there is half the battle."

"And what if it makes no difference? Maybe this is the path you need to follow." My insistence makes her stiffen in my arms.

"Who are you to tell me what I should do with my life?" She gets up and starts to back away, face blazing.

My hands spread in apology. "Someone who cares about you. I'm not making the choice for you, just pointing out you aren't happy where you are and maybe considering alternatives isn't such a bad idea."

Her phone buzzes. Fumbling it out of her bag, her eyes widen as she looks at the text. "It's from Rebecca."

"Who's that ?"

With a catch in her voice, she says, "My, my mentor."

She reads the message a second time, just as another comes in. A determined look replaces the disbelief, and she types on the screen. An extensive set of back-and-forth texts follows. When she finishes, she drops the phone in her lap, breath whooshing out. Energetically, she jumps out of the chair.

"Let's go to Vancouver." Then we walk back into the hotel to debrief with our friends.

I wonder what made her change her mind?

CHAPTER
FOURTEEN

The beginning is always today.—Mary Wollstonecraft Shelley

Micki

> REBECCA: I know you're planning on coming back, but don't.

> ME: What!!?? Why?

> REBECCA: The partners will be out of the office on a retreat. Hayden is going as "assistant."

> REBECCA: Fred is practically dancing around the hallways. His gloat is epic.

A PHOTO OF FRED, feral smile, arms raised in a victory salute, accompanies the text.

> REBECCA: A really great report on progress might help, eventually.

> ME: I'm thinking about spending a little time in Vancouver?

> REBECCA: Why not? As long as you have a connection, you can be anywhere.

> REBECCA: I'll let you know when everyone is back in the office so you can make a triumphant return with a report ready to go.

Yesterday I was involved in a terrorist attack, stayed up late while the event was dissected, heard another nail being hammered into the promotion coffin, and committed to meeting JL's mother in Canada. Today, my feelings are bittersweet because this is our last day in Paris. I have mixed feelings about this city, and I'm not sure if I need to come back with a clean slate or never return.

Tomorrow we start a new chapter in Vancouver. I don't know what JL has told his mother about me, and I'm afraid to ask. My brave facade has cracked and I'm not sure I can fix it. Life is a Tilt-A-Whirl, and I don't know which end is up.

At the briefing last night, Max explained the supposed threat from Nasim Faez was fabricated by Yavuz, who wanted revenge for the death of his sister, Zehra, Max's lover in Istanbul. He blamed Max for her death and plotted his revenge for ten years before being able to carry it out.

Hooking into an already planned attack at the Victor Hugo House was fortuitous, but I'm sure he would have found another way if that circumstance hadn't dropped into his lap. He and his brothers all died in the showdown in Goussainville. No more threats from that source.

I sleep surprisingly well, maybe because JL has an arm

around me all night. The sunshine encourages me up and into the shower, even though JL is still asleep. At least I think he is until he joins me, washing my hair and scrubbing my back.

We all want a change of scene, so we breakfast at Café Charlot on the Rue de Bretagne. Inside, the dark wood of the furniture contrasts with the white subway tiles on the walls. The weather is mild, and we sit outside under the big red, white, and black umbrellas. Max hovers, frequently looking over the top of *Le Monde* to make sure Cress eats all of her L'omelette de la Maison, stuffed with vegetables and a side of crispy fries. Insists she drinks the freshly squeezed fruit juice. Calls for more coffee when her cup is empty. Reaches to touch her between bites of his eggs Benedict and sips of tea. Too touchy-feely for me, but Cress probably needs the comfort right now.

I check my email and listen to the conversation with half an ear, while JL reads the satirical weekly *Le Canard enchaîné*. I wonder how Mom and Dad are doing in the condo and whether they are looking for a temporary rental house.

Even with the mess at work, Sam's threats are uppermost in my thoughts. I should just tell JL I have to go back to Chicago and sort out my life, but I won't. Whatever job threat Hayden poses, at least he won't murder me. Right?

"Are you enjoying your breakfast, ma chouette?" JL's concerned expression makes me wonder what sort of faces I'm making while munching on pain grille with saumon fumé. He's scoffing down a platter of charcuterie and cheeses. I am on my second grand crème and JL slurps café au lait while he folds up the paper to deal with work emails and one to his mother.

He checks his watch. "We have an appointment with

Inspector Poulliot, then plenty of time to soak in the romance of the city of lights."

"Cress," I call over where my friend moodily pushes food around on her plate. Normally a hearty eater, I can see the shock of last night has killed her appetite. She looks up questioningly.

"Are you going with us to explore Paris after we talk to Inspector Poulliot?"

"We saw Poulliot at the crack of dawn. Now we need to do some quiet things," Max says, "and pack for the trip to Venice. Taking a page from your book, we're spending the day in Montmartre. Tonight, we have a reservation for dinner at Tour d'Argent. Our last memory of Paris needs to be a slap-up meal. I assume you'll join us."

"You're sure?" JL is feeling him out to see if this is a genuine invitation or if they really want a romantic dinner alone.

"Of course. I wouldn't have mentioned it otherwise."

I screw up my face in a wry smile. Paris is gray this morning, heavy clouds promising rain later in the day. "I think we'll walk around the city." JL nods his agreement. "Can we borrow an umbrella from the hotel if rain starts?"

"Probably, although the parapluie vendors will rise like mushrooms. Flimsy, but we're leaving tomorrow, so it doesn't matter if it breaks." JL grins.

We haven't had rain, but I've seen pictures of twisted, bent umbrellas, discarded like broken-winged blackbirds, forlornly ready to trip unwary passersby.

"We're off," Max says, helping Cress out of her chair. He whispers something in her ear and she shakes her head. Arm and arm, they decamp to wave down a taxi.

After our discussion yesterday, JL returned my cell. Now

it rings and I answer reflexively, not paying attention to caller ID. Maybe my parents, checking up on our plans.

Before I say a word, an assumed Southern drawl, sugar sweet but oily, raises hackles. "Slipped past your defenses." A sinister chuckle. "Guess you ain't payin' attention, darlin'. Hearin' yer voice, babe, maybe you can guess what's risin' here." His breathy vocalization swells with lascivious menace.

JL taps my arm and signals I need to put this on speaker.

"Heard there was some brouhaha in Paris, and I was wondering whether you was nearby. Don't want anything to happen while you're away. That would spoil the fun." He chuckles. Despite myself, I can't hang up. "Can you imagine what I'm doing right now?" The accompanying panting and lip-smacking moan brings bile up my throat.

JL's warm hand envelops the back of my neck, breaking the spell. I choke back a gasp and hit end. Hyperventilating, I throw the phone toward JL. Putting a hand up, he catches it easily, keeping his eyes on me.

I expect him to reprimand me for answering, but all he says is, "Salopard."

A giggle grips me as I grope for the glass of water sitting on the table. Why I feel the need to laugh when I'm hurting is a mystery I can't deal with now. The swallow of water extinguishes the sound. If I try to speak, I'm afraid bile will pour out. The phone rings again. "Hello?" JL's greeting sounds distinctly unwelcoming. Then he listens soundlessly, finally saying, "I'll put her on."

"Your dad," he whispers, handing me the phone.

"Micki?" The growl is very familiar.

Confirmation the news hit the U.S. papers. Dad still gets all his news that way. Wonder if it was on the front page of the *Chicago Tribune,* complete with graphic photo, or buried farther back in the international pages?

"Hey, Dad. How are things working out at the condo?"

Text messages are scrolling across the screen. Work colleagues. Guess word of the attack has spread far and wide. I can see the start of a long text from Paul, Cress' and my best friend from school. More stuff whizzes past from volunteer acquaintances and staff at the women's shelter where I do workshops on legal resources. I turn off the screen.

Momentary relief at the short period of wordlessness disappears when Dad roars with all the bellicosity of Patton exhorting his men. "Your mother is going crazy. We're both going nuts."

I gurgle, but no words come out. Closing my eyes, I see the men in fatigues, face masks, automatic weapons. Gag from the memory of the acrid odor as the bullets whiz around. Feel JL push me under the table, the cloth rubbing against my hair, shoulders, back, as I creep away, knees rubbing on the carpet. Remembered screaming blots out Dad's voice. Then I feel JL's thumb rubbing circles against the back of my hand. His voice soothes. "Calme toé, ma chouette. C'est tiguidou." Except for calm and owl, I don't understand the words, but the icicles I thought would pierce my heart melt away.

The world comes back, and I see the café, sunlight pouring in from the Place, dispossessing the earlier clouds. The hiss of the espresso machine as shots are pulled blends with conversations in French, English, and languages I can't identify. From my phone, I hear, "Answer me. What the fuck is going on over there?" He's yelling loud enough for both of us and maybe everyone else in the café to hear him, even though I've turned off the speaker.

My dry, swollen tongue makes pushing words out impossible. Awkwardly, I manage to grasp the glass and water spills into my mouth. I sputter as some goes down the wrong way.

JL gently removes the tumbler from my tenuous grip, pours more, and sets it within easy reach while I wipe away the moisture filming my eyes from the violent cough that follows.

After a few more demanding growls from the other end, I manage to remove the cell from my lap and squeak out, "Uh, well..."

At way too many decibels, the two words I hear are raw with relief, not anger. "You're okay?" A deep, ragged breath follows. "We weren't even sure if you were alive after we read about the attack. Why didn't you call?"

I wrestle my lips apart, but all that comes out is another inane "uh." JL watches me with concern.

My near silence provokes another growling outburst. "That's it?" I can visualize Dad's reddening skin and the throbbing vein in his temple. Maybe he should just scream obscenities and throw stuff. I worry he'll have a stroke one of these days.

"What the hell is going on over there? You were at that museum, weren't you? I'm on my thousandth cup of coffee. Your mother's in a tizzy. She can't even come to the phone. She's borrowed your across-the-hall neighbor's dog and they're running along the lakefront instead."

JL wrenches the phone out of my frozen fingers. "Mr. Press? This is JL Martin. I am with your daughter, and she was not a target. Now she's fine, just overwhelmed. Give her a minute and she might be able to answer."

"Hummphff," comes from the other end of the line.

Pressing the mobile back into my hand, JL gives me a

pat. After another cough, I say, "I'm okay, Dad. JL got me out of the room and the police rounded up the terrorists."

"On the news, the reporter said terrorists kidnapped an American, a woman."

"Not me." Maybe he'll accept that, and I won't have to give him my secondhand account of Cress being dragged out of the dinner by someone we thought was a friend, the car chase, and the rescue in the abandoned village near Paris.

"What happened to her? No updates yet."

I keep the anguish and relief out of my voice, as if this woman is nothing to me. Just dry statements. If Cress' name is released, they'll know along with the rest of the world. I'll face those recriminations later. Right now, my cup more than runneth over.

"She was rescued in a village outside Paris. Police killed the kidnappers."

The sound of a sigh gusts into my ears. "That's good news. We're glad you'll be home tomorrow. The world is a dangerous place, and you'll be safer here."

Sam's text threats belie that sentiment. I don't mention them or the phone call. No point in adding to the angst billowing through the phone in waves.

"What flight will you be on? We can pick you up at the airport."

"Not coming home right away," I mumble.

What sounds like static on the line is Mom panting. She must be back from walking the neighbor's dog. "Speak up, darling. I can't understand what you're saying."

"I'm not coming home right away." My chest contracts and my throat constricts as silence greets my response—and then the volcano erupts.

"What do you mean you aren't coming home tomorrow? Are you in the hospital? Or are the police making you stay as a witness?" Dad's shoutiness makes my ears ring.

Underneath, like a bass line, I hear Mom ask, "Are you staying in Paris?"

"What about work?" Dad asks the $50,000 question.

"Rebecca told me to keep working remotely."

"Was this before or after the 'incident'?"

"Before. All the partners will be at some kind of retreat for a week, so no one will be in the office to impress."

"Wouldn't you be going if you were there?"

"No. It's just the partners." They don't need to know about Hayden's coup, going as the assistant.

I glance at JL. His jaw tightens and there is a noticeable tick in his cheek.

"May as well stay over there then."

"JL's concerned about my safety, so I'm going to Vancouver with him. He has to visit his mom. Then he can come back to Chicago with me."

I put the phone on the table, prop my chin in my hands, and gaze into heavily fringed, bottomless dark brown orbs that twinkle at me as if he's managed to capture the Milky Way in their depths.

A rumble from the phone makes me spring out of my seat like a jack-in-the-box. Dad's impatience is legendary.

"How wonderful. I hear Vancouver is very beautiful. This certainly takes your relationship up a notch, or three." Mom's fizzing like she's Dom Pérignon and someone just popped her cork.

"Alice, calm down. This might not mean anything, Maybe JL really is just concerned about Micki traveling alone." Dad has gotten quiet, like he doesn't want JL to hear his misgivings.

"I didn't think of that, Des." Mom has gone from ebullient to deflated in less than sixty seconds.

"Got to go," I tell them, then switch off the phone, turn to the man offering me support and bury my face in his buttery soft Chicago Fire sweatshirt.

He whispers against my hair, "Tout va bien se passer, ma chouette. Ne pleut pas, ma chère."

I understand about a third of that but get the gist. A deep moan escapes. "Sorry, I should have told you about work."

"I wondered why you changed your mind about Vancouver. Now everything makes sense."

I can't help a cry of anguish. "Yeah, well, what you don't know is Hayden is going to the retreat. Rebecca keeps intimating I need to have a backup plan—ideally a new job to go to when Hayden gets the partnership. Everything is so screwed up."

"This is the darkness before the dawn, as they say. They didn't hurt you last night. I'm sure new opportunities are just around the corner, and I know Maman will embrace you like a daughter." I feel his warmth as his smile burns away the clouds.

CHAPTER
FIFTEEN

First impressions matter. Experts say we size up new people in somewhere between 30 seconds and two minutes.—Elliott Abrams

JL

MICKI SPENDS the flight typing on her computer. She dragged out her computer as soon as we were told we could turn on electronic devices. She swore under her breath when meals were served and scowled as the cabin attendants passed by without picking up her tray.

Some report for work. She snapped when I asked about it. She wasn't kidding when she warned me that work comes first. I'm hoping to change her mind.

Now, laptop stowed, nose pressed to the glass, she looks down on Vancouver Harbour as the plane rushes toward the airport. Her silken blond hair sweeps back and

181

forth across her shoulders. The scene unfolds as we soar over the Canadian landscape, a perfect blend of tall buildings, green space, and water, surrounded by mountains.

I can't keep my hands to myself, running my fingers up and down her back, enjoying the feel of her quivering muscles respond to my touch, wish I could stroke cool, velvet skin.

She never takes her eyes off the view out the window as we begin our descent. I'd forgotten this is her first trip abroad and her second time crossing the Atlantic. She rocks back and forth with excitement. The window seat gives her the perfect ringside view.

In the meantime, I've been questioning my decision to bring her. Two messages from Maman have reminded me of the "surprise." And although I told Micki Maman will love her, that might be wishful thinking on my part. I could have arranged for security back to Chicago. GSU will provide security here too, although not as heavy since I will be part of the team. While I want her to meet Maman, the main reason for my visit is to do something about my hoser uncle, like move the salopard out of Maman's house. Maybe not the best introduction.

We have a sudden drop and her breath catches, she reaches for my hand and squeezes the hell out of it. I wince but don't disengage. Anxiety rolls off her like high surf.

"Do you think something's wrong?" A verbal tremor betrays her fear.

Still letting her try to crush my hand, I slip the fingers of the other under her chin and turn her face toward me. "These dips happen. If something was wrong, either a cabin attendant or the captain would come on and tell us." Then I give her a kiss to concentrate on.

Not so successful because as soon as we separate, she

asks, "What if they don't want us to panic so they're keeping quiet?"

Her flight anxiety is a surprise. She's flown many times in the U.S., so I assumed she was a seasoned pro. I lean forward and touch my lips to her temple. "Believe me, if something was wrong, we would be told how to prepare." In the meantime, the plane is back on an even keel as we smoothly come closer to landing. She looks back through the window.

"What do you think? Is my hometown beautiful?"

"I thought it would look more like Chicago," she mutters, "But it's impressive." Her blue eyes sparkle and it's like drowning in an ocean of stars.

"Very different terrain," I tell her. "Flying over the harbor is not like looking at Lake Michigan. Except, they both have very tall buildings near the water."

"How about the airport? Should I expect an O'Hare-type environment? Or De Gaulle? Every big airport is kind of O'Hare to me—crowded, long distances to reach gates, just all hassle."

"We'll go through passport control, then customs. Not sure how long that will take. I've arranged for a rental car so we will have wheels while visiting Maman.

"More of a driving city, then?"

"Yes. Also, they do random luggage checks here. If they ask to open yours, just go with it. They aren't singling you out for a reason."

"Does your mom live near the water?"

"Not too far. You'll see when we arrive."

∿

Micki

My feet feel as if I've walked The Proclaimers five hundred miles by the time we reach baggage claim at Vancouver International Airport. It's is filled with nervous travelers, watching suitcases roll down the chute and come around on the conveyor belt. Fingers crossed their belongings haven't been lost en route. Everyone ready to pounce when they see their case. Since most of them are black, that can be a challenge.

I can't help looking around, as if Sam will jump out a me like a clown in a fun house. Relieved he didn't show up in Paris, somehow Vancouver seems more reachable.

My ears plugged, I'm dizzy from the flight. Everything looks a little distorted and I hover as close to the chute as I can get, waiting for my beat-up maroon bag to sail out. JL offers to grab it for me, but I shake my head no. Establishing control is my priority. If I let him do everything, I won't be able to take care of myself once we go our separate ways. I try to make myself believe this can last, but my heart has a hard time convincing my brain.

An ache rises at the thought of not being together. The more time I spend with him, the more time I want to spend.

JL's black leather duffel sits between his feet, and I glance over my shoulder to watch him watch me. He bounces on the balls of his feet, ready to rush in if I need him.

When we met last year, I was still with Sam but JL's magnetism was hard to resist. Once things fell apart, I slowly let myself be pulled in. Ever since, we've been circling each other like wary tigers. Now I cling to JL as a safe port in a storm. I'm well and truly ensnared, even though I can't help feeling one day the web that brings us together will unravel and I'll be alone.

My topsy-turvy life is light-years from where I want to be—gainfully employed doing work I love, in a stable relationship, and most of all free of fear.

Now, not-so-fresh off the plane from Paris, I question the decision to meet his mother and deadbeat uncle. Am I fooling myself into thinking this is one of the building blocks of a stable relationship? I can't really believe Louisette Martin will look at me and see a perfect match for her son.

From what he's told me, she's a proud French Canadian and a devout Catholic who longs for grandchildren. Two strikes right off the bat. And although JL would make an amazing dad, not that he's ever said anything, at forty-six, the risk in having children is not one I want to take.

The words, "Hey, dreamer," snatch me out of my reverie. I haven't been watching and my guardian spirit lugged the case off the belt. It's so overweight the wheels can't keep it balanced. I rush over to help as he wrestles the soft case into submission. He keeps a death grip on the handle, shooing me away.

"I've got it." Then he rolls over to where his duffel sits, forlorn, and sets it on top. "First customs, then locate our ride."

My computer bag slung over my shoulder, I rub my stomach and make smacking sounds. "When do we get poutine?" When he laughs, I feel my cheeks heat and know my nose has turned bright red.

"Poutine? Have you ever even had it, ma chouette? Besides the distinctly ersatz variety at Stan's?"

"It's very popular in Chicago."

He leans the bags against his tight abs and scratches his head. "Never even thought about finding real poutine in Chicago. Where do you find it?"

I throw out my arms as if I've just crossed the finish line in the marathon. "The Gage on Michigan Avenue has it for their weekend brunch. And it's delicious." Then I pull his hand off his head and twist my fingers in his. "This is Canada, home of poutine."

He frees himself from my grasp and strokes his chin. "Do you think you're in Quebec?"

My face sags. Is this really just a regional thing? Maybe I should have read up about it, but I didn't know I was going to Vancouver until a couple of days ago, and life has been a little hectic.

He's going on and on while my stomach sinks to the soles of my feet with humiliation. "This is Vancouver," he says. "Don't you want candied salmon sticks, oysters, B.C. rolls, Nanaimo Bars, Japadog?"

I pout. "Are you telling me there's no poutine in Vancouver, Beau?"

Then I notice his face has morphed into an impish grin. "Poutine is French Canadian."

Not willing to give in to feelings of idiocy, I grab the front of his jacket, but the bags are a barrier. I kick them aside, unconcerned when my suitcase clunks to the ground. Then I kick his duffel out of the way and pull him close. My eyes glare like Medusa, my voice hardens, and I declare, "You're French Canadian, and you're from here." I try to rock him back and forth, but he stands his ground like a boulder. "Is there or isn't there poutine in Vancouver?"

With a sigh, he removes my fingers, steps back, and stumbles over the duffel. While he fights to keep his balance, I move forward and poke him in the chest.

JL's almost black eyes darken further. Then, as if by magic, his face lightens, and he rubs his stubbly jaw. "Yes, ma chouette, there is poutine. Anywhere there are French

Canadians, there is poutine. For sure my maman will have that and tourtière for us as a welcome."

～

JL

When we finish with customs, we walk outside. A black SUV waits by the curb, uniformed driver behind the wheel, aviator sunglasses hiding much of his face. Another man leans against the rear bumper. When he sees us approach, he lopes over and grabs the bags.

"Bonjour, JL." His smile is wide as his booms out around the carpark.

"Yannick. Been too long." He gives a side hug, then I feel an arm slip through mine. "Micki, this is Yannick Moreau. He is one of my guys in Vancouver."

Yannick's lips twist into an amused grin. "We grew up together."

I draw her forward. "Yannick, I want you to meet Michelle Press from Chicago."

"Enchanté, Mademoiselle." He holds out a hand and when she reciprocates, gives it a squeeze.

"Not sure what you're doing with this reprobate," he tells her as we settle her into the passenger seat. I climb in beside her.

She levels him with a look. "He's not too bad. I like the accent."

Yannick huffs and ups the accent ante. "If that's the attraction, you can be spoiled for choice here." He pauses. "And I'm much better looking. My nose has only been broken once. JL's nose is just a misshapen blob from the many, many times it has been pummeled."

"So, he's braver than you?" she teases.

"Non, just not as smart. I know how to give blows and avoid receiving them."

"Enough. Don't pay any attention to this blowhard, ma chouette."

"Okay, Beau, whatever you say."

"You call him Beau?" Yannick starts laughing.

By now we've reached the car rental place.

"What type are you getting?" Yannick asks.

"A Porsche. Come in with me so you have all the info. Micki, stay with the driver until we bring the car around, okay?"

She frowns but doesn't come with us.

"Is this serious, chum?" Nosy fuck. I purposely misunderstand.

"Don't think there will be any trouble here, but there's an outside chance the douche will show up."

He's unrelenting, like a cat stalking birds. "Not the surveillance, dumbass. The girl."

I rub my hand against my head. "I think so, but I'm afraid Maman has other ideas."

"Have they met?"

I push open the glass door and walk up to the counter. "Not yet," I tell him.

He makes that clicking sound that shows disapproval. "But she knows your friend is with you." His flat stare dares me.

"She knows, but…"

"But what?"

"She just knows I'm bringing a friend."

"Ah. Well, that confrontation should be interesting. We'll be watching so we can rescue you when your maman beats your ass."

The man behind the counter sniffs. "May I help you gentlemen?" His British accent is so sharp and polished, he can't have been here long enough to have the edges rubbed off.

"JL Martin. I have a car reserved."

He taps at the keyboard, then peers at the screen. "A red Porsche for a week. Will you be driving across the border?"

"No." I hand him my driver's license and U.S. passport.

He looks down, then glances at me in surprise. "American?" While he's making a copy to go with the paperwork, I call out, " Both, actually."

"Will your friend be driving it as well?"

Yannick exhales, and a propulsive blast of air hits the guy in the face. "Non."

The agent steps back, eyes wide, but quickly recovers. "Why are you in Vancouver, Mr. Martin?"

WTF! This is not passport control or customs. Just a bored nosy parker. "Visiting my mother." All true, but his smile tells me he's unconvinced. Well, fuck him.

"I would have thought she'd live in Montreal or somewhere." He smirks, as if he's caught me out in a lie.

"Not all French Canadians live in Quebec," Yannick huffs.

"She lives here," I say. I clench my fists, temper frayed.

Yannick claps me on the shoulder. "Let's just finish up." His eyes are hooded and he purses his lips. Is the warning for me or the asshole behind the desk?

I sign a bunch of papers, insist on two copies, and promise to bring the Porsche back with a full tank. Moving at a fast clip to work out my foul mood, we go out back where lines of sparkly clean cars sit, waiting for travelers to claim them.

The Porsche, parked next to a gleaming gold BMW, looks like a sweet ride and the minute or so as we roll around to the front confirms it. While we transfer the luggage, Micki gets into the front seat. Once we're both belted in, I connect my cell to the car audio system and wave off Yannick. "I better not see you hugging the curb."

"We'll be unobtrusive but close enough to be effective."

"Tell Jean-Claude I need to know where he bought his aviators."

"I'll have him text you." With a screech of tires, they exit the rental place. They'll be in Kitsilano before us.

"Hey, Siri. Call Maman."

"Calling Louisette Martin," Siri answers.

While the phone rings, Micki asks, "Who's Jean-Claude?"

"The driver."

Puzzlement spreads over her face. "Why didn't you just ask him?"

"His role is chauffeur. A customer wouldn't ask that."

"But who would hear once we were driving?"

"Probably no one, but you can never be too careful. And he likes to stay in character."

"He's an actor? TV? Theater?"

"He wishes, although he was an extra on a TV show once. As a getaway driver."

We're still sitting at the curb, laughing, when Maman picks up.

"Où es-tu?" she demands before I can open my mouth.

Hoping to encourage her to do the same, I answer in English. "Just picked up the rental. We'll be there in about an hour, depending on the traffic."

"Qui sont nous?"

Again, I lean into English. "I told you. I'm bringing a

friend." The glance I give to Micki is warm and not so friend-like.

Trying to keep irritation at bay, I snap out the response, "And my friend doesn't speak much French." Don't even bother to tell her about the security detail that will shadow us everywhere, even though there is no sign Sam is in Vancouver.

"Of course. Is your friend staying with us or at a hotel?"

From the coolness in her tone, I'm sure she hopes for the latter. "With us," I tell her, then reach for Micki's hand and give it a reassuring squeeze.

Not missing a beat, Maman trills, "Fine, I'll make up the bed. And I have some surprises for you."

A pang hits where my heart rests. Some surprises? A harem? "The sooner we're underway, the sooner we'll be there." Then I throw a little French her way, "Á bientôt, chère Maman."

"Ciao, ciao."

Micki sighs as I turn the key on the cherry-red Porsche Carrera S. "Too bad you couldn't rent a motorcycle like the one you have in Chicago. Might be fun to go buzzing around in the mountains."

"You like my bike, huh?"

"Oh yeah." Her voice rises with excitement.

"Too bad that's not practical for this trip. No place for the luggage. And it's often rainy."

She twists and looks back. "We're being followed."

I glance at the rearview mirror. "Yannick. I thought they'd gone ahead, but they must have dropped back. I'm not expecting anything, but better safe than sorry."

"Do you have enemies here?"

"Haven't lived here in so long that any enemies would have forgotten me by now. My only concern is you."

Micki scoffs, "Sam would have to sell a boatload of art, a body part, or rob a bank, to buy a ticket."

"Maybe he socked money away while he sponged off you."

She winces but doesn't answer.

Contrite, my automatic response is just as stupid. "C'était stupide de ma part. Je suis vraiment désolé, ma chouette." Her eyes are big question marks. Crisse, I'm as bad as Maman. "Sorry, ma chouette. Just telling you it was a stupid comment, made even more asinine by apologizing in the wrong language."

Moving one hand off the steering wheel, I squeeze her fingers, then put my hand back where it belongs.

"I'll have a burner for you to use until you have a new phone and number. GSU routed the burner number through the company. If Sam somehow connects, they will monitor the call."

A shudder ripples through her. "After that last call, I never want to hear his voice again." The utter disgust tells me everything.

"How explicit was he?" I ask.

"All innuendo. Everything was tone of voice and double entendre. Nothing we could use in court. I didn't think to record it either."

"Too bad. I want to see his ass nailed to the floor of a jail cell, with the toilet just too far away to reach."

"Eww."

We take a slightly out-of-the-way route so I can show her Mitchell Island in the Fraser River, drive past Langara College, and point out the VanDusen Botanical Garden, Queen Elizabeth Park, and Granville Island Public Market before we cut back west to Kitsilano. I'm hoping to take her mind off Sam—and meeting Maman.

The reiterated threat of a surprise makes me want to take an even more meandering detour around the Greater Vancouver area, but even if we waste a few hours, the sword of Damocles still hangs over me. I gun the engine and we race to meet our fate.

CHAPTER

SIXTEEN

To be a queen of a household is a powerful thing—Jill Scott

Micki

A GABLED HOUSE, the siding painted dusky blue with white trim and a welcoming red door, sits a good hundred feet from the street, steps leading to the porch jutting out into a curated flower display of daffodils and tulips. A manicured lawn rolls toward the sidewalk paved with large stone, enhancing the country cottage look. The tops of tall maples and oaks that poke out from behind the steep, pointed roof remind me of home. There's no fence but a vigorous hedge, JL says is forsythia, edges the sides of the property. The right-hand front windows have leaded panes. The smaller upper floor is probably an attic.

"Does your mother garden?"

"No," JL says. "I pay for a guy who does all the yard work. Maman has mild COPD."

"The house is beautiful." I'm reminded of Chicago bungalows. Never realized they might be common elsewhere too.

"It's a Craftsman bungalow. Inspired by architecture from India, they started in California and spread all over the Northwest before moving to your neck of the woods."

I feel bouncy with excitement. This seems like a good omen for the trip. "We should do a tour when we're home. I read somewhere there are still 80,000 of them around. So cool that your mom lives in one."

By the time we are on the sidewalk with our luggage, the front door pops open and a short, slim woman looks out. JL told me she's seventy, but while her skin is somewhat weather-beaten, she looks ten years younger. Over a white T-shirt and denim skirt, she wears a black apron, the bib top proclaiming her Queen of the Kitchen. Her cropped, silvery hair is a mass of tight curls and I wonder if she has it permed. "Déguédine!" she calls out in a raspy, impatient command. I wonder if she smokes.

"Bien sûr, Maman," JL calls to her. He whispers in my ear, "She wants us to hurry up."

I expect to see her beam with welcome, but her lips are pursed as she looks down on me from the small porch. I paste on a smile, push in the handle of my suitcase, and trudge toward the steep, narrow wooden steps. When JL tries to grab the bag from me, we end up in a little tug-of-war, which he wins.

"Why don't you have the ramp out?" he challenges the woman on the porch.

"I'm not a cripple," she snarls.

"I didn't say you were, but the ramp would make

walking easier." Under his breath I hear him grumble, "Replace the steps with a permanent ramp."

When I start forward, I understand his point. The ten steps are narrow and steep, but the railing helps me keep my balance when only half of my foot fits on each step.

At the top, I look into the narrowed eyes of JL's mother before noticing another woman, about our age, hovering. She's taller than Madame Martin and model-thin. Her resemblance to Audrey Tautou is striking. Bobbed brown hair and short, straight bangs flatter a narrow chin and forehead, and high cheekbones. Dressed in skinny distressed ankle jeans, topped by a bright pink cropped sweater that shows a strip of her flat abdomen, her á la mode style enhances the impression she could be making a living on the runway if she was twenty-five years younger.

I flash a questioning look toward JL. He never said anything about siblings. Superficially, she could be his sister, or maybe a cousin. I scoot to the side so he can stand next to me on the porch. He puts down the bags and moves forward to embrace his mother.

"Bonjour, Maman." He kisses her on both cheeks, but she doesn't reciprocate. Instead, she moves back and crosses her arms across her chest.

He sniffs ostentatiously. "Still smoking? I thought you'd agreed to stop after the doctor told you your lung capacity was deteriorating."

One hand creeps down to the pocket of her apron and she fiddles with something inside. But instead of answering, she asks, "Qui est cette femme?" Her voice is rough and accusatory.

My heart sinks briefly, then warms at the big smile that lights up his face as he throws an arm around my shoulders. "C'est ma blonde, Michelle."

"Ta blonde?" she exclaims. "Mais non. Impossible."

Eyes wide, the woman's jaw drops as she takes a step back. Her open mouth displays slightly pointed teeth. Predatory. Is she a vampire? Too much *Buffy* and *Twilight* I guess. Still, I'm relieved there is no sparkling, although she's not out in sunlight either.

Jaw clenched, JL starts. "Ce n'est pas possible."

His mother says, in careful English, "It is possible."

My heart plummets. JL said his mother had a surprise for him. At least she didn't jump out of a cake. Questions dart around my brain like a pinball, but without the lights and bells.

Why did JL call me his blonde? The reaction of his mother makes me wonder what difference my hair color makes. Does she buy into the stereotype? Think I'm an airhead? Or vapid? Or maybe just American? This conversation is already beyond me, but the hostility in Louisette Martin's voice makes me want to find Yannick and Jean-Claude and have them take me back to the airport.

JL smolders, and not in a good way as he faces the woman. She cringes.

"What are you doing here, Angélique?" His voice is rough with emotion. I wish I knew what that meant.

Licking her lips, she looks down at well-worn sandals. "I've been helping your mother." Then she puffs up like an angry cat. "More than you do for her."

Before he can respond, his mother chides her, "Angélique, JL does what he can."

"With money only, from a distance."

"Who are you to criticize me, Angélique?"

If looks could kill, she'd be lying on the floor—a crumpled, burnt heap. "After all this time, why can't you let go of the past?"

"Stop it, both of you. Angélique has been very kind to me the last few months since her divorce. You should be happy someone is here to help me, JL. Especially since you refuse to move back from Chicago."

"We've been over this, Maman."

"Well, I for one am happy Angélique has come back into our lives."

"She dumped me years ago for the man she's now divorced from. No reason for her to come back into our lives."

Angélique is a study of how to look downcast and defiant at the same time. "Not that man. My second husband."

JL's jaw drops. "Sec-second husband? But you were such a devout Catholic."

She lifts a shoulder. "Times change."

He looks at his mother, but she just waves away any concern. "Men frequently marry several times. Why shouldn't women have the same chances? Of course, she can have a place in our lives. Just because Angélique made a mistake when she was young is no reason to punish her now."

JL's mother gives me a long, assessing look. "I thought your friend would be one of the men from work, Max, perhaps. And what sort of name is Micki? A mouse?" She snickers at her joke. Been there, heard that, trying not to wince.

"The name her family and friends use."

"Vous appelez Michelle si vous préférez, Madame," I interject in my best French.

Unimpressed, Louisette Martin's glare is a warning beacon. Her chest heaves as if breathing is difficult and she coughs several times. Then she turns on her heel and pushes past Angélique, who follows like an obedient dog.

When JL waves me in, I hesitantly cross the threshold and stop, leaving him just enough room to bring in our bags. Angélique moves down the hallway.

"Go on," he says softly. "The living room is just to the right."

I edge forward slightly, but with no intention of walking farther into Martin territory. "Not without you." Angélique, who must have bat ears, smiles.

The bags thunk onto the tile. "Fine," he huffs and slips his arm through mine, giving it a squeeze.

Louisette's voice rings out sharply. "JL? Où est tu?"

"Ici, Maman. Une minute, s'il vous plaît."

Giving me a look that pleads with me to be brave, JL steps forward. His grip is like a vise. I have no choice but to go with him.

Her face tight, Louisette points to a ladder-back wooden chair. "Bonjour, Michelle. Asseyez-vous."

JL guides me toward the love seat and pulls me down next to him, entwining our fingers while his mother glowers.

She turns to the woman watching from a chair near the fireplace and finally switches into English. "Angélique, when do you have to pick up the children?" Smiling at JL, she says, "Angélique has two adorable sons, eight and ten." Her eyes sparkle as if she is speaking of her own grandchildren.

"Bonjour, JL. Tu as l'air différent. Très viril," Angélique simpers. JL seems not to notice the way she fawns over him. If I had said that he would have flexed a bicep. When she looks me in the eye, I see blazing hatred.

"It's been close to twenty years." As he says these

words, he sticks resolutely to English. His tone is pleasant, but JL fixes his gaze on his mother, not on the girl begging for his attention.

"I need to leave in a few minutes, Tante Louisette. No sports today."

"And you will all come back for dinner."

"No, we don't want to impose. Especially on JL's first night back." She wrings her hands.

Louisette gently takes the woman's hands in hers. "You will come back. It is no imposition. And I want André and Christophe to meet my son."

Loosening my grip on JL's hand, I say, "Nice to meet you, Angélique. I am Michelle Press." Not formally introduced and not knowing how good her English might be, I speak slowly, trying to make my voice pleasant and even. It's not a reflection of the way I feel, neither pleasant nor even.

With no trace of a French accent, she says, "Pleased to meet you too, Madame. Where are you from?" Maybe it's my imagination, but I think I hear the ghost of the words, "and when are you going back there?"

My spine stiffens. "Chicago. Where JL lives."

And then we sit, silent, silent, silent, while Angélique walks out the door.

JL

When I first see Angélique, heat rises from my belly through to the top of my head, not with desire, with anger. Furious, I can't bear to look at the ex-fiancée who threw me over for a more available, and richer, guy.

When I see Maman's complacent expression, my fists

clench. "Seconde chance," she mouths. *As if. Why Maman thinks Angélique would appeal now is beyond me. I've forgiven, but not forgotten. One look at Micki should have disabused her of that idea.*

At the same time, Angélique smooths her bobbed hair, then touches her fingers to lips quirked into a small smile. Her stick-thin, angular body is unappealing compared to Micki's lush curves. She assumes a meek expression, but I notice something feral in her eyes, as if she is the predator and I am the prey.

For years I have been telling Maman to stop trying to find me the perfect woman. And my former fiancée. Give me a break. Now we're here—my choice and hers facing off.

I love my mother. But her concerns are not the ones that matter to me. Religion and nationality are not markers to ensure my happiness. And she's found someone who can give her ready-made grandchildren. Somehow I must convince her Micki is the perfect daughter-in-law.

My chest loosens when Angélique leaves, although I know the reprieve will be temporary. She'll soon return, with her sons.

"Vous voulez un café?" Maman asks.

"Anglais, s'il te plais."

Maman frowns.

"I'll have café au lait. Micki?"

"Just a glass of water, please." The brightness I love about her dims, but there is nothing I can say, at least with an audience.

"Angélique helped me make the poutine and tourtière for dinner." Maman's cat-who-got-the cream voice projects satisfaction. "These are two of JL's favorites. Perfect for his return."

"Visit, Maman, not return. Micki is very excited to try real French-Canadian food."

"Especially poutine." Micki regains some animation with the promise of dinner.

A fruitless glance toward the front door yields no sign of my uncle. "By the way, is Uncle François here?"

"He said he would be home for dinner." Her answer is offhand, but I can't help wonder. Is he out drinking, or buying drugs?

"What does he do with his time? He must be at loose ends now that he has left Montreal."

"He has some new friends here," she says. "Introductions from his pals in Quebec."

Knowing what his Montreal friends get up to, this isn't a promising start.

"I've taken him to some events at Maison de la Francophonie as well. And last month we went to the Festival du Bois."

"Is he interested in French-Canadian culture?" I'm dubious. In my remembrance, Uncle François saw cultural events as a way to boost his nefarious activities.

She shrugs. "He goes. Maybe not enthusiastically, but when I ask him, he's agreeable."

"And this doesn't worry you?" I ask.

"He hasn't caused any trouble."

How do you know? I wonder. Maman always tended to turn a blind eye. "Why did you let him come?" I can't keep the accusation out of my voice.

"When he was released, I invited him. He has no one except us, mon chou. Who will help him if not family?"

"But, but ..." I sputter.

"But what?" she says sharply.

"He's no blood relation to you." I start pacing the small living room.

"He is your father's brother."

Out of the corner of my eye, I see Micki eye me anxiously. I give her a reassuring smile, then turn back to Maman. "You told me he has been violent on several occasions. I would like him to have his own place. Is he on any lists for subsidized housing?"

"Not that I know of." Maman grimaces, presumably at what she thinks of government housing.

"Any job searches?"

She grabs a corner of her apron and twists it. "He says he's looking."

"And you believe him?"

"What choice do I have?"

Throw him out. Before frustration gets the better of me and I say something I'll regret, I tell her, "While you make the drinks, I'll run the luggage to the room."

"I have made up the guest room. Michelle will sleep there." The finality in her voice makes me wince as she addresses Micki. "I hope this will not be a problem for you?"

"No, Madame Martin." Micki sounds subdued but not angry.

"Come with me. I'll show you the house." I reach for her hand, but she doesn't take it, although she follows me out of the room.

The bedrooms are on the other side of the hall from the living room. Mine faces the front lawn, Maman's in the middle, and the guest room is in the back, closest to the full bath. Maman made sure we're separated for the length of the visit. I didn't foresee this as an issue. But then, I hadn't expected Maman would have Angélique at the house, either.

The narrow hallway means Micki walks behind me, heels dragging against the wooden floor.

"Never thought Maman would have a problem with us sharing my bedroom."

She peeks in but doesn't answer. When I turn to see what's happening, she's stands still, one hand rubbing the opposite arm. Her face is blank.

"Micki?" Except for her hand movements, she could be a piece of sculpture. I step toward her. When she drops her arms. I slip my arms around her waist and pull her into me. Like a block of ice, she stands stiff in my embrace.

"I'm so sorry. This trip was supposed to cheer you up." I pause. Is that a sniffle I hear? I touch her cheek but feel no trace of moisture. "We don't have to stay here. I'll get a room at the Corkscrew Inn. Close to here. I can go back and forth when I need to. You can work and avoid Maman completely." I kiss her temple.

Her face slowly crumples in misery. She is no longer stonelike. I startle when wetness penetrates my shirt. Micki hardly ever cries. She's upbeat and always has plans B, C, and as far down the alphabet as she needs. Now her tears spill out like Shannon Falls, the third tallest in British Columbia.

"If I can move my uncle into some sort of temporary residential facility and onto a list for a permanent place-ment, we can spend a few days in Victoria and go home from there."

"Won't your mother be hurt?" Her voice hitches.

That Micki cares about Maman's feelings just shows what a good person she is. Brusquely, I say, "She'll survive."

"And Angélique?"

"What about her?" I can't see how she comes into the equation.

"You didn't notice the stars in her eyes when she looks at you? She sees you as husband number three. Anyway, I have work to do, so I'll just hole up in my bedroom most of the time."

My laugh brings Maman into the hallway. "What are you doing out here?" The pointed look Maman casts at the luggage says it all. She blows out a breath. "Michelle, your room is at the back."

"Tiny. And no desk."

At my snarl, Maman's eyes widen, and I immediately regret my tone.

She stalks out onto the front porch, and I see her reach into her apron for a pack of DuMauriers and the engraved lighter Papa gave her. Reflexively, I move toward the door, but stop myself before I make yet another scene.

Her cheeks damp, Micki pulls up the handle on her case and trudges toward the end of the hallway, disappearing through the doorway of the last room. As I throw my duffel through the open door to my bed, I hear her call down the empty, echoing hall. "I can work on the bed."

My heart sinks a little. Then I walk back to the living room to wait for Angélique's return.

CHAPTER
SEVENTEEN

Running away will never make you free.—Kenny Loggins

JL

BACK IN THE LOUNGE, Angélique has stealthily returned, along with two skinny boys, all floppy dark hair and enormous black eyes fringed with long lashes. They move behind her chair as I walk into the room. She looks too composed as she sits primly in the fireside chair, palms flat on the arms, legs crossed at the ankles. There is no sign that she is about to erupt until..."

"You should be ashamed, JL Martin." Sparks fly from her almost black eyes, and I feel heat rise along with my indignation.

"Ashamed of what?" I try to control my voice, even if my anger burns in my gut like live coals.

"Staying away so long. Allowing your maman to smoke

when it's so bad for her health. Bringing home a woman without warning." She ticks off my transgressions on her fingers.

"Only three?"

She flushes at my sarcasm but quickly recovers. "Three mortal sins," she snaps. "I'm sure you're guilty of many venial ones, too." The older boy pulls at her sleeve. "What is it, André?" she snaps.

He whispers something in her ear. She snaps, "Go into the kitchen. Tante Louisette has probably left you a little treat. Then do your homework."

The two boys run off as if devils are chasing them.

I consider her carefully. "If I am such a sinner, why do you want anything to do with me?'

"To help you repent," she says, as if the answer is obvious.

My abrupt laugh doesn't go over well.

"You have no respect. Yet another sin." The last syllable comes out like a cobra's hiss.

I cast a searching look around the room. "I don't see your basket. Or a pungi."

Confusion spreads over her face. "Je ne comprends rien."

"You remind me of a cobra rising out of its basket at the sound of a flute. I'm staying well back from your venomous bite."

She huffs and looks away.

"It is true I don't visit Maman as often as I'd like, but when you're in business, you can't just drop everything. As for the smoking, Maman is resolute. I have been after her for years to stop. If you have more influence, perhaps she will listen to you."

Her eyes bug out at that thought. We sit quietly for a

bit, and then, in an anxious tone, she asks, "And the woman?"

"What about her?" I'm back to belligerent, crossing my arms across my chest.

"Your maman wants grandchildren. That Micki won't give you any. And I have two she already loves."

"Maman doesn't get a vote." My voice hard, Angélique flinches.

Footsteps sound in the hallway. Maman coughs and glares at me. "What don't I get a vote about?"

Unmoved, I glare back. "Micki. And for God's sake, stop smoking." Then I walk out of the room to the sound of coughing.

Micki

The twin bed is narrow, the mattress a slab of concrete. With her angular figure, Angélique would be more comfortable than I am. A scratchy gray army blanket over white sheets peeks out from under a green, yellow, and cream chenille spread. The wallpaper is made up of repeating geometric designs in the same colors. Everything harkens back to the 1960s. Only the anti-war slogans are missing.

Frozen in time. And so am I. Soft murmurs waft down the hall. I can't make out any of the words, but I'm sure JL is back with his mother and Angélique, drinking his coffee, while Louisette sings the praises of the girl she expects him to marry. I'm not sure, in the end, if he'll be able to resist.

So far I haven't seen him soften, but we've only been here a few hours. Not because of Angélique's looks, her malleable temper, or her children. Resisting his mother's desire will be the sticking point, and giving up his family may break our little fairy tale.

My laptop calls. But I don't have the Wi-Fi password, assuming Louisette has one. And would I find someone hacked my computer? I have a VPN installed. How secure is it, really?

My text tone sounds. I look at the sender. Cress. I notice a few were from the last couple of days while JL had my phone. I debate opening the app. That should be safe, right? As long as I don't click on the texts? Uncertain, I watch messages appear and disappear on the lock screen.

CRESS: Have you landed in Vancouver?

CRESS: We had to go back to London, but we're still going to Venice.

CRESS: WHY AREN'T YOU ANSWERING?

CRESS: EVERYTHING OKAY?

CRESS: We're on the Orient Express. Squee.

CRESS: Amazing!!!!! Lunch in the English countryside, fizzy wine, and our own steward.

CRESS: Tomorrow we'll be in Venice.

CRESS: LET ME KNOW YOU'RE OKAY, DAMMIT

My finger hovers over the keys. Not sure if I should respond or not. I want my life back, to answer my own questions, make my own decisions and yet...

Damn Sam to hell—in fact, to not just to some run-of-the-mill version but to one of the circles of Dante's *Inferno*.

My mind spins to possibilities. It's been years since I read the book so I google to refresh my memory.

The first circle isn't really punishment since Limbo is for people who were alive before Christianity, like Plato and Julius Caesar. The second circle is Lust. Much more appropriate although the punishment, being blown back and forth by the wind, doesn't sound dire enough.

I skip along to the seventh circle, Violence. After all, Sam did hit me and set fire to my parents' house. This circle has three rings, and in the middle one, profligates are chased and torn apart by dogs. Promising.

After considering the ninth and last circle, Treachery, where the punishment is being frozen in a lake, I decide being torn apart by dogs is a fitting punishment. I never knew I could be so bloodthirsty. But after my encounter with JL's mother, I don't feel empathetic or charitable.

Guess I've been sitting here for quite a while because darkness steals into the room. Heavy steps come down the hallway. I look again at my phone, debating whether or not to answer Cress. Was it less dangerous when I googled Dante, or was that a mistake? I'm not sure how a hacker would track me. Out of the corner of my eye, I see a shadow loom in the doorway.

The light in the hallway illuminates his face faintly. He stares at the phone in my hand. "Micki? Why are you sitting all alone in the dark? I've gotten several frantic texts from Max because you aren't responding to Cress." JL sounds like he's swallowed gravel. His shoulders droop as he walks in, arms outstretched.

My breath hitches. "Didn't know if it was safe to answer." I don't mention my Google search.

"You should have come back and asked." He sounds

testy and I wonder what sort of conversation has been going on in my absence.

"I didn't think your mother wanted me back in the living room." I pick up my phone and hit messages.

ME: JL's mother hates me.

CRESS: Thank God you're not dead. I thought Sam had shown up in Vancouver.

ME: I could deal with that.

I turn off the device and throw it on the bed, giving JL a twisted smile. "There, I broke out of my exile and sent Cress a message."

"What? I said ask, not just do it." A frown mars his oh-so-tempting lips. I want to kiss the frown away. His next words let me know he's pissed off. "This isn't exile." He rolls his shoulders and continues in a milder voice. "And we'll be eating soon. Come and have some creton and cheese. And meet Angélique's sons."

"What's creton?" I picture a mixture of something and cheese, like sardines and cottage cheese? My mom liked to mash them together. Maybe like a sandwich?

"Pâté. And I think Maman put out Kabritt and some local brie."

I stretch and wipe my sleeve across my face. "Probably look like hell. Should I put on some makeup?"

"You're fine," JL says, combing through my hair with his fingers. "So silky," he murmurs.

I flash back to the scene on the porch. "Question."

"Anything."

So many. But I'll go with the one most pressing.

"Should I answer Cress from now on? Or should I wait until the burner arrives? Or should I ignore her?"

He pulls out his own cell. "Let me contact Max. GSU may have to be the intermediary until you get a new phone and a new number."

We look at each other. When did easy conversation disappear? A sound like geese breaks the silence. "Max? Yeah. Okay. Glad it's all arranged. I'll expect Yannick. Give our love to Cress." He clicks off.

"GSU arranged for Yannick to bring a new phone in the morning. Lots of security, so even with your number, Sam shouldn't be able to track you. Once you have it, you can text Cress whenever."

My life highjacked, I can only hope relief is in sight. "Thanks." Only one word, knowing my graciousness index is at minus fifty thousand. "I hope it's an iPhone."

Instead of moving away, JL rests his fingertips under my chin and presses his lips to mine. They are cool, dry, and unbearably tender. I pull away.

His eyes flash a question, but I don't answer. With a resigned air, he says, "It's an iPhone 5S. In the new color, gold. Max said they're downloading everything from the cloud, and it will be all ready to go. As soon as you've verified everything is there, I'll deactivate this one."

My face feels brittle when I try to smile. "Thanks." I pause for a second. "Another question." He sighs. "When we arrived, your mother asked who I was, and you said..."

A wolfish grin makes me think this question is okay. "Ma blonde, I called you my blonde."

My burning curiosity makes me press. "Yes. But why? What difference does my hair color make? Or is that another nickname, like chouette?"

"Hmmm." He scratches his head, as if considering. "Interesting question."

"Then answer it," I demand, my voice a little louder.

"Your mother's reaction was pretty strong. Does she prefer brunettes?"

"Les brunes? No, I don't think so. Although Angélique..." He pastes on a totally faked puzzled expression.

All the frustration of the last few weeks boils up. I bolt off the bed, put my head down, and barrel into him.

"Ooof." The wuffling sound reminds me of a big Bernese mountain dog my friend Paul used to have. Cuddly, soft, and comforting.

We both go down, him on his ass, me in his lap. Then he rolls so my back is against the floor. He hovers over me, hands next to my shoulders and knees on either side of my hips. We're both giggling.

A deep, hitching breath comes from the doorway, combined with a little scream. Tremolo vibrating in her high soprano, Angélique strikes an accusatory note. "I thought you came in here to ask Michelle to join us for un petit goûter." I push my way up off the floor. She leans against the doorframe, lips puffed in a generous pout.

"That was my intention." JL gives her a smug smile as he helps me off the floor. "But then we started talking..."

Her skin pales under the carefully applied makeup. "Didn't look like talking to me," she whines, tapping her fingers together.

Ignoring her fidgets, I focus on JL. "You never answered my question, Beau."

"N-n-non." Angélique has one hand pressed to her chest, the other against her mouth. Stuttering sounds vibrate as if her breath has caught in her throat. "B-b-beau? C'est impossible."

"Just a nickname," I tell her, trying to be offhand.

JL is silent.

"It's an endearment," she snarls, eyes glowing red. Her

sharp little fangs gleam in the incandescent light. "I won't let you call him that. It's been my name for him since we first got together in school."

My jaw drops. "Is that true?"

JL nods, shamefaced. "I didn't think it mattered. And you picked out the name."

"Did you call her chouette?"

"Yes, it was his pet name for me," Angélique screams.

At the same time JL says, "No, I never called anyone that before you, Micki."

Squeezing my eyes shut, I put my fingers in my ears. I don't know what to believe. Does it matter if he's no longer with her? Guess it does, because when I hear her call him Beau again, my stomach turns over.

"Beau's mine. You will see. Tante Louisette will never let you have him."

A chill goes over me as if a hyena snaps at my heels, and I wrap my arms around myself. Why is she so intent on winning JL back? Then a possible motive knocks the air out of me. JL is worth a lot of money these days. Is that why she's pegged him as husband number three?

JL ignores her, takes my hand, and presses a kiss to my knuckles. "I will stop toying with you, ma chouette."

"Don't call me that." The smirk on Angélique's face means she thinks she's won.

JL's expression is full of tenderness. "All right. If I can't convince you, I'll come up with something else." He scratches his jaw. "Ma blonde means my girlfriend. It has nothing to do with your hair color."

"Non," Angélique cries. "JL, je t'ai aimé toute ma vie. Tu m'es promis."

"How can you say that? You broke that promise. You." JL moves toward her, but she runs out of the room.

"André, Christophe, put on your coats. We're going home."

"But, Maman, we're hungry," a treble voice calls out.

"We'll stop at McDonald's on the way home."

JL freezes, hands clamped to my wrists in an unbreakable grip. His mouth works soundlessly. Then, with a bellow, he declares, "Incroyable. Elle ne peut pas être sérieuse." I can tell he's trying to convince himself.

I pull back but can't work free. When his fingers slacken, pain shoots down my right arm as my muscles release. My neck aches. My left hand wavers between rubbing my arm or my neck. With a sigh, I drop back onto the bed.

JL grabs my wrist and gently pulls me to my feet. "So, you are ma blonde, yes?"

"Bien sûr. Bien sûr." I try to add Beau, but the word sticks in my throat. Instead, I take his hand and cross the threshold, back straight and head high.

~

JL

I rub Micki's hands until feeling flows back in her crushed fingers. Then we walk into the living room, hand in hand.

Maman must have just come in. I shiver from the lingering chill she brought from outdoors, along with a whiff of smoke.

"Maman," I say warningly. "Tu m'as promis que tu arrêterais de fumer."

Her lips purse as she throws the packet at me and gives us the stink eye. Of course, it's empty. She bares her teeth in a not-so-humorous grin.

Angélique is back by the fireplace. "I thought you were leaving."

"No. Tante Louisette insists we stay."

His mother taps a foot. "I can't believe you were so rude, JL. Living in America has not improved your manners."

"Where are the boys?"

Maman smiles broadly. "In the kitchen, playing video games on their iPad. I gave them a petit goûter."

Then she motions Micki to sit down and picks up a tin-glazed faience Quimper plate. The salad-size dish is part of a tea set I bought her while stationed in Europe. I had a week of leave just after Angélique broke our engagement. Maman flew over and we spent it in Paris, seeing all the sights. The Breton peasants, in their eighteenth-century garb, are cheerful reminders of good times after bad. She fills it with creton, wedges of cheese, and woven wheat crackers.

"Triscuits," Micki says with delight.

"You know them?" Maman is incredulous. "They are a French-Canadian..." She waves her hand around, trying to think of the English word she wants. "Chose," she says, giving up the struggle.

"Thing," I say. "Chose means thing."

I can see from the look on Micki's face that she wants to tell Maman Triscuits are American. But she bites her tongue. "We eat them all the time. They're my mother's favorite."

"Tiens! Amazing. Your mother is a woman of good taste. Is she from Canada?"

Micki chokes and Maman doesn't pursue it. I don't know Alice Press' ancestry, but I'm sure she's not French

Canadian. I'm just relieved Maman and Micki have something in common, even if it is only a cracker.

"What's this?" Micki points to the slice of creton.

"It's the creton."

"When you mentioned it before, I tried to guess what it was. Never thought of this." She spreads a bit on a cracker and pops it into her mouth, crunching the biscuit happily. "Yum. Did you make this, Madame?"

"Louisette," Maman says stiffly. "Yes, I made it. Homemade is always better."

"Would you like something to drink?" I gesture toward a console table where bottles of red and white wine sit.

When Micki nods, I pour a good amount of Nota Bene from Black Hills Estate Winery into a balloon glass. She always chooses red over white. Maman sips Alibi, a white from the same vineyard.

"We visited the winery and brought back a couple of cases after the wine tasting," Maman tells her.

"I'd love to go. Vineyards are one of my favorite things," Angélique speaks, her voice loud and rapid, showing a little spirit, although her words are not too convincing since she's clutching a glass of water.

"That part of BC is very interesting—desert and interesting microclimates. Perfect for wine cultivation. You'd like it, ma chouette." I catch Micki's gaze and her face lights up.

Angélique puts the glass down with a shaking hand, ready to protest.

I circumvent her. "Maman, did you ever hear me call Angélique ma chouette?"

She purses her lips. After a few moments, she shakes her head. "No. I don't think I ever heard you use that at all."

I beam in triumph while Angélique squeezes her pink,

swollen eyes shut. Then, recovering, she picks up the glass, takes a sip, grimaces. She no longer sits primly, rather, she huddles in the armchair. Despite her fierce announcement in the bedroom, she seems defeated. The water finished, she puts down the glass with exaggerated care. Her gaze fixes firmly on her hands, picking at her cuticles.

Pine, cherry, and oak scent the air as a healthy blaze chases away the late afternoon chill. The soothing sound of gentle rain patters on the roof and against the windows. November and December may be the wettest months, but April definitely has its fair share of precipitation.

Besides the crackle and pop of the fire, the only other sounds are the crunching of Triscuits and high-pitched boyish giggles that waft in from the kitchen.

CHAPTER

EIGHTEEN

Chapter 18

All you have to do is say, 'I'm going home,' and you're the most popular girl at the party.—Elaine Stritch

Micki

PEA SOUP with dumplings known as doughboys is the first course. The large yellow peas in broth with diced leeks, celery, carrots, and pork belly look appetizing, but all I taste is salt. The tourtière and poutine smell wonderful. But the ground meat in the tourtière has a grainy, fatty, unpleasant feel and the poutine gravy has a metallic taste. The salad seems crunchy in all the wrong ways, and the vinaigrette is unpleasantly sharp.

JL enjoys every morsel, mopping everything up with bread, making his mother smile broadly, but I can barely manage more than a few forkfuls of dinner after a small spoonful of soup. Louisette's baleful looks at my plate don't improve my appetite or my taste buds.

"Not to your taste?" she remarks scornfully.

"Sometimes new tastes need to be assimilated," JL says. "I'll eat some of yours, ma chouette." He tips everything onto his plate and quickly makes it all disappear. The boys follow suit, but Angélique also eats tiny portions.

By the time we're finished with the salad, JL is antsy. His uncle hasn't turned up. He keeps looking away, as if he can actually see the front door, and even gets up a few times to look out the living room window.

"Sit still, mon chou. If your uncle comes, fine. If he is with his friends, playing cards, that's fine too."

"But Maman..." JL says.

"Don't say anything. Your uncle is a grown man and can make his own decisions."

Face like a thundercloud, JL stirs sugar into his milky coffee. So much sugar that he makes a face when he tries to drink it. He throws down his napkin, ready to leave the table.

Angélique had started her car earlier, before Louisette convinced her to stay for dinner. "We should leave, Tante Louisette. But the car is making strange noises."

"Leave it here and JL can try to get a mechanic over in the morning. Good thing the boys don't have school tomorrow."

Another obligation for the obliging son. JL looks at his mother sourly. "I have a friend who can figure out the problem, Angélique."

"When you finish, drive Angélique and the boys home." Louisette's request brooks no refusal.

"Get your coats, everyone, and let's get going."

When I start toward the hall, Louisette stops me.

"Michelle, you will stay here and help with the dishes, if you don't mind."

Schooling my face to hide the tide of anger that rolls over me, I say, "Of course not." I pick up the dessert plates and saucers, piling the cups on top.

Angélique flounces out, quickly returning with her raincoat on and a large purse dangling from her shoulder. The boys are wearing jackets that aren't quite heavy enough for the weather, and they drag their backpacks by the straps instead of wearing them. Angélique makes the boys walk out first and slips her arm through JL's. "Ready...Beau." Then she smirks as they walk out the door.

"Beau," Louisette says, beaming. "You always called him that, Angélique. See how my JL blushes?"

I swivel my gaze away and carefully place the dishes next to the sink. Louisette washes, every peek from the corner of her eye a criticism of my incompetence. Too slow, too sloppy, the dishes aren't sufficiently dry.

When I almost drop the pie plate, she shrieks as if there is a huge hairy spider hanging down in front of her face. "Be careful. That dish belonged to my great-grandmother, and I cannot replace it."

JL isn't back yet, his uncle hasn't turned up, and I need to escape. Dishes done, I throw the towel over the back of chair. "Bonne nuit," I tell Louisette and take myself off to bed, planning to fire up my laptop and put in a couple of hours of work, but I fall asleep almost immediately and never even hear JL get back.

Sun peeks through the thin linen curtains. The house is very quiet. I forgot to ask for the internet password, so I read for a while. When my stomach starts to growl, and the need for coffee becomes unbearable, I dress and quietly creep toward the kitchen. To my surprise, Louisette is already there, whisking a batter.

"JL loves crepes," she says without turning around. "The coffee is made if you want some."

I pour a cup, adding just a tiny bit of milk, then sit at the table, watching her strong biceps flex as she beats the batter.

"Now it needs to rest," she says, placing a cloth over the bowl. Louisette fetches her own cup and sits across from me.

"You were asleep when JL got back?" she asks.

"I fell asleep almost as soon as my head hit the pillow," I tell her.

She sips, then leans forward, forearms flat against the table top. "Look, Michelle, I want to be honest with you."

Honest. I know this is not going to be good.

"When JL returned home, last night, we had a long talk. I think he realizes he still has feelings for Angélique. That is why he was back so late."

That can't be right. I start to tell her she is a liar. But she forestalls me. "JL understands his obligations to his family. I am sure he will move back to Vancouver."

I gulp to keep from shrieking. "Did he say so?"

"Not in so many words, but I can read his heart."

With a shake of my head, I negate all she is telling me. Then she says, "Angélique called and will be over soon."

"But she doesn't have a car."

"Her parents are picking up the boys for the day and will drop her off here. That way, when the car is fixed, she'll have it."

Makes a kind of sense, but my stomach starts to burn. Jealousy.

"I am sure he will ask for the family ring soon. It's my

mother's ring." She sits back and drinks more coffee. I never thought euphoria had a scent, but Louisette stinks of it.

Just then, the doorbell rings. Angélique?

"Are you expecting someone?" she asks me.

I shake my head no.

When Louisette comes back, Yannick is close behind.

"Ah, Madame Micki. So good to see you." Of course, it's too early for the showdown with Angélique.

I realize Yannick has brought me the new phone as he hands me the Apple box. "Here you are. I've been told everything should be set up but to wait until you check it over. It's already charged."

Louisette looks at the box curiously. "A new phone? Don't you already have one?"

"It was stolen," I say quickly as I take everything out of the box. The screen comes to life asking for my passcode. When I put in the numbers, the home screen appears. After checking out a couple of things, I put everything back in the box. "Perfect. Thank you, Yannick."

Angélique walks into the kitchen and gives Yannick an appreciative look. I realize she must have a key to the house.

"You should have had your parents stop in, Angélique," Louisette reproaches.

"They are taking the boys out to breakfast and the zoo." She pours coffee and slips onto an empty chair. "Who is this?"

"Yannick Moreau. I'm one of JL's colleagues." Yannick shakes her hand but doesn't kiss it.

"I remember you," she says. "You were that school friend who was almost in the Olympics."

She flaunts a sparkly ring she wasn't wearing yesterday. Maybe it's one of her two wedding rings. Noticing my look, she smirks at me with satisfaction, turning her hand back and forth so the light bounces in rainbows.

Louisette gasps. "Angélique." She doesn't seem to know how to go on.

With a gush, Angélique says, "JL told me this was your maman's ring when he gave it to me last night."

Louisette stammers, "But, I, he... Why didn't he tell me last night?"

"He wanted me to tell you. The boys are so thrilled he will be their father. They liked him right away."

Louisette's eyes soften. This is the happy ending, however they got there. She throws her arms around her daughter-in-law to-be, tears of joy running down her cheeks. They suck the air out of the room as the enormity of the betrayal makes me sway. I put my hand on the top of a chair rail, closing my eyes against the now dancing wall-paper flowers..

On the one hand, I can't believe this is happening. On the other, maybe this is for the best. I don't have time for a relationship, or the emotional wherewithal to cope. I have to save my reserves for the confrontation I know will come with the partners over the promotion.

Flight is uppermost in my mind. I can almost hear my footsteps pounding down the walk to the SUV sitting at the curb. A little voice tells me, *Take your chance, Micki. JL will have a happy family and forget all about you.*

Yannick looks bemused as I steer him out of the kitchen, where Louisette can't hear us.

"Yannick, I have an emergency and I need to go back to Chicago. Could you wait by the car, and I'll throw my stuff together so you can take me to the airport?"

"What about JL? Does he know?"

"He got in very late last night and he's still asleep. I'll text him from the airport."

A dubious expression washes over Yannick's face. "Fine. Jean-Claude and I will wait for you outside."

I stand on my tiptoes and peck at his cheek. "I'll be out before you know it."

He saunters out, yelling, "Bye, Tante Louisette. Tell JL I'm sorry I missed him."

I run back into the guest room, throw my pajamas, toiletries, and e-reader into the case, zip it up, and slip out of the house with my jacket over my arm before Louisette sees me. Once I settle in the back seat, I use my new phone to find a flight home. I mark a couple. Just hope I can get a seat.

Jean-Claude drops us off at check-in with my suitcase.

"Text me when you're ready to be picked up," he tells Yannick. "I'll be at Tim Horton's."

Not able to change my ticket online, I stand in a long queue, not sure what flight I'll be able to take. Yannick finds a seat across from the line of desks where he guards my case. After half an hour, I snag an agent.

I shove my ticket at her. "I need to change my flight."

She thumbs the jacket and pulls out the somewhat crumpled piece of paper. Her tired smile looks pasted on. "Chicago. When do you want to leave?"

"Today. Whatever flight you have available." I summon my woe-is-me expression and whisper, "Family emergency."

Her fingers fly over the keyboard. She looks at the screen and rechecks my ticket. "You're in luck. The next flight has one first-class seat available. Otherwise, the plane is full. Do you want it? You'll have to hurry because they're boarding soon."

I nod. Inside, though, I'm shouting yes with a double fist pump. Adrenaline is keeping my spirits up.

"Luggage?"

I point to where Yannick sits with my case. "One bag." I motion to him and put the bag on the scale.

"Perfect." The printer clatters and spits out a boarding pass. "Just to the left for security. Bon voyage." She hands me the boarding pass and my passport. We clear the security checkpoint. Like Case at O'Hare, he will accompany me to the gate and onto the plane.

Once through, we rush to the departure lounge, where people line up to board. It's déjà vu. This could be O'Hare except the announcements are in both French and English, and Yannick is not exactly Case.

"Attention passengers for Flight 478 from Vancouver to Chicago. Because the plane is full, we request you to bring larger carry-on bags to the desk to be gate checked."

Yannick takes my passport and ticket, then explains my situation to the agent. When he gets back, he shoves the paperwork at me. No point standing in line when I'll be in the first group to board. "Why are you leaving so soon?" The abruptness of the question startles me.

"I told you, I have a family emergency."

"Your father is dying?"

"No. No one is dying."

"Can't be much of an emergency." So judgy.

My adrenaline crashes and I regret everything. "You can ask JL." I turn my attention to the woman with the microphone, waiting for my group to be called. When I changed my flight, I almost switched from first class to economy, but they had a first-class seat available and there was no charge for the flight change. Being miserable in first class might be better than in coach. I can drink my sorrows away for free.

The agent calls out three names, including mine. We're motioned over to board early.

Yannick grasps my elbow as we walk down the jetway. At my seat, he places my computer bag within easy reach, takes my hand and kisses it. "I hope you've contacted JL."

Resentfully, I think, *not your business*, then realize that it is. JL is his boss and I've made Yannick do something that will piss off JL. "Yes, I sent him a text."

There may be a glimmer of relief in his face as he says, "Au revoir, Madame Micki. Have a pleasant flight home." He says nothing more, but disapproval hangs in the air like a thundercloud as he exits the plane.

I pull out my phone and text my parents.

> ME: On my way home. See you in a few hours.

> MOM: Should we meet you at O'Hare?

> ME: I'll have a ride.

> ME: Any luck on a rental?

> MOM: Yes. Tell you when you get here.

> ME:

> ME: See you at the condo.

Then I send another text, this time to Cress.

> ME: Flying back to Chicago.

> CRESS: ??????

Just then the cabin attendant comes by. "Would you like champagne or a mimosa?"

I take a glass of champagne and orange juice, then read Cress' newest text as I sip.

CRESS: Tell me what's going on.

ME: JL's mother informed me he is engaged to someone else

CRESS: WTF

"Good afternoon. This is Flight 478, Vancouver to Chicago. At this time, please make sure your seat belts are fastened and turn off all electronic devices."

ME: Got to go

I put my phone in airplane mode and slip it into the pocket next to my seat. Then I close my eyes and try not to think of anything.

Case waits for me when I disembark at O'Hare. Knowing a little about how GSU works, I'm sure Yannick was on the phone to Chicago headquarters as soon as he saw me onto the plane.

"Nice to have you back, Ms. Press. Where's your luggage?" I can't tell whether he is being serious or ironic.

"Baggage claim."

"No problem. Let's grab your bag and make tracks for the condo." He pauses. "Everything's been quiet since you left. Maybe the guy knows you have been away?"

"He knows, all right. I got texts and calls in Paris."

"Good thing he's not waiting for you here, although I'm sure I could take care of him."

A creepy-crawly feeling spreads over me, and I look

around, even though my last-minute plans mean Sam can't possibly know I'm back.

Once we locate the correct carousel, we wait for the luggage to come through. I twist around, looking to see if we're being followed.

"Relax," Case says, trying to reassure me. The goose-bumps on my arms tell me I'm not.

I start a list in my head. First order of business is to let Rebecca know I'm back.

~

JL

I get back late after taking Angélique home. I know I should never have agreed to go into Angélique's house for coffee and a drink. She asks me to say good night to the boys when they're ready for bed. They want a story, so I read them one. Angélique sits on the stairs, waiting, and starts crying as we walk down. Even though I feel nothing for her, guilt pounds me for being so dismissive all day. I'm sorry she takes this so hard, and I agree to one drink. She takes out an open bottle of Caribou, left over from Carnaval.

When we're done, she begs me to stay, and I have one more drink. I manage to keep her from climbing all over me and finally escape into the rain. The drive back is hellish.

Head pounding, I strip off and shower, then take some ibuprofen. Now everything feels fuzzy as I walk up the drive. Maman huddles in her rocker on the porch, swathed in a heavy sweater, a lap blanket keeping out the cold.

"Why are you out here, Maman?"

"Just waiting to make sure you got home all right.

Angélique called and said you were drinking, and she was worried."

"She was sad, and I agreed to a drink or two. Then I left." My voice rises. "Nothing happened. See you in the morning."

Exhausted, I fall onto the bed. Not long after, yelling and banging pull me out of sleep. I stomp out of my room to find Uncle François in the living room, yelling and throwing things around. When he tosses a porcelain figurine against the wall, it's time for confrontation. He's drunk and high as a kite.

"Uncle François," I bellow to capture his attention. "Is this any way to greet your nephew?"

He squints through bleary eyes with no recognition. "My nephew is JL Martin. Who the fuck are you?"

I poke him in the chest, and he takes a swing at me, overbalancing and landing on his ass. "Look at me. I am JL Martin. Your nephew."

Eyes blurred by drink and drugs, he stares up, then shakes his head. "He's a skinny little boy, so high." He holds his hand three feet off the floor, and I guffaw.

"It's been too long, Uncle François. I'm a grown man now."

Suspicious, he studies my face. "Maybe..." His reluctance makes this more difficult. He may think I'm a cop or a narc.

"Why are you breaking up Maman's house"

"Need a drink," he mumbles, managing to stand.

"You've had more than enough."

He swings again. I grab his arm and twist it behind him. Then I push him out of the room and toward the attic stairs. "Up we go. You need sleep, not another drink." I push him into his room, pull the key out of the lock, and relock the door from the outside. He yells and pounds, but I go downstairs and put the key on the kitchen table.

Eventually, he exhausts himself, and I fall back to sleep.

Clouds cover most of the sky, but the room is bright enough I can tell that it is late, even before I check my watch. One in the afternoon—not possible. I never sleep that long. And I'm still in my clothes. Must have toed off my boots and fallen right into bed. Then I remember the confrontation with my uncle. He's a danger to himself and everyone around him.

Maman sings along with Edith Piaf as I wander into the kitchen for coffee. I'm surprised to see Angélique sitting at the table, playing with a ring, slipping it on and off her finger. My mug, emblazoned with Le Meilleur Fils du Monde, sits on the table, steam gently rising from the surface. I give Maman a kiss.

"Merci, Maman. Tu m'as sauvé la vie."

Then I realize Micki isn't in the kitchen. I pick up my cup and start toward the living room.

"Where are you going?"

"Looking for Micki."

"She's not here." Maman's tone is offhand.

I peer out the kitchen window to check the backyard. "Taking a walk or something? Or is she in the guest room?"

She shrugs. "Gone."

Gone? Like shopping or something? Was she desperate and got Yannick to take her sightseeing? Guilt washes over me. I should have come back immediately last night. Too bad Angélique seemed distraught. My heart starts to pound. Did Maman set this up?

"She took off with your friend, Yannick. She had her luggage with her." Angélique gloats.

I take my mobile out of my pocket and sit down. When I turn it on, harp sounds announce text messages.

One is from Micki. Another from Yannick. A third from Max. As I start to open the app, a fourth one appears from Case. Has the sky fallen in while I've slept? I pick up the mug. Coffee might clear my fuzzy brain. I concentrate on the text from Micki. It makes no sense.

> MICKI: On my way back to Chicago. Have a nice life.

> YANNICK: Micki asked me to take her to the airport. Said she had an emergency.

> MAX: What the bloody hell? Cress is beside herself.

> CASE: Just collected Ms. Press from the airport. Will be in touch.

The sky has fallen, and my life has officially gone to shit. I key in Micki's new number. It rings and rings, no answer, so I text.

> ME: Why did you leave?

> MICKI: Nothing to say. Better if we just go our separate ways.

> ME: We can make things work.

> MICKI: With you married in Vancouver and me fighting for a partnership in Chicago. Unlikely.

> ME: But...

> MICKI: I know how important family is to you. Au revoir.

Frantically, I text, call, leave a message, all the while cursing Angélique and Maman. Micki's angry, scared, overwhelmed. I need to talk to her, but she's cut me off and out.

I call Max in Venice.

"Pronto." He's going all Italian.

"Max, what's going on?"

"That's what we want to know." The noise from wherever they are makes him difficult to understand.

"Where are you?"

"Finishing dinner. Why are you calling so late? I texted you hours ago."

"Stayed up too late, overslept," I mumble.

All I hear is crowd noise. Then a sudden silence.

"Had to find somewhere quiet. The owner is letting me use the office."

"I don't understand what's going on. Micki's gone and everything else is in an uproar."

"What do you expect when you bring her home to meet your mother, then immediately get engaged to someone else?"

The explosion of profanities I produce has Maman and Angélique staring at me. I have no intention of apologizing either. "Max, I need to have a conversation with my mother. But if you speak to Micki, please tell her I am not engaged. She's not answering her phone, or I'd tell her myself."

"She's blocked you, mate. I'll have Cress pass on the message."

I put down the phone and mentally rain fire and ice down on the two women standing in front of me.

"Did you tell Micki I was engaged?" My bellow can probably be heard down the street.

"You gave Angélique my engagement ring," Maman

says decisively. "Last night. I just don't know why you didn't tell me when you got home."

Angélique holds out her hand, turning it back and forth so light from the diamond careens around the room, bouncing off the stainless-steel appliances.

This is ridiculous. I wasn't drunk. Engaged. No way that happened. The ring should still be in the jewelry box in Maman's top dresser drawer. But I have no time to unravel this mess. I ask just one question. "Is my uncle in the house?"

Maman nods. "Yes, he is sleeping off a bender in the attic room." She gives me a curious glance. "I found this on the kitchen table. Did you lock him in his room?"

"He came in drunk and was trashing the living room. I persuaded him to go upstairs and locked him in. Glad you didn't release him."

I look up the social services number. If I'm going to get back to Chicago, I need to take care of this. Moving Uncle François out of the house is the main reason I'm here. As angry as I am with Maman, I can't let him stay with her. When someone answers, I say, "Bonjour, Madame. My name is Jean-Louis Martin, and I would like to find out about getting my uncle on a public housing list and find him temporary accommodation in the meantime."

She asks me some questions.

"He moved here from Montreal last year, is sixty-five, alcoholic, takes drugs, and can't find work. I am willing to try to convince him to go into rehab."

She asks more.

"He's living with my mother, but it isn't a safe environment for her. He has some very dangerous associates and has been known to become violent." After last night, I'm a believer.

More questions flow over the airwaves.

"I am visiting Vancouver. I live in the U.S., and I need to go back. I only have a few days leave from my job to take care of this."

She says she will call back, so I give her my number.

Maman looks at me disapprovingly. "Well?"

"I should hear back sometime later today. The woman I spoke with thought they could do something on an emergency basis."

"He can refuse." She sounds like she might encourage that.

"If he does, then we call the police. He is a danger to you. And probably to anyone else who is around him."

She folds her arms. "Your uncle is not that bad."

I pull up her sleeves. Fading bruises decorate both forearms and probably go up to her biceps. She pulls them back down, glaring.

"He's been in and out of jail for drug selling, grievous bodily harm, minor theft, and who knows what else. You can't deny he has hit you. And last night he tried to break up the house."

"That was the first incident since he came here this time." She looks away evasively.

"These bruises are old? How old? Years? Unlikely. He's a ticking bomb. And I can't stay to protect you."

"I want you to move back." Her hands are on her hips, her lips pushed out. She must see this as a bargaining chip, but I'm not playing. My whole life is in Chicago. She knows this.

Angélique never moves, but her eyes shine with interest. Now she butts into the conversation. "If your uncle is as bad as you say, you owe it to Tante Louisette to stay."

I ignore her, then adopt a beseeching tone. "Maman, move to Chicago."

"No. I'm not leaving."

Then I confront the matter directly. "Did you take the ring out of the dresser, Maman?"

"No. I thought you did."

"I would never do that without asking."

Angélique fidgets but says nothing. Neither of us are willing to accuse Angélique outright. Maman gazes at her, but if disapproval prods her conscience, she doesn't let it show

Standoff until, twenty minutes later, the call comes through. I can bring my uncle in tomorrow. Fingers crossed, he agrees to treatment while they find him a place to live.

Then I call my copain at the garage and ask him to check out Angélique's car so she can leave.

CHAPTER

NINETEEN

Do not dwell in the past, do not dream of the future, concentrate the mind on the present moment.—Buddha

Micki

AFTER A WHIRLWIND OF RELOCATION, Mom and Dad are in a rental house in Skokie, a suburb west of Evanston. Close enough for them to monitor the construction work on the house. I hide out in the condo. When Rebecca heard I was back, she advised me to continue working from home.

Max and Cress changed their plans and are spending a few days in London after a return trip on the Orient Express. When I need a break from hours of reading documents, I visit the zoo, the farm in the park, the Lincoln Park conservatory, and check out new movies.

When I get the call to come into the office tomorrow, I'm not sure if it's for a meeting, good news, or terrible news. If the partners decided, and Hayden is the new partner, do I want the pain if I stay on? I've done nothing about finding another job.

Grabbing Liam, I fire up the geocaching app. "Let's go to Lincoln Park. I want to do some treasure hunting."

"For what?"

I study the app. "Let's do the Shakespeare statue."

A frown of disapproval creases his face. "Not a treasure you can bring home, and not exactly hidden."

"A photo will do." I start toward the door, and he catches up. But when he steers me toward the SUV, I say, "Thought we'd walk up."

"Kind of warm, don't you think?"

I snort. "Sixty-five isn't that bad. Come on."

The forty-five-minute walk, followed by the geocache search, makes us warm. But I have my photo. A small box nearby contains Shakespeare-related postcards. I take one of the famous Cobbe portrait and leave a small letterpress sheet of Sonnet #116.

Let me not to the marriage of true minds
Admit impediments. Love is not love
Which alters when it alteration finds,
Or bends with the remover to remove:
O no! it is an ever-fixed mark
That looks on tempests and is never shaken;
It is the star to every wandering bark,
Whose worth's unknown, although his height be
    taken
Love's not Time's fool, though rosy lips and
    cheeks
Within his bending sickle's compass come:
Love alters not with his brief hours and weeks,

But bears it out even to the edge of doom.
If this be error and upon me proved,
I never writ, nor no man ever loved.

Then we walk back to the condo where Sean meets us.

"You look done in, big guy," he teases Liam.

"Yeah. See you day after tomorrow, Ms. Press."

"How long have you been here, Sean?"

"'Bout half an hour. Lady came by to see you." He reaches in his pocket and pulls out a small spiral notebook. "Name of Rebecca Masters. Said you need to give her a call as soon as possible."

I pull out my phone, which is off. When the screen comes to life, Rebecca's message is on the screen.

REBECCA: Meet me at Glunz."

ME: On my way.

REBECCA:

"Okay, Sean. We have an appointment."

When we get there, Sean finds on-street parking for the SUV and walks me in to the restaurant. The wine shop is right next door, but Glunz, established in 1888, sells much more than wine. Rebecca is at a small, highly polished table that rests on old hardwood flooring. In front of her is a pint glass of the draft beer on offer. A large bar sits in the back of the smallish space.

"This is pretty good." She lifts the glass and salutes me.

"I'll have the sangria," I tell the server.

"You'll love it. It's the Glunz family recipe."

Rebecca nods but doesn't say anything. After too much

silence I break down. "Did you ask me here to get drunk or to hear about Paris?"

"Neither." She drinks some more, the liquid going down rapidly. When the server places the wine glass in front of me, she hands him her glass. "I'll have another. Along with coconut shrimp and fries. Hope that's okay, Micki."

He moves away just as Frederick Lanscombe walks in the door doing an exaggerated double take when he sees me.

"Back from your travels, I see. I had the impression from Rebecca you were going to be away a little while longer."

"My plans changed, so here I am. I have a preliminary report on Greenberg's social media accounts. I'm still working through the email. He has five different accounts, four through his office computer and one more that's only on his laptop.

The server places a foaming glass in front of Rebecca as Fred snaps out, "Buffalo Trace, on the rocks."

By the time he gets his drink, and the food arrives, we've been uneasily studying each other for at least ten silent minutes. I finger my neck, aware something is up.

Rebecca takes the lead. "Fred wanted to a have a private conversation before the decision about the partnership is made public."

I take a swig of wine and wait. And wait. And wait.

Fred sips his bourbon. All the time in the world. When all that's left is ice, he signals for another, and I watch him go through the ritual a second time.

Then he clears his throat. Meanwhile, Rebecca and I have been nibbling on the flatbread.

"As you know, we only have space for one new partner at the present time."

Yeah, yeah. Get on with it. Not that I really want to know. But I have to know.

"You are an exceptionally well-qualified candidate."

That sounds good. My spirits raise a bit.

"However."

My stomach plummets.

He licks his lips as if I'm a prime piece of steak. "The partners have offered the position to Hayden Forbes-Cartwright. We see him as more likely to bring in prestige clients. Despite glowing reviews from some of the other clients on your work, Congressman Greenberg is not impressed with your work on his case and that weighed heavily on our decision."

"Did the fact Hayden is Tyler Miller's nephew weigh heavily in the decision?"

Rebecca chokes on her beer. Fred glares. "Personal relationships were not in the equation."

Yeah, right. I pick up my glass to take another sip of wine and realize it's empty.

Fred throws back the rest of his drink. "You've worked as a valued member of our staff for eight years and I wanted to give you the privilege of a personal meeting. We all hope you'll stay on as a senior associate."

I look him in the eye. He shifts his gaze away. "Another opening should come up sometime in the next four years and you'll be in an excellent position for promotion."

Liar, liar, pants on fire. May as well resign now. My jaw is granite. If I don't loosen up, I'll crack my teeth.

JL

When we arrive at the clinic, the receptionist directs us

to the social services area, where the counselor immediately takes us into a small office. Uncle François and I take up most of the room and a good chunk of the air. He alternates between sheepish and belligerent when I call him out for his behavior. He gives me a flat no to being evaluated. Then I tell him I want to move Maman to Chicago, and he blusters before his resistance collapses.

A hostile glare accompanies his bellow. "I will go with you to the U.S."

"You think the American authorities will let you in? Even if they gave you a tourist visa, they'd never let you stay..." I let out a humorless laugh. "You can't hide the past."

At that he deflates like a pricked balloon. "Fine. Maybe they can find me accommodation back in Montreal. No point in staying in Vancouver once Louisette is gone."

I don't mention she hasn't agreed to move. Let him think it's a done deal.

"Your full name?" the social worker asks. She is around fifty, with an air of competence, perhaps from the broadcloth navy suit. Her graying blond hair is pulled back into a businesslike bun. She has a file folder in front of her, with a white form to the side.

"François Jules Martin."

She writes on the folder, then says, "Tu préfères québécois ou Anglais?"

"English is fine." He's hunched over in the hard-backed chair, which rocks a bit from side to side. I can see the craving build for the next drink or the next hit. Or both.

She moves to the form, takes a few more details, then says, "I understand, M. Martin, that you would like to relocate back to Montreal."

"Yes." Even with just the one word, the gravelly note

is evidence of decades of hard living. He clears his throat. "I have friends there. And my sister-in-law may emigrate to the U.S. No point in staying here in that case." He sends me a look, reaches for a nonexistent pack of cigarettes, then puts a fist on the desk in disgust. "My nephew has made it clear I would not be able to move to the U.S."

"Are you willing to go into a rehabilitation facility for up to two months?"

"I understand that is part of the deal." He's starting to shake. Is it the prospect of rehab, moving, or merely the need overwhelming him. He clamps his lips shut as his fingers desperately push into his biceps to keep the trembling under control.

"You and your nephew can sit in the lounge while I make the arrangements. We should have you scheduled to move to a facility in the next two hours."

"What about my stuff?" Uncle François asks.

"Your nephew can bring your belongings after you have been admitted. Of course, they will be searched to make sure there are no drugs or alcohol." She leads us into a utilitarian lounge with a few chairs and a small coffee machine. Instead of sitting down, he paces, muttering under his breath. A volcano builds and suddenly he slams his fist into the cinderblock wall.

"Tabarnak." Then he hits the wall again. "Calisse." This goes on until his knuckles are scraped raw, droplets of blood spattering the linoleum floor. He spews until he has no voice left, then slumps down to the floor, his back against the wall he just abused.

Once he's quiet, I point to the coffee machine. "You want something to drink, Uncle François?"

"Water..." Still restless, he struggles to his feet and

continues to pace, strangled sounds echoing through the room.

On shelf above the coffee are bottles of water. Room temperature, but better than nothing. The only sounds in the room are his footsteps and mine. I loosen the cap, hand him the water, and pace with him.

The door opens and a cheerful, rubicund man in his twenties walks in. Holding out his hand, he says, "François Martin?" Uncle François stares at him from puffy, reddened eyes but doesn't take the proffered paw.

"And you are his nephew, Jean-Louis?"

"Yes." I do shake with him.

"I'm Father Thibault."

Uncle François steps back. "No priests."

"I'm not here to bring you religion." Father Thibault's soft voice is soothing. "If you want to talk, fine. If not, we can all just sit here until all the arrangements are ready."

He abruptly collapses into a chair. "I won't go into a Catholic facility." Uncle François' hoarse voice wavers, but his words are precise.

"You don't have to." The priest has an emollient, reassuring tone. "Once the doctor evaluates you, a number of places will be available. Your nephew has indicated he would prefer you go into private accommodation."

"Can't afford it." His voice slurs, making him harder to understand.

I spread my hands wide. "Don't worry about that."

He growls like a grizzly bear. "Don't want charity. Just dump me in the garbage."

We sit there, mute, until a nurse comes in. "M. Martin, please come with me. The doctor will do a full medical evaluation, and we will escort you back here to wait for the results."

"Can my nephew come with me?" He's moved into the whining phase.

"Sorry, but that's not allowed. He will be here when you get back."

I help him up. The nurse takes his arm, but he pulls away. There is a little struggle before he gives in and is led off. The priest and I eye each other.

"You are very good to do this for your uncle," he says.

"Not really. I don't want him living with my mother, so I am doing it for her." Not that she appreciates it. I get more coffee. At this rate I'll be shaking as much as Uncle François. After I gulp down the lukewarm liquid, I excuse myself to find the toilet. When I get back, the priest is still waiting.

"I'm surprised to see you at a public clinic," I say as I pick up a bottle of water.

"I'm a volunteer. Many people need reassurance, whether or not they are religious, and I feel that is part of my calling."

An hour and a half passes. The receptionist comes in. "M. Martin, please come with me."

Father Thibault gives me a thumbs-up as I go back to the counselor's office. Uncle François isn't there.

"Please sit down, M. Martin."

I wait, trying not to fidget, while she looks through some papers.

"Because your uncle is in withdrawal, we need to hospitalize him until we can transfer him to rehab. I want to go over the options with you."

I rub one thumb over the other as I regard her. "I want a place with an excellent reputation that he can get into quickly. I need to get back to Chicago, but we must resolve this first."

She nods and passes over a list of programs. Leaning

over her desk, she taps the third one down. "This is an excellent facility, although expensive."

"I'm not worried about that. How soon can they get him in?"

"They can take him in three days. That's the minimum waiting period for private facilities. The other ones I spoke to would need seven days before they could transfer him."

"Fine, let's go with that one."

"Do you want to go out there and see what it's like?"

Maman would like that, but at this point, I don't care. "No. I'm sure it will be acceptable." I switch from rubbing my thumb to stroking my throat. "Where is he, by the way? Do I need to drive him to the hospital?"

"He is going by ambulance." She scribbles on a piece of paper. "He'll be at Vancouver General. You can visit him there."

"And the transfer to rehab?"

"They'll pick him up from the hospital. No visitors for the first thirty days. But you can drop off his stuff any time in the next three days." She stands and walks me out. "Have a good trip back home."

I shake her hand. "Thank you for all your help."

CHAPTER

TWENTY

A stiff apology is a second insult... The injured party does not want to be compensated because he has been wronged; he wants to be healed because he has been hurt—Gilbert K. Chesterton

JL

I CAN'T LEAVE for at least three more days, and with Uncle François on his way to the hospital, I don't want to go back to Maman's house either. She has sent me a string of texts, which I've ignored. We haven't spoken since I found out how Angélique maneuvered Micki to leave. In her own way, she is just as guilty in my eyes.

I couldn't believe how easily Maman and Angélique convinced Micki. Maman didn't even have to suggest that she go. Yannick arrived at the opportune moment with the phone. Micki didn't hesitate, just took advantage of his presence and left immediately. I should be furious with her, but instead I'm heartsick. The world is a different, and worse, place.

My phone rings. I look at the dashboard screen. Yannick.

"Just the man," I tell him before he can get a word out. "Meet me at Caffè Cittadella." I leave him no time to disagree, ending the call before he can answer.

I pull in and park with no idea whether Yannick will already be there or not, but wherever he is, I know he's coming. After all, I'm his boss, although I like to think that as my oldest friend he'd come anyway. In the shadow of a modern glass-walled office building, the 1894 house, rehabbed into a two-story café, could be right out of a San Francisco street scene. Micki would love this place. My breath catches. What if I can't get her back? I clench my jaw against the flood of emotion. Then I make a fist, bang it against my chest. Osti de colon. Positivity, idiot.

When I get Micki back, we'll come here for breakfast. Then again, even if I get to explain the monstrous fraud Angélique perpetrated, even if she agrees to try again, she may never agree to come back here. That leads to another thought. How will she feel when I tell her I want Maman to move to Chicago? Calisse. I need to learn how to manage relationships.

My stomach growls, reminding me I haven't had anything since a quick roll and coffee for breakfast at Social Services. Middle of the afternoon and the place is quiet while I look over my choices. Yannick sits down just as I have decided on tomato soup and grilled cheese with café au lait.

I expect him to say something, but he just sits back in his chair, waiting for me to open the conversation. Neither of us is willing to break the impasse. When my lunch and Yannick's glass of beer arrive, we thank the server. I eat my soup.

Yannick glares. "You're an ass, JL."

Tomato soup sprays everywhere from my mouth and nose—down my shirt, into Yannick's face, all over the tablecloth.

"Pardon?"

"An ass." He hastily wipes off the soup before it drips down his neck and into his collar.

"Why do you think so?"

"How could you let that charming woman run back to Chicago? And what did you do to cause her to leave in the first place?

I've been blotting my shirt with napkins and a damp cloth the server brought over, but it may be too stained to be saved. Unless Maman... Nope, not going down that road.

Now I fix my attention onto Yannick. "Listen very carefully," I snarl. "I didn't do anything. I didn't let her run. It was a clever setup by Angélique."

"I know her." Yannick rolls his eyes. "That Angélique Rigaud has always been a schemer."

"She made Micki believe we were engaged. That's what made her leave. I want to explain, but she's blocked me."

"Why didn't you catch her at the airport? You could have called me. I would have kept her from leaving."

"I overslept. By the time I found out..."

"Stop. Stop. TMI. Eat your lunch and let me talk."

I spoon up more soup.

"Let me sum up. Things happened. Then other things happened. Now you are miserable. I'm guessing she is too. In the meantime, she's back in the danger zone and you're here. Now you need a plan, which revolves around you getting back to Chicago ASAP."

"Je n'ai pas besoin de tes conseils, occupe-toi de tes oignons!"

"Believe me, JL, onions aren't the half of it. You need all my advice because you're royally fucked."

I scrape the last drops out of the bowl and drop the spoon back in. The noise summons our server, and she picks up the dish.

"Are you finished with that, too?" She points at my uneaten sandwich.

With one hand on the plate, I wave her off with the other. "I haven't even started."

She backs up, then turns around and leaves.

A bite of the now no longer warm sandwich is still satisfying. Once I swallow, I say, "Can't fly out until Friday."

"You need to go tonight, or at the latest, tomorrow."

"My uncle is in the hospital and has to wait to be admitted to rehab until sometime on Thursday."

"So?"

"What do you mean, so?"

Yannick rubs his eyes, then squints at me. "Is the rehab place expecting you to bring him?"

"No, they'll bring him over from the hospital."

"Are you obligated to visit him and get him settled?"

"He can't have any visitors for at least the first thirty days."

Yannick is leaning over the table. He sticks out his right index finger and starts stabbing me in the chest.

"Why. Do. You. Need. To. Be. Here?"

"Hey, stop that."

I slap his hand away and rub the sore spot on my chest. We're silent while we drink our respective beverages. Then, enlightenment. I slap my forehead. Fool. Yannick is right. What do I need to do? Have it out with Maman, take Uncle François' stuff to the rehab, change my ticket, return the car, let Case know my arrival time at O'Hare.

Yannick waves a hand in front of my face. "Where did you go?"

"Just thinking. Let me see when I can get a flight."

I start on the internet, but in the end, I call the airline. Air Canada can get me out on the first flight tomorrow morning."

"What time is that?"

"Eight thirty."

"You need to return the car?"

I nod. He looks at his phone. "Let's go now. Then I'll drive you back to your mother's house." He winks. "Maybe she'll invite me for dinner."

Yannick as a buffer isn't a bad idea.

"The only thing is..."

"Stop. You are just trying to find obstacles."

"No. I need to get back to Chicago and straighten things out. But I'm supposed to take his stuff to the rehab facility."

"We'll pack it up after we return the car. You give me all the info, and I'll get it there by Friday. Unless..."

"Unless what?"

"Unless you feel you have to do that yourself. In which case, I'll fly to Chicago and see Micki." His lascivious grin is another small burr under my thinning skin.

"Tu me prends pour un poisson!"

"Certainement." He makes a hand gesture of a fish swimming.

We both laugh.

~

I know Maman will be in the kitchen, so we plan to come in through the back. But she's standing on the deck I built her, smoking. Her frown morphs into a smile when she sees Yannick.

"Who is this stranger?" Even though she saw him the morning Micki left, Maman pretends she hasn't seen him in years. She drops the cigarette on the deck and grinds it out with her foot. Yannick grins wide as he hugs her. Stepping back, she gives him a long look, then says, "Mon coco, what are you doing with this méchant?"

"Trying to put him back on the right path," he teases.

I move in and give Maman a kiss on her left cheek, and then her right.

"So where is the Angel?" Yannick jumps right in.

I wince.

Maman is having none of that. "JL, what is going on with François?"

"He's in Vancouver General. Withdrawal. On Thursday, he will enter a private rehab facility."

"When can I visit him?"

"No visits for at least the first month."

She gasps, then goes into a long coughing spell. "So long?"

"After that, there should be limited visits, if he improves."

She latches on to the brochure I was given when Uncle Francois and I decided on the residential facility that looked most promising. "Like a country club or a resort. He'll be living better than you."

"And after?"

I thought I was prepared to give her my ultimatum. Now I'm not so sure.

"Whatever you're making for dinner, Tante Louisette, smells wonderful."

Trust Yannick to come up with the perfect distraction. Maman preens, smoothing her apron. "Bouilli."

Yannick kisses his fingers. "Magnifique. You must have intuited I would be here. Bouilli is my favorite dish."

"And Tart au Sucre for dessert."

She turns to me. "The table is set, JL. Bring out the pot and ladle."

"Do we need an extra setting? After all, you didn't know Yannick would be here."

"There are five place settings," she says, her voice heavy with accusation and I wonder why Angélique hadn't stayed. "And now we have a guest to use one."

I feel her eyes burning into my neck. As I walk to the stove, Yannick says, "I'll take the basket of bread and the butter. Do you need me to pour the water?"

"The water is already in the glasses. Do you want some wine? JL, get some wine and wine glasses."

"Non, merci, Tante Louisette. Water is enough," Yannick says.

I ladle stew into each bowl and set them back on the plates. Yannick passes around the bread, and we all take chunks of butter. The sounds in the room are chewing and slurping.

Then, always the instigator, Yannick breaks the mood. "This is so good, I hear an angel singing, Tante Louisette."

Maman gasps. Her spoon clatters onto the plate and she presses her hand against her chest. I glower.

His expression is one of innocent confusion. "Did I say something wrong?"

Recovering her breath, Maman pats his hand. "You said

nothing wrong, Yannick. Your words just reminded me of something sad."

"Pardon, ma chère. I didn't mean to cause you any distress."

Sure, you didn't. My mouth pulls slightly to one side, lips pursed. While Maman stares in my direction, Yannick gives me a conspiratorial smirk.

Time to get all the drama out of the way. "I need to pack up Uncle François' belongings to take to the rehab center. Mostly clothes, I think."

"You can take a few things tomorrow and the rest will remain here until François returns." Maman thinks she has everything planned out.

"Yannick will take his stuff. I'm leaving tomorrow morning."

"What? You were supposed to stay until at least Friday."

"I need to get back to Chicago. Things are sorted for uncle. And he won't be coming back."

"He'll survive this experience and here is the only place he has to come back to."

I look her squarely in the eye. "He's going back to Montreal. Social services is working to find him a place once he leaves the facility."

"Is this your idea?" she shouts, which brings on a coughing fit.

"No." It's not really a lie, but it is stretching the truth a little. "He wants to go back."

"Once you move here, we'll be a proper family."

"I'm not moving back. How many times must I remind you that my business is in Chicago?" I give her another look. "And Micki is there."

A howl tears out of her. "I don't want you to marry Micki. You need to marry Angélique."

"Even if I can't marry Micki, I won't marry Angélique. She's a liar and a cheat. She knows I have money now. The whole idea is repugnant."

"Her boys are..."

"Nothing to us. And she stole your ring."

Furrows line her brow. "Borrowed it."

Alternate crying and coughing doesn't help. "She's everything I want in a daughter-in-law—she is Catholic, French Canadian, has wonderful sons, and she'll be around to take care of me."

"It's the boys you're attached to. The rest is immaterial, and she's just looking for her next comfortable nest. I like the boys, but not enough to marry that gold digger."

Mouth drawn into a stubborn line, she spits back at me, "JL, I know what's best. And that's Angélique. Please think it over."

"If you love her that much, you marry her. She already has the engagement ring." I throw my napkin into my half-eaten bowl of stew. "Yannick, can I stay with you tonight?"

"Sure, as long as you don't mind the couch."

Maman sniffs and walks out of the dining room. Pots and pans bang in the kitchen sink.

Fifteen minutes later, we're out the door with my duffel and Uncle François' case. The last thing I see is Maman standing in the kitchen doorway, eyes red, arms folded. I don't walk down to her, and she doesn't come to the door.

There are no goodbyes.

CHAPTER

TWENTY-ONE

Take all the time you need to heal emotionally. Moving on doesn't take a day, it takes lots of little steps to be able to break free of your broken self. — Tere Arigo

Micki

MAX AND CRESS let no grass grow under their feet. Two hours back from London and they've turned up at the condo. A crisp knock at the door has Liam looking out of the peephole. He unlocks the lock and unchains the chain.

"Didn't expect to see you here," Liam says, opening the door wide. Cress runs over and hugs me. I must look really sad because she's not a hugger.

"How was the Grand Canal?" I ask.

"Grand. And a Canal." She looks around the room. "I expected to see your computer and papers everywhere. Are you taking a work break?"

"Not exactly."

Max has been talking to Liam, who gives a little wave and walks out to stand in the hallway

"We thought you might want to stay with us for a while."

Huh? "Why would I? This is a perfectly nice place."

"But lonely. Come stay with us and we'll coddle you."

"Your new home awaits," Max tells me with a sweeping bow.

"Where's your top hat? And your cape?"

"In the trunk with his monocle, cane, and white silk scarf," Cress declares while the crinkles around Max's eyes show his amusement.

In the blink of an eye, they've carried me off. Liam and Case wait patiently next to their cars. Then we make a very small caravan to Max's house. Liam scores street parking and Case pulls around to the underground garage, an unusual feature that was one of the main selling points when Max moved to Chicago.

Jarvis sits in the living room, the cats cuddled up with him on the huge cream couch. In most rooms, it would take up at least half the floor space, but this room makes it seem just the right size. Perfect for Max's six-foot-five frame and deep enough for two.

"Thanks for bringing them back, Jarvis." Cress walks over to pet Dorothy and Thorfinn. They seem uninterested in her return. "You've stolen their hearts," she scolds.

"Hi, Micki." Jarvis gets up, the cats scrambling away from his big feet. I give him a little wave.

"I toyed with the idea of keeping them, but cats are heartless." Jarvis gives a big stretch, then sits back down. The cats, like yo-yos, immediately climb back into his lap. "They know their place in the hierarchy and it's far above us. I'm sure a judicious amount of groveling will convince them to grant you grace."

"You could just take them with you when you leave," Max teases.

"I'm not leaving without another crack at your wine cellar. Bring out a bottle of that $2000 red you kept locked up while you were away. It's not too much to ask." Jarvis readjusts his lounging position, showing he's in for the long haul.

"It's much too much to ask," Max says as he leaves for the basement, where he cellars his vintage wine collection under lock and key.

"By the way, Micki, you're looking for a new job, right?" Jarvis has a twinkle in his eye.

"How do you know that?"

"Hackers know everything." He languidly moves from the couch and whispers in my ear, "There may be an interesting nonprofit opening for a legal consultant coming up in the next few months. If you're interested, I can put a word in."

"What kind of consultant?"

"I can't give you any details. But showing interest won't hurt."

This sounds too good to be true. On the other hand, his sister is a recruiter for nonprofits, so he probably gets inside tips. I give a mental groan as I'm reminded of insider trading and Congressman Simon Greenberg. "Guess I'm willing to throw my hat blindly into the ring. Don't have anything to lose."

Cress walks in from the kitchen. "Did you say something about needing a job?"

"Yeah." Glumly, I look at my shoes, now covered with a stretched-out Thorfinn.

"We need the whole story in gory detail."

"What do we need?" Max puts his arms around Cress, pressing her back into his chest.

"We need to hear why Micki, instead of celebrating being the newest partner at one of the stuffiest law firms in the country, is looking for a new job."

"Not now. Maybe soon." I grab my bag and haul it up the stairs before either Max or Jarvis can help me.

My temporary bedroom, the Provence room, is even more sumptuous than staying at a posh hotel. When Cress moved in with Max, she looked at half-empty, undecorated rooms and made redecorating a priority. This room, all yellows and blues, has enormous windows that let in plenty of light from the garden. The furniture is French provincial, with a king-sized bed that has a duvet cover decorated with Van Gogh's *Starry Night*. A beautiful Aubusson carpet covers the hardwood flooring. Just like elite hotels, there's even a small refrigerator with bottled water and a basket of snacks, all without a card telling you how much each item costs.

They'd probably let me stay indefinitely, but I need a job and my own place. And JL. I need JL. I throw myself face down on the bed and have my little pity party.

JL

Yannick's sofa is old and too soft to be comfortable. In the end, I throw the cushions on the floor, wrap up like a mummy in the duvet, and try to ignore the cold rising from the uncarpeted tiles. His dog, Brioche, wakes me up with her slobbery tongue. She wants something but I don't know if it's a walk, breakfast, or just playtime. The sound of rain beating against the aluminum siding makes me reach for my phone.

> AIR CANADA: Your 8:30 flight to Chicago is delayed. It is now scheduled for 11 a.m.

> ME: Fuck you and fuck the rain. (Not sent)

Yannick sounds like a moose in the woods, loud snores rolling down from his second floor. When he bought this little house, he gutted the whole second story and turned three tiny bedrooms into one large room with a state-of-the-art self-care center, as he calls it—Jacuzzi, sauna, power shower—instead of a master bath. His basement is a professional-grade gym. This is definitely a bachelor pad.

I let Brioche out, and she's back in minutes, already soaking wet. The copper-colored standard poodle shakes herself off and now I am just as wet. I lock her into the kitchen and fetch towels. Once we are both merely damp, I make coffee in Yannick's fancy espresso machine. Two doppios later, I check my phone again.

AIR CANADA: Your flight is now scheduled for 1 p.m.

ME: Tabernak. Va te faire foutre (not sent)

Yannick walks in, stretching. His T-shirt rides up and he scratches his stomach. "Ah, café."

I start the machine to make him a cup.

"It's late, JL. Why didn't you wake me? We'll barely make it in time for your flight."

"Plenty of time," I say with an accompanying growl. Brioche must think I'm talking to her and she growls back.

"It's seven and your flight is at eight thirty."

"Air Canada wanted us to sleep in. My flight is at one."

"Calisse."

"I've told them that." I laugh, handing him the unsent text messages.

"Coward. Why didn't you send them?"

"And have my ticket revoked?" I hand him the cup and make a third double for myself. "What's for breakfast?"

"Now that we have time, I have eggs, croissants, potatoes, ham, back bacon, and sausage. Bread too, if you want toast."

"Let's just eat it all."

My mobile rings. Max. Forestalling the inevitable, I don't bother with hello. "Coming back today."

"When? I'll meet you at O'Hare."

"When Air Canada stops holding me hostage. The rain and wind are heavy enough that my flight has already been delayed twice. How's the weather there?"

Yannick slips a plate to me—fried eggs, toast with butter and jam, fried potatoes with ham, rounds of back bacon, and two fat sausages, well browned.

"Sunny here, but windy."

I spear a sausage and take a bite. "Not too bad then." With a mouth full of succulent meat, I must be hard to understand. Not that I care.

"You eating?"

"Yeah, so? It's early here."

He makes a humming sound. 'We're going out for dinner after we pick you up. Japanese. Cress has a yen for ramen and sushi."

One of Max's bad jokes. I laugh. Unlike Cress, I appreciate his sense of humor. I know Micki does too. A pang runs through me. "I really want to see Micki as soon as possible. Maybe you could just drop me off at the condo. It's more important than dinner." I put the bacon on top of the toast. Bacon and jam go well together, at least in my book.

If I can see her, I can get her to listen.

"She's staying with us."

"Why?" I scrape up the last of the egg with potatoes.

"We didn't want her to be alone." Max's voice is as arid as the Gobi Desert.

I choke as egg and potato go down the wrong way.

Yannick pounds me on the back.

"What's going on?" Max asks.

"EERRHH, cough, cough, EERRHH, hack, uhhhhgggg."

"JL, are you all right?"

"Hem, Ahem, Ahem, Hem." I swallow and the choking subsides. "Fine. Something went down the wrong way."

"Yannick give you the Heimlich?"

"Just pounded me on the back. He might have broken my ribs with the Heimlich. This way he just dislocated my spine."

"Can't afford to have you out of commission." He switches gears. "Tonight, we're going to Tanoshii in Andersonville."

Maybe Max is giving me a hint. "Isn't that one of Micki's favorite places?"

"You're right. I'd forgotten. Cress suggested it. Near where she used to live." He sounds totally unbelievable.

This screams setup, but I don't care. "Max, I thought you were a better liar."

He just laughs. "Let me know when you take off and I'll meet you at the gate."

"Using your influence for your own ends."

"I'm off. Cheers." And he's gone.

"Sounds like manipulation is on the up in Chicago." Yannick's on his back with Brioche resting on his belly. They've been wrestling. He pushes off the floor with one hand, showing off he's kept the agility he had as a gymnast. "Rain's stopped. Any more messages from Air Canada?"

I thumb the screen. "Nope. May as well get going. Sitting there is better than sitting here."

Neither of us mentions Maman. I finger my phone while I wait to board, but I don't call, and neither does she.

CHAPTER

TWENTY-TWO

It doesn't really matter whether we reflect the light through our authentic gifts or whether our authentic calling is to spread it. What matters is that tonight the world is dark, cold, and bleak. Your flame burns so brightly. Share your Love and warmth with others. Watch the Light return.—Sarah Ban Breathnach

Micki

MY IDEA of bliss is never to cook. But tonight, the corollary is to stay in with pizza, wine, and snuggly cats. That dream will never be fulfilled since Cress wants to go to Tanoshii for sushi and maybe some noodles. Max is, as always, ready to concede to her desire. But he has some work to do, so Dawson, a fairly new member of the team, will drive Cress, Jarvis, and me to the restaurant, where we will meet Max.

"I can just stay here and order out. You have a romantic meal with Max popping succulent morsels of raw fish into your mouth."

"Forget that. You love Sushi Mike's."

Sushi Mike is the owner of Tanoshii. His creations are fabulous, so tempting. But I don't want to give in too easily. "I don't have anyone to feed me fish," I whine.

Cress plays her tiny invisible violin. "We're all going."

She glances at Jarvis, who says, "I'll feed you fish, Micki."

"By the way, Max invited Elizabeth Talbot along so she can update Max on what's happening with the sabotage investigation."

Jarvis crosses his eyes. How does he do that? "Elizabeth and reports. Max really knows how to ruin a promising meal."

"Sabotage? At GSU?" JL never said a word.

"Cybersecurity issues." Jarvis is curt.

Cress enjoys his discomfiture. I wonder why. "Elizabeth's an old friend of Jarvis," she says with a grin. From both of their expressions, an old friend is stretching things. "She's a consultant, and Max asked Clay to hire her to help with some issues."

I see my opening and I squeeze myself through. "If it's a work meeting, maybe you and I should stay here."

Cress nibbles on her lower lip. "The whole point of this is *I* want to have sushi at Tanoshii. If anyone else wants to work, they can go back to the office after we eat."

A timely but unwelcome reminder that I am meeting with Rebecca tomorrow before the big announcement. I still haven't decided on my next step. The logical thing would be to stay while I look for a new job. Then Hayden's face leers at me and logic doesn't really come into it.

Cress struggles into her coat. "Dawson is waiting in his fiery chariot to waft us up to our old haunts."

I never ate at Mike's with Sam. His disdain could reach

from Howard Street down to Congress. "Just bait, darlin'. What's the point? A good fish fry is a million times better than small bits of raw fish wrapped in rice." Unpleasant experiences to dwell on.

We aren't going far enough north for me to see my old building. Haven't been back. The memories are too painful. The realtor handling the sale had it staged, and I haven't set foot inside since moving out in January. She contacted me when I got back to say the closing was going to be soon.

We've just settled into the back seat when my phone rings. Instead of pulling away from the curb, Dawson lets the car idle. "Unknown caller." I announce it as if my news is as important as a new World War. I won't answer, but most of these are really hang-ups.

After two rings, the phone goes dead. I've had five in the last couple of days. No one has been able to trace the calls. Jarvis says whoever it is uses a nested-chain multi-hop VPN that masks the IP addresses and routes the call through a bunch of different servers. I'm convinced it's Sam, but no one knows where he is or how he could have gotten this number.

"Spyware," Jarvis says.

"What?" I've missed most of this, but that word sends a chill right through me.

"We've been checking but if it's on your phone, whoever put it there is a master."

"Not likely then. Sam is not a master techie."

Jarvis scrunches his face, lips moving soundlessly. "When we get back, I'll root around a bit. I have contacts on the dark web who might know if he paid someone. He's had help hiding himself. We've been digging and not finding much about him."

Huffing to catch my breath, I push my icy-stiff fingers

around the case. *Wrong number. Wrong number. Just a wrong number.* If only my brain would believe the wishful thinking. But the primitive core sees a humungous pulsing red light while a voice like siren screams, "Danger! Danger! Danger!" My muscles bunch, adrenaline pushing me to run. "He can't afford it."

"True, at least not from his artist account. But I can't help wondering if he has access to other money."

Cress touches my hand. "Shit, you're freezing." She reaches into her pocket and pulls out a pair of tartan gloves. Prying the phone out of my death grip, she hands it to Jarvis, who immediately starts typing things on my keyboard. The screen turns black with white letters and numbers scrolling and scrolling.

While he's engrossed in trying to ensnare my stalker, Cress slips the gloves on my unresisting fingers. Her gesture and the warmth of the wool sprinkle fairy dust all over me.

Just as the adrenaline drops, Dawson screeches to a halt outside the restaurant. "Move in quick," he says.

Handing back my phone with a shake of his head, Jarvis asks, "Is there a threat?" Then he turns to look through the rear window, fingering a small bulge in his pocket. OMG, does the computer geek have a gun?

"I don't see anyone, but that doesn't mean no one's there. Get the ladies inside and I'll park the car." Dawson's order is uncompromising.

A black cloth banner with the name of the restaurant hangs over the sidewalk on Clark Street. We hustle under the narrow black awning and through the doorway into a tiny space where everything is brown maple. A car backfires. The sensation on my skin is like a hot dog splitting as it cooks. Cress stops so suddenly, she practically falls into an elderly man bent over a cane who has stepped off the curb. Jarvis grabs her upper arm to steady her. "Sorry," she says, a quaver distorting the word. Remembrances of the shooting at the Palmer House last December must be over-loading her nervous system.

The hostess approaches. "Everything all right?"

Jarvis gives her a reassuring nod. "We have a reserva-tion for Grant."

She goes back to the podium and looks at her list. "Yes, Grant. One of your party is already seated."

The restaurant has put several tables together. A woman sits in the farthest of the six chairs, three on either, a tablet in front of her, laptop open. She doesn't look up as we approach, deeply engrossed in her screens. Her straight chestnut hair reaches the middle of her back and hangs loose. I have no idea who she is but hazard a guess she's Elizabeth Talbot, the woman Jarvis doesn't want to see.

"Hi, Elizabeth," Cress calls out. A quickly raised head reveals an expressionless face, wide-spaced hazel eyes, and translucent skin. When she recognizes Cress, a smile trans-forms her.

"Cress Taylor? So nice to see you again. I hope you and Max had a wonderful trip."

"Parts of it," Cress responds dryly. "The terrorist attacks, not so much. But the rest was lovely."

"I heard. Sorry about the awards dinner."

"Water under the bridge, kind of. Anyway, I know Max was relieved you agreed to consult with GSU." She pulls out a chair. "But let's talk about something more interesting. What are you doing besides computer stuff?"

"I'm part of Chicago Bird Collision Monitors." She taps the laptop case. "That's what I'm doing now. And I read in my spare time."

"Have you found anything exciting recently?"

"Birds or books?"

"Either, although I'm probably more interested in the books."

Cress gives her a Cheshire cat grin. The way she does the slow fade is amazing and Elizabeth stares, mesmerized.

"Funny you should ask. I remember we talked about biographies of women who have done all sorts of research in computing. After that, I read *Queen of Nowhere*. That Caterina Cornaro was really something."

Hearts dart out from Cress' eyes. A definite bonding is beginning here. Meantime, Jarvis has been shifting from foot to foot.

Standing with his arms crossed like an unmovable object, Jarvis says, "Hello, Lilibet." For some reason, his greeting reddens her cheeks.

She glances up from under her lashes for a moment, then refocuses on the tabletop. "Hi, Jar. Didn't see you." He scowls at her brazen lie.

Then Max walks in, and the world stops.

Whatever I expected this evening, seeing JL Martin wasn't part of it. I can't take my eyes off his scruffy face, glassy eyes with bags like backpacks, and an unhealthy pallor. His shoulders sag and the corners of his lips are downturned. But for all that, he is drinking me in, his eyes with a glint of hope like a shiny coin glittering in a sea of rubble.

Tanoshii is a BYOB and Max hands a carrier full of bottles and cans to the hostess before he looks around, puzzled. "Why are you all standing here?"

We scramble for seats. It's like musical chairs with me trying to avoid JL and Jarvis trying to avoid Elizabeth. In the end, Jarvis sits across from Elizabeth, while Max grabs the center, across from Cress. JL and I are across on the other end. Girls one side, men the other. A kick in my ankle lets me know JL wants my attention.

Jarvis and Elizabeth sit tight-lipped. She's closed her computer and put it in a caramel-colored brief bag. Arms tightly pulled into their sides, they concentrate on the menu, but I see the covert glances when each thinks the other isn't looking. A server comes by and stops next to Max. "You brought drinks?"

"Yes, Mike gave me a list of the sakes and he'd put something together for us."

"Sure. Do you want an explanation in advance or just as each selection comes out?"

"We'll just take it as it comes with the explanations at the time."

JL pushes his chair back, moves around to Cress and whispers in her ear. She smiles and I see Max scowl. Then JL helps her out of her seat, and she sits down across from me. "Easier for conversation," she says. "I want to know all about Vancouver."

JL, in the meantime, has moved his new chair so the top rails are touching. Then he slides to the edge and casually lays his arm across the top. His sleeve brushes against my neck, shivers run up to the base of my skull, and I feel hairs rise at my nape. An involuntary shiver makes me flinch, not in rejection, more like overstimulation. My nerve endings tingle as he blows across my ear, and I clamp my lips together to suppress a deep moan I can feel in my chest.

Fuck. This man. I can feel electricity run through me and I'm almost willing to forgive him anything. A vision of his mother glaring and Angélique gloating displaces the room. Then my brain short circuits as our fingers entwine.

"We need to talk, ma chouette. Après le diner?"

I want to shake my head no or just run out of the

restaurant, but I don't. Because I want to stay more than I want to go.

❧

JL

Paper-thin slices of sashimi glisten on a bed of white vinegary rice—salmon, fatty tuna, yellowfin, and eel show off their varying charms. I pick up a piece of glistening salmon with my chopsticks and hold it to Micki's mouth, feeling the pull as she snatches it. Her eyes are hazy with enjoyment as she savors the morsel coated with wasabi, a piece of ginger perched on top.

"I see you found someone to feed you fish," Cress says. Then she grabs a piece of eel Max holds out to her.

"She has." I gaze at Micki's mouth.

Ma blonde swallows. "Merci, mon loup." I start at the name.

If she notices, there's no sign of it. "Thought you wanted to know more about Vancouver, Cress?"

"Too busy enjoying this fabulous spread." She beams like Glinda, the good witch, as she focuses on my hand caressing Micki anywhere that isn't totally indecent. "And I thought you called JL 'Beau.'

"Doesn't work so well. He's more wolflike than anything."

J'adore. With a wolfish grin, I prepare another slice. In the meantime, she has forgiven me, and holds a ruby red morsel of fatty tuna between her chopsticks and, when I open my mouth, slips it onto my tongue. A little groan rumbles in my throat.

The rich taste of the toro lingers, tender flesh melting like snowflakes as it slides down. The contrast between the vinegary sushi rice grains and the silken texture of the tuna is almost a religious experience.

I lean into her and touch my tongue to her parted lips, tasting the strawberry flavor of the lip gloss that coats the bright red lipstick beneath over the vinegar. My shoulders stiffen and my arms feel heavy as I imagine carrying her out of the restaurant and whisking her off to bed.

Since I came with Max, we can't ride into the sunset on my bike. Instead, swallowing my frustration, I spear a piece of yellowtail and feed it to her. "Love you," I mouth as she accepts my offering.

As dinner goes on, our intimacy dissolves. Hard to be in a party of six and carry on as if we are in private.

"Damn it, Jar." Elizabeth rises slightly and reaches across the table, trying to slap my colleague. "You are the biggest asshole I've ever known. Crawl back into the tree stump you sprouted from."

"You're comparing me to fungi?"

With a snort, she says, "You're not evolved enough for fungi; you're just slimy mold. I should have known you wouldn't have changed. I'm sorry I ever agreed to Clay Brandon's offer."

What the hell happened while I was wooing Micki? Max, frowning at his second-in-command, drums the fingers of his left hand on the table. "Jarvis, you need to concentrate on reconstructing the update and let Elizabeth do what she's hired for—working on the malware issue. You know better than most people this is a team effort, not a solo ascent."

"Fine," Jarvis says, the scowl accompanying the syllable belying the bland agreement. "But I don't know why we need to share an office. There must be some little cubicle she can perch in like the bird of prey she is." He snickers at his obvious reference to her bird rescue work.

Max throws him a thunderous glare. Cress whispers something in his ear and he slumps forward, resting his head in his hands.

"Crisse, Jarvis. Try to act your age. Sulky teens are not wanted here."

A pained expression crosses Jarvis' face. "Can't she work remotely? Like back in St. Louis?"

Max raises his head. "Of course not. Hell's bells, man, you should know better than that. Even with the best security, we can't be sure there wouldn't be a breach. And she needs to be available for consultation. Stop being a bloody berk. The faster we get this resolved, the sooner you and Elizabeth can go back to pretending you've never met."

Then, with a sigh, Max casts me a look. "And you, JL, do you think it's appropriate to practically have sex in full view? I was starting to think you were going to sweep everything off the table, lay her out, and eat sushi off her."

Micki leans into me, shaking with silent laughter. Calisse. I harden at the feel of her body quivering against me.

Cress squeezes Max's arm, shaking her head. and his face falls. Then she whispers something that lights him up like fireworks, fizzing and sparking.

Servers bring continuous courses of sushi enhanced by cup after tasting cup of sake. Mike's explanations enhance the experience. Each new offering comes in a fresh set of serving pieces made of elegant ceramic or porcelain.

We're a table piled with unfettered emotion fueled by alcohol, feelings running like flames from one to another. Anger and the bliss have combined, and we are all in a frenzied state.

"Let me know what I owe you." My fingers play over the GSU app on my phone as I gauge the arrival time of Sean, who's on call. "We're leaving now." Staying risks a meltdown, leaving may lead to paradise.

Max's earlier frustration has vanished and his eyes crinkle. "Sure, carry your damsel off to your love nest. But remember her curfew is midnight."

"What if I want to keep her out all night?" *What if I want to keep her forever?*

"If Micki wants that, she has a key. But she needs to let Cress know. I'm not the dad, staying up all night, waiting to let her in. But Cress will worry something has happened."

I give him a thumbs up and mouth how grateful I am for arranging this chance for amends. My phone tells me we are two minutes from liftoff.

TWENTY-THREE

We must develop and maintain the capacity to forgive. He who is devoid of the power to forgive is devoid of the power to love.—Martin Luther King, Jr.

Micki

I'M tipsy with sake and beyond sushi satiety. JL helps me into my coat, puts the strap of my bag over my head and, one broad hand on my back, guides me out onto Clark Street, pools of illumination from street lamps creating pockets of chiaroscuro. The sidewalk seems curiously empty, and few cars trail up and down the street.

With a professional air, JL scans the area, and sees something that makes him wave at the driver of an SUV. He moves into a protective stance while we wait for the driver to come to the curb. He looks inside at the driver, and I expect him to move away in alarm. My head is too fuzzy to understand their terse exchange.

Then, with a muttered "Sean," JL opens the back passenger door, helps me in, and buckles my seat belt, before getting in on the other side.

A shout from just outside a dark doorway has JL urging the driver to get going. I think I hear my name, but I can't be sure..

A shadow detaches itself, but we're away. I watch as the now-still dark figure pauses statute-like at the curb. I choke back a comment and decide silence is the better part of valor.

Then with a roar like a maddened bear, feet pound down the concrete, but whoever is out there can't get us. Not this time.

The brief rush from the possible danger makes my heart pound violently, then, suddenly feeling safe, I fight to keep my eyes open.

"Do you think it was Sam?" I murmur.

"Could just be a drunk panhandling. Or someone wanting wallets and phones."

I finger the key alarm I always have with me. Being a random target reminds me of city dangers and is both reassuring and disquieting.

Once we're on our way, he takes a lock of my hair and rubs it through his fingers. "Do you want to stay the night?"

I exhale. I'd love to just say yes, but caution dampens the desire. "After we talk. If I find I can forgive you, I'll stay."

"You gave me a new sobriquet. Isn't that forgiveness?"

"We'll see."

Driving to JL's high-rise condo is tame compared to the exhilaration of clinging to his waist, fingers through his belt loops, on the back of the bike. Whether we can have a coherent conversation is questionable, and I wonder if he hopes physicality will replace explanation and repentance. Repressing a small burp, I nestle into his shoulder, knowing this tacit acceptance is unwise but irresistible.

Another black SUV idles on the circle drive at the entrance to the building. JL gets a text and sends a reply. "All clear," he says. Our driver comes around and hands me out to a waiting JL, who has scrambled from the back seat and run around to take my arm. Two shadowy figures exit the other SUV and follow us inside. Once we are at the desk, they nod to JL and leave. I hear the slam of their doors before they drive away.

A GSU security guy swivels on a high stool. His back-and-forth motion makes me feel like Cress' description of the Drake Shake on the way to Antarctica.

"Evening, JL." *Roll.* "All quiet here." *Shake.* "We had your place swept about thirty minutes ago." *Twist.* "No visitors either." *Urgggh.*

"Perfect, John. Can you open the doors, please?"

Before I know it, JL sweeps me up and carries me to the now-gaping doors of the all-glass elevator that only serves the top floor. Too surprised to struggle, I stay still in his arms as the car swoops upward like a hawk loosed to hunt its prey.

When the doors open, JL puts me down, but the pseudo-seasickness followed by the rush skyward has destroyed my balance and I can't manage to stand. There is a door at each end of the wide, short lobby. Clay Brandon lives in one of the two suites and JL in the other. Lifting me back into his arms, he strides down the hallway to the door labeled JL Martin, stares at a little screen, and the door swings open.

"Biometrics," he says, as if I asked. "The sensor recognizes my eye pattern. Very clever, secure, and hands-free." Then I get a first look at the cloud palace JL calls home. After getting to know Max, who barely furnished his place on Gold Coast and then, when he won Cress, left the decorating details to her, I thought JL would have very minimalist guy furniture. But there is no giant black leather sectional, or even a gigantic TV screen. The living room walls are mostly floor-to-ceiling windows, with great views over the lake and Millennium Park. No blinds or drapes, just the drama of the water and sky.

His couch is a four-piece sectional in olive leather with a chaise on either end. Matching ottomans rest nearby. Gray double drawer end tables, with a shelf underneath, keep things easily to hand and are matched by a long cock-tail table. Four armchairs are scattered around the room, upholstered in cream with an olive print. Along an interior wall is a shelving unit with spaces for books and drawers for storage.

"No TV?" I ask.

"It comes up from the top of the storage unit if I want to watch something."

He gently lowers me onto a chair and then manages to remove my jacket. "Do you want to stay here, or move to the sofa?"

"Here's fine." The slur in my speech is disturbing. How much sake did we have?

"I need to explain what happened in Vancouver."

"Mmmm. Okay." My eyes close.

"Micki, are you listening?"

"Uh huh. Listening."

JL gives an explosive huff. All I hear are footsteps but I'm not sure where they're coming from or going to. The sound could be from anywhere.

The scent of coffee permeates the fog. Something warm presses against my hands.

"Come on, Micki. Take a sip."

Panic. Where am I? Who's here? I don't feel safe, and I rear back against the chair, my hands flail, and as I hit out, a voice yells, "Tabernak." The sound of crockery shattering cements the utter chaos of the moment.

My eyes pop open. JL, coffee all over his nice white shirt, stares at the floor. A flowered mug is in pieces. Big pieces, little pieces, shards, chips. He bends and begins picking up the larger pieces. Moving toward the kitchen, he says, "Stay where you are until I get the rest of this cleaned up. I don't want you cutting your feet."

Why would I cut my feet? I notice my feet are bare. What happened to my shoes?

Broom in one hand and a glass in the other, he hands me water, then vigorously cleans up the remnants of the coffee mug. Now sober, I watch his shoulder muscles ripple while he works. Clinking signals he has dumped all the tiny bits into the trash. I sip my water and he makes more coffee.

Then I jump in with both feet. "I'm meeting with Rebecca early tomorrow morning."

"Good news, I hope."

"Not good and not news. When I got back, I was told Hayden Forbes-Cartwright will be the new partner."

JL's mouth drops open in surprise. "I was sure they would choose you. What happened? Was it the trip?"

"They rigged it. Two partners convinced most of the rest to choose Hayden. Doesn't help that one partner is Hayden's uncle."

JL sits on the arm of my chair and strokes the back of

my neck. "Why do you need a meeting if you already know?"

"To discuss if I should stay."

"And Rebecca can help with this?"

I nod. "We'll discuss the pros and cons of my staying until I find another job, hanging on until there's another partnership opportunity, or just leaving."

"The last sounds the least workable, financially at least."

"It might be the most desirable." I rub my palms against my eyes. So tired. "Hayden will make my life miserable, and I'm not sure hanging on is worth it."

"But you'll have no income, no insurance."

"I can get an insurance extension for a number of months. And I have some savings. If I'm lucky, I'll find another job within the next six months or so. Or I could threaten to sue for unfair hiring practices. They might settle, even though I doubt I could win a case."

JL

I'm stunned by Micki's flat statement, but we have more to deal with than her job.

We sip coffee and stare at each other. Yawning hugely, she says, "I think sake is not the drink for me."

"We all had a lot to drink. That much of anything alcoholic would have the same effect." I prop my left ankle on my right knee and rub the still-warm cup against exposed skin. The combination of the smooth ceramic and the warmth from the retained heat help me focus. "Micki, let me explain to you what happened in Vancouver."

Her head bobs in agreement and one knot in my chest disappears.

"First, I love you. I am committed to a life together. You are my person, and I hope I am yours as well."

She's utterly still, lips slightly parted, eyes huge.

"I was stupid that night. When Maman asked me to drive Angélique home, my intention was to drop her off, watch to make sure she got into the house safely with the boys, and return home. She asked me to walk them in. The neighborhood isn't great, so I agreed. Once she put them to bed, she started crying, so I stayed for a drink." A pause, and a chance to figure out what to say next.

"And?" Her eyes are eyes are fiery with suspicion.

"And nothing. I sat with her until she seemed to be calm, then I left."

"She arrived while your mother and I were drinking coffee. Told me you were engaged. Showed me a ring. A family ring, platinum with a square-cut diamond. Your mother was over the moon. Then Yannick arrived with my phone and the solution seemed so simple." She gulps, while tears run down her cheeks and drip off her chin. "Your mother couldn't wait for me to pack my bag."

"All lies. When Angélique was helping Maman..." My neck heats when I think of my mother's actions. Not dishonest, perhaps, but certainly callous.

"Angélique went through Maman's dresser and found the ring. Then she hatched her scheme." I cough and drink more coffee. "Unfortunately, despite Angélique's fraudulent claim, Maman still thinks I should marry her. She's become too attached to the boys."

Micki rubs at her wet eyes, her runny nose. A strangled sound rises and falls. It's a cry of pain and betrayal. "I can't marry you, JL. If your mother won't accept me—"

I press my lips against hers. She's not allowed to say these things. To think these things. She is the most important person. "My mother's acceptance isn't important. Please forgive me," I whisper. "If I have to choose, I choose you."

The telephone rings.

I let it go to voice mail.

It starts again.

Voice mail.

The third time, Micki grabs my phone. I shake my head no, but she answers anyway. I expect to hear Maman haranguing, even though Micki hasn't put it on speaker. She listens intently, then tries to hand me the device. When I refuse to take it, she looks around, then mimes writing. I open the shallow drawer in the coffee table for a piece of paper and a pencil. The pencil point breaks, and she silently begs for another writing instrument. Frowning, I hand her a pen.

"Go ahead," she says, then scrawls what might be a name, whether a person or a place I can't tell.

"Yes, I understand," she says after writing what looks like a series of numbers. "Let me read this back."

I hum to block out her voice. There's a pause and we are both still and silent.

"Yes. I will let him know." And she ends the call, leans toward me, elbows resting on her knees. "JL, you have to go back to Vancouver."

What the fuck? "I just got home. Why should I go back? Maman and I are not speaking, and until she apologizes, there will be no speaking. I've just told you that you're it for me."

Her eyes look hazy with unshed tears. "You're it for me too. But you have to do this. Your mom..."

My chest fills with flames as I think of Maman and what she did to me, to us, so I wave off her words. "Non. Pas interessant. Je resterai toujours ici."

Micki slaps at my arm. "Listen to me. You have to go. Louisette is in the hospital. Maybe a heart attack."

I close my ears to her pleas. "Probably another fake, trying to get me back to Vancouver."

"I talked to the doctor at the hospital."

"Could be she got one of her friends to call and impersonate a doctor."

Opening her hand, Micki proffers a damp ball of paper nestling on her palm. When I smooth it out, there are the numbers and an unfamiliar name, slightly blurred from her tears.

"Call, please. It's the hospital in Vancouver." Then she curls up in the chair like a wounded animal.

Fumbling my phone case open, I use one finger to hit each number. The rings seem interminable, reinforcing the idea Maman is just fine. My finger hovers over the end button but just as I go to swipe, a voice answers. " Vancouver General Hospital. How may I direct your call?"

Connected to the doctor who just spoke with Micki, he quickly fills me in. Maman has congestive heart failure, but not a heart attack. The doctor put her on diuretics, and they are keeping her under observation for a few days. It's well after midnight. I tell him I won't be able to leave until later today. He assures me that will be acceptable. She is stable and they won't send her home before I arrive. She will need someone with her for a while after she's released.

I cast a questioning look in Micki's direction. "I'll have to stay there for a while and try to convince her to move to Chicago."

Once she gets over her surprise, Micki accepts what I

now see as inevitable. "You should get in touch with immigration, so you understand the options before you propose she move."

"Do you think it will be difficult?" I know Micki doesn't specialize in immigration law, but she may have some idea.

"You're an American citizen, so she can probably come as an immediate family member. At her age, it won't matter that she can't work, and I don't think there will be any financial requirements. I have a friend who does health law who can look into the insurance implications." She leans back with a sigh. "She already hates me. How will she feel when you uproot her?"

"That's on me, not you."

"People are not always rational, and she could feel I'm pushing you to bring her here."

"Do you want to go with me? I hate to be away for some indefinite amount of time. My heart is already feeling the loss."

"No. I think you need to be there without me."

Each word is a little laceration. She's my shelter and I want to pack her in my bag. My guys will protect her, but I feel anxious Sam will find some way to get to her. Resolutely, I put aside visions of Vengeful Sam. Sam the Sniper. Sam the Bomber. Sam the Stealthy Stalker lying in wait. Instead, I retrieve my phone and call the GSU twenty-four-hour logistics line.

CHAPTER

TWENTY-FOUR

*Always deal with the honesty, the truth of what something is,
and then you've got all kinds of choices.—Michael J. Fox*

JL

I LEAVE Chicago in the sunshine at 7:30 a.m., after dropping Micki off at her condo, where Case waits to take over. My heart is a slow leak of pain.

Vancouver is damp. No rain right now, but puddles are everywhere. Yannick meets me at arrivals, and we weave through early morning traffic to the hospital.

"Have you spoken to the doctor?"

"A few hours ago. I expect an update when we arrive."

Yannick fidgets with the radio, switching from station to station.

Tired, irritable, and missing Micki, I snap, "Just pick something."

He frowns and settles on an oldies station playing "Lucy in the Sky with Diamonds." "Did she have a heart attack?"

"No, congestive heart failure. She'll be on pills forever, but at least she doesn't need surgery. Now anyway."

Pointedly, I stare out the side window of Yannick's black RAV4, crooning to "It Never Rains in Southern California." I'm done talking about Maman's health. I'll need to follow up on Uncle François' situation, too. After I speak with the doctor, I'll call the rehab center. And maybe social services to see whether they will get him back to Montreal. Then I'll tackle the big job—convincing Maman to move to Chicago.

The hospital is a ten-story modern brick and metal building with clean lines and immense windows fronting the street. Yannick parks in the garage across the way and we make our way to reception. Inside its institutional, just like any other hospital. The floors are tile, the counters wood and plexiglass.

Pinned to the bright yellow sweater of the woman at a window marked information is an identification plaque that says "Volunteer." Her bobbed white hair has rainbow highlights.

I'd hold out my hand, but it would barely fit through the aperture, so I tap instead. She's so absorbed in typing that she starts at the sound, a small pile of files fluttering to the floor. "Excuse me." Then she bends down to retrieve the papers. Carefully placing them next to the keyboard, she turns to me. "May I help you?"

"My name is Jean-Louis Martin, and my mother is a patient."

"What is her name?"

"Louisette Martin. She's probably in the cardiac unit."

With a few taps, the woman brings up Maman's record. "She is in the east wing, room 881." She writes something on a card and hands it to me. The room number, in case I forget. Then she detaches two badges that proclaim us visitors from a cardboard sheet. Yannick and I clip them on our shirt pockets.

"Don't take these off until you return them to this box at the end of your visit." Pointing to the side, she says, "Take that bank of elevators. On the eighth floor, turn to the right and stop at the nurses' station to sign in."

By this time, there is a short line of tapping feet behind us, so we slip off toward the lifts. Slow lifts. Dilatory, as if passengers are holding the doors open so they can finish their conversations as they leave. Most of the little lights that show the floors are off. Only one of the eight cars seems to operate. Finally, after it has gone all the way to the top and down again, we can ride up. Several other people turn up.

"Hold the door, please," a man calls out. Yannick mutters as he pushes the button. Every time he removes his finger, someone else runs up. By the time the doors close, we are ten people and stop at every floor. Could have walked up faster.

The corridor is long and my hands clench and unclench at the prospect of the doctor's report and trying to talk to Maman. I don't know what state she is in, and I'll have to be careful not to lose my temper and upset her.

The nurses' station is a brightly lit island with nurses, doctors, aides, and technicians milling around the counter. Phones shrill, beeps sound from electronic equipment, and there is constant chatter over the commentary that is a constant undertone from the PA system.

Room 881 is the last one on the corridor and is the only private room at this end. Maman sits up listening to the doctor. I regard her for a long moment, then lean against the jamb, not wanting to interrupt, but I must make some sound because both the doctor and Maman turn to the doorway.

"JL, mon chou. I wasn't sure you would come." Her eyes are heavy, lids half closed, voice gravelly with relief.

Not knowing what to say, I just walk over and kiss her on the cheek. The doctor holds out his hand. " Nice to meet you, Mr. Martin. I'm Dr. Fitzroy. Glad you could get a plane out so quickly." We shake.

"Sit down." Maman's voice wibble-wobbles. "I can't see you without straining my neck." Even in her frail state, she attempts the authority of a lion. "Dr. Fitz was just explaining what happens when I'm released."

I settle in a blue vinyl chair and Yannick is able to get into the room. No more chairs, so he leans against the door-jamb. "Bonjour, Tante Louisette." He flutters fingers in a little wave. "You look lovely."

Maman beams, then leans back, face white, lines bracketing her mouth. "You are such a charming liar, mon cher. I look just revived from the grave."

Fitzroy breaks in smoothly, "Madame Martin. Perhaps you may go home tomorrow now that your son is here to take care of you. I'll check you out in the morning, and if all is well, the nurse will give you printed instructions, prescriptions, and a schedule for rehab. Your son can then bring you back in a week for further evaluation."

"Thank you." We strain to hear Maman's whisper. " I think I'll have a little nap." A nurse comes in to help her lie down, taking her blood pressure after slipping an oxygen monitor on her finger.

"I'll walk you out, Doctor." I give a little wave to Maman, but she doesn't see.

When we reach the lounge, he turns to me. "Did you have some questions?"

"How feasible would it be to move her closer to me?"

"You're in Chicago?"

I bob my head. "I'm looking into the immigration process. But will her health permit a move?"

"Yes, but not for at least a month."

A month. That's twenty-nine days too long. "Can't she travel sooner?"

"That's not advisable." He frowns, trying to head off any insistence on my part.

"I can't stay here for a month," I protest.

"Does she have other relatives who could help out?"

"No."

"She could move into a nursing home, where she'd get good cardiac care." He pulls out a pad of Post-it notes from his shirt pocket, makes a note, and pulls the top one off, affixing it to the sheet on the clipboard he's holding.

That would be a possibility. Then I could get her house on the market and make arrangements for transportation.

"Once she agrees, try to set up a health team before she arrives. And you will need to understand the insurance there for visitors since she will probably have to come as a tourist, then apply to stay. Not that I am an expert on the subject."

"I'm consulting some specialist lawyers about how all that would work. I might be able to add her to my insurance as a dependent. And arrange some home health care once she arrives."

"Does your mother want to move to the U.S.? Are you proposing she live with you?"

I lift a shoulder. "She wants me to move back here, but my business is there. I mentioned it once, and she was reluctant. I'd like to broach it soon, but without causing a setback."

"Bring it up but be prepared in case she reacts badly. You might have to back off and let her get used to the possibility."

"Could she get upset enough to have a heart attack?"

Fitzroy gives a head shake. "I don't think so. Just come at it as a suggestion and be prepared for her to take time to get used to the possibility." He puts a hand on my shoulder. "She knows she can't live alone, so she may be more receptive than you think. Good luck. I'll see you tomorrow when she's discharged."

CHAPTER

TWENTY-FIVE

Freedom is the oxygen of the soul.—Moshe Dayan

Micki

WHO KNOWS how long JL will be in Vancouver. Time stretches out like taffy. Restlessness makes me want to be somewhere else. My conversation with Rebecca led me to resign. I informed Fred just before the announcement of Hayden's promotion so he wouldn't tell everyone I was staying on as senior associate, and he offered me a generous severance package if I agreed not to sue for unfair hiring practices. Salary and insurance benefits were the main things.

After a lot of thought, I declined. If I took the offer, I couldn't pursue any legal action. Then I spent time with the firm's HR director, filling out paperwork and applying for

COBRA before clearing out the few personal things in my office.

Because I refused to initial the non-compete clause, Rebecca and Fred descended on my almost vacant office at the same time. He harangued me while Rebecca tried to make him shut up. In the end, she got him to agree to forego the clause.

I'm back at Max and Cress' house. They convinced me not to stay alone. But right now, on day three, at 5:30 a.m., the Provençal Room is too familiar. The luxurious mansion is too comfortable. I want to go somewhere. By myself. No friends, no bodyguards. Just solitude away from the house that seems more like a prison. I slip on jeans and a long-sleeved T-shirt, socks, and walking shoes.

Deep carpeting in the hallway means my footsteps are noiseless. Max and Cress' bedroom door is closed. I stand next to it, listening. Silence. Probably just sleep noises inside. Too soft to hear through the thick oak. With careful movements, I walk down the stairs, keeping to the runner. One step creaks and I stop, wait, but no one moves.

When I look out, a GSU car is at the curb, but I don't see anyone inside. I slip on my jacket, grab my cross-body shoulder bag, make sure keys are inside, and slip out the front door. No movement from the car. I walk over and see Case sound asleep on the back seat. Then I walk to the corner and summon an Uber to take me to Lou Mitchell's. Breakfast alone in a crowd seems just the ticket.

The Uber driver is friendly and talkative. Gray hair peeks out from under a Cubs cap. "You from around here?" he asks.

"Yes, But I grew up in Evanston."

"Me too. Humboldt Park."

Just an Uber ride, but a feeling of normality creeps over

me. A regular car, with a regular guy driving it. I settle back in the late-model Toyota Corolla and watch the downtown streets whiz past. The sense of freedom gives me goosebumps of joy.

He pulls up on Jackson and I check the sidewalk, just to be on the safe side. A small knot of teens cluster around the Dunkin' Donuts a few doors down, smoking. My driver looks at them. "You want me to walk you in?"

"Thanks, but I think I'll be okay. It's only a few steps."

"You take care of yourself. And try a waffle. That's what I have when I get the chance to eat here. They're A number one. The homemade marmalade is superb, too."

The donut group ignores me as I walk purposefully under the historic sign, reminding diners they do all the baking in-house. At six thirty, the place is already jumping. The smell of freshly baked donuts and frying bacon, accompanied by the chatter of happy diners, makes me feel at home. A short line ensures my wait is brief. I decline a chance to sit at the counter, and I'm led to one of the few open tables, clutching a small box of Milk Duds and a donut hole. Milk Duds, only doled out to women and children, is a tradition started by Lou himself, a friend of the candy maker. For the record, he said it was for the Greek tradition of greeting guests with something sweet. His family insisted he just liked the ladies. The donut holes started later, but never replaced the candy.

While I savor the seductive coffee aroma that wafts from my first cup of their special blend coffee with pure cream, I take my time over the menu. The history is amazing. They opened in 1923 before Route 66, which started practically on the spot in 1926. It's known as the first stop on the Mother Road and has been listed on the National Register of Historic Sites since 2006. I only wish JL was here with me, so I take a picture and send him a text. With the two-hour time difference, I'll be safely back with Max and Cress before he reads it.

> ME: At Lou Mitchell's diner. Not sure why we've never had breakfast here. It's one of my favorites.

> ME: The menu says: Enough fresh eggs have been cracked, made into omelets, cooked in skillets, and sold for breakfast at Lou Mitchell's to go side by side more than a few times around the world.

> ME:We've poured enough cups of our signature coffee to fill the Chicago River and our delicious pancakes could fill Wrigley Field. And to think, it all started with one man's food dream in Illinois.

> ME: YUM!!!!

I eat my donut hole, savoring each of the three bites I take for the tiny confection. Powdered sugar dots my T-shirt and brushing at it smears the sugar everywhere. I look around but I don't see Sam in his designer overalls.

Eyes tight shut, I pretend to be invisible. Can't see you so you can't see me. When I open them into surveillance slits, a small fruit bowl with a prune and an orange segment has appeared above my knife and spoon.

After much debate, I order a mushroom special hobo skillet, which is an omelette with the potatoes mixed in. I ask them to add spinach to the eggs and bring a side of bacon. When I'm finished, the waitress brings the bill. "Get you anything else?" she asks.

"More coffee, and ..." My pause is brief. She has her pencil at the ready. "A waffle, and, I know chocolate chips are for the pancakes, but could I have them and whipped cream with it?"

When the plate-sized Belgian specialty appears, it is gooey with chips. Moving the whipped cream to the side, I slather on marmalade and then push the cream back to cover everything. I clean my plate. I'm celebrating, dammit.

By the time I work my way through the enormous breakfast, groaning from greed, the early morning regulars are gone.

I waddle down to the CTA bus terminal on the corner to catch the 151. So many footsteps behind me as other commuters rush to cross the street to Union Station or to catch other buses at the terminal, so I just keep on my straight path.

A faint impression out of the corner of my eye makes me turn around once to see if Sam is chasing me, but shadows distort, and I don't see him on the crowded sidewalk. I keep on walking and gratefully board the bus, even though it won't leave for another ten minutes.

A few people lean in and ask the driver if the bus stops at one place or another, but there is only one other passenger when we take off. By the time we approach Water Tower Place, riders crowd in, jamming the aisle. I've paid no attention to who might have boarded and feel uncomfortable. My plan was to go straight to Max's house, but I enjoy my escape too much.

I get off at Chestnut and walk over to Fourth Presbyterian Church to sit in the cloister. The short walk helps relieve the bloat from my overindulgence at breakfast. The outdoor space is inviting, even in chilly weather, and I check out all the early flowers. Then I sit on a bench and enjoy the April sunshine after a couple of rainy days.

Text messages beep and my phone rings. Did JL get my text? He has, and he's pissed.

> JL: What the fuck? Why are you out alone?

> ME: Felt cooped up.

> JL: Too bad. Answer your phone.

The phone had stopped but now it's ringing again. GSU is the caller.

"Hello?" I sound more hesitant than I'd like.

"This is Case. Where are you?"

"Fourth Pres on Michigan Avenue. Sitting in the cloister."

All I hear is breathing. Could this be Sam fooling me into divulging my location?

"I'll be there in five minutes. Stand at the corner of Delaware and Michigan and look for the black SUV." He hangs up.

When I get back to Max's house, he's pacing outside. He shouts, waving his arms. "Where the hell were you?" When I get close enough, he grabs my hand and hustles me inside, calling out to Case, "Call JL and let him know his wandering client is safe." He mutters to himself, "You'll be lucky to have a job after this."

Cress is in the living room, mouth pinched, wringing her hands.

"What the bloody hell were you thinking?" Max's face is hard.

Maybe I acted like a rebellious teenager instead of a forty-six-year-old professional woman, but I don't care. I'm not going to be intimidated. "I'm a grown woman and I needed to get some time alone, not in this house. I feel like I'm in prison."

"You snuck out." His snarl chills me, bringing home the realization of how dangerous Max really is. "Anything could have happened to you."

My natural resistance kicks in. "But it didn't." I turn to go up to my room. Over my shoulder I shout back at his scowling face. "I can move out if you want."

"Don't say that, Micki." When I swivel toward Cress, her face has crumpled. "We're just worried. No one knows where Sam is. He could have attacked you out there."

"How did you travel?" Max, in a milder tone, asks.

"Uber to Lou's."

"And?" Max gives me a gimlet glare.

"Uh, I took the 151, but just to the church."

Cress' jaw drops. Max's face reddens. "Excuse me, did you say you took the bus?"

"Yes. It was empty when I got on." I set my shoulders and loosely make fists.

"Did you see anyone familiar get on?"

My head swings back and forth in negation. "But I wasn't paying much attention, and the bus got crowded.

I thought he was furious before, but now Max's anger boils over. "I can't believe you were so negligent. Careless. Stupid."

"Max, stop." Cress' wail gets his attention.

He takes off his glasses and cleans them with a microfiber cloth. That action allows him to get himself under control. "Did anyone get off and follow you?"

"At Water Tower Place? Lots of people, but no one followed me as far as I could tell. No one came into the cloister," I tell him.

"No protection. You could be dead right now." Max

underlines the danger. The quiet menace is scarier than the explosiveness that came before.

"Did you say Case could get fired over this?"

"Up to JL."

"Not his fault. I took advantage."

"That's selfishness on your part. He fell asleep. That is his fault." Max's tone is uncompromising.

"Okay, okay, I get it."

Max glowers, unconvinced by my lukewarm acknowledgement. But the scariness has drained away.

Cress puts an arm around me. "Come sit down and tell us about your adventure."

I tell them how I escaped, the friendly Uber driver, breakfast, including the awesome dessert waffle, and hanging out in the cloister."

When I finish, Max still sounds upset. "You thought that was worth risking your life?"

I flush like a chastised ten-year-old.

"We need to go to Lou's," Cress says, trying to calm things down. "The breakfast is to die for."

"And you could have," Max says to me, unforgiving.

Like a little kid, I tell him, "But I didn't. Here I am, full to bursting, and very much alive." *Nah, nah, nah, nah, nah, nah* sings in my head, but I decide not to add insult to injury.

TWENTY-SIX

Isn't it nice to think that tomorrow is a new day with no mistakes in it yet?—L.M. Montgomery

Micki

My phone sings, but the generic ringtone tells me it's not JL. My heart hurts as I think of him in Vancouver, uncertain about his mother's condition. While I'm not fond of Louisette, I want her to recover.

When I look at the screen, I see Unknown Caller. Sam? I don't think he has this number, the fourth I've had in the last few weeks. Probably a sales call of some sort. While I debate, the sound stops. Whoever called leaves a voice message. One that surprises the hell out of me.

"This message is for Michelle Press. I'm Kath Brandon, Clay Brandon's wife. Jarvis Howard tells me you are looking for a legal job with a nonprofit. JL raves about how wonderful you are. And you're interested in social justice issues."

She clears her throat. My curiosity sharpens as her message goes on. "GSU has been setting up a nonprofit foundation with that mission, and I'd like to meet with you about the possibility of bringing you on as the head of our legal team."

Practically dropping the phone in my excitement, I press callback.

"Hi," a cheerful voice greets me. "Is this Michelle Press?"

"Yes. I'm returning your call."

A sharp exclamation follows the sound of breath whooshing out. "I take it you're interested?" I wonder if strings are being pulled to find me a job. Is this some kind of pity interview? Or a favor for JL?

"I'd certainly like to discuss the possibility."

We meet at her rooftop garden in the building where JL's condo is. Sean pulls into the garage where there is a row of spaces for GSU cars. We take the elevator to the foyer and the desk guy opens the elevator.

"I'll hang here with my pal Jonesy."

After another rocket ride to the top floor, I see a door that leads to the roof. Kath Brandon is a tall, blond woman in her late thirties. When my footsteps clatter onto the slate floor, she gets up from her gardening bench, puts down a trowel, and strips off heavy gloves. I admire her trim, wiry figure and neat bob. My stick straight hair is no match for the shining sheet that curves perfectly at chin length. My fingers twitch with the desire to "fix" my hairdo, so I fold them in my lap to avoid temptation. Her jeans, GSU T-shirt, and short rubber boots are perfect for the activity and she's as elegant as if she dressed in designer clothing.

She touches my hand briefly instead of the usual air kisses that even almost strangers favor. " I'm so glad you could come. And the weather is decent enough for us to sit outside." She motions me to a café table with two wrought-iron chairs fitted with woven willow seats. "Your body-guard stayed down in the lobby?"

"Yes. I think he's friends with the concierge." The mention of Sean reminds me of Case and my escape to freedom. Max, JL, and Cress really ganged up on me. Case has his job, but JL reamed him out. Not surprised he wasn't my driver today.

"I'm so glad I am finally getting the chance to meet you, Ms. Press."

"You can call me Micki." I hope I'm not starting on too informal a note for this meeting. Jitters strike. Haven't interviewed in years, and not sure if this is an interview or more something else. My leg bounces but I try to hide the movement.

"I'm Kath." I can hear the warmth in her voice.

She notices I'm staring at her. "Something wrong? Is my blouse inside out?"

"Of course not. You look perfect. But Cress mentioned you're pregnant."

"It's early and I'm hardly showing yet." She grins and smooths her palms down her almost flat belly. "Pretty soon, though, I'll be as big as a house."

"I doubt that."

"Believe me, I have plenty of experience. Clay calls me Moby Dick."

I look around at raised beds and lots of unplanted space.

"Not much to see yet," she says cheerily. "The potted dwarf trees will come up from storage this weekend, and I'm preparing the beds for this year's plantings." She points to one bank. "That will be a cutting garden so we can have flowers in the house. The next grouping is an herb garden.

Our chef likes to use a lot of fresh herbs. He likes fresh vegetables too, but we just grow heirloom tomatoes and salad vegetables up here."

She takes me by the shoulders and turns me around. A large sandbox sits in a corner with a pail, miniature wheelbarrow, and implements nearby. "That's the children's garden. I give them mixed seeds to plant, and we see what comes up."

"Amazing. Mom only let me weed after I pulled up all of her zinnia seedlings." I make a sad face.

"I love to garden, and this is the best I can get in the city. We have a house up in Wisconsin too—with a much bigger garden—and a gardener to do the hard work. The kids and I spend a lot of time there in the summer with my parents. Clay comes up when he can."

A squeaking noise, like a rusty chain, comes from a dumb waiter and signals lunch. From its interior, Kath produces artichoke salad with shrimp and sip Prosecco. Crusty bread sits in a basket conveniently to hand, with a bottle of extra virgin olive oil. I pour some on my bread plate, dip a corner of the bread, and sigh. "This tastes so fresh."

"From the newly released bottling."

Knowing the new harvest won't be available in the U.S. for a few months, I wonder how she gets access. Kath must be able to read something in my face, when she smiles and says, "We have friends with an olive grove. They always ship some oil to us after they finish the first pressing."

Following the salad, we have chicken Milanese with risotto. When the empty plates have gone back down, a woman comes through the door with a tray holding a carafe of coffee, a pot of tea, biscotti, and a plate of truffles and jellied fruit candies.

Kath hands me a demitasse of espresso, then pours a reddish liquid from the tea pot into a bigger cup. "Rooiboos," she says, taking a sip. "Let's get down to business."

My brief bag is under my chair. I pull out a folder and hand to Kath. "My résumé."

Her slender fingers take it from my grip. "By the way, this is not a formal interview. I've done enough research to make up my mind. This is more of a getting to know each other meeting."

She glances at the sheet I handed her. "That covers school and work history. I should tell you, GSU did a thorough vetting and, besides JL, Cress Taylor and a few other people sang your praises. I had a conversation with Rebecca Manners. Even Fred Lanscombe had nice things to say about your ability. But as a great believer in making sure we have a great fit, I want to see whether we're compatible. Tell me why, after a career with a major, conservative law firm, you want to go into nonprofits. And why social issues are important to you." She puts down the folder and, head tilted slightly to one side, gives me the bright-eyed stare of a bird assessing the worm opportunities.

A lot to unpack, but a sip of Prosecco and a bite of a biscotto give me a few seconds to think about my response. I take a deep breath.

"That could be a twelve-part miniseries. But I'm guessing you don't want the eighteen-hour version."

"Can I watch it on PBS?"

"As soon as I can get Ken Burns on board."

She laughs. Not a polite tinkling laugh, but a full-on belly laugh. "Well, go on with the abridgment."

I give her a quick rundown on growing up with social activist parents. How volunteering at a woman's shelter in college opened my eyes to the injustices that so many women face and convinced me to go to law school. My own recent experience with being a "battered" and stalked woman. Cress' graduate school boyfriend, who victimized her. I don't mention her name since it's not my story to tell. Then I tell her about the competition for the partnership.

"Wow. I don't think twelve episodes would do it justice," Kath says as I run down like a windup toy.

Leaning forward intensely as I unspool my history, now I settle back into the chair and guzzle water. "What about you? What drew you to this mission?"

"My sister. A group of college boys murdered her in high school."

My breath catches, and I reflexively reach for her hand and give it a squeeze. She returns it with a shaky smile.

"Moving on." Her artificially brisk tone makes my heart ache. "I thought I'd tell you a bit about the foundation and then, if you're still interested, we can discuss the actual job."

"Great. From what you said on the phone, the mission of the foundation seems to fit very well with my own goals." I pause, rub behind my left ear, then blurt, "If I become a candidate, who will I interview with? Is there a board, director, GSU admin personnel?"

"Fair question. Right now, I'm the entire foundation, along with a borrowed secretary and an unpaid intern. If we come to an agreement today, that's it, no other hoops. There is no formal interview."

My jaw drops and my eyes kind of bug out. "Wha— wait— You're the sole decision maker?"

She gives a decisive nod, clears her throat, and goes on. "There's no board yet. That's one of the projects for the near future. I heard about what happened at Miller, Lanscombe, blah blah, and when Jarvis told me you were looking for a new position, I jumped on the possibility of hiring you. From everything I heard, you fit my checklist perfectly."

She picks up a piece of bread and tears at it. Crumbs shower down onto the table.

"I don't want a pity offer or a handout."

"That's not what's happening. I've been on the hunt for the perfect person to fit this job, and I'm pretty sure you're it. At least on paper. You have great references. And now it's just the chemistry."

A warmth of fellow feeling creeps up. This may be a good fit for me.

"I've been working on this project for a while and Clay has been really supportive. At first I just wanted to do something that would make a difference in the community, but volunteering didn't seem to be enough. That's when I got the idea of the foundation. I have an MBA from Northwestern and haven't been able to put it to good use."

She offers me more coffee but I'm hyper enough already. Pouring more coffee into her tiny cup, she takes a minute sip. "I told Clay about my idea to open a progressive women's shelter, and he suggested creating a foundation that could fund it and other programs.

I thought a program tied to GSU would cause conflicts, but Clay was eager to show security was more inclusive than just corporate offerings. He persuaded me to turn my idea into the nonprofit arm of GSU. Not having to worry about the initial startup cost has made everything much easier."

She takes a breath, and when I don't have questions, she continues, "We have office space in the Rookery Building and an old hotel in Avondale that's being rehabbed into safe housing for women who need it.

"The creche and daycare are on the first floor of this building and are open to company employees and women who need, but can't afford, childcare. Mostly children who aren't school age, but we hope to add an after-school program as well. My intern is working on a proposal for a summer program for kids."

"How much staff do you plan to have?"

"That's another early step, figuring out positions and then hiring."

"Would I be involved in that part?"

"I would hope so. Once we have a few administrative people, the next step is legal aid. And that's where you would come in."

I hold up a hand and she stops. "Would that mean I would be handling legal aid or would staff lawyers do the actual work?"

"You would have a couple of options. If you want to be in the trenches, that's fine, but I'm envisioning your role as the director. You would have staff and be responsible both for the legal aid team and for working with the GSU corporate lawyers on any legal issues that involve the foundation."

The idea is exciting, and she's talking as if I've already accepted the position.

"I'm getting ahead of myself," Kath says, the corners of her mouth turned up into a small smile.

The warmth has dropped to a chill. Maybe I misunderstood?

I rush to speech. "I know my problems with Sam are a complication."

Kath's eyes are sad, almost pitying. "The only complication is I can't do a big PR splash if you're hiding from him. Let's hope JL's guys and the police can find him and lock him away."

"But…"

"No buts." Kath pulls out her own folder. "Here's the fine print, including a proposed salary. Read it over and let me know if you have any changes, additions, or deletions to propose."

"Is there a problem if I have a relationship with a GSU employee?"

Kath's drink of water goes down the wrong way and she coughs. When she finally gains control, she says, "If it was a problem, I wouldn't be able to run the foundation."

"Thought you might be a special exception."

"Why don't you take it home, read over everything, and then we can meet again."

After settling on coffee at Hero Coffee Bar tomorrow at ten, I take off for Max's house on the Gold Coast after checking my text messages. Nothing from Sam. I take a relieved breath, followed by a pang of sadness when there's nothing from JL either.

LIAM IS THE BULLDOG TODAY, but Hero, newly opened on South Dearborn, is proving a challenge. There's no place for him to put the SUV. He visually checks out the narrow courtyard that leads to the entrance.

"Shit," Liam exclaims. Then, shamefaced, he says, "Pardon my French."

I giggle. Having googled how French Canadians use Catholic terms in a wholly unexpected way, I know JL's epithets are much more graphic.

The street is clogged with cars as Liam double parks to let me out. A couple of cars honk. Liam gives them the finger and one of the drivers taps the rear bumper. Liam lets out a roar and pushes open the door. "Hop out and run in quick as you can." Then he stalks toward the red sports car snuggled up to the rear of the SUV.

I look carefully, but don't see anyone who looks like Sam, then move swiftly toward the entrance.

"Gotcha." Sam's voice rings like the crack of doom as he throws his arms around me, his grip like a steel band. Where the hell did he come from?

Kath approaches the building. Liam has jumped out of the car, ignoring the honking and yelling that follows. Sam tries to drag me away. So far he hasn't produced a weapon, but I see a bulge in one pocket and eye it uneasily. Seems too small for a .38 or a Glock, but maybe a derringer. That strikes me as funny. Sam changes his grip and twists my arm. "What's so funny? You think this is a joke?"

I have no voice, so try to shake my head no, but I'm pulled so tight against him no words can get out, just a gurgle. "Can't understand you, cunt." He twists harder and I moan, listening for the crack of bone.

Kath screams. Her hands are spread over her belly protectively. "Help. Call the police. He's trying to kidnap her."

Someone gets the wrong idea and tackles Liam from behind. He goes down and two guys kneel on his chest.

"No, not him. The guy over there." Kath waves wildly, but they don't move.

"Get. The. Fuck. Off." Liam pants and pushes, but they are immovable.

Whistles sound as I fruitlessly bite and kick at Sam. He has an arm around my neck, tightening it as I struggle.

I manage to squirm a little and loosen his grip. "Why? Why are you doing this?"

He giggles. Giggles. "Don't like to lose. You tried to best me, and now you'll pay. I'm always the winner."

Just as the police run up, Sam pushes me toward them. As I fall against the leading officer, he yells, "I'll get you next time, bitch." He takes off just as a cop pulls the guys off Liam.

The foot chase from two other officers is unsuccessful, and Sam melts away. All that's left is a bruised throat, the memory of his rancid breath, and the threats still ringing in my ears.

Kath takes my arm. "We're going into the coffee shop," she tells the cop standing closest to me.

"We need to ask some questions."

"Ask them in there." She walks inside, grasping my arm, so I have no choice to go with her. Two policemen and Liam make up the tail of the parade.

Efficient as always, she finds a table that is not only empty but secluded and sinks onto a cushioned seat with a sigh. "Not the best thing to happen when you're pregnant."

She rubs her eyes, then summons a server. "What kind of herbal tea do you have?"

"Rooiboos and chamomile."

"I'll take the Rooiboos. What do you want, Micki?"

"Do you have green tea?"

The server nods. "Gunpowder or Genmaicha?"

"Genmaicha."

We let the men give their own orders. Liam gets coffee and the others go for glasses of water.

I managed to hold on to my portfolio and now I pull out the manila envelope. Nudging Kath's hand with the edge, I get her to take it from me. "I'm prepared to accept your offer."

With an outward breath of relief, she puts it into her bag. "No counters? No demands?"

"It's a substantial offer. I wouldn't know what else to ask for."

"My seven-year-old daughters would say a golden key, a tiara, and tea with the queen."

"How about a unicorn?"

"I think you have that already."

Puzzled, I decide I'm too shaken up to work it out.

The tea arrives and the questioning begins. Two hours later, I go to the women's room and examine my neck. There are bruises where his arm squeezed it. I touch them and my neck is tender. Wish I'd worn a scarf. Then again, Sam might have strangled me. When I get back to the table, Kath is still there.

"I thought you would have signed and gone home by now."

"Do you need to go to Immediate Care? Your neck looks bruised."

"It's not that bad," I lie and grab a pen.

We sign statements and leave, Liam still apologizing for letting Sam get the jump. Kath waves down a cab. Somewhere along the line, Liam moved the car. As we walk to the parking lot down the way, I wonder how Sam knew where I'd be.

CHAPTER
TWENTY-SEVEN

I believe forgiveness is the best form of love in any relationship. It takes a strong person to say they're sorry and an even stronger person to forgive.—Yolanda Hadid

JL

THE HOSPITAL ROOM IS DARK, although not exactly quiet. Machines whir and beep, monitoring Maman's heart. She looks tiny, lying on the bed. I thought she would be up, eating breakfast, but instead she is still asleep.

Yesterday, my head was spinning from the situation and the travel, so I didn't ask many questions, but now I want to know more. Dr. Fitzroy motions me out of the room for a chat. "How did she end up in the hospital?" I ask.

"She told me a friend came for dinner. Just as they sat down to eat, your mother complained of dizziness and trouble breathing. Fortunately, the guest had the presence of mind to call an ambulance."

Angélique? "Do you know her name?"

He looks down at the clipboard. "Angélique Rigaud."

I clamp my lips shut, grateful she was there when Maman needed her, but unsure how I am going to thank her without raising false expectations.

"Do we really need to wait a month before she can come to Chicago?"

"Four to six weeks for air travel." His statement is uncompromising.

"I need to get home, and Maman lives alone. If I had access to a private plane with a nurse and all the medical facilities you recommend, would she be able to travel sooner? We could have a medical team ready to work with her in rehab immediately."

"Mr. Martin, I..."

A nurse pushes past us with a cart. I can tell the tray is Maman's breakfast. She closes the door behind her. Vital signs, then food.

"Well?" I am unable to keep my impatience from breaking out.

His fingers whiten as they grip the clipboard. "Even in those circumstances, I wouldn't advise it. But let's talk with your mother and see how she feels."

When we reenter her room, Maman has whole wheat toast without butter, fat-free yogurt, and fruit. I'm surprised to see tea, but I can see from the color that it is herbal. She puts down her toast and holds out her arms. "JL, mon chou, I'm so glad you're here."

I kiss her cheeks, then sit in the guest chair. The doctor looks at her chart.

"How do you feel, Madame Martin?" he asks.

"Much better. Do I get to go home today?"

"We'll do a few tests and if they go well, your son can take you home." He shuffles a bit. "You understand you will need to have someone there?"

"Of course, that is why JL has come home."

"Maman," I interrupt, "I can't stay here too long. I need to get back to Chicago."

She frowns. "I thought you would move home now. Angélique was such a darling, getting me to the hospital."

I shake my head. "I want you to move near me."

Her pallid face looks like wallpaper paste. "Don't be silly. I can't move. And neither can Angélique."

I want to shout, but I keep myself in check. "Angélique has nothing to do with this," I say through clenched teeth.

"She saved my life. We owe her."

My stubborn side clicks into gear. "We don't owe her."

A nurse runs in. "Mr. Martin. Keep your voice down or you will have to leave."

"Sorry. I didn't realize I was shouting."

Her soft-soled shoes shush along the floor as she leaves.

I grit my teeth. "Maman, make a choice. I would like you to move to Chicago. But if you refuse to go, the other choices are to move into a senior citizen complex or move in with Angélique and her boys. I am not moving back to Vancouver or marrying Angélique." I pace back and forth. "You can have Angélique, or you can have me."

"I can't move in with Angélique," she huffs.

"Do you want Angélique to move in with you?"

"You would stay?"

"No, Maman. My life is in Chicago."

"Because of Micki?"

The room temperature shoots up to 150 degrees. "I'll be back." I choke and walk out to cool off.

The doctor, who has been hanging around in the lounge, puts his hand on my shoulder. "Not going well?"

I growl. "That's an understatement."

Fitzroy gives me a wry smile. "I'm not sure an ultimatum was the wisest approach."

I collapse into a chair and scrub my face with my palms. "She gave me no choice." I let out a moan. "Not sure how to move forward." I remove one hand to fumble for my phone.

"Mr. Martin?" A brisk voice hails me from the lounge entrance.

Abandoning the quest for my mobile, I look up at the woman in crisp nurse's garb who regards me expectantly.

"Can I help you?" I ask.

"I just came from your mother's room. She wants to speak with you and is worried you left the hospital. I told her I would try to find you."

Getting to my feet, I repeat my mantra. *Be conciliatory. Be conciliatory.* I want to find some way out of this impasse without surrendering the thing that's most important to me—my future with Micki.

A muscle in Maman's right cheek twitches as I walk into the room. She holds out a small, heavily veined, shaky hand and I take it between mine. Her skin feels like tissue paper. I stand next to the bed, neither of us able to begin a conversation.

After what seems like eternity, Maman rasps, "Sit down, mon chou."

I drop her hand and pull over the chair. Once I'm positioned, she holds out her hand again, the connection seeming so necessary, even if we can't communicate any other way.

Her voice a mere whisper, she says, "I am so sorry. And so selfish." Silent tears roll down her cheeks.

"You were doing what you thought would bring the most happiness, and you believed your idea of happiness and mine would be the same." I clear my throat. "Now we have to find some way to both be happy."

"Why do you want me to move to Chicago? If you aren't going to move here, perhaps that means things stay just the way they are."

My feet shuffle as I move the chair backward and forward. "Nothing will stay the same. You can't live alone."

"I don't need to. François can return."

"That's not a solution. Once he is well enough to leave rehab, Uncle François will move back to a facility in Montreal. If you don't move to Chicago, assisted living here would be a possibility." I squeeze her hand gently. "But I can't be here often, and I want you nearby. You can't live alone, and being in Chicago means I can make sure you have all the best care. And Micki and I will, well, you won't be alone."

Sniffles erupt along with a few tears as I tell her, "I know you want grandchildren." I pause and gaze into hope filled eyes. "I have some ideas about that, too."

"You and Micki? You'd be willing…?"

She doesn't finish the thought—a request I'd have to say no to. But I have some other ideas. "Let me put some plans in place. And I have to talk to Micki about the immigration piece."

"I don't understand."

"Micki is a lawyer. She can find out how to make everything work because you should be able to claim status as the mother of an American citizen."

"You've given up your Canadian citizenship?" Her voice is low, but the sourness of Maman's face could curdle cream.

"Once a Canadian, always a Canadian. I have dual citizenship now. It would be the same for you. You don't lose your identity."

"What's your plan?"

I can't believe she is giving in so easily. Perhaps now that she knows I will never marry Angélique, she is choosing me. Warmth pervades my chest. She and Uncle François are my only family. I've done my best for him. That's all I can do. Maman is a different matter, and I'm relieved I won't lose her. I give her hand another squeeze.

"You need to be settled as soon as possible, and the doctor agreed if I can provide a flight that has the proper equipment and medical staff on board ..." Is this a little white lie? The doctor didn't forbid the travel, just didn't advise it for a longer period than I want to wait. "We're working on the timing. If it can't be soon, in the meantime you'll get cardiac rehabilitation in a nursing home. I'll take care of all the arrangements."

"What about the house?"

"I'll contact a real estate agent for the sale, and then you'll have a nice nest egg to invest." It's my house but I don't begrudge her the money.

"And you'll help me find my own place to live?"

"You can stay with me for the time being. And then, if you like the location, Clay can set you up with one of the apartments in the building."

"This is all so fast, JL. I'm not sure..."

"Maman, we want you to be with us."

With a little of her usual feistiness, she snorts. "Not so sure Micki feels that way."

"If you accept her, she will be more than happy. And you'll like her parents too."

"Ah yes, Madame Triscuits." Maman reaches toward

the side table, then realizes she won't find any cigarettes to soothe her anxiety. Instead, she mutters, debating with herself, "I need paper and a pencil. And a box of Triscuits."

At the nurses' desk, a volunteer hands me a small pad and a stubby pencil. It's not very sharp but serviceable. Pulling the tray table over, I put down the implements. "Water, Maman ?"

"Yes, that would be nice." She takes a sip through the red plastic straw, then picks up the pencil, tapping against the paper.

"I'll be back in a few minutes. Just going to see if I can have another word with Fitzroy."

She doesn't look up, just scribbles away. "Don't forget the crackers."

"Yes, yes. Triscuits coming up."

Fitzroy stands at the station, chatting with another doctor. "Just the man I want."

"Let's go to my office." He turns on his heel and walks off. I follow down a long corridor with many closed doors. When he opens the door at the end of the hallway, we enter a small room with a desk, a visitor's chair, hanging bookshelves on one wall, and filing cabinets on the others. His collection of medical diplomas and certifications in cardiology as well as cardiovascular and thoracic surgery are impressive.

Maman has been in good hands. I'm almost sorry to take her away. Almost. The window has a deep embrasure with a display of family photos.

"I know you want to discourage me from moving my mother too soon, but unless you think she has a high probability of dying, I'd like to make arrangements to do everything in the next week."

Eyes narrowed, he examines my face. "Has she agreed to move?"

"She's writing up a list of pros and cons. I left her to it, but I'm pretty sure there will be more pros than cons when she finishes. And getting her settled as soon as possible would be preferable to moving her, then moving her again. If she could go directly from the hospital to the airport, that would be ideal."

"If your mother agrees and she's stable, I'll work out the logistics with you."

"Give me a date so I can get the plane here."

He looks puzzled. "Why not just charter one?"

"My company has a plane, so I'd rather use that. They can get it outfitted in Chicago and have the medical staff on board and prepared." I stand, then remember one more thing. "Maman would like some Triscuits."

"The woven wheat crackers?" He frowns. "They're high in sodium, but I'll see if there is an acceptable replacement."

We shake hands. I've been away for an hour and when I get back to the wing where Maman's room is, a nurse hurries up to me.

"Your mother has been asking for you, Mr. Martin. I told her you were meeting with the doctor, but she is getting anxious."

As if on cue, alarms sound. People start running around. Dr. Fitzroy is paged. I grab the nurse's arm. "Is it my mother?"

"Don't worry, Mr. Martin. I am sure she will be stabilized quickly. Sit down in the lounge and someone will take you back in a few minutes."

I pace the small lounge. Walk to the window. Drum my fingers on the glass. Walk to the coffee machine. Examine the dregs. Repeat. I stop when I hear footsteps tapping down the linoleum. Fitzroy frowns at me.

"Your mother's blood pressure spiked."

"Is she all right?"

"We're giving her a supervised course of intravenous antihypertensive meds." His arms are folded and his foot taps in no particular rhythm.

"You're going to forbid her traveling?"

"No. If she's agreed to go, doing it quickly to avoid more anxiety is the best course. If you can arrange for transportation two days from now, I will make sure she's well enough to go."

I want to hug him, but I shake his hand. "Thank you so much."

"I just hope I'm not making a mistake." He turns on his heel and leaves. Then stops and calls over his shoulder. "You can see her now, but try not to get her excited. And there is a low-sodium version of the crackers—Triscuits with a hint of salt. Not totally healthy, but better than the normal type. Just don't let her eat too many at one time."

When I walk in, Maman is flat in the bed with a new IV. "Maman. I'm so sorry to have caused this."

She opens her eyes slightly. With a raspy whisper she says, "Not your fault. Make the arrangements." Then she closes her eyes. I am dismissed.

I kiss her cheek and hustle back to the lounge, surprised Dr. Fitzroy has returned.

"Well? What is the verdict?"

"She's agreed to go. I'll have the plane here the day after tomorrow."

"She'll be ready," he assures me.

I have a lot to do, and a ticking time bomb may go off in

Chicago at any moment. I take off for the hospital café—coffee and list making.

When Micki calls, I'm just finishing up.

"JL, I ..." Sobbing comes through, and anger rises in me.

"What did he do now?"

Her voice is tiny as she tells me what happened outside the coffee shop. I want to run out of the building, grab a ride to the airport, and fly out immediately. Not going to happen. I can't be with both Micki and Maman yet.

All I can give her are soothing platitudes as acid eats at my insides.

TWENTY-EIGHT

Nobody has ever measured, not even poets, how much the heart can hold.—Zelda Fitzgerald

Micki

CALLING JL HELPS, but not as much as I'd hoped. He won't be back for two days. Two days of Sam being out there somewhere. Carrying a gun, a knife. Ready to ambush me.

The phone on the side table next to my chair suddenly starts to rock and roll. I peek at the screen. Unknown Caller. Once it goes to voice mail, I block the number. Clinking sounds come from the kitchen, then Cress comes in with a tray of glasses and a pitcher of iced tea.

Carefully sliding the tray onto the low table in front of the couch, she looks up at me. "What's wrong?" The alarm in her voice alerts me I must look as shocked as I feel.

"Unknown caller."

"Shit. You think it's Sam?"

"Who else? I added Kath to my contacts." My neck has a mind of its own and my head bobs up and down, up and down, like a demonically possessed puppet. Bobblehead Micki. "Now that he's emerged from his hole, he probably wants me to keep reliving the attack until he strikes again." My face feels damp, and I rub an arm across my forehead. "But how did he get this number?" I whisper.

"How many people have it?"

My forehead wrinkles as I try to count up the contacts. "JL, GSU, you, Mom and Dad, Kath Brandon."

"That's it?"

"I think so." Something niggles the edge of my thoughts. "Maybe, uh, not someone I gave it to, but I had to call the firm and..."

"They could have your number then."

"True, but Sam has no connection with them."

"If they have it in a directory, maybe he could hack in and find it." A pleased expression suffuses Cress' face, as if she's found the secrets of the universe.

A short barking laugh erupts that I can't control. "Sam, a hacker? You have to be kidding. He can barely send email." I pause. "Jarvis did think he has someone from the dark web working with him, so I suppose it's possible."

"What are you going to do now? Call JL?"

"Done that. And we've been texting, but with his mother in the hospital, he's not able to say when he can get back."

"Max is upstairs. I'll have him take a look." She pours me a glass of lemonade and patters out of the room, calling for Max. I take a careful sip, then lean my head back and contemplate the nightmare that never ends.

A dark shadow looms over me. "Hand me your mobile,"

Max says, exhaustion in his voice, even though he looks as dapper as ever.

I hold it up and he snatches it out of my grasp. "I'll be back," he calls out as he strides out of the room. Muttering combines with footsteps pounding up the stairs.

"More tea?" Cress asks after Max is no longer in sight

A half-filled glass sits wetly on a coaster. The ice has melted. "I don't think so."

She puts the glasses back on the tray and disappears toward the kitchen. Reappearing with the ice bucket and a different pitcher filled with a reddish liquid, she makes the ice tinkle invitingly. "Time for something stronger." Her cheerful demeanor strikes a false note in the circumstances.

We sip Negronis and wait for Max. The cats bathe me in pity, one on my lap, the other stretched across my shoulders. Occasionally, they readjust, swap places, or stroke my cheek with a velvety paw.

A hollow place spreads from the pit of my stomach up through my chest and into my throat, where a lump chokes me. I touch my eyes, expecting them to feel wet. Instead, they are dry and burning. Furious blinks make no difference. I am desiccated, withered, wizened, sere— Georgia O'Keeffe's *Cow Skull with Calico Roses*.

Max has my phone so if JL has tried to reach me, there's no way for me to know. I'm bereft.

When the front door bell rings, Cress seems unsurprised. "Be right back," she says, her voice sounding like a loudspeaker against the reverberations from the carillon sound. She trots off, both cats trailing after her. Max shouts something from upstairs but I can't decode his words. "Got it," Cress shouts back.

The front door opens. I hear a soft murmur from the hallway, then a distinct snick as she reactivates the lock.

Cress' shoes click-clack as she moves from the tiled foyer and morphs to a shhh-shhh once she hits the hardwood. Back in the living room, she curls up in the big armchair and lays her head back. "Dinner. I put it in the warming drawer. Are you hungry?"

I shake my head no. The idea of eating makes me nauseous.

"Whenever Max finishes, we can eat. It's pizza from Pequod's. You might feel more like it if he can figure out stuff about Sam."

Can't imagine ever wanting to eat again. In fact, I'm not sure I can go on at all. When I tell that to Cress, the look on her face is a mixture of horror and pity.

"Micki. Stop this. You are not the suicidal type. You face adversity head on. In fact, you are the most annoyingly positive person I have ever known. And didn't you tell me the perfect job seems to have fallen into your lap?"

"Yeah," I admit. "But right now, that doesn't seem at all important."

"If you're serious, Max and I are carting you off to see someone pronto."

For the depths of my gut, I summon a weak smile. "This feeling of despair is just so overwhelming. I don't know how to cope."

Cress moves over to the couch and sits next to me. After a hug, she just holds my hand until Max finally clatters down the stairs.

His big frame darkens the doorway. "That was a merry chase." His sarcasm isn't even thinly veiled.

The expectant look on Cress' face is probably mirrored on my own. My fingers are crossed. "Burners," Max says, his voice flat. "Multiple burners. And the text messages are sent from public terminals from libraries all over Cook County."

A wail I can't repress splits the air. Cats scrabble off the couch in alarm.

"I do have a bit of good news," Max says as the siren-like quality of my voice winds down.

Cress pats my back, then hands me a glass of water I hadn't noticed before. I sip and splutter as Max moves over to the armchair, pulling Cress with him and settling her on his lap. Another pang of loneliness and desire pierces my chest.

"We've been doing some deep digging into Sam's background. We're hampered by having to work on a big GSU issue, but Jarvis and I try to dedicate some time to this as well. Sam's hidden things pretty well, but we're finally making progress. He's definitely not the man you thought he was."

Confused, I glance over, trying to interpret what he's saying.

"Your Sam Beaton didn't exist before 1986. We found a birth record for a Samson Beaton from 1966 who died in1986 and we think your Sam stole that identity. It's called ghosting. Somehow, he got that person's Social Security number and managed to get a complete set of documents. We've been doing facial recognition to see if we could match his current persona with his original identity."

"Did you find a match?" My voice shifts from vibrato to tremolo to squeak.

"With a couple of possibilities, we should have more answers soon." He stretches his six-five frame, folding down, reaching up, hands flat against the top of the frame. "That's all I can do tonight. Let's eat something." She drags Max to the kitchen, and Max carries in two pizza boxes, a container of wings, and a bowl of onion rings. Cress follows with a bottle of Prosecco and three flutes.

Pequod's never disappoints. Besides the wings and onion rings, we have a large caramelized-crust pan pizza topped with spinach, pepperoni, sausage, mushrooms, olives, and onion. Max insists on pineapple and ham, so he has his own small pie. Cress and I turn up our noses.

"Just think how great it would be if they would do tuna and sweet corn with red onion," he taunts. "Very popular in Scotland."

"You Brits come up with the most disgusting combinations." Cress makes a sick face.

Too many Negronis followed by glasses of Prosecco, combined with too much pizza lulls me to sleep, where all my dreams are of climbing cheese mountains dripping with tuna and corn, then floating in a sea of bubbly wine while Sam taunts me from the shore.

CHAPTER

TWENTY-NINE

O' What may man within him hide, though angel on the outward side!—William Shakespeare

JL

STILL SEETHING over Sam's latest attack and Liam's ineptitude, I call Yannick to pick me up.

"Aren't you spending the day with your maman?" he chides.

A pang in my chest reminds me Maman's current condition is my fault. "She's had a slight setback, so she'll be sleeping most of the day." I take a breath. "In the meantime, I have a lot to accomplish, and I need you to help me. Text when you get to the hospital."

"Be there in a few." He rings off.

Instead of the company SUV, he's driving his black Corvette Stingray with the red racing stripes. The rain has stopped. Water beads up on its highly polished surface from the overladen trees, while sun sparkles on the drops. He pulls into the circular drive, coming to a flashy stop as the tires spray water from the puddles. I jump back from the resultant wave, then get into the front seat, examining my slacks for damage.

"Where are we going?"

"I need to see a real estate agent, or two."

"Your maman has agreed to go to Chicago?"

"At least in this moment."

"Strike while the iron is hot." He punches my arm.

"Keep your hands on the wheel."

"When?"

"When what?" I've totally lost the thread.

"When are you taking her?"

"Day after tomorrow. Can't go any sooner."

"You're glowering. Did something happen?"

"Sam appeared and attacked Micki. I'd leave right now if I could."

Yannick hits the brakes. The stop is so hard I'm worried he'll trigger the air bags.

"I don't understand. Why don't you just go?"

"The medical plane will be here in two days. I need to travel with Maman. Micki is in Max's house, which is like a fortress. Sam has disappeared, again." I rub my temples. "No reason for me to rush off at this moment. Instead, I need to get the house listed, then take off."

He puts his foot on the gas. "My pal, Joseph, is your best bet. I don't know if you remember him. He's a few years younger than us, from the neighborhood, and will know the value of every house, including Tante Louisette's."

The six-story office building dominates a corner on Mainland Street. The ground floor, filled with restaurants, ethnic food stores, and other shopping, showcases their wares with windows artfully designed to entice the passersby. We go in a business entrance and take the elevator to the top floor. A glass door is emblazoned Joseph Campbell, Realty. It occupies the whole space and even in the elevator lobby I am dazzled by sunlight streaming through tall windows. Yannick pushes through the doors.

"Suzi," he cries. "Is the reprobate here?"

"Why didn't you call first, Yannick?" she scolds. About fifty, she sits at a low desk with graying hair in a stylish bob, but her smile undercuts the lecture.

Yannick takes the hectoring in stride. They've obviously known each other for years. "Well, is he? By the way, Suzi Campbell, this is my best friend, JL Martin."

We get through the niceties and stand at the desk while she pokes a button on what must be an intercom. "Joe, could you come out here, please?"

An indecipherable crackle comes through the box.

Suzi focuses on Yannick. "Haven't seen you in a while. Are you thinking about selling that party house of yours and moving to something more grown-up?"

Eyes rolling, he says, "Ha, ha, ha. My house is definitely adult."

"Exactly." Her lips twist, light blue eyes twinkling.

Yannick pokes me in the chest. "JL needs to sell his mother's house."

Biting her lip, she says, "I'm so sorry for your loss."

"No loss. I am persuading Maman to move to Chicago, where I live."

Boot heels thud against the carpeting. Tall and saturnine, a blond man in his early forties strides out. Incongruously, he wears a black cowboy hat, which he pushes back with one finger. "No seats offered, no coffee? Where are your customer skills, my dear?"

"Go stuff yourself, Joe."

"This is why I'm not married." Yannick claps a hand on his friend's shoulder. "Joe, this is my bud, JL Martin."

"Did I hear you have a house to sell?"

When I nod, he goes on. "Come on back to my office and we'll chat." He casts a glance at his wife. "And would you please bring us some coffee, my love?"

She sticks out her tongue, like an eleven-year-old. "That's my girl," Joe says with a laugh. "Always young at heart, even if she's a dozen years older than me."

"I look better for my age than you do." The lightness in her voice takes the sting out of her tart retort.

"True, true. I coddle you, while I've had a hard life." He motions us to follow him into the office behind the desk.

"Take some seats, gentlemen." Joe leans back in a grandiose office chair. "Where's the house?" The space has banks of windows on three sides, offering a spectacular view of water, mountains, and sky.

I throw out the address and wait to see if he can identify it.

"So, Kitsilano. You should be able to get a good price and once it's on the market, a quick sale. Usually two weeks or less."

"Not one of the big, fancy houses," I caution. "A Craftsman bungalow, three bedrooms. Four if you count the finished attic. Two baths downstairs and a toilet and sink in the attic space."

"I know exactly what you mean. I still live in Kitsilano and handle a lot of sales in the area. Probably close to a million, maybe more. I'll be able to give you a better esti-mate once I see it."

"That much?" Maman a millionaire. I can't get my head around it.

"Could be closer to two mil. Kitsilano is very desirable these days. Gentrification. Not the hippie community of the past."

"Have time now?" Yannick focuses a laser gaze on Joe, willing him to say yes.

Joe blinks furiously, then rubs his eyes.

"JL has to get back home in the next few days. No time like the present, eh?" Yannick's sly prod gets the agent to hold up a hand, then he sidles around the desk and out to the lobby.

When Joe gets back, a portfolio and a For Sale sign are under his arm. "Suzi says I have no appointments until much later in the day. You drive and I'll follow."

Like ducklings, they follow me out. "Should we take both cars or just drop you here?"

"Might as well all go together." Joe looks at the Corvette with anticipation before climbing into the back.

Our trip from the office to Maman's house is fairly quick. House dark, the beater in the driveway is a surprise.

Joe frowns, disgruntled. "You have another agent coming?"

"No. You are the only one we've contacted."

Joe spends a little time looking at the front of the house, muttering, and taking photos with his phone. "I'll have a professional out for the sale pictures. These are just for reference."

"Fair." I'm not concerned about who takes the shots. I'm itching to find out about the car. This is the problem with an empty house. I suspect someone is creeping around inside.

"Do you have a gun with you?" I whisper to Yannick.

"In the trunk. Do you want me to get it?"

"Better safe than sorry."

He comes back with a .38 Special and a Glock and hands me the Special. Joe looks over. "What the..."

"Shhh. Keeping walking around out here, Joe." Yannick runs around to cover the back door and I carefully walk up the front steps, glad my running shoes won't make much noise. The front door is unlocked, and I curse softly as I ease it open. Once it's free of the frame, I kick it, wincing as the heavy wood hits the wall.

"Come out," I yell, holding the gun in a ready position.

A high keening noise comes from nearby. "JL? Is that you?" Angélique edges nervously forward, hands up, just like in the cop shows.

I lower the weapon. "Yannick. You can come back now. No one is going to run out."

My pal saunters around to the front. Meantime, Joe has come up on the porch, giving me a quizzical look.

"You can put your hands down, Angélique. Tell me why the hell you're here."

She turns and walks back inside, and we trail behind.

Once in the living room, she plops into her usual chair. We all stand stiffly, looking at her. I fold my arms. "Well?"

"Your maman called and told me she is going into a nursing home for a while so I thought I would bring her a few things and check to make sure everything is all right with the house."

"Where are the boys?"

"With my parents. At Stanley Park."

"How did you get in?"

"I still have a key." Her eyes regard me warily. "She never asked for it back."

Two grocery sacks sit on the floor near her feet. Curious,

I try to see what's inside. She pushes them to the side, but one falls over. I catch a glint of gold. "Did Maman ask for anything specific?"

"No, she didn't ask at all. Just doing her a favor." She shifts around in the chair. Then, gazing at Joe, she asks, "Aren't you that real estate agent who's on the television?"

Big grin, arms thrown wide, chest puffed. "I am indeed."

Her frown is as big as Joe's grin. "Does your mother know you plan to sell the house?"

"Of course. I wouldn't sell it from under her, even if I am joint owner."

"Is she staying in the nursing home permanently?"

"No, she's moving to Chicago."

Angélique curls into herself and a deep moan reverberates around the room. "I don't believe it. Tante Louisette would never leave Vancouver." She means Maman would never leave her and her sons.

"We're leaving tomorrow."

"I will lose everything I love. I won't let you do it."

"I have to go back to the hospital later, so I'll bring all this with me." I wave at the bags as if it's no big deal. "You might as well go now. And thank you so much for taking Maman to the emergency room the other evening."

She sniffles, gropes for nonexistent tissue, then wipes her nose on her sleeve. "Of course."

I hold out my hand, palm up. "Key, please. You won't need it again."

Practically throwing it at me, she skirts the fallen sacks and races out the door.

Yannick peers at the contents. "Funny things to take." He lifts out a porcelain figurine and a pearl and gold necklace.

"Joe, why don't you start looking at the rooms while I deal with this." An idea hits me. "Joe, do you know someone who does estate sales?"

"Do I know someone..." He guffaws. "Do I, Yannick?"

"Suzi."

"Great. Let's keep it in the family, then. I'll find out what, if anything Maman wants to keep, and you can sell the rest."

In the meantime, the porcelain figurine goes back onto the mantelpiece. Then I pick up the bags by their handles to return Maman's things to her room.

"Gonna tell her?" Yannick twists the augur sticking out of my chest.

"I don't see disclosure doing anything except causing a relapse. Maybe someday, when she's happy in Chicago, but not now."

Maman doesn't need to know Angélique has lost her halo.

CHAPTER

THIRTY

You can keep as quiet as you like, but one of these days some-body is going to find you.—Haruki Murakami

Micki

DOROTHY CURLS ON MY LAP, her warm, vibrating body soothing. I need a pet. The text message dings, and I startle. Dorothy looks annoyed as she resettles herself.

> THE DEVIL: One other small piece of paperwork to be signed.

The cat nudges my hand, demanding attention but I ignore her. Frozen, I can't stop looking at the screen. Even if there is some overlooked piece of paperwork, the message would never come from him. Either a secretary or HR would get in touch, probably by email.

JL will be back soon. He called last night with an update

on his mom. I'm not sure how I feel about her moving to Chicago, but he's seeing a realtor today. Maybe I should call him? Not that there's anything he can do from Vancouver, except the sound of his voice would make me feel so much better.

Dithering, I wonder if I should consider it spam and dump it. Or have Max look at it. I don't really want to call the firm and ask what's going on.

Cress heads for her special reading chair with a cup of tea and her Kindle. "What's up? Why are you sitting there like an ice sculpture?"

When I don't respond, she comes over behind me and looks over my shoulder at the screen.

"Who's the devil?"

With a gulp, I tell her, "Fred Lanscombe."

"And you call him that because...?"

"Because he is."

"Isn't he the managing partner? Why would he text you?"

"Good question. Maybe he's been hacked."

"Let me get Max."

"I've bothered him enough with my issues." The protest falls on deaf ears as she briskly runs up to his office. Any excuse for a little kissing.

My face in Dorothy's fur, I feel a damp tickle on my neck. Thorfinn, his rough pink tongue licking me, wants in on the action. We're a living depiction of solace in a time of despair.

Silently, a shadow looms over me. Long thin fingers remove the phone from my hand. Footsteps recede. A tea mug is pushed under my nose. I sneeze.

"Shit." Cress yelps as the mug splashes hot liquid over her hand and onto my lap. "What the fuck was that?"

"It's your own fault. What were you thinking? I can't help it if the tea made me sneeze. I react to linden."

"Just trying to help."

Dorothy digs in her back claws and my reflexes kick in, dumping her onto the floor, into a spreading pool of hot liquid.

"Yowch. Hiiiiissssss." She bats at my leg with a wet paw, then flounces out.

Running feet. Cress is back in a flash with towels for me and the floor.

Max pounds down from the second floor. "Jarvis is coming over. This is getting too complicated. Erik will have to take over on the cybersabotage while Jarvis helps me work this out. He'll try to figure out the text message while I continue the hunt for Sam."

"Don't stop important work for me."

"Threats to you are more important than threats to software." Cress gives Max a meaningful look.

Briskly, Max adds his two cents. "Erik is very capable, if not the genius Jarvis is. Elizabeth will help him. I just wish I could trust everyone else. I know we have an inside threat, but we haven't identified the culprit yet."

Six hours later, Cress and I have gone through a pitcher of lemonade, followed by dirty martinis. A little tipsy, I keep apologizing about inconveniencing everyone. Twice Cress has tottered up the stairs to invade Max's office, only to come back with a flea in her ear. The second time, she trips on the stairs and hobbles the rest of the way.

My voice slurs. "You okay?"

"My ankle hurts, but it's not broken. I don't think." Then she lets out a mewl that brings the cats back.

"Two growly bears. You wouldn't think Sam could

cause this much mayhem. I never liked him, but I also never thought he was very bright."

"Cunning. And scary. Two words I never thought I'd use about him." An involuntary shiver makes me wrap my arms around myself. "Think I'll get a sweater."

Cress props her leg on a pillow and goes back to reading and I trudge to the stairs. I'll hang on to the banister. Not going to fall like Cress. I'm not the clumsy one.

The sound of keyboards clacking in the library entices me to abandon my search for warmth. The library doors are open and Jarvis' broad back swivels as he switches back and forth between three screens and several keyboards. He mutters and I edge closer to hear him. "How did you get access, you fucker? Who did you pay?"

Bang. He slams his hand against the desktop. "Crap." He cradles the injured appendage. Footsteps sound, some thumping down the stairs and others in an irregular tap from the living room. Max and Cress arrive at the same moment. He pushes past as if I'm invisible. Cress limps behind him.

"What the bloody hell, Jarvis?" Max rasps.

"Did you find something?" Cress quivers with excitement, or maybe apprehension as she leans against Max for support.

I rub my arms, again noticing the chill.

"All I can find is he used Lanscombe's account, but I can't figure out who he's been dealing with on the dark web or imagine how he found them. They must be really good to hide their tracks like that. Absolutely no trace."

Max hands me my phone. Like a charm, I clutch it in my hand, willing a message or call from JL. Nothing.

"I think I can answer that question." Satisfaction oozes out of Max.

Jarvis swivels around in the big desk chair, facing the three of us. "What? Who?" Instead of sounding thrilled, Jarvis' grumpy expression reflects losing some imaginary race.

"Let's shut everything down and reconvene in the lounge for a drink. And I'll tell you a story." Max puts his hand on Cress' back and guides her down the hall. I trail behind, the sound of Jarvis' grumbling punctuating my path.

Reluctance slows my steps. Instead of eagerness to find out how Sam is managing to terrorize me, I want to emulate an ostrich. Getting the sweater takes a little time and when I reach the bottom of the stairs, pulling on the cardigan, I almost walk into Jarvis, who clomps into the living room, seemingly still pissed off at Max's apparent cyber victory.

"By the way, Max turned off your phone."

He did, and I never noticed. I slipped the phone into the pocket of my sweatpants when Max handed it to me. Now I put the heavy rectangle into my cardigan pocket where it bangs against my hip as I walk into the room. I don't turn it back on. If I'm going to pay attention, I don't need distractions.

Several bottles of wine sit on the drinks cart, along with white wine and red wine glasses, reminding me of the wine party at Louisette Martin's house. Cress has put out sliced sausage, a couple of blocks of cheese, crackers, and chips. Jarvis has made a beeline to the wine and fills a big balloon glass almost to the brim with a dark ruby red liquid. He sips to make sure it doesn't spill over.

Cress, her ankle wrapped up with an ice pack, has a glass of something bubbly.

"Prosecco," she says, holding up the glass to admire the play of the tiny bubbles. "Want some?"

Must be the drink of the moment. Even though we've been drinking cocktails, I enjoyed the Prosecco I've had the last few days, so why not? Eschewing my usual red, I nod. Max jumps up with alacrity. Soon, I'm ensconced in one of the armchairs with my drink and a selection of cheese and crackers.

Cats twine around ankles, trying to decide which laps look most inviting. Thorfinn sits between Max and Cress on the couch, while Dorothy continues to wander. Her intermittent chirps sound like a radar system.

Settling in, Max downs his shot of whisky and drops the glass onto the end table. Head back, eyes closed, he clears his throat.

"After a lot of digging, I decided to see if anything Sam told you about his background was true." He pauses and rubs Cress' cheek with a thumb. "Like many con men, he kept too much."

Jarvis snickers. "Elementary mistake, but great for us."

"Uh-hum." Max practically purrs. "He went to school in Highland Park, not Lake Forest. And he kept his first name, Samuel."

"Highland Park?" Jarvis rolls his eyes, disbelieving.

"Don't tell me you believed all that back country, good ole boy baloney?" Cress' acid comment makes me want to laugh.

"Well, the overalls, ball cap, Appalachian accent..." Jarvis protests.

"When he became a 'folk artist,' he changed his image," I explain. "The accent has always been a little hit or miss."

When Max breaks in, a hint of briskness reminds me of

his professionalism. "Funnily enough, six guys named Sam went to school with the Samson Beaton, who died."

"How convenient," Cress interjects.

"Could be." He scratches at the unusual scruff around his jaw. "Beaton committed suicide. Drowned in Lake Michigan in a boating accident with some schoolmates At least that was the verdict. Two of them are of interest in this case. No proof anyone helped him along, but no proof he wasn't either."

"If it was one of the six, and not some other guy, how did you figure out which one?"

"One of them is a Samuel Lanscombe. The name rang a bell. They both played on the school baseball team. In fact, Beaton was tipped as a future pro. He was one of the friends in the boat."

My mouth drops open. "Lanscombe. You're shitting me," I squeal before I slug back the rest of the wine and snort when bubbles go up my nose. Such an unusual name. Can't be a coincidence. Fred's what? Son, nephew, distant cousin? There must be a connection.

Instead of throwing out my suspicions, I focus on something else. "Sam loved to brag about how good he was as a baseball player in high school but gave it up for his art."

"Second rate," Max offers as a brief aside. "Besides the last name, that's how I knew I had the right guy. Beaton had no strong connections with the other Sams."

"He said he'd cut himself off from his family." I roam the room twirling the flute.

"Lied about that, and other things," Jarvis adds. Max must have clued him in before I got back down.

Picking up the story, Max says, "But this Sam Beaton did. His best friend was Sam Philips, who... Wait for it."

"Max, this is unfair. Tell us." A slug in the shoulder accompanies Cress' demand.

"Fine, fine. If you're going to commit GBH, I'll confess."

And then he's silent, drinking a second glass of whisky. Once it's empty, he finally goes on. "He was the other guy in the boat. And after graduating college, Sam Philips moved to France and changed his name to Phillippe Samuel."

"Name sounds familiar." Jarvis scratches his head.

"Catacomb Galaxy." Max smiles with satisfaction.

"The hackers?"

"Two connections that would definitely benefit Sam Beaton."

"And he's never been caught. Kind of a dead end."

"We know he could have tracked Cress in Paris. And might help on the dark web side. That's progress."

The plate on my lap slides to the floor, cheese and salami everywhere. Dorothy and Thorfinn are on it immediately. We're all too paralyzed to stop them. Cress looks on passively as they lick the plate clean, then hoover up the crumbs on the rug.

"Go on." I want Max to finish the story.

"He established the new identity within months of Beaton's death but didn't start using it until his art started to sell. And we can connect this Sam Beaton with a bank account in the name of Samuel Lanscombe."

"Once Max clued me in, finding the accounts was easy. He has quite a healthy balance." Jarvis chortles. "His father, name of Frederick, deposits a monthly allowance. Plus, the investments and savings as Sam Lanscombe."

Max adds the crowning piece of evidence. "There are also substantial payments to a numbered Swiss bank account. Presumably Catacomb Galaxy."

Father. Fred Lanscombe is his father. A blinding realization makes my head spin. "All those years he sponged off me." Max picks up the empty plate, then cradles Cress. Jarvis focuses on his screen.

I just want JL. Loneliness fills every corner of my being. Worse thoughts pour in. I blurt, "He could have afforded to come to Paris ... and Vancouver." I double over. What if he had, following me around, spying? Hanging out with his high school crony. Or they might have hired someone else to do it. "Why didn't he?" *Why, why, why?*

"He's a lazy SOB and he knew you'd come back." Jarvis gives himself a metaphorical pat on the back.

"Sending you threatening messages and making prurient phone calls without having to exert himself would be just his speed," Cress spits out.

"Fred is aiding and abetting?" My mouth twists like I've been sucking on lemons.

"Probably not in the stalking, but certainly providing contact information, even if passively, and cash."

Passively? "What do you mean about the contact information?"

"Sam probably has access to his dad's phone, or at least his account. So he could find you that way." Jarvis' explanation makes my muscles lock up momentarily.

"Fred may have provided the hiding place, too. Should have suspected something when your former firm kept asking for your contact information." Max's words hit like a mea culpa.

I lift an eyebrow in absolution. "They had logical reasons to ask, because of the termination. They needed to send me documents, and I gave your address. And I asked for the recommendation that gave them my current number." Another thought strikes me. "Sam must know I'm here. Why hasn't he made a move?"

"We live in a fortress. Sam would realize attacking this place would be pointless and risky. But he could hide in the neighborhood and track you."

Cress' face squinches in speculation. "Do you think they hired you in the first place because Sam asked his dad?"

"I knew Sam casually for a couple of years before I interviewed with them," I say, slowly. "We didn't start dating right away, though."

"He plays a long game," Max says. "Just speculating, but maybe his father mentioned you as a promising candidate. He might have checked you out, then pursued you."

My past crumbles before my eyes. I don't know what's real and what Sam constructed.

I glance at the flute I'm still gripping, pour a second helping, gulp it down, and pour a third. "Do you know where he is?"

Max sits forward. Cress slides off his lap and comes to rest at his feet.

"'Fraid not. I think he has yet another identity, just for this eventuality. And I'm positive the text from your former boss is really from Sam. He either 'borrowed' or stole his dad's phone. Must be wondering why you haven't responded."

"Should I?" I don't want to, but maybe that's the way to catch him.

"No." Max's response explodes into the silence. My breath whooshes out.

"We let him stew. At some point, his frustration will explode and he'll make another move. He's preparing the dénouement. We can be patient. In the meantime, GSU has some guys watching his father in case they get together."

"Are you bugging Fred's phone?"

"That would be illegal. And doing a wiretap on the head

of a law firm would beg for a lawsuit." Max's eyes twinkle. "We've passed on information about their connection to the police, so they might do something."

"Haven't they told you anything?"

"No. I wouldn't expect it. They might tell you something as the victim, but even that's doubtful." He looks at me with pity. "Turn on your phone, Micki. All we can do is wait."

The cheese I munched earlier curdles in my stomach and the wine seems to have gone to my head. I grit my teeth and slide the orange button down to turn my phone on. Wait. Again. Even though the pieces are coming together, waiting is all that seems to happen.

CHAPTER

THIRTY-ONE

When everything seems to be going against you, remember that the airplane takes off against the wind, not with it.
—Henry Ford

JL

MY TIMEX, a gift from Maman when I graduated from high school, reads 4:00 p.m. through the scratched crystal. Yannick drives us back to the hospital so we can update Maman on our progress.

We signed the contract with Joe. He did the listing on his laptop. The sign is on the lawn. Not sure what she will think about the house when I tell her Joe estimates two and a half million. He'll have an inspector tomorrow to check everything out. The open house will be this weekend. By then, we'll be in Chicago.

A bit of breathing space gives me time to text Micki. I

351

want to arrange a long call for tonight. Even if we say little, just her breath on the other end of the line will ease my heart. The email from Max, telling me who Sam is, makes me itch to get back. We need to flush out the fucker and get him locked away for the rest of his life.

ME: Miss you so much.

MICKI: MISS YOU TOO

ME: You free for a call tonight?

ME: I need to update you on what's happening.

MICKI: I have news too. What time?

ME: Nine Chicago time?

MICKI: Can't wait 😘

ME: 🙂

By the time we finish, Yannick is maneuvering into a parking space far away from other cars.

"Not taking any chances with my darling." He runs his hand over the hood.

The clouds are back, the skies tipping the pitcher. We make a run for it but he's parked far enough out that by the time we make it into the foyer, we're soaked.

Water drips into my eyes. "We can't stay here like this."

"Instead, you want to inundate my leather seats?"

If Yannick glares, I can't see it. "I'll call an Uber if you want."

"Then the car will still be available when we get back. Perfect."

Paper towels are pressed into my hands. "Maybe these

will help a bit," a masculine voice says. I wipe my face and look into the smiling face of the receptionist, who has come out from behind the welcome desk.

"Can I help you with anything else?"

"Dry clothes?" Yannick asks.

With an assessing gaze, the receptionist says, "The shop carries T-shirts and flip-flops, but I don't think they can outfit the rest of you."

"We'll leave, change, then come back in more suitable clothes." I brandish my phone. "Three minutes to takeoff."

Yannick grabs all the paper towels and wads them into a ball, then does a perfect overhand shot into the trash barrel—the perfect segue to our exit.

We go to my hotel. Fortunately for Yannick, we can wear the same size, so he borrows jeans, a T-shirt, and dry socks. When we return, the rain is as heavy as ever, but the driver drops us off under the canopy, so we arrive dry. I start to make a comment, but a different receptionist makes that pointless. We walk past but the woman calls us back.

"May I help you?" Not really a question, the way she lobs the remark at us.

I freeze while Yannick whirls in her direction. "We know the room number but thank you." His voice is polite.

She fishes out two badges and holds them in the palm of her hand. "You'll need these to access the floors."

"Forgot. Sorry."

Yannick darts forward, grabs the badges with a muttered thanks, and heads toward the bank of elevators, tossing a badge at me.

When we reach Maman's room, the bed has been raised. She watches TV while talking on the phone.

When we walk in, she ends the call and mutes the box.

"You're looking better, Maman," I say, then kiss her

cheek.

Yannick pulls over the two guest chairs, dropping into one like this is his living room.

"Who were you talking to?" I try to keep it casual.

"Angélique. She is so distressed that I am leaving Vancouver."

"You're like a second mother to her, Aunt Louisette."

Maman preens a bit.

My voice harsh, I say, "Fortunately, she has a mother, so she should be able to manage without you."

Maman flashes me a worried glance. "She said you took her key, JL."

"The house is going on the market. There's no reason for her to be in there." I don't want to tell her about Angélique's attempted theft.

"You don't have a say." Her voice is weak as she struggles to get the words out.

Trying to avoid another incident, I hold out my hands placatingly. "I have a say. I am the legal co-owner of the house."

Maman gasps for breath. She's forgotten, years ago, I paid off the mortgage and the house is in my name.

She slides down a little onto her pillows and closes her eyes. I then tell the nurse at the station we will be in the cafeteria if Maman wants me later and I give her my cell number.

At this time of day, the hospital coffee is neither warm nor fresh. After a tentative sip, we decide to switch to tea, ignoring the water-beaded bottles of beer beckoning from the cooler. I text Clay to find out how the arrangements are going for the flight and Maman's apartment.

> ME: Is the plane on the way?

CLAY: Another hour. You aren't using it until tomorrow, so why worry?

ME: Maman's doctor insists on checking out the setup, the staff, and the crew.

CLAY: ...

CLAY: ...

CLAY Plane inspection scheduled for 10 a.m. tomorrow, Vancouver time.

I text Fitzroy.

ME: 10 a.m. Will that work?

FITZROY: Fine. Where?

ME: I can pick you up. It will be easier.

FITZROY: From the hospital?

ME: Of course.

Back to Clay.

ME: All set

CLAY: Great. Apartment is ready for your mom. The twenty-four-hour nursing staff is on call.

ME: I owe you.

CLAY: You don't.

No point arguing. I'll find a way to pay him back, eventually.

With the mobile back in my pocket, I down the dregs of

my lukewarm tea. "Let's go. I want to say goodnight to Maman and explain the arrangements. Then you can drop me off at the hotel. I'm dead and ready for the undertaker."

"I'm exhausted too. Do you have one king or two queens?"

"Two queens. I take it you want to stay?"

"Yeah. Long drive back to my place."

"You snore."

"So do you."

"What about Brioche?"

"Texted my neighbor. She'll feed and walk her." He smirks. "I can borrow shorts from you."

Maman is dozing when we get back. "She's pretty stable right now," the nurse says. "Although there was a visitor who upset her a little."

"Visitor?" Uncle François is in rehab. Who else would visit her?

"Was it a woman around our age?" Yannick asks.

"With two little boys?" I add.

"Yes. Her name was Angel or Angela or something like that. And the boys were adorable."

I suppress a growl. "How long did she stay?"

"Not long, a few minutes. Your mother fussed over the children, but then the woman asked for something and started crying when your mother refused."

Tension starts to ebb. "Then what."

"She said something like, 'I can't believe you chose him over me. You don't really think of me as your daughter after all.' The boys looked nervous, and your mother started having breathing issues, so we made her leave."

Furious, I want to have it out with Angélique, but I won't. She'll be out of our lives tomorrow.

CHAPTER

THIRTY-TWO

The English language has 112 words for deception, according to one count, each with a different shade of meaning: collusion, fakery, malingering, self-deception, confabulation, prevarication, exaggeration, denial.—Robin Marantz Henig

Micki

IMPATIENCE MAKES THINGS HAPPEN. Reining in my own is hard. Sam doesn't bother. When I turn my phone back on, text message notifications scroll past like marathon runners. Some are from "Fred Lanscombe." Others from Unknown Caller. I laugh when I see the ones from Tom Collins and Margarita Screwdriver.

Max sips Grant whisky and stares into space. When my message tone goes off wildly, he puts the glass down and walks over. "Don't open them," he warns. "Just hand me your phone. We'll take care of this."

357

"Are you planning to flush him out?"

"We'll try." Jarvis' mouth turns down, and he almost looks like a killer rather than a geek.

"I'm supposed to have a call with JL at nine. Can I do that?"

"Not a problem," Jarvis assures me. "I can give you a burner. I'll text him the number. That way, we can spend as much time as we need to set up our trap."

They disappear up the stairs to Max's office with a platter of nachos and my cell.

"Cyber widows," Cress remarks, taking an eggplant bruschetta.

"Speak for yourself," I tell her.

Time drags. I stare at the phone Jarvis gave me, run my fingers over the glass, push some keys. The device lights up. A message appears on the screen. "Connect here to make phone operable."

I stare at the letters, trying to make sense of the words. Wouldn't Jarvis have set up the phone for me? Then again, maybe this is extra security. I glance in Cress' direction. She's sipping tea, absorbed in something on her phone. Should I check with the guys? I don't want to disturb them. The message keeps blinking at me, so I hit the connect button.

"Phone is now usable." The message lingers for a few seconds, then disappears. That's all right then. I lay the phone down on the side table and go to the kitchen for some hot chocolate. Dorothy hops onto my lap as soon as I sit down.

The guys haven't reappeared or even given us an update. I try to read but my attention wanders. Cress turns on the playoff game but that doesn't keep our attention either. I go up to my room and stretch out on the bed, phone on the pillow, next to my ear.

Right at nine, the burner I've fiddled with all evening trills, startling me even though I expect it. My top teeth bite into my bottom lip as I push accept. "JL?"

"Micki? You sound, uh, ..."

The phone drops to my lap. My right hand massages a sudden tightness in my chest and my left index finger rubs against my bottom lip. Stickiness tells me I am bleeding. Guess I bit down too hard. I run my tongue along the injury, hoping that will staunch the blood. "I'm okay," I manage to choke out.

"Sam has reemerged?"

"Not exactly. I'm getting lots of messages. Max and Jarvis have the phone and they're trying to set a trap."

"Hmmm. I hope it works." He's silent for a minute. "We're flying in tomorrow. It's a medical flight on the GSU plane. Tell Max we'll land at the private terminal about 7:00 p.m. I'll arrange for some of my guys to be there."

I'll be there too, but I don't say anything. JL will try to forbid me. Especially after my freedom run. That argument can wait until after the fact.

"Can't wait to be with you," he murmurs.

"Won't your time be taken up with your mother?"

"Some of it. There will be round-the-clock nursing. And she'll have her own place. Clay had Kath set up one of the apartments for her."

"Convenient." Can't think of anything else to say. I can hear his breath and he can hear mine. What I want is to feel his heartbeat. When our hearts beat in unison, I know we will be together always.

"Micki." His voice is so serious I worry something is wrong. "Micki. I want to keep the call open all night so we are sleeping together, even if we can't be in each other's arms. Hear each other breathe. Talk if we wake up. Just feel the connection."

The door to my room slams open. Cress, panting, sags onto the doorframe. "Hang up, Micki. Max says hang up now."

Fear clutches my gut. "Gotta go."

"I heard."

I cut the connection.

THIRTY-THREE

I think once you start to think that you're the man, and you know it all, and your style is unbeatable and stuff like that, that's when you get caught and clipped and get humbled really fast.—Jon Jones

JL

MAMAN HAS a comfortable bed specially designed so once they transfer her to it at the hospital, she stays in it for the entire trip, all the way to her new apartment. We have two nurses and a doctor for the flight. The plane looks more like a state-of-the-art hospital than a luxury private aircraft. I guide Fitzroy onto the plane and his eyes go wide as he sees how we were able to emulate an Angel MedFlight setup.

"I could have a traveling hospital. Be the doctor on call anywhere in the world. This is incredible."

Cardiac monitor, oxygen, ventilator plus suctioning

equipment, IV medications for pain control, cardiac intervention, shock management, blood pressure support (IV fluids/pressors), and trauma management supplies are there for any exigency. I sit in the back, near Maman, holding her hand, even though she sleeps through most of the flight.

Just as we land, I get a call from Yannick. "Just thought I'd let you know, Angélique has been arrested. She broke into Tante Louisette's house and tried to set it on fire. The police found a stash of stuff in the boot along with a tin of gas and some accelerant. What is it with fire as revenge? Didn't you say Micki's ex set her parents' house on fire?"

"Yeah, with a grenade." I rub the top of my head. Guess I need a haircut. Then I wrench my attention back to Yannick. "Rage, I guess. If you can't have something or someone, just destroy it. Just like Sam is doing to Micki. Fire does a good job too, and you can be far away when things turn bad." Just one more problem for the shit pile. "Is there much damage?"

"Joe checked it out. He's hired cleaners and a carpentry crew, and they should be done in a few weeks. The insurance will contact you soon. Of course, that sets back everything for the sale. You may have to make another trip up."

Tabernak. "Can't be helped. I'll talk to Joe after I settle Maman. We're just pulling into our parking space, so I should be off the plane soon. Maman will spend the night in the hospital to be checked out. I'll move her into her apartment tomorrow."

"Any chance for me to move to Chicago?"

Crisse. "Not now." I stifle a groan. "Ask me in a month."

The late April evening is cold and windy as the sun fades away. We park near the Signature Building, a one-story textured brick structure that caters to private planes.

Once everyone is off, the plane will move to the hangar and the medical equipment will be removed. Being tenants gives us access to 200 airports around the world. Right now, the flight has an ambulance pulled up next to it with EMTs ready to move Maman. They've been told the special bed goes with her.

Walking down the gangway, I pull on my mid-weight coat and a toque to survey the scene. The landscaping is minimal with few bushes and trees, nowhere to hide. That eases my worries. At the entrance to the building, I know Liam and Sean are the lookouts. Then a group of people approach the aircraft. What appear to be three tall men resolve into Clay Brandon, Max Grant, and Metin Hazan. Hail, hail, the honchos are here. With them are two shorter people—Cress Taylor and, I can't believe it, Micki. Micki, who isn't supposed to be here. She runs toward me, arms outstretched.

In the distance, a horn honks as a van approaches at high speed, heading straight toward the plane. The driver swerves and squeals to a stop. At first, nothing happens. The windows are darkened, and I don't see a driver. I shout for Liam and Sean, who run toward the vehicle, guns drawn. They shoot at the tires and the van rocks.

Clay pulls out his phone and hits some number, probably 911. "Police," he barks, then feeds information. An EMT comes out onto the gangway. "Mr. Martin. Your mother wants you."

I run toward the gangway. "Get back on the plane." Then I pull the guy inside.

"What's going on?"

I rub the back of my neck. "Not sure, but it looks like a dangerous situation. Is something wrong with my mother?"

"She's restless and eager to get off the plane." I hear his own anxiety underlying the words.

I push past him and kneel down by Maman's bed. Her hand is cold, and I chafe it between mine to warm it. "We'll have you out of here soon. Right now, you're safer inside."

The crew is watching out the windows. I move to see Liam and Sean try to sneak up behind the van.

Clay, who has been standing on the gangway, calls back, "JL. He's coming out." Then he pulls out his Glock, holding it loosely at his side.

When I join Clay, Sam walks slowly, stiff-legged, toward the plane, hands out like he's a supplicant. Instead of the usual overalls, he's dressed in jeans, a T-shirt with a plaid button-down open over it, and a jacket. No hat. Formalwear for the occasion?

When he's close enough for us to hear him, he yells, "Don't shoot an unarmed man. I need to see Micki. Tell her to come out."

"No way, you asshole."

He glares at me, then melts slightly, like a snowman during a warm spell.

"I have to talk to her. Explain." He forces out another word. "Apologize."

A hand touches my back. Micki pushes through and stands in front of me, hands on her hips.

I hiss under my breath. "Get back."

She ignores me. "This will take more than an apology." Tremors run through her into me, but her voice is strong.

With my fingers resting against the base of her neck, I feel her relax, although at the sound of Sam's voice, her muscles contract again.

"No matter what I do, you won't come back to me?" What starts as a whine turns into a snarl.

"No. Even if I forgive you in the next hundred years, we're done."

Sirens scream and red and blue lights flash in the distance. The cavalry, in the form of the police, have arrived.

His face contorts. "Damn it. I'll have you, even if we both die for it." Pulling out a Glock from under his shirt, he backs up toward the van.

The cop cars pull up, out of range of the shooter. The sirens continue briefly and we all blink as the lights strobe. An officer climbs out of one of the cruisers and pulls a bullhorn out of the back. "You're surrounded. Throw down the gun and move away with your hands up."

Everything goes quiet. Sam seems frozen. Sean and Liam creep closer, but that draws his attention. He dives back into the van and starts up the engine. But with two flat tires, the van doesn't move.

After a few minutes, the officer with the bullhorn calls out the same message. "Drop the weapon and put your hands up."

In front of me, Micki hasn't moved. She glares at the van and yells, "Give it up, Sam. You don't want to die and neither do I. Just throw out the gun and make a plea bargain with the DA's office."

"Will you represent me, darlin'?" Out of the open window, his voice sails out into the darkening night. His incongruous cheeky grin shows up bizarrely as his over-white teeth gleam in the fading light.

"I thought you despised lawyers?"

"I do, but I need one now. Who better?"

"Have your father find one for you." The rejoinder is flat, but Sam recoils as if stunned.

"What do you mean?"

"I know who your father is. I know everything, Sam. All the lies, all the betrayals." She stops and I can't believe what she says next. "Did you kill Samson Beaton? Drown him in Lake Michigan? Steal his identity? Is that the only death you've caused?"

Sam sticks the Glock out of the window. I push Micki back through the door. "Take cover, Clay." Liam and Sean close in from either side. Clay drops to one knee and aims at Sam's ghostly white face. The cops fan out behind the truck, moving in a phalanx while Sam's attention stays on me.

"Where's your friend, Philippe?" Max stands at the end of the ramp, arms folded.

"Don't know who you're talkin' about." When he raises the Glock and aims at Max, the action undercuts his words. Hand shaking, he misses everyone within range. Still, he's not finished with his false bravado.

He looks away from Max and focuses on me. "I'll shoot you first, Frenchie, then get my woman." He waves the Glock again, and I can just see the oversize magazine in the dim light. "I've got plenty of bullets in this baby and more magazines too. Micki will come back once you're out of the way."

"Don't fool yourself. She'll never come back to you. Even when you're both dead, she'll be in heaven, and you'll be in hell."

"Blow it out your ass." Then he flips something on the mechanism, steadies the gun on the window frame, and pulls the trigger. The modified Glock, now in automatic mode, wavers wildly as bullets start to spray. We dive for cover. Clay drops to his belly and squeezes off a couple of shots. They hit the van, causing Sam to roll up the window once his magazine is spent. A bullet cracks the windshield.

He must have reloaded because he opens the door and rolls out onto the ground, shooting all the while. Sean and Liam jump on him. The gun, magazine depleted, falls from his hand. The police move in, put on the cuffs, read him his rights, and push him into the back of a blue and white.

All the while, he howls for Micki. "It ain't over. Just wait and see. My dad has clout. I'll be out before you know it. I'll find you. I'll find you. I'll hunt you down to the ends of the earth." I can see him frothing under the sodium lights. "You're mine. Don't forget that, Miche. YOU'RE MINE."

He gives an unearthly cackle and I see her face blanch as he uses an old, unwelcome nickname.

Then his voice, hoarse from screaming, falls silent.

As the cruiser takes him away, Sam glowers through the rear window, teeth bared like the wild animal he is.

Micki's in the back of the plane with Maman. No tears, but she quivers like autumn leaves in a windstorm. Everyone in the aisle moves aside to let me through. When I reach her, slip my arms around her waist, she clings to me. "All over," I growl. "He's on his way to jail. No escape this time. No bail. Nothing." She backs away, unsure in the whirlpool of my anger.

I want to hit something, but being around all this delicate equipment, I have nothing to take out my frustration on.

"Take it easy, mate." Max's hand is on my shoulder, although I don't take my eyes off Micki. His voice calms me down. "At least he didn't set the plane on fire."

Light footsteps patter near. "Is he dead?" Max moves away from me as Cress settles into his arms.

"Dunno." He kisses the top of her head. "I don't think Clay hit him. Don't much care, either. Still, I'd rather see him locked up for life. In solitary confinement. Or, better yet, sharing a cell with that bitch Tina. Put two psychopaths together." His eyes sparkle with mischief, and Cress laughs.

"Yeah, she attacked me, and he attacked Micki. They would be a perfect pair."

"You two attract the nutcases. Why's that?"

"White knights, too." Max gestures to me, then points to himself.

"I shot at the van to shake him up. Doesn't that make me a knight, too?" Clay's lips turn up in another small smile. "Too bad there aren't co-ed prisons."

"Maybe in the future." Metin glows in the aftermath of the excitement. "Fewer jail breaks with connubial bliss." I'm surprised at the girlish giggle from my usually sober colleague.

Maman calls out, "Mon chou, come here." I squeeze Micki's hand.

"Go see your mother," she breathes against my neck.

Instead, I call out, "Going to find out what's holding things up," then walk down the gangway.

Micki

I'm trying to reassure Louisette when JL comes back with the EMTs. They were out on the runway with the police and Sam.

They busy themselves getting Louisette strapped down safely so they can move her off the plane. In the meantime, she glares at her son, standing nearby with his arm around me, nuzzling my hair.

"Is this because of your job?" Louisette throws the accusation at JL, the query developing into a cough. "You told me you sit behind a desk, but that's not true. You should find something safer."

"Maman," he says sharply. "Relax or you'll have a relapse. What will I tell Dr. Fitzroy if you die at the end of the flight?"

I interrupt, "It's me. I'm the reason all this happened."

"You? I don't believe it." Louisette shakes her head in negation, prompting another small cough. Then, with a calculating look, she says, "JL says you're a lawyer. Did you put a criminal away who wants revenge?" The relish in her voice chills me. But her breathing is steady, and that's more important than her ghoulish imaginings.

"Too much television, Maman. This is not a murder mystery."

"My ex has been stalking me and he upped the ante."

"A love tragedy. Those are good too."

"Maman." JL's protest falls on deaf ears as she produces a wheezing laugh.

The level of emotion has ebbed. The EMTs give Louisette a sedative and take her to the ambulance. When I look out, the police are gone. Not a trace remains of the shootout at the O'Hare corral. Sean and Liam have brought the GSU car over. "Hop in," Liam says. "We'll take you to the hospital."

Clay and Metin push past. "I told Burak I'd get his wife home safely. He wasn't best pleased she insisted on being here."

"I don't get much excitement, these days." She slips her arm through Clay's.

"Tell Kath I'm looking forward to our next meeting," I call out as they stride away. Clay gives a little wave as they disappear into the dusk.

Max and Cress have vanished in his Porsche SUV.

The ambulance peels out, siren blasting, and JL helps me into the back of the GSU vehicle. Exhausted by the drama, I don't want a lecture about my recklessness in coming to the airport.

"Time for a debrief," he says.

"No, it's not." It may never be time, but definitely not now.

"It is," he insists. I move out of his reach and look out the window.

Instead of cajoling me, he stares in the other direction, lips pursed.

When we arrive at the hospital, JL tells the guys to drop off the car and go home. Their job is done.

"Sean," he says, leaning in to the driver's side window, "See me Monday. I think you're done with training." Sean flashes a big smile as JL goes on, "Great job, both of you."

They wave and pull out of the circle drive. We watch until the taillights disappear through the darkness. JL takes my hand, and we walk through the revolving door, where JL's mother waits.

CHAPTER

THIRTY-FOUR

If you want a happy ending, that depends, of course, on where you stop your story.—Orson Welles

JL

NEXT ON THE agenda is Frederick Lanscombe. Sam called Daddy Dearest as soon as they gave him his one call. Fred's been frothing at the mouth, giving statements to the media, telling them Micki, attracted to Sam's money, lured him into this. She's a gold digger who set him up.

Wonder who they'll line up for the defense? There are possible murder charges on the line. Micki shouldn't need a criminal lawyer, but GSU will provide a legal team if necessary. A friend has offered to help her with a civil suit against Fred and his son.

A little war council is necessary to deal with Fred the Dickhead. He is guilty of collusion and aiding and abetting, even if he didn't know his son's ultimate objective. We can't meet on his home turf. Finding the best neutral ground is a crucial step. Clay invites him to a lunch meeting at the University Club. Whether he thinks we want him to hire GSU security, or offer software systems that might fit their needs, isn't clear. As long as he shows up, we're in business.

At the appointed time, two days after the confrontation at O'Hare, Clay, Max, and I convene with Clay's PA, Elena, in a meeting room set for six. Frederick may or may not bring anyone with him.

Built between 1907 and 1908 by the well-known Chicago architecture firm of Holabird and Root, I would normally take time to appreciate the formal staircase and rich setting of the large foyer. Not today. The bank of elevators is the goal. I exit on the sixth floor and locate conference room D. The room, a narrow rectangle, paneled in dark wood has red carpet overlaid with an oriental runner. The opulence is heightened by the gold fabric of the draperies over the slightly vaulted windows.

We pull the dining chairs away from the table into a semi-circle. A credenza has water, tea, and coffee available. We sip, look at each other, but no one really wants to say anything. A power game ensues when our guest arrives half an hour late, with three other people in tow.

"Sorry," Lanscombe says, not sounding sorry at all. "Partners' meeting ran a liddle lahng."

I've never met him, but I assumed he was an older version of his son. They are nothing alike—except they are both shallow façades. From his supercilious expression, I can see Lanscombe has no respect for anyone in this room, not even his colleagues. Heavy gold cuff links wink in the light as he shoots his cuffs. And then he does it a second time to make sure we all see how rich and important he is.

The designer suit is classy, almost too classy. There's a sheen to the fabric that offers a glitz unexpected in a man pushing retirement age.

He's fit, unlike Sam, with slightly too long silver hair, a long narrow face with a pugnacious jaw, hawk eyes under heavy brows, and too-thin lips. He projects ersatz Eastern patrician until he speaks. Then he's pure Southside Chicago.

Clay shakes hands as Elena slips out to alter the arrangements. When she returns, Clay makes introductions. "The head of WatchDog, Inc. and co-owner of Global Security Unlimited, Jean-Louis Martin. Head of CyberSec, our cybersecurity division, Max Grant. And this is my personal assistant, Elena Doukas."

Frederick inclines his head in a regal gesture, then waves a hand toward his cohorts. "Rebecca Masters, Mark Hargrove, and Tyler Miller. All senior partners."

We fall silent as the staff removes the table that seats six and returns with a larger round table that seats eight. The staff reset the top with an undercloth in the same design as the drapes, that brushes the floor with a shorter white tablecloth overlaying it. White napkins sit atop menus bordered by heavy cutlery, wine goblets, and water glasses. While staff bustles about, getting everything rearranged, a manager arrives. "Mr. Brandon?'

Clay unfolds from the deep armchair.

The manager updates the status of the meal. "We've alerted the kitchen, but the extra guests will delay lunch. I hope that's acceptable."

"Perfectly fine. Thank you so much, Tony. Could we order drinks now? And maybe something to nibble on while we wait?"

"Of course. I'll send someone in right away."

After a couple of bobbing bows, Tony takes his leave. A few minutes later, a server comes in from the bar and takes drink orders. The understanding is no business will be discussed before or during the meal. Instead, Clay and Max savor barrel-aged single malt whisky. Miller orders champagne and shares it with Lanscombe and Hargrove. Rebecca Masters and I get draft beer, and Elena sticks with iced tea. A tray with crackers and cheese is available.

Twenty minutes later, Frederick Lanscombe's jaw drops to his chest when Micki walks in, followed by lunch. "What the hell is she doing here? Don't tell me she's your legal counsel?"

Dressed professionally in a Chanel suit, hair swept up into a perfect twist, Micki looks like a million dollars—American, not Canadian.

"Nice to see you, Michelle." Clay bows over her hand. "I'm sorry Kath couldn't join us, but she's visiting some women's shelters today."

Micki's face lights up, accentuating her natural beauty. "I'm joining her after this. Can't wait to get to work." She casts a cool gaze over the team from the law firm. "Hello, Rebecca. Nice to see you. Tyler, Mark." They all incline their heads slightly in acknowledgement. She turns to Lanscombe. "Well, hello, Fred. I thought you might be visiting your son." She spits out the last words, as if removing a nasty taste.

Puzzlement spreads over the faces of his partners. Frederick clears his throat, forestalling questions. The fulcrum has shifted, and he's scrambling to regain the power position. "Mr. Brandon, perhaps we could move things along. I'm a busy man."

"Dr. Brandon, actually." Clay doesn't suggest using first names. "Lunch first, counselor. Then we'll get down to business." Lanscombe walks over to the drinks tray, puts down the half-empty flute and pours a double scotch. Drinks it down. Pours another, drinks that too. He sets a third at his place.

Instead of letting everyone order their own meal, Clay asked Elena to consult with the University Club food service to set the menu. The food is excellent, but Fred Lanscombe looks like he's eating ashes. A steak-and-potato man, it turns out he's a legend for the number of things he dislikes. And Micki knows them all. When the platter of raw oysters perched on crushed ice and salt is put on the table, the green of his face reflects against the white cloth. While the rest of us enjoy the briny delight, he holds his napkin to his lips.

After a small taste of the bitter bed of frisée, he toys with the salad of fig, goat cheese, and walnuts, with a fig vinaigrette. The main course is poached salmon with a hollandaise sauce, flanked by tender asparagus, and tiny potatoes. He forks up a potato, only to find they're filled with sour cream and caviar. Reaching into the bread basket for a last-ditch chance, a grimace shows how much he dislikes seeds on bread. Caraway rye and sesame-covered butter rolls are the offerings. He drops the roll as if it is a hot coal.

"If you could have chosen the meal, Fred, what would we be eating?" Micki's smile is so sweet I can feel my blood sugar rise.

"Yes, well, we'd start with iceberg lettuce and thousand island dressing. Then a nice medium steak and baked potato with butter. Dessert would be vanilla ice cream."

"A classic American meal." Max's posture signals boring.

In the meantime, most of the conversation is about

the newest play at the Goodman, predictions for the Cubs and Sox, speculation on how the Blackhawks will do in the playoffs, having won the Stanley Cup last season. Rebecca recommends a Korean-American restaurant, Parachute, that is opening next month in Avondale. Micki gushes over Cress' new book, which will be out next month.

Lanscombe doesn't take part." Mr... uh... Dr. Brandon, I'm afraid I haven't been able to eat any of this meal." He mumbles something about allergies and diverticulosis. Micki's been spot-on. He doesn't have either but uses them as excuses to avoid eating things he doesn't like.

Fake commiseration oozes from Clay. "Really sorry about that. I can have Elena ask the kitchen for a sandwich if you prefer. I know the children's menu offers grilled cheese and tomato soup."

Lanscombe huffs, "Don't bother. I'll just have some coffee. Then perhaps we can stop farting around and get to the reason for this gathering."

Clay waves a hand and conjures coffee and dessert, a luscious set of three tarts—lemon, pear, and sweet potato. We tuck in, all except Lanscombe, who waves away the plate.

"Gives me heartburn."

Table cleared and coffee cups refilled, Miller stands up and leans over the table, hands pressed down for balance as he gets in Clay's face.

"Why exactly are we here, *Dr.* Brandon? My impression was you are planning to present us with a proposal to upgrade our computer system with new security tools." Tyler has enjoyed his meal and now he's ready to go a few rounds.

"Really, Mr. Miller? I don't believe I suggested any such

proposal." Clay sips his coffee. "Max, did you prepare a cybersecurity proposal?"

"No." He folds his arms, then leans back. "Perhaps JL has a proposal for a new security system—alarms, security guards."

"Definitely not. The Aon Building provides all that, and I would never work with a company that abuses their employees."

The other law partners swivel their heads to face Lanscombe. "What is he talking about?" Mark Hargrove's suave tone is at odds with the hardness around his mouth.

Rebecca breaks in, "Let's not be coy. We all know he's referring to Ms. Press." She gives me a curt nod. "I can assure you, Mr. Martin, Ms. Press was offered a very good severance package as well as the recommendations that ensured she was hired by..." She turns to Micki. "Who is it that hired you?"

Micki frowns. "I was hired by the GSU Foundation, Rebecca."

"Of course. So, Mr. Brandon is now your boss." Rebecca is playing her role well. She can't afford to be seen as being on our side.

"Not at all," Clay breaks in smoothly. "I have no influence with the Foundation. It was set up to be an administratively separate entity from the corporation."

"But your wife is the director?" Tyler Miller's belligerent posture is more laughable than intimidating.

"True, but if you knew Kath, you'd know she makes her own decisions. I wouldn't dream of interfering."

I focus back on Lanscombe and stare at the beads of sweat popping out on his forehead. "This is not about the firm or the adequacy of Ms. Press' separation from your firm. It's about the damage your son has caused to Ms.

Press and her family." By the time I finish, the droplets have turned into a rivulet, running down the side of that prominent nose.

Face turning beet red, Fred Lanscombe looks like he might have a stroke. "Baseless charges. I will restore my son's reputation and have this woman"—he shakes a finger at Micki—"arrested for entrapment."

Micki bangs her fist against the mahogany tabletop. "If you call hitting me in the eye, sponging off me for years claiming he had no money, tearing down my feelings of self-worth, stalking, sending abusive texts, making abusive phone calls..." She runs out of breath, but recovers before he can get a word in. "Not to mention throwing a grenade through my parents' window and setting their house on fire." Her hand waves as she tries to fan herself. "I'm sure I'll remember more when I give my deposition."

"You lying little—"

I try to cut him off before he can continue, but Micki is in a take-no-prisoners mood and yells over both of us. "Shooting at Dr. Brandon's plane when it was transferring Mr. Martin's mother here from a hospital in Vancouver was heinous."

Fred looks around wildly at his colleagues, but none of them meet his gaze. "We'll sue you for defamation, Micki. No jury will convict Sam of a crime.."

"That is for the criminal justice system to decide. Personally, I think you overestimate your leverage." I give Micki a thumbs-up and a wink.

If looks could kill, I'd be dead.

"However, there is also the question of a civil suit. Ms. Press is planning to sue you and your son for damages of..." I pretend I don't remember the amount we discussed. "Micki, how much are you asking for?"

She levels a cool look at her former boss. "Not that much. Ten million seems about right."

Lanscombe sputters like boiling fat. "Ten million. Ridiculous."

"If you want to settle out of court, I'll give you the name of my lawyer." Micki collects her coat from the rack. "Thanks for lunch, Clay." Then she sashays out the door.

∾

Micki

My feet want to fly, but I force myself to maintain a stately pace. My stomach flutters, like I've swallowed a swirl of autumn leaves.. Fierce, angry conversation drifts out from the conference room, so I hurry to the elevator and jab the up button. The lawyers will be out of there in a minute, and I don't want to run into any of them. From the glares of his partners, the Devil will get his due. Forced retirement would not surprise me. I'll bet he gets a golden parachute when he goes. It might pay for the lawsuit.

Out of the corner of my eye, I see Rebecca edge out the door, just as the elevator opens.

"Micki, Micki, wait." I hold the door and she rushes up to give me a hug. "I'll call you so we can have a celebratory drink. By the way, all your digging helped find what Greenberg is really hiding."

"Something bigger than the possible financial malfeasance?"

"Much bigger. He's hiding a bigamous marriage and an illegitimate child. Not a good look for a wannabe senator."

"Is he going to be outed?" I know the firm can't do anything, but leaks happen.

"I've heard he has a couple of disgruntled aides, so it's possible."

As the saying goes, watch out or karma will bite you in the ass. Chuckling, I take the elevator to the eighth floor and join my parents, Cress, and Kath. JL's mom is at the creche, but we'll all be together for dinner later.

Mom meets me and gives me a hug. "Love you, sweetie." We link arms and walk down to the arched windows that overlook Michigan Avenue, where Dad and Cress have taken over a leather couch and one of two facing club chairs. She reads something on her phone. He taps his toe against the underside of the low table in front of the couch.

Out in the hall, a group chatters, their voices getting more distinct as they near the door. Clay strides through, followed by JL and Max. No Elena. Probably went back to the office or home. I wonder if she felt uncomfortable taking part in that charade?

When he sees Kath at the other end of the room, Clay's steps quicken. He swings her around, laughing, as he tells her what happened. "Should have seen his expression when Micki walked in."

"Nothing compared to his reception of the meal." A big smile shows how much Max relishes the memory.

"No." JL holds up a hand to stop all this. "The best, the very best, was his face when Micki told him she's suing him for ten million."

"Ten million!" Dad turns to me. "Brilliant, honey."

"Who knows, maybe we'll even get it. A decade from now."

"Any word about Sam?" Cress squeezes in next to Max in an oversized armchair. JL picks me up from the other club chair, settles in, and cuddles me against his chest.

"Psychiatric evaluations to decide if he's fit to stand

trial. He won't be seeing anyone but his lawyers and doctors for the foreseeable future."

"Thought you were visiting women's shelters?" Max looks bemused.

"Just a subterfuge," Kath says. "Micki and I will start that next week."

My enthusiastic bounce produces a groan from JL. "Be more careful, ma chouette. Delicate objects down there." I kiss him, not sure what's happened to my aversion to PDA.

"Fun times, everyone." Clay snatches Kath's hand. "Time to go home to the kiddies."

"You're joining us for dinner, right?" JL gives him the hard stare. "We picked a kid-friendly place just for you."

I groan. "Hope it's not Chuck E. Cheese."

"Crosby's Kitchen."

"We'll definitely be there. The kids love Crosby's." Kath grins and Clay nods in agreement.

Once they've left, we speculate about Lanscombe's fate.

"What do you think he'll do now?" Cress asks.

"Stew, resign, support his son...or not."

"Do you think he might try revenge, too?" Cress shudders at the thought.

"I doubt it. If I was still working there or at another major law firm, he might try to destroy my career. But that won't work now. Once word is out, his reputation will be ruined. I think he'll just slink off into the night, like the weasel he is.

CHAPTER
THIRTY-FIVE

My characters shall have, after a little trouble, all that they desire.—Jane Austen

Chicago, July 2014
JL

It's a steamy Sunday night in July, but air-conditioning will make karaoke at Stanley's tolerable. We spent the afternoon geocaching, and this feels cool in comparison. Riding through the warm summer darkness, Micki's arms tight around my waist, cheek pressed against my back, casts a magical veil over the world. She's over the moon about being on the ground floor of GSU's new social justice foundation.

Moving out of her condo to my place happened right after our meeting with Fred Lanscombe. She managed to find someone to sublet quickly. She even agreed to a dog.

Our miniature husky puppy, Fairbanks, chews on everything. His cuteness makes up for the destruction. Puppy training starts in a few weeks.

Maman, reassured Uncle François is safe and happy in Montreal, is adjusting to Chicago. She keeps telling me one big city is much like another, although I think this is her way of convincing herself as well as reassuring me. She's found a Francophone group, places to buy high-quality maple syrup, cheese curds, and the sausages she likes and shouldn't eat.

Trying to relocate to the Chicago office, Yannick has come in for the festivities.

And Sam, well Sam wasn't granted bail and is in jail awaiting trial on various felonies including two counts of attempted murder, stalking, and carrying a gun at an airport. His father is still arguing he is not fit to stand trial, so far unsuccessfully. If convicted, Sam could spend a lot of time in prison.

Parking around the corner, I make sure we salute the mashed potato mural, just like I did when we had our first date here last March. Then I pull ma chouette close and murmur into her hair, "Happy?"

"Delirious," she says, pulling away and slipping her arm through mine. "Let's go in."

When Micki and I walk to the back room, the gang has assembled. Maman chatters away with Mrs. Press about whether Triscuits are the perfect cracker. Really, I think they're mostly bragging about children. Cress and Kath lean toward each other with serious faces as they look at Cress' phone. Probably deciding on their songs.

Max, Clay, and Mr. Press have a variety of forks, knives, and spoons laid out. The terms tight-head prop and scrum-half clue me in Max is explaining rugby. I notice Micki's father's attention is wandering. Then he catches sight of us. "They're here," he calls out and waves his arms above his head.

Everyone crowds around us, hugging, backslapping, and air-kissing. You'd think we hadn't seen them in years rather than less than twenty-four hours ago. Fourth of July weekend has been a full calendar of breakfast and neighborhood parades, the Windy City Smoke Out, followed by fireworks at Navy Pier on Friday, a barbecue on Saturday at Micki's parents' newly remodeled house, and today's events.

Platters of fried pickles, chicken, and ribs are already on the table. Michelle's dad and Clay collect the drinks. I take a breath. My life is so full of joy I can hardly sit still as I listen to Maman mixing French and English with abandon.

I gulp down my shot and walk over to Clay. A shoulder punch captures his attention. "You arranged everything, right?"

A rare smile spreads over his face. "All taken care of. The guys will make sure we have seats right in front. Here is the lineup." He hands me a sheet with the singers and their numbers. Micki's parents are leading off with "This Magic Moment," followed by Clay and Kath with "It Had to Be You." Not surprisingly, Max and Cress are singing The Proclaimers "I Wanna Be." Ever since Max's big apology to her last Christmas, that's their song. I'm penultimate unless Micki sings. The finale will be Maman, with "La Vie en Rose."

After I hand back the list, Clay says, "This room will be ours until closing." He leans back and takes a sip of bourbon. "Your mother seems okay. Does she like her apartment?"

"What's not to like? It's bigger than her house, fully

furnished, and up-to-date. And the daycare is just the thing she needs. All the bébés, she's in heaven."

I swallow down my shot. "No more interference in my love life. Micki's help with all the immigration application papers made a big difference in her outlook." I glance over at Maman, who is hugging Micki for some reason. "And finding out what a little schemer and thief Angélique turned out to be. The disappointment didn't last as long as I expected."

"What about Angélique's sons?"

"With their mother standing trial, the grandparents have custody. The father has visitation rights. I feel sorry for them. Such nice boys."

The band is warming up so Max herds us all toward the stage area. They arranged a group of chairs just to the side. The owner ambles over and gestures to the seating. "Calling your name, I think," he says. Then he takes Maman's arm and leads her through the rapidly increasing crowd.

Micki shoots me a quizzical look.

"Clay told me he was going to arrange something so my mother would be comfortable and away from the crowd." We file in after her.

Her blue eyes soften. "So thoughtful."

The microphone crackles and the emcee starts his spiel. Once he's introduced the band, he motions Micki's parents up to the stage. "Our first performers are Desmond and Alice Press." As they start bopping to the swinging beat, Micki grabs my collar and pulls me close. "That's their song."

"Their song?"

"Ye-e-e-s. It was the first dance at their wedding."

The audience is entranced when they hear "forever 'til the end of time." It's a great start.

Kath and Clay push through the throng as the emcee announces them. Another oldie but they sell it well.

Instead of announcing Max and Cress, the band just starts the opening of the Proclaimers' popular song. Feet stamp as Max, pushing his highland burr, starts. His resemblance to David Tennant doesn't hurt, and Cress harmonizes nicely.

After they go back to their seats, the emcee announces, "JL Martin with "Truly, Madly, Deeply," by Savage Garden."

I clear my throat, take the mic, and turn my gaze to Micki. "This is for mon amour," I say, to awws and ahhhs from the assembled karaoke lovers. A glance at Maman shows me her eyes glitter with unshed moisture. I twirl the mic by the cord a couple of time. The crowd quiets as I put every bit of emotion I feel into the lyrics. At the end, I hold out my hand and motion her forward. "Please say yes."

The atmosphere is hushed with expectation, longing, and hope. My limbs shake like branches in a high wind. What if she turns me down?

Micki's eyes are unnaturally bright as she comes forward. Instead of taking my hand and answering, she motions to the emcee, whispers something I can't make out. He nods and goes over to the band. "Nothing's Gonna Stop Us Now," blares from the amps as Micki climbs up onto the stage and belts out the lyrics. Everyone in the place joins in with her resounding yes.

I'm on my knees and as she finishes, I pull her down beside me and slip the ring on her finger to the sound of "La Vie en Rose."

∼

For more of the GSU gang, check out *At First Sight* and *At the Crossroads*, available in e-book, paperback, and audio. Look for Jarvis and Elizabeth's story, *At the Breach*, in 2024. And please consider leaving a review. Not only do they help the author, but other readers appreciate them when deciding on what book to read next.

Turn the page for Chapter One of *At First Sight*

AT FIRST SIGHT

CHAPTER ONE

Chicago, November 2013
　Cress

I step off the private elevator on the fortieth floor of One Financial Plaza in my new shoes. New shoes—ridiculous, bright-red, three-inch stilettos. What was I thinking? Oh yeah, Everest. Maybe the best restaurant in Chicago. One of the thirty or forty best in the U.S.

As I passed the store window, the shoes lured me in. My willpower collapsed like a condemned building. This is so not me. I've only had them a minute, and they're cheese graters for feet.

A quick roll of my ankle on the slick granite floor reminds me why I don't wear high heels. My arms splay and rotate like a windmill. The shopping bag that holds my serviceable flats and my small evening bag spins off my wrist. One shoe skids away. *Crap, crap, crap.*

The brown kraft-paper bag is a missile that hurtles

toward a man on his way to the restaurant entrance. My mouth opens in soundless warning as it speeds toward an invisible bullseye.

Thunk. The bag bounces off his arm.

My evening clutch pops out, wide open. Damn that broken clasp. Change rings against hard wood and granite, spraying in all directions. I drop to my knees and crawl after the quarters and pennies. Out of the corner of my eye, I see him spin. A frown twists lush lips.

"You all right?" A foot in a brogue polished within an inch of its life rests a millimeter from my fingers as I reach for more coins. A shoe, a red shoe, is in his hand.

"Lost something?" He holds it out to me. His rich British accent sends a prickle down my spine. I tip my head up to give him a quick once-over.

A spark flashes through eyes that remind me of a walk on the beach in winter. A face bisected by a high-bridged aristocratic slash of a nose. My face tingles. The tips of my ears are warm. I grab the shoe, drop it on the floor, and hide my face in my hands.

"Fine. Sorry. I lost my balance and the bag escaped." My fingers muffle the sound.

He starts to bend down. His hand brushes my ear.

Zap. I scoot backward.

He straightens up and shakes his hand. "Pins and needles."

With effort, I wrench my focus back to the coins. My good luck charm, a Victorian black opal pendant I bought when my first book sold, slides back and forth against the sanded silk of my shabby chic little black dress. Streaks of fire reflect off the granite floor as it swings. I brush stray discs into the pile.

"Just trying to help."

"I can manage. Thanks, though."

A loud male voice calls out, "Hey, Max. Get in here."

"Half a mo'."

I wave him off. "Your friends want you."

"But..."

"I've got this."

"Sure?"

"Yeah. Go on."

He straightens, turns, walks into the restaurant.

I stare at his back in the perfect gray suit. The color matches his eyes.

The heap of change winks at me. I slip on my shoe and pick them up so no one else falls. Little traitors.

Purse and shoe box stuffed back into the shopping bag, I stagger through the wood-framed doorway.

The tables are all full. I have a word with the maître d' before he shows me to a center table where four people give me a standing ovation. Heat burns my cheeks. The other diners stare, some annoyed but more amused. In fact, complete strangers join in, clapping.

A group of men in elegant suits, ensconced at a round table positioned to enjoy the spectacular view, whistle loudly. My nose wrinkles. Over-aged frat boys.

With my unruly curls and my almost too-thin frame, all these people may wonder if I'm some D-list celeb. I look like a starved model, but the genes tell the story. I have the appetite of a hockey player after a game.

My best friend, Micki, leads the cheers. She is a statuesque platinum blonde, all curves, killing it in a red-sequined dress. My shoes would be perfect.

She glances toward my feet. "Nice shoes. New?"

"Yeah. Big mistake."

"About time you started to wear grown-up shoes."

We wear the same size. I'll wrap them up for Christmas. One pair of fancy shoes, light wear.

Her SO, Sam, is three inches shorter and resents it. My other best friend, Paul, is medium height with a monk's tonsure and average features that are transformed when he smiles. His wife, Ellie, is twenty years younger than the rest of us and short. I'm a giant next to her. She has long purple and pink hair with nails to match and a sharp, foxlike face.

The staff stare, wide-eyed, jaws dropped. I mouth an apology.

"Sit down already," Sam growls. He's dressed in an untucked plaid shirt and dark jeans. His gut hangs over his belt. I wonder how he even got in.

I slide into the chair pulled out by the table captain and check out the room. Enormous windows showcase the city. My best friend has done me proud.

I shoot a look at Sam.

"What? The only rule here is shirt and pants." A grin splits his face, and he pulls out an oversized clip-on bow tie. "Miche worried they might not let me in without a tie, so I brought this just in case."

He waves the red clown tie festooned with yellow, blue, and green polka dots in my face, clips the monstrosity to his shirt pocket like an obscene boutonnière, then runs his fingers through his sparse, straw-like hair.

"How many times do I have to tell you that a miche is a large loaf of bread?"

"You're tellin' me that's not a compliment? Bread is the staff of life." He smirks.

"Stop it." Micki raps his knuckles with her talons.

"Just teasin'." His fake drawl makes me cringe.

The rest of us sit down just as the sommelier comes

over with a bottle of *Veuve Cliquot*, which she pours with a flourish.

Micki lifts her glass. "To Cress. Congratulations on being nominated for the most prestigious award a historical novelist can win."

"To Cress." They all lift their glasses and drink.

The server comes over. She seems slightly taken aback when she looks over our table, head slightly lowered, a glance from the corner of her eye. Her hand sweeps the air over the unopened menus. "Ready to order?"

Paul takes over. "We'll have the tasting menu with wine."

"All of you?" She picks up the menus, almost as if she wants to hide behind them.

"Yes." Paul gestures around the table. "All of us."

Sam's face twists. "Why not a bourbon tasting?"

"Wine. What a great idea." Micki squeezes Sam's hand so hard he winces.

"Okay." The woman scuttles away.

Ellie, Paul's wife, tosses her hair back and sniffs. "What got up her butt?"

"She looks familiar somehow." Micki stares after her. Paul nods.

Sam gives a dismissive wave. "Probably she's worked somewhere else we've eaten."

Micki turns and cranes her neck for another glimpse. "I eat here pretty often with clients, and I've never seen her here.

My spine tingles. The way she seemed to hide was weird.

"What is this award?" Ellie's eyes are bright with curiosity.

My apprehension drains away and excitement bubbles

up. I reach for my water glass. My hand hits the stem, and it keels over. Water gushes over the table. Sam gets the brunt of the deluge.

"Christ, Cress."

"Sorry." I put my hands over my mouth.

"You're fire engine red." Paul blots his shirt.

People hover around, mop up the table, hand napkins to Sam, and pour me fresh water.

Once everything is back to a kind of normal and Ellie stops giggling, I go back to my explanation. My hand snakes out for my glass. Micki taps my wrist then moves the glass closer to my bread plate.

"About ten years ago, the *Société des Romanciers Historique*, an international organization located in Paris, decided to start an award for the best historical novel of the year. Not sure why their year is September to September, but anyway..." My voice trails off. I rub my nose.

Ellie goggles. "Do you have to be so pretentious, Cress?"

I catch my tongue between my teeth before I can stick it out at her.

"They named the award for two famous historical novelists of nineteenth-century France."

Her eyes glaze over. Why did she bother to ask if she isn't interested?

"Go on, Cress." Paul rubs his hand over his bald spot.

"Anyway, it's named for Victor Hugo, who wrote *The Hunchback of Notre Dame*, and Alexandre Dumas *père,* who wrote *The Three Musketeers.*"

"Why is he called a pear?" Ellie's face looks totally innocent.

Ellie's gaze wanders around the room, but like a homing pigeon, her attention goes back to the group at the window table, lingers on the wolf-whistlers. I glance over.

Four handsome men in their forties lounge in the black armchairs and sip cocktails. I peek at the man who faces our table—the guy I hit with my bag. Almost black hair, glasses, a blue Oxford cloth shirt with the top button undone and a tie, loosened. Check him out again. Squint. Can't be sure, but it looks like Balliol. A striking oval face, high cheekbones, and a chiseled, squared-off chin. Movie star good looks.

Micki checks him out. "Hey, he looks like David Tennant with glasses and dark hair."

"Who?" Ellie looks confused.

"Yeah, Dr. Who." Micki throws her a wicked grin.

"Uh…" If anything, Ellie looks more confused.

"Just some British sci-fi. Let it go," Paul advises her.

I pull my eyes away and clear my throat. "It's a really prestigious award, and I'm one of the five finalists for this year."

"But the pear."

"P-E-R-E. French for father. Now stop being silly." Paul's voice is impatient.

Ellie's cheeks pink. Micki chortles. Sam is glazed over with indifference.

"I'll be on *Morning at 7* Friday to talk about the book and the award." The words come out in a whoosh. I slump and push back the damp curl that clings to my cheek.

Our server hovers at a nearby table. I finish my hurried explanation, and she moves off. When she realizes we've noticed her, a flush rises on the back of her neck.

Sam raps lightly on the table to get our attention and starts an interminable story about an art exhibit where he will show his "found art" installations. I'm a little ticked but not really surprised that neither he nor Ellie wants to know about the book. Micki and Paul suffered through everything while I hid in my cave to pound out words, occasionally creeping out to whine.

On and off through course after course of delectable Alsatian specialties and far too much wine, the fishbowl sensation waxes and wanes. The middle-aged businessmen glance over on and off. Maybe they expect firecrackers next. I catch glimpses of our server, who hovers around the tables near us far more than she needs to. In the end, I shake off the discomfort and celebrate with my friends.

By the time the mignardises and petit fours arrive with coffee, I can hardly move. Our server has disappeared from the room, most of the tables are empty. Paul signals to the maître d'.

"We're ready for the check." He flourishes his black AmEx card.

"Your meal has already been paid for." He gestures toward me.

"What?" Paul frowns.

"My celebration, my treat."

Paul and Ellie offer to drive me home to the far north side, way past their own house in Old Town. A bus home doesn't seem like a great idea. Don't want to cram into Sam's truck either.

At home, I put the new shoes in the box. *Remember, Cress, wrap them up for Micki.* I pull the dress over my head and hang it in the closet. I don't set an alarm.

Crack of dawn. My head throbs and my eyelashes glue my eyes closed. Dorothy and Thorfinn jump on my stomach. Double whammy.

"Fuck. Get off." I push them to the floor. Four green eyes glare at me. Dorothy hisses. Bad cat mom.

I stagger into the kitchen and pull a large glass out of the cabinet. A prairie oyster and a couple of ibuprofen are just the ticket with a big glass of ice water the chaser. Dig a bag of frozen peas out of the freezer then shuffle to the chair in the living room.

The pain recedes and my stomach settles. Micki shows up and suggests we go out for a hangover reviver before she drags my unwilling body downtown to pick out a suitable dress for my TV interview.

At Strings in Chinatown, I order spicy tonkatsu ramen to clear my still-fuzzy head. This is probably the third hangover I've ever had, and the worst.

"I may never drink again."

Micki rests her hand on my wrist. "You still have a pulse. This will pass, and you'll forget all about it until the next time."

"No next time." I pull my hand out of her grasp and hold up it up to stop her. "This is the worst morning of my life."

"Three hangovers in forty-five years is nothing. You'll drink again."

I drop my head into my hands. "No way. Never."

She giggles. "Your birthday is soon—we'll get you drinking again by then."

I pick up the check. My best friend offered to take the day off from her busy law office just to help me, so it's the least I can do.

Acknowledgments

I appreciate the great feedback from my early reader, Pam Gennusa, and my beta reader Gay Lynn Cronin. The Dark & Stormy critique group kept me going while I pushed through the first draft and corrections. Béatrice Detiege generously offered to check my French. All the comments and questions made this book so much better.

My editor, Karen Hrdlicka, worked her magic and helped me make decisions on some sticky questions. Any lingering mistakes are mine.

Thanks to all the people who have helped along the way — early readers, cheerleaders, betas, writing groups, critique partners, and fellow writers. I couldn't have done it without you. If it takes a village, mine is large, and I'm grateful to everyone in it.

About the Author

Sharon Michalove writes romantic suspense and traditional mystery as well as being a published historian. After growing up in suburban Chicago, she spent most of her life in a medium-sized university town, working as an academic professional as well as teaching history. She was married to a composer and frequently uses her knowledge of music, history, and food to enrich her novels. A hockey fan, Sharon moved back to Chicago in 2017 so she could go to Blackhawks games and spend quality time at Eataly Chicago.

Keep up to date—subscribe to my newsletter here.

ALSO BY SHARON MICHALOVE

Global Security Unlimited Series

At First Sight

At the Crossroads

"It's Just a Guise" (short story)

"A Heartfelt Christmas" (short story)

Murder in the North Country

Dead in the Alley

Dead in the Studio (coming 2024)

Anthologies

"Colonel Fitzwilliam Meets His Match" in *Austen Tea Party*

"Aegean Persuasion," in *Tales from the Golden State of Mind*

"Partridges and Gold Rings," in *Mistletoe and Markets* (available for preorder)

"Melting the Iceman," *in Second Time's A Charm: A Second Chance Contemporary Romance Anthology* (available for preorder)

"Code Silver" in *Protect My Heart* (coming July 2024)

COFFEE, ECLAIRS, AND CONVERSATION

I have a discussion group on Facebook. Join me and other readers at Coffee, Eclairs, and Conversation and chat about food, books, travel, and cats.

www.ingramcontent.com/pod-product-compliance
Lightning Source LLC
Chambersburg PA
CBHW051312190726
48290CB00001B/115